JONATHAN HARVEY

The
SECRETS
WE KEEP

PAN BOOKS

First published 2015 by Pan Books
an imprint of Pan Macmillan
20 New Wharf Road, London N1 9RR
Associated companies throughout the world
www.panmacmillan.com

ISBN 978-1-4472-3847-8

3 5 7 9 8 6 4

A CIP catalogue record for this book is available from the British Library.

Printed and bound by CPI Group (UK) Ltd, Croydon, CR0 4YY

Visit www.panmacmillan.com to read more about all our books
and to buy them. You will also find features, author interviews and
news of any author events, and you can sign up for e-newsletters
so that you're always first to hear about our new releases.

THE SECRETS WE KEEP

Jonathan Harvey comes from Liverpool and is a multi-award-winning writer of plays, films, sitcoms and Britain's longest-running drama serial.

Jonathan's theatre work includes the award-winning *Beautiful Thing* (Bush Theatre, Donmar Warehouse, Duke of York's; winner: John Whiting Award; nominated: Olivier Award for Best Comedy), *Babies* (Royal Court Theatre; winner: *Evening Standard* Award for Most Promising Playwright; winner: George Devine Award) and *Rupert Street Lonely Hearts Club* (English Touring Theatre, Donmar Warehouse, Criterion Theatre; winner: *Manchester Evening News* Award for Best New Play; winner: *City Life Magazine* Award for Best New Play). Other plays include *Corrie!* (Lowry Theatre and national tour; winner: *Manchester Evening News* Award for Best Special Entertainment), *Canary* (Liverpool Playhouse, Hampstead Theatre and English Touring Theatre), *Hushabye Mountain* (English Touring Theatre, Hampstead Theatre), *Guiding Star* (Everyman Theatre, Royal National Theatre), *Boom Bang a Bang* (Bush Theatre), *Mohair* (Royal Court Theatre Upstairs) and *Wildfire* (Royal Court Theatre Upstairs). Jonathan also co-wrote the musical *Closer to Heaven* with the Pet Shop Boys.

For television Jonathan has created and written three series of the BAFTA-nominated *Gimme Gimme Gimme* for the BBC, two series of *Beautiful People* (winner: Best Comedy, Banff TV Festival), the double-BAFTA-nominated *Best Friends*, *Von Trapped!* and *Birthday Girl*. He has also written for *Rev* (winner: BAFTA for Best Sitcom), *Shameless*, *The Catherine Tate Show*, *At Home with the Braithwaites*, *Lilies* and *Murder Most Horrid*. To date he has written over one hundred episodes of *Coronation Street*.

Jonathan's film work includes *Beautiful Thing* for Film4 (Outstanding Film, GLAAD Awards, New York; Best Film, London Lesbian and Gay Film Festival; Best Screenplay, Fort Lauderdale Film Festival; Grand Prix, Paris Film Festival; Jury Award, São Paolo International Film Festival).

But perhaps most telling of all, he also won the Space-hopper Championships at Butlins Pwhelli in 1976.

His novels are *All She Wants*, *The Confusion of Karen Carpenter*, *The Girl Who Just Appeared* and *The Secrets We Keep*.

For Paul Hunt

ACKNOWLEDGEMENTS

Continued thanks to Wayne Brookes, Camilla Elworthy, Jeremy Trevathan and all at Pan Macmillan who continue to believe in me and publish my books. I am incredibly grateful and slightly taken aback. Also to my agent Gordon Wise for his continued sage advice, and to Michael McCoy and Alec Drysdale for looking after all my other writing.

Thank you to my old schoolfriend Justin Bioletti for the loan of his surname.

For those who took the time to chat to me about various elements of the book, from what it's like to run a club, to how a new model might go about landing the dream job, or what happens when you leave a suitcase in left luggage for years, or what the police procedure is when someone goes missing: my thanks go to Amma Amihyia, Conan Corrigan, Steven Doherty, Mark Foster and everyone who answered my random questions on Facebook and Twitter.

Many years ago I adapted Lorraine Gamman's book *Gone Shopping: The Story of Shirley Pitts – Queen of Thieves* for the big screen. Although it was one of the best films never made – well, I would say that – the stories in it have never left me. They were my inspiration for the, albeit tiny, section of this book where Danny comes to London and works for

Jonathan Harvey

a gang of shoplifters. If you've never read that book, do – it's fantastic.

Thank you to Kathy Burke for always encouraging me to go a bit deeper and darker. Also to my friends who put up with me being antisocial as I 'have a deadline to meet'.

To my family in Liverpool, thank you for not being as dysfunctional as the one within these pages, and for giving me a better start in life than Danny.

And finally to Paul Hunt. Officially the nicest bloke on the planet. And he didn't even pay me to say that. Thank you.

Oh. And to you who picked up this book to read. Thank you. And I'm not being funny but . . . that colour really suits you.

PROLOGUE
Danny, 2009

The cliff face is a cut rock of cocaine. Not that I can see the cliff now, but I've seen it in images online, in the planning of this moment. I feel like I'm floating. That's how high up I feel. Green grass, stone sky, clear today, coastline as far as the eye can see. There were images where a fog had come in. Thick as cotton wool. People stood on top of the cliff as if perching on skyscrapers. Yet this is natural beauty. Though nothing feels natural or beautiful about what I have planned for today.

Mine's the only car here. Good. I don't want witnesses to my cowardly behaviour. I see a phone box. Beside it, a sign.

The Samaritans.
Always there day or night.

Then a phone number. A bus stop. I imagine a bus arriving. People stumbling off, nearing the cliff's edge. A ring of the bell and the bus drives on as the lemmings drop.

Not everyone's idea of a good day out.

It's cold. For May. Mind you, it's early, I wanted to be here before any other contenders got here. I pull the zip up on my jacket so it grazes my Adam's apple. And not for the first time wonder how it came to this. And yet, there's a dreaded inevitability to it as well.

I see a wooden floor. Ill-fitting chunks of carpet. The wood looking like ripped-edged lakes between them. Mam with her beehive disappearing behind clouds of smoke as she watches her soaps. Murmuring to the women on the black and white screen. Shouting out sometimes. Topping up her glass from the jug as regularly as she lights her fags.

The bell ringing in the playground as we're called back in from break. A lad in calipers not making it to the toilets on time. A pissy puddle that lasts for days. He has a week off school coz of the ribbing.

The prefabs. The courtyard. Standing in line like soldiers when all we'd been were bad lads. A mixed-race lad getting in the back of a Rolls-Royce. The windows steaming as it drives off.

The euphoria of my first time on a dance floor. My first clubbing experience. Wanting more. And more. Till that was my life. The highs. The money. The laughs. The lows.

Natalie. Fresh as a daisy the morning after our wedding. In the First Class Lounge. Looking at me blinking, going, 'Did yesterday really happen?' Yes, my sweet, it did. But look at us now.

Us and the kids. A beach club in Ibiza. Cold beer and warm heads. Greek salads in the Spanish sun. Cally's giggles. Owen's serious face. Me desperate to get him to break a smile. Clown, that's me. Always the clown. Never really wanted a family. Got one and look what I did to it.

And look at me now.

I know what I do next is going to cause them pain.

Why didn't I stick to my motto? Look after number one. Just worry about yourself. Don't get involved with other people and . . .

I'm a coward and I can't go back.

And no matter how much they might end up hating me, it won't be as much as I hate myself right now.

And her. The pressure. And the things I've done. What I did to Owen. What Cally knows. What they don't know. What I know. What I've seen. Who I've let down. It's too much. It's time to go. It's time to make amends.

I hear the crack of tyres on gravel. A car has pulled in next to me. I don't want to look, to see their face. The engine stays running.

Redemption time.

PART ONE

Natalie, 2014

'Welcome to suburbia, kids,' I say brightly as we watch the removal men unloading the last of our possessions from the back of the van. They hoist it aloft and carry it solemnly towards the house on their shoulders, like pallbearers bearing a coffin. I hear Cally tut loudly. At sixteen she hates being called a kid, even when I say it ironically.

'I can't believe they got so many things out of that tiny space,' Owen says.

'Now that's magic!' I say, trying to sound like Paul Daniels. I hear Cally tut even louder. I don't have to look. I know she's rolling her eyes.

'It's like Mary Poppins' handbag.' Owen giggles.

'Oh shut UP, bumder!' Cally snaps, then she turns her anger to me. 'I can't believe you've brought us here. It's *embarrassing*.'

Every time she emphasizes a word like that she means to puncture me. I should be used to it by now, but today my guard must be down – they say moving house is as stressful as bereavement – so it's like a roundhouse kick to the guts.

'You didn't seem to mind when we came to view the house three times.'

'I must've been on *drugs*.'

'It's nice.' Owen tries to compensate for his sister's rudeness.

'That's easy for you to say, you don't have to live here,' she spits.

'You know I can't keep away from you, Cally.'

'Oh shut UP, bumder!' and she flounces off towards the house. She does a good line in flouncing, my daughter.

'It's your cheery disposition at all times!' he calls after her. 'It's infectious!'

'Piss . . . OFF!'

I look to Owen and grimace as we hear the new front door slam.

'Well. She's gone inside. That's a start,' he says, a little act of encouragement, then links my arm and drags me along to follow her. Have I made a mistake? OK, so the cul-de-sac is a step down from our last place; well, several steps down, but that wouldn't be hard. This circle of individually designed Eighties mock-Georgian houses has its own bucolic charm.

Or does bucolic mean it gives you the plague? God, I hope not.

As we reach the garden gate a woman appears from nowhere, scuttling towards us. She's tiny, like a munchkin, and wears Fifties winged glasses. She is carrying a vast Tupperware container, the transparent sides revealing a lumpy cake within.

'Mrs Bioletti?' she chirps, all smiles and flicky eyes, sussing out myself and Owen very quickly, the smile never once leaving her lips. Only problem is, because of her height it's like she's checking out our nipples.

I smile back. 'Hello.'

'Welcome to Dominic Close. I'm Betty Caligary. Number seven. I've been here since the estate was built.'

She says 'estate' oddly. Like it's a French word. *Éstat.* Presumably this is to differentiate between the sort of the place this area wants to be – smart, swanky, aspirational, like a country estate, rather than a common or garden council estate. It makes me laugh.

'Original cast, you might say. I made you a carrot cake. It's just a little thing I do. To say hello and I hope you'll be very happy here. We're a tight-knit bunch.'

'Oh, thank you,' I say warmly as she passes me the incredibly heavy box. 'It's really . . .'

But she cuts in, 'And you must be Owen.'

'I am,' says Owen. I hear the defeat in his voice. My heart sinks.

'So sorry for all your troubles. Nasty business.'

'Thank you,' I say. How does she know? How?

'I Googled you,' she says conspiratorially, as if reading my mind. She pinches my arm, then turns on her heel and retreats. As she does she calls back, 'My phone number's on a piece of paper in there. Anything you need, just give me a tinkle!'

'Thank you so much!' I call after her.

I look to Owen.

'She Googled you, Mum.'

I nod. So that's it. My identity is out there in Dominic Close.

'She Googled me,' I agree, unnerved.

'Oh well. It's good they know,' says Owen. 'Means you don't have to keep explaining yourself.'

How did I produce such a lovely, charming, rational young man?

'Come on. Let's get inside and have some of that cake,' he says with a wink.

9

And in we go.

When I was a little girl I used to have this silly dream of being famous. I wasn't sure how this was going to happen; sometimes I thought maybe I'd be a pop star, sometimes an Oscar-winning screen idol, possibly even an Olympic gymnast (but a pretty one, not one with a face like a bag of spanners). Other times I considered becoming Prime Minister (again, a pretty one, bow on the blouse collar possibly. I felt there was an opening in the market for that). For most people these childhood fantasies never come to fruition, so it was ultimately quite the surprise that in my mid-thirties I became – sort of – famous. And by none of the above routes.

On the 18th of May 2009, my husband Danny left our old house to go for a pint of milk and never came back. I'd like to be able to say that the last time he spoke to me was significant, that as he left the house he turned one final time and told me how much he loved me, how much I meant to him, how I had been the peaty soil from which his petals flourished. In fact, I was in the bath at the time listening to *Popmaster* on Radio 2. I heard him calling goodbye and, this is the embarrassing bit, I didn't even reply. I've never told anyone that. When I described it to the police I said I'd called back, 'See you, Danny!' but the truth was I'd been concentrating on the radio quiz, trying to remember if Haysi Fantayzee had had their top ten hit in 1983 or 1984. Either way I'd been wrong – it was 1982. By the time I realized Danny had been calling, the front door had slammed and the moment had passed.

Don't worry. That's the only thing I lied to the police about. I didn't omit any gruesome facts like I'd actually killed him, chopped him in a mincer and served him in a lasagne for dinner. And I'd only twisted the truth in that tiny way so I didn't look like a complete cow, ignoring my husband, and therefore forcing him to run away. *Well, Natalie, who wouldn't want to disappear when his wife snubbed him for a slightly dodgy Eighties pop song, hmm?* I could hear the police saying.

There is one thing that plays on my mind. Something I never mentioned to the police at the time because it seemed so minor, and I thought I'd got it wrong. The night before he disappeared Danny had said with a sense of urgency, 'Nat? I've got to tell you something.'

We were in the kitchen. I was cooking. I forget what. I turned to look at him. For a second he wavered, and I worried he was going to say something bad.

Then he burst out laughing and said, 'Ha, got you!'

And we both laughed. But I couldn't help but worry for a very long time that maybe he'd been about to unburden himself of some grisly secret.

But he hadn't been. He'd been winding me up.

These days I don't like to dwell on the pain of those first few hours, days, then months after we realized he was missing. It's too painful, still. One minute Danny was there, next minute he was not. He left the house and didn't come home. He didn't take his phone, his cash point card and credit cards were never subsequently used, and a few days later his car was found hundreds of miles away near Beachy Head, a beauty spot popular with people who want to commit suicide. The police naturally assumed this meant he had killed himself and every time they called they needn't have said anything, just played a sound effect of a massive hardback book slamming shut – case closed.

But by then I had become a reluctant media sensation. Danny and I had, back in the day, run a club in Manchester called Milk that had been franchised round the country. We had made a bit of money. There was a touch of glamour to the story. My children were photogenic, and we looked good on newspaper pages, despite having piggy red eyes from crying. I went on *This Morning* and begged Danny to come home; they kept asking me back even after the discovery of the car, 'for an update' or 'to review the papers'. I turned them down, but by then it was too late – I was recognized wherever I went.

Oh look, it's her. The one whose husband disappeared. The nightclub one.

There she is. With the kids. Poor thing.

It was a very strange feeling to walk into your local gastro-pub because you couldn't be bothered cooking and feel everybody's eyes upon you. And why? Because they felt sorry for you. Or worse, they disapproved of you.

Why isn't she stopping in like a proper widow?

If he is still alive, as she claims, why isn't she out there looking for him instead of ordering deep fried camembert?

I bet she killed him.

Everywhere I went I was judged. Or I felt I was. If one of the kids was playing up, it was evidence of my dreadful parenting skills – no wonder my husband left me. Or if I dared to smile, I was getting over this disappearance thing far too quickly and therefore a bit of a psychopath – and again, no wonder he buggered off.

The papers kept reporting the story, which I was grateful for. Something told me that yes, Danny might have got out of his car and thrown himself off that high cliff. But another part of me saw him parking there and catching a bus to . . . who knew where? According to the papers he was 'severely depressed' and our family was experiencing financial difficulties – on the verge of bankruptcy, they actually said – and this was why he'd gone missing, and the story kept running. People felt an affinity with us and the all-too-common despair felt in austerity Britain. The only problem was, none of it was true. I'd made the mistake of saying to one reporter that Danny was 'a bit fed up' the week before he went. But this was only because he'd smashed the screen on his mobile phone and had had to cough up a hundred quid to get it fixed. By the time he went missing, the phone was fine. But why spend all that money on something you weren't going to use? That didn't make sense. And as for our finances, they were flourishing really. When we sold Milk we had made enough that neither of us had to work again. Not bad for a couple approaching forty.

Yes, we had debts. Big debts. With no income coming in, we had continued to spend, and we'd decided that the time had come to downsize. But it hadn't caused us any pain. We had enjoyed the ten years we'd had in the posh house with the massive garden, we had enjoyed being profligate and getting the weekly shop from the better class of supermarkets. Now it was time to tighten our belts and buckle down and be sensible. But it didn't worry us. We had come from nothing, and we would return to nothing; we'd be returning to a very comfortable form of normality.

Except that 'we' used to be four. And now 'we' are three. And since Owen left home to move in with his boyfriend Matt, 'we' are really only two.

Some days I wish I had my mum to speak to. To tell her how I feel. To tell her I miss her almost as much as I miss him. My mum's name was Sheila, and after my dad walked out on us when I was still in nappies (she subsequently usually only referred to him as 'that knobhead'; his name, in fact, was Derek) she brought me up in a very ordinary low-rise block of council flats in Stockport. She did a succession of bar jobs when I was at primary school, which meant that she was often out in the evenings, when I would be looked after by a variety of her mates from the local amateur dramatic company, of which she was a leading light. It was a colourful childhood, as Mum loved eccentric people and anything that went against the grain. Ours was a world of Easter eggs for breakfast and impromptu discos with my dolls at midnight. When I started secondary school, her gift of the gab and self-confidence led her to abandon the pubs and take a job doing telesales for Yellow Pages, which was then based in Stockport. She made an efficient saleswoman, apparently, with her warm, friendly manner and good sense of humour. She also never took any shit. She called a spade a spade. These days people might say she 'told it how it was' – if that didn't have overtones of reactionary mouthing-off about nothing. She was wonderful. She was all I had.

I started going to bars and clubs in Stockport and then Manchester from around the age of fifteen. I loved not necessarily to drink but to dance, and could spend all night up on a podium shaping it out to 128 beats per minute. Mum didn't mind, as long as I always came back when I said I would and told her who I was going to be with.

Then when I was seventeen, Mum got ill. Ovarian cancer. She lost all her hair and started wearing a succession of outrageous wigs. She was like Mum, but fainter. Towards the end, a neighbour called the local priest out. Mum wasn't religious but she also wasn't rude, so she humoured him for twenty minutes before he asked if he could say a prayer for her. She was wearing her bobbed wig that day, and gave the impression of being quite prim and proper. It was one of her more convincing hairpieces, even if the impression was less convincing.

The priest took my hand. And her hand. And then dragged them together as if we were about to play 'One potato, two

14

potato' and then he broke into his rather long-winded prayer. It felt like we were there for half an hour. I could feel Mum's hand shaking. I think he took this for tiredness, because he gripped on tighter and prayed more vehemently. I knew her better. She was trying desperately not to laugh.

And when the priest came out with 'And dear Lord, bless every hair on Sheila's head . . .' she could stem the flow no longer, and she snorted an involuntary guffaw which startled the priest into silence. Before winding the proceedings up with a rapid 'in the name of the Father' and so on.

After Mum died I lost the flat I'd been brought up in as although it was a council flat, Mum sublet it from someone from the am-dram group and they wanted it back. I took solace in my other family, the people I'd met through the clubs. I lived in a succession of squats in central Manchester before making the brave move South to London with a couple of club kids who'd heard of a squat in a beautiful block of flats in West London going begging. It was the late eighties, and lots of loft apartments and offices lay empty. And it was at a party in one of these that I met a gorgeous guy just a year or two younger than me who was addicted to jelly bean sweets. This was Danny. He claimed he'd seen me out and about around London, working the door of a club near Piccadilly Circus. I had no recollection of him. But before I could say so he'd offered me a sweet. The rest, as they say, is history.

For years he kept a jar of these sweets in the fridge. I used to bicker with him that there was no need, those sweets don't really go off, but he said he liked the colour they brought to the fridge. They were his sweet of choice and he enjoyed the ritual of opening the door, pulling the nipple shaped lid off the jar in the door, and furtling around inside for a handful of the multicoloured beans. After he disappeared I didn't dare move them from their home. If that fridge was jelly-bean-free it meant I had given up hope. He would return. He would furtle and eat again.

Last week I discovered that they do sort of go off. I tried a bit of furtling myself and found that they'd all stuck together. One homogeneous mass of rainbow-coloured coagulation. I threw the jar in the bin and felt lousy about it.

Today it's five years, three months and eighteen days since he disappeared, but even now I can describe in minute detail what he was wearing when he left. I had to say it over and over again to the police, in appeals, to the press. I'd seen him gelling his hair in the hall mirror while my bath was running. Evisu jeans, black bomber jacket from Schott, pale pink Ralph Lauren polo shirt, Nike Airs in baby blue. The distinguishing gold tooth, right at the back, so you only caught a glimpse of it when he was throwing his head back and laughing. Which he did often. He liked a laugh, did Danny. And then there was the necklace. The one I'd given him on the night of the millennium. Silver chain with a dog tag on. On the tag four letters were engraved. D N O C. Mine, his and the kids' initials. On the back it said *please return to* . . . and our address. It was a little in-joke about Danny's dreadful sense of direction. Well, he is lost now. And nobody's bothered to return him.

I got some smaller versions made for the kids, but I don't think they wear theirs any more. I don't like to ask. He never took his off, though.

Any time I think about Danny, I think three things:
Where is he?
How is he?
And the worst:
Is he?

That last question is the hardest. Even if I kind of know the answer.

And then there's, jelly beans aside, the life choices I've had to make. Something as simple as having a haircut can result in months of agony. In the end Cally told me to 'stop fucking about and get on with it.'

Aren't teenage daughters kind? So I bit the bullet. And now instead of looking quite unusual – middle-aged woman with lots of hair but not the intellectual capacity of Mary Beard – I just look like everybody else. And d'you know what? After being stared at for five years, that feeling is sweet. Although when Cally saw the new cropped look she commented,

'Oh my God, no wonder Dad left, you're a total *lesbian*.'

'Good job your brother can't hear you saying that,' I said.

'No he can't. He's probably off somewhere listening to musicals and bumming *lads*.'

My son punches his sister a lot.

And then last year I had to start wearing glasses. After trying to read the instructions on a microwave curry and having to move it close and then far and then bringing it back halfway, like I was playing an invisible trombone, I thought I'd better get my eyes tested. And now not only do I have to wear glasses just to see normally, I have to wear another pair when I'm reading. So not only do I now look just like every other harassed mother of two, I also have not-so-cool specs into the bargain. Danny really will never recognize me now.

'You look like Velma from *Scooby Doo*,' Cally said dully when I returned from the optician, not looking up from her iPad.

'Velma's cute,' countered her delightful older brother as I left the room.

But not before I heard Cally reply, 'No she's not, she's a dog.'

Cally used to be lovely. She was eleven when Danny went and, hand on heart I'm not just saying this because she's my daughter, she was so sweet. And I can say this now because she's my daughter, but these days she's an out and out cow. I put it down to her missing her dad.

I'm unpacking boxes in the living room with Owen when Cally comes in with a face pack on.

'Cally. We're meant to be unpacking. And you've done a face pack?'

Cally folds her arms, mirroring my body language and spits back, 'Cally. We're meant to be unpacking. And you've done a face pack?'

One thing she's good at is mimicking. She can do Cheryl Cole, Ann Widdicombe, Lorraine Kelly, Sharon Osbourne, Kylie Minogue. And me. It never ceases to wind me up, but I've stopped rising to the bait. I just glare at her.

She glares back. Then:

'I just want to point out,' she unfolds her arms, though thankfully she's just being herself again. Well, I say 'thankfully' – I know what's coming: 'that Dad has no chance of finding us now you've moved us to this manky old estate.'

'It's not old,' tuts Owen.

'It's not old,' she mimics him.

'It's not!' I back him up. 'Anyway, we've been through all this.'

'We've been through all this,' she mimics.

'Cally, drop it,' says Owen.

So she does. Well, she drops the mimicking me bit.

'If he's had a bump on the head and he comes . . . staggering back to the old place, riddled with amnesia, he doesn't stand a chance. On your own conscience be it!'

She runs from the room.

'Take no notice, Mum,' says Owen.

But I know she has a point. It's my second-favourite fantasy: that he's had a bump on the head and doesn't remember who he is. We'll bump into each other in Sainsbury's and he won't recognize me. I'll show him press cuttings about when he went missing, and slowly he'll start to trust me and fall back in love with me. My favourite fantasy is that he is living in a cottage near Beachy Head, mortified by what he has done, and one day he will work up the courage to phone home and say sorry.

And she's right. He won't be able to find me. And when he does, he'll take one look at me and go, *What happened to your hair, Nat?*

Age happened to my hair.

Why are you living in a suburban cul-de-sac that looks like something out of a No-Frills Desperate Housewives?

Because we brought the kids up in a big posh house in the country and it was too big for just me and Cally and it made financial sense to sell and save the profit to live off. And we were going to downsize anyway, it's just that you buggered off without so much as a by your leave . . .

What is a by your leave?

I don't know, stop interrupting me. And then when you went I kind of froze and didn't do anything apart from look for you and campaign for missing people, and I stayed put. And then last year I thought, you might never be coming home and so what did it matter if we moved? And there were so many memories of you there. This is part of my new life.

Thanks.

Yeah, well, thanks for sodding off and never coming back. Really appreciate that, Danny. Nice one.

I realize Owen is talking and I can't hear him.

'Sorry, dear?'

Dear? What am I? Ninety?

'I was just saying. It's obvious Cally's winding you up at the moment. Me and Matt are going to Birmingham tomorrow. Why don't we take her with us?'

'Birmingham?' I say incredulously. 'Why are you going to Birmingham?'

'Clothes Show Live. Matt got tickets through work.'

'She doesn't really like clothes.'

'I know, but it's a day out. And that designer from *Kings Road*'s gonna be there.'

Cally loves *Kings Road*, the fly on the wall soapy documentary thing about a load of spoilt brats. I hate it, but at forty I don't think I'm particularly the target demographic.

'Or d'you need her here helping unpack?'

'She'll be neither use nor ornament, Owen; if you can get her to go, do it. Might cheer her up.'

'I'll go and get us some of that cake.'

Owen heads out to the kitchen and I pull two framed photos from a tea chest. The first shows Owen, aged thirteen, winning a tennis tournament in Cheshire somewhere, I don't remember where now. His sunny face beams out at me, light hitting his cheeks from the gold cup that's almost as big as his head. I don't think I've ever seen him smile like that since his dad went. The other is a photo of me and Danny taken from the pages of *Dazed and Confused* with a headline: 'Milking It'. We felt we were so cool back then, having our pictures in this hipster's bible. The thing I think when I look at it now is a) how badly dressed we were (it might have been the Nineties, but platform trainers were never a good look) and b) how bloody young we look. I also appear to have about three different hairstyles on the one head.

Youth. Platform trainers. What did we know?

I look at Danny. He's wearing a sort of satin dungaree suit. The stylist for the shoot provided it, he would never normally have worn anything like that. I look at his twenty-something face and feel a stab of pain in my chest when I take in how handsome he was. It's like I've never seen him before and it's my first time, and yet rolled into that sensation is the realization that one day he won't be around any more. And he might be dead, he might be alive, but I just don't know.

I used to have this picture on the wall of the little toilet in the old house. I'm not sure I'll hang it anywhere now. Too painful.

A huge cube of boxes almost fills the smallest bedroom. They contain all the lever arch files that contain all the accounts and files to do with Milk up until we sold it. I've been nervous about throwing it all away because I can't remember how many years my accountant said I had to hang onto it for. I'm probably safe to chuck it now, but for some reason I packed it all for the move anyway. I make a mental note to email the accountant later.

As I put the frame back in the box I hear a weird slicing noise coming from outside. I look through the window to see an odd sight. A rake of a woman is gliding across the cul-de-sac on a pair of skates, an envelope in her hand. She stops at the gate to our drive and then daintily walks the final few feet to the front door. The bell rings. I go to answer.

'Hi! I'm Harmony Frayn!' She does a double take. 'Oh. You changed your hair.'

I want to punch her. How dare she be so over-familiar.

'How can I help you, Harmony?'

Harmony has got to be anorexic. And the skating has made her very red of face. What face there is. Mind you, even though she is the size she is, it doesn't stop her wearing skin-tight jeans that, let's just say, leave very little to the imagination. She has a topknot and freckles and is wearing a jumper with a treble clef on it. She looks like one of those skeletons medical students have in their halls of residence bedrooms, dressed by Primark.

'I bought you this!'

She hands me the envelope. It has quite childish, swirly writing on the front which says:

Natalie Bioletti VIP
♡ ♡

and then some love hearts.

'I'm not a VIP,' I say.

'Oh, but you are.'

The urge to punch her is even stronger now. Even if she does look days from death.

'Everyone who moves into Dominic Close . . . we like to make them feel special! Can I come in and look round? This house has been empty so long I've forgotten what it's like inside.'

She is practically pushing me out of the way but I block the door with an iron arm.

'I'm sorry. No. It's . . . all a bit of a mess at the moment.'

'I don't mind mess.'

'Why don't you wait till we have a housewarming?'

'You're having a housewarming? Awesome! Do you want me to sing? Me and Melody? My twin sister? We sing, we're really good, we've been on *X Factors* three times with our group Mirror Image. Simon Cowell said we were a bit karaoke but Melody said he was just hacked off coz he wasn't sure how to market us.'

'I'll see,' I say, when what I really want to say is, *it's X Factor, not X Factors.*

I have no plans to have a housewarming. Even less so now.

'Anyway, thanks for the card, Harmony.'

She sees me looking suspiciously at her feet.

'They're skates!' she beams.

'I know.'

'Did Betty from number seven bring you one of her carrot cakes?'

'She did.'

'Awesome!'

And then she lifts up her hand and I think she is going to punch me. I flinch but she screams, 'High five for Dominic Close!'

So I high five her limply, then, rather rudely, I step back and shut the front door. I listen to the slicing sound of her pushing herself home across the cul-de-sac.

'Who the FUCK was that?' Cally says when I turn around. She's standing at the top of the stairs with a face like thunder.

'Harmony Frayn,' I say perkily, as if that explains everything. And from the look on Cally's face, it does.

'Oh GOD. I want to kill myself.'

'Oh, shut up, Cally,' I say, moving back into the living room. And then, as an afterthought, 'And don't say fuck.'

An hour or so later I head upstairs and my heart stops beating for a second. It looks like Danny is stood in the bedroom, his back to me, wearing one of his favourite coats. He's staring out of the window, looking out across the Oaktree Estate, so-called because if you view it from the sky, the main roads and cul-de-sacs off it form the outline of a many-branched oak tree. IS Danny weighing up whether he approves of this new setting? Or . . .

23

But then he turns and it is of course Owen. He looks embarrassed to have been caught trying it on.

'Sorry.'

'No, it's fine. D'you like it?'

'Course I like it, it's Barbour.'

I never threw Danny's clothes out. I've been meaning to, but . . .

'You can have it.'

It's been so hard. What if he comes back? What will he wear?

'I'm not sure the biker look's really me.'

'Oh, stop with the false modesty, you look great.'

'I look butch.'

'You are butch,' I say, and go into the bathroom. I put the loo seat down and sit to regain my composure. It's then that I hear the doorbell ring again. A few seconds later I hear heavy footsteps descending the stairs, then I hear Owen talking to someone on the doorstep. When I hear the front door closing I brave it and head out.

'Who was it?' I call. He looks up from the hall.

'Harmony Frayn.'

Oh, for God's sake.

'What did she want?'

'She says don't worry about a housewarming. Her Mum's going to do a party in our honour on Sunday afternoon.'

As my daughter would say: WTF?

I'm beginning to think Cally was right. It was a mistake moving here. I've been here five minutes and already the neighbours are taking over my life.

Cally

My mother is SO embarrassing. Owen is taking me on a day out to the NEC where there will be fast food outlets and really cute eating places and street food stalls probably, and what has she done? She has made us a PICNIC.

I really wish she would die.

I know she's like an ORPHAN. And never really had her OWN mum. And so didn't have a role model to work out how you do this family shiz but c'mon guys! A packed lunch? SERIOUSLY?

Normally the idea of being cooped up with Owen and his so called boyfriend Matt the Prat all day would drive me literally mental but:

One. They're taking me to Clothes Show Live.

Which is amazing because apparently you just walk round the NEC and see loads of famous people and fashion shows and there are stalls with loads of freebies on them and you get hundreds and hundreds of goody bags with amazing things in them like hair straighteners and foundation and breast implants and it's really really cool and I'll be able to use the bags as school bags for like the next a million years. Result. Bags for life or what?

Two. Them taking me out gets me out of the hideous Oaktree Estate.

As I said to Mum, they can't even spell. Oak tree is two words for puck's sake. I really don't like it. Every road looks the same. Poo-brown box houses. They are, they are literally like shoe boxes propped up on one end. And the colour of poo. Well. Poo if you've not been eating too healthily and they've gone a sort of milky coffee colour. OK, they're cappuccino-coloured houses. And they don't all look like shoe boxes, I suppose. But my point still stands, like I said to Mum when we moved. How will Dad find us now? He won't. And this is why I officially hate the Oaktree Estate and everyone who lives there. I want to go back to our old house. Not coz I'm a ridonculous snob or anything, because that house was AMAZEBALLS compared to the current one, but just because DAD WOULD BE ABLE TO FIND IT. I am amazed Mum hasn't taken this into consideration. She is worse than the Gestapo.

Four. OK, she's not worse than the Gestapo.

I know she couldn't afford to keep us in the big house. But I have left a letter for the new owners telling them to look out for Dad and to give him my new mobile number if he ever turns up unannounced. Seeing them might throw him. And I included a photo of him just so they'd know what he looked like. I didn't tell Mum I was doing this. Not that she'd be cross or anything. It's just. Well, you never know how she's going to react. And I'm sure she thinks I should just pull myself together or something. I have tried, but it's harder than you'd think sometimes.

Ooh yes, and Five. When we get to Clothes Show Live, Rufus De Villeneuve will be there.

Oh my God he is completely amazing and fit and stylish

and I just know that if I see him I will literally fall to the ground and have an epileptic fit or faint or something. He's like really old (33 or something) but he's really buff and has this massive beard that on most men would make them look like Father Christmas or something but on him makes him look like someone who makes you go, like, hold me back coz I'd so do him in every room of the house!

Of course Owen and Pratley McShatley reckon he's a full-on massive bender. But I'm like, what the fuck do you know? And they just laugh.

Don't get me wrong, they're not laughing because they find me, like, funny and stuff. Seriously, they're laughing because they think every man that walks this planet is totally into taking it up the pipe.

I say this to them. I also call Matt a retard, and World War Three breaks out. Matt's driving the car and he is threatening to pull over on the hard shoulder of the M6 as he is 'so angry with you, Cally' – deal with it, dog breath. And Owen's neck has gone red (I'm sitting in the back and can only see the back of his head as he's too lazy to turn round) and he's telling me what is and isn't acceptable.

1) I can't be reductive and say being gay is all about anal sex.

Yeah yeah, whatever you say, Owen.

2) I can't call Matt a retard because it's offensive to people with alternative abilities or something.

I know it's offensive, that's why I say it, you IDIOT.

3) And I better not even think about calling Owen a ginge because that's tantamount to racism apparently.

Oh drop dead and die, hot pubes. Are there countries full of naked gingers walking around starving to death because of the colour of their hair? No. I don't think so. THAT's racism.

4) I'm really lucky they've brought me today because everyone at both their works wanted the spare ticket but they've chosen me and I should be grateful.

Oh God I'm so sorry I'm not grovelling at your shrine, gays! I know you only invited me coz Mum can't stand the sight of me and wanted me out of her hair so she could arrange all her hideous knick-knacks in her new Wendy house. Deal with it!

I wouldn't mind, but I haven't even mentioned the fact that I've noticed Owen is wearing one of Dad's coats. Well, that's not strictly true; I did say, 'I can't believe you're wearing that,' under my breath, but I'm not sure he heard me. And even if he did he wouldn't have said much, coz his comebacks are so lame. I've overlooked that in the name of having a nice day out, but seriously, Owen won't let anything drop! I can't be arsed to argue with them so I bury my head in my phone and check my Twitter and Facebook.

I love Twitter. I've got 325 followers, which is more than some of my friends have got but much less than Macey McIntyre's got. But then someone said she'd paid like a thousand pounds to get a thousand followers. I'm not sure how that works so I can't do that but 325 isn't that bad. I've already tweeted the bum cheeks out of going to Clothes Show Live ON A FREE TICKET so I check my mentions to check that everyone at school is suitably jel. And they are! I've changed my avi to a picture of Rufus De Villeneuve and that's got me loads of comments too. I retweet some of them.

Fab avi Cally.
LOL at your pic Hon.

God I love Twitter. It's just so real.
I see another mention:

Drop dead Cally you skinny alien.

It's from a girl in Year 10 but she's only joking so I decide against blocking her. People are so funny. And if I block her I think that might mean one less follower, so . . .

Facebook's really quiet today. I don't think anyone goes on there any more. In my feed I see that Mum has put the status:

Got the house to myself today. And breathe.

What a bitch. And she's got 28 likes for it. I wish there was a dislike button. I would press that like ten million times and see how she breathes then. God she's annoying. Instead I write her a private message:

Mum maybe you should think twice about writing stuff like that on here in case people think you're happy that dad has gone missing. #justsaying

And then I press send. God she winds me up.

Matt has put some weird music on the stereo.

'What's this?' I ask.

'Belle and Sebastian,' he replies. And they both start humming along.

I remember when my brother was a laugh. He's only five years older than me but now he thinks he's got to act like my dad or something. Which is bang out of order because even Dad never behaved like that. My dad is a laugh and is dead cool and always called me Princess. Mum was the strict one, he was the soft one. But then, being married to my mum, is it any wonder he ran away?

I write another tweet.

Brothers are SO annoying. #cantchooseyourfamilydotcom

My brother isn't just a gay, he's a professional gay. He runs a website that helps people do the gay thing better and ever since he got into all that it's like he's been to homo hospital and had major sense of humour bypass surgery. He may as well not run his stupid website, he should just be honest about what he really does, which is be a fully paid-up member of the PC Police. I know I shouldn't take the piss out of people with special needs but he is so easy to wind up it's hilarious, and I only do it to annoy him. And it works! No honestly, I love people with special needs. Keesha Lomax has got a cousin who's got that Down's Syndrome and she's SO SWEET. Last time I saw her she let me put make-up on her and put a false bun in her hair like the Peru Two and she looked SO LOVELY. Keesha's mum was less impressed though and rang my mum and told her I had treated Patsy like a doll and I should be ashamed of myself. Mum gave her some bullshit about me not being myself since my dad left but she still grounded me. God. You try and help people make the best of themselves and it all gets thrown back in your face. Patsy loved it. She was so happy she cried. AWWWW I LOVE HER.

Time for another tweet.

OMG Literally can't believe in less than an hour I'm meeting the entire cast of Kings Road.

Everyone at school will be sooooo jel when they read that. I'll be like the coolest person in the entire universe. I'm already quite cool coz my mum's been on the telly and my dad was in the papers and it was really amazing because when

Dad ran away like, yeah it was really intense and I hated it and I'd rather he didn't, but for ages the teachers let me get away with loads of things they wouldn't usually. They excused me from tests and didn't go mental when I was late with homework, and I hardly had to do any PE coz I'd just turn on the waterworks or say, 'I couldn't find my trainers coz I think my dad took them.' And it was really cool. And all the girls think it's really cool having my brother being a massive bumder, and being on posters and everything.

Basically when he was 18 he posed for this poster about coming out for some gay charity trying to encourage more people to do it and it was actually quite a good shot and all the girls were like 'Oh my God why are gay boys so fit?' and 'I can't believe he's your brother, that's so cool.'

And even though I was like 'Oh it's disgusting' everyone thought I was joking, so in the end I was like 'Oh yeah he's amazing. Like, I totally heart him?' But fortunately that's died down a lot lately.

'Can you pass us a sandwich please, Cally?' Matthew says.

'What did your last slave die of?' I grumble. And then hilariously shout 'THAT WAS A JOKE!' and punch him in the neck. Oh my God, giggles! Only now apparently I'm not even allowed to touch him when he is driving as we could have a 'serious accident' coz we're on the motorway and not only would I kill the pair of them I'd kill myself as well and ten or twenty innocent lives if a minibus was passing.

Honestly. I just can't win.

I grab a sandwich from the plastic bag on the seat beside me and hand it to Owen to hand to him.

'Just in case I touch him,' I say.

'You're a fucking nightmare,' he says.

'And you're Rafael Nadal. NOT!' I go, and I piss myself coz if there's one thing likely to wind Owen up it's reminding him HOW SHIT HE IS AT TENNIS. LOLZ!!!

God. I am, like, well funny?

Owen is fidgeting with the lining of his coat. Even Matt's finding it irritating.

'Stop fidgeting,' he goes, and I go hysterical. I love it when they argue.

'DOMESTIC!' I shout and I can tell Matt's trying not to laugh.

Owen stops. And then after a bit he starts again. Eventually he pulls something out of the lining of the coat. It's a small piece of white paper with writing on it. Tiny. He sits there turning it over in his hands. And then I realize that he has started to cry.

Oh God. The MORTIFICATION. What if someone sees? What if someone really cool drives past (which wouldn't be hard as Matt is the slowest driver in the world) and sees me in the car with this loon? It's too much to bear.

'What's the matter, Bubsy?' Matt goes.

Bubsy. They have THE most ridiculous names for each other. I can't bear to find out what's set him off now. I ram my earphones in my ear and listen to some proper music. One Direction. Then I don't have to listen to them being so CRAP.

I have that daydream again where Harry Styles is proposing to me and he's looking really scared in case I say no. All the girls at school are looking and I'm like *God Harry, this is SO embarrassing.* And he starts to cry and then I laugh my head off and go *RINSED!*

I look at my phone. Mum has replied to my message on Facebook.

As you know, Cally, my settings are set to private so it's only close friends who see what I write. I also have a false name. Unlike you, I don't have a desire to broadcast everything to as many people as possible.

If you say so, Mother! She didn't even put a kiss! No wonder I feel so unloved! So I jab back, really hitting the phone.

I love you who do you love or what?

And press send. It's amazing what I have to put up with.

Owen

Sometimes I wish I knew what was going on in Matt's head. He's so poor at communicating it's hard to tell. It's like all he can deal with is the good stuff, the happy stuff, the silly stuff, and when that's not on offer he hermetically seals himself away. Like today when I was sitting in the car crying because I'd found that ticket in the lining of Dad's coat, what does he do? Calls me Bubsy like that's going to make everything OK, squeezes my leg and then just leaves me to it. Even though most of the things Cally says are incendiary, at least she is honest about her feelings and lets us know them. And some.

'Owen. It's just a left luggage ticket from years ago,' Matt says that night over a stir-fry. We only ever seem to have stir-fries. Quick, functional, healthy, no messing about. Very Matt.

'I know, but it tells a story.'

He tips his head to one side and I know what he's thinking. 'Oh, here we go. Owen mopes some more about his dad and I don't know what to say, so I try not to yawn and lose interest.'

'What story's that?' he asks, raising a far-too-full glass of white wine to his pursed lips.

'Well . . . Mum and Dad obviously put some stuff in left luggage once.'

He nods, though I can see he doesn't understand.

'I know it's not earth-shattering but . . . it just brings things up, you know?'

He takes another swig of wine. Soon he will be slurring his words and leaving big gaps between each one.

I'm too hard on him sometimes. It's a lot for him to cope with, I suppose. It might be easier if I was grieving properly – had Dad died and there'd been a funeral there would be something finite about that, there'd be a grave, closure, forward movement – but there's not, there's the eternal question mark.

'I'm sorry,' I say, sensing I'm confusing him rather than, say, wasting his time.

'You don't have to apologize, Bubsy.'

There we go again. Bubsy. As if that makes everything all right. He then frowns. Something is confusing him.

'Is it the demo tomorrow?'

We're taking part in a demo against a UKIP candidate who's coming to speak at the university. He has blamed the recent poor weather on the advent of gay marriage.

'No, that's next weekend.'

He hiccups then nods, relieved. Then repeats, 'You don't have to apologize, Bubsy.'

I nod. Maybe he's on a loop. Better not to encourage him.

'Wasn't today mad?' he says, incredulous, shifting the tone of our conversation and moving us onto safer territory.

'Mental,' I say, for it was. And as if on cue, my mobile rings. I check the caller ID and answer.

'Hi Mum.'

'Owen, what's this about Cally being scouted for modelling?' Mum is sounding impatient, pleasantries have been dispensed with, no beating around the bush tonight.

'Yup. It's true. I bet she hasn't shut up about it.'

'She's gone for a sleepover at some hideous posh girl's. She's phoned me, I think she's drunk. Rambling on about having the last laugh. What happened?'

'Well, we went to the Clothes Show and . . .'

'God, I wish I'd been home when you dropped her back.'

'This woman started following us round and . . .'

'Abba? Is she called Abba?'

'She is.'

'What sort of parent names their child after a pop group?'

'No, she's African. It's a real name. Just one B.'

'Oh.' Mum is suitably chastised.

'She's from Sierra Leone,' Matt pipes up.

'Sierra Leone,' I repeat. 'Well, her family are. She was brought up in Colchester.'

'Bloody hell, you got her life story then.'

'Well, yes. I think she was doing the hard sell. Buttering us up, but she seemed OK.'

'She was really nice!' Matt is almost shouting now.

'Well, whatever she said, Cally now thinks she's the next Kate Moss. She's full of it tonight.'

'I thought she might be, but it was all pretty genuine.'

'Cally?' Mum is clearly flabbergasted.

'She's a perfect model shape, apparently.'

'Cally?'

'Yup. Aba's going to call you on Monday.'

'Is she now.' And the way Mum says it means it's not a question, but a threat. I can't help but laugh.

'Apparently the Clothes Show is a hotbed of talent. All the modelling scouts go there and lurk behind pillars spying on all the teenage girls.'

'Maybe I should give Operation Yewtree a call.'

'Mother, you are an outrage!'

We share a soft chuckle. Matt starts clearing the plates noisily. I'm not sure whether that's to make a point that I'm ignoring him, or because of the amount of wine he's knocked back.

'As you can imagine, Cally was a nightmare from start to finish today. And she was even worse when Aba had spoken to her.'

'Oh God. I wish you'd never taken her now.'

'I'm sure Matt thinks the same thing.'

'What?' Matt calls from the kitchen, furious at feeling left out. 'What?!'

'Nothing!' I call back.

'What you doing?'

'Just having our tea.'

'What you having?'

'Matt made a stir-fry, now we're gonna catch up on *X Factor*.'

'I can't believe you're my son sometimes,' Mum laughs.

'I'm a disgrace to my family,' I agree.

'You're twenty-one, not forty-one.'

'Oh, Mum? I found something today. In Dad's coat.' Well, now seems like as good a time as any.

'What?' she sounds scared.

'Oh, it was just a little piece of paper. A left luggage ticket for Manchester Piccadilly.'

'Really?'

'From years ago.'

'When?'

'2008.'

'I thought the police had been through everything with a fine-tooth comb.' And then she adds, 'I thought I had.'

'D'you want it or shall I chuck it?'

'No, I may as well have a look at it. Was it in the pocket?'

'No, it was in the lining. There's a little tear under the inside pocket. It was in there.'

'Weird.'

'I know. I'll bring it round tomorrow. Might jog a few memories. Made me cry.'

'Ah.'

'I'm fine.'

'Well, we were always going on the train. I don't remember leaving stuff in left luggage, though.'

'Well, you can look it up in your diary.'

I hear another phone ringing at her end.

'Oh, Owen, I've got to fly. Lucy's calling on the mobile.'

'All right, Mum. Love you.'

'Love you, babes. D'you think you can make this vile housewarming thing tomorrow?'

'I'll check with Matt.'

'OK. Speak in the morning.'

And I hang up. Matt is returning with a new bottle of wine and a corkscrew.

'What do you have to check with me?'

'One of the new neighbours is throwing a party for Mum tomorrow. Wants to know if we can go.'

Matt rolls his eyes.

'All right, I'll go on my own.'

'I didn't say I wouldn't.'

'See how you feel tomorrow.'

'You don't live there, you live here.' And then he adds, 'Allegedly.'

I say nothing as I hear the *schlopp* of the cork exiting the bottle neck. Matt comes in with the new bottle and bangs into a plastic storage box near the doorway. Hacked off, he then kicks the box.

'Don't do that.'

'Well, if we could keep stuff in the loft like normal people,' he moans.

'Not now, Matthew.'

'Well, it's a waste of bloody good space.'

'Please.'

'I'm gonna put everything up there one of these days, it's ridiculous.'

I decide not to argue with him, hoping soon he'll stop.

'Why do you have a phobia of lofts?'

I shrug. Although of course I know full well why.

Matt flops down beside me on the couch.

'So what did she say about the ticket?'

'Not much.'

'She can't remember it?' Matt asks, pouring himself a new glass and not bothering to top me up.

'She'll be giving herself a hard time about that.'

'*X Factor*?' he says, and although it's a question it's also a statement of intent.

Halfway through the first song I see that Matt has fallen asleep. A flush of longing washes over me; he looks like a dormouse, lying on his back, softly clenched fists lying on his chest, mouth open. He looks so adorable when he's like that. The desire to wake him is strong.

Come on, it's the girl group next. You like them.

And then I think of the long hours he's worked this week in the restaurant. This is his first day off since a week last Friday. But then I see the bottle of wine on the coffee table.

I am twenty-one and have a coffee table. I am twenty-one and I'm so boring my boyfriend has to drink to feel some excitement, feel something.

I am twenty-one, and maybe my boyfriend drinks so much so that he doesn't have to have sex with me. That is possible.

And then I'm flushed with another sensation. Panic. Mum's words echo in my ears.

You're not forty-one.

And I wonder if I'm wasting my life away with the wrong man.

I go outside. The pitch-black sky feels thick like velvet. The odd stars scattered across it glint like halogens peeping through. Something about the whole thing feels man-made, unreal. And then I see the three brightest, Orion's Belt. And I remember that night. A panic rises in my chest. It always does. I swallow big breaths of the cold night air. And hurry back inside.

Matty is still asleep. Snoring now.

I put a DVD on to cheer myself up. It's the 1993 Wimbledon Men's final, the year I was born. Sampras beat Courier 7–6, 7–6, 3–6, 6–3. I know the match inside out. My favourite bit is the third set when I always still get nervous that Sampras is going to lose everything. And then he pulls it back just when you think he's going to succumb.

I look over at Matt and think, *Yes. I will claw this back.*

But I don't really know what I mean.

I twiddle the chain I wear round my neck. I always do that when I'm worried. It's my little comfort blanket. It's the chain Mum gave me on the millennium. She gave us all one. It's not the most attractive thing in the world. But I'm used to it now.

Is that how Matty feels about me?

I return to the hypnotic game and suddenly I am anaesthetized.

The panic has gone.

I position myself on the floor. I lie there, head crooked up against the edge of the sofa. Knees tucked up, toes touching the coffee-table legs. It reminds me of when I went with my dad once to pick Mum up from somewhere. I can't remember what she'd have been doing, but I hid in the back of the car, in the hatchback bit where she usually put the shopping. I enjoyed the sensation of lying down and looking up, of seeing the sky and the streetlamps, and then keeping quiet as Dad made out to Mum he'd come on his own. Then halfway home I'd jump up and shout *surprise* and Mum'd jump out of her skin, then laugh her head off. I must have done this many times as a child, and every time I would think I was so clever. I took to lying in odd places around the house, waiting to surprise Mum, Dad or Cally. Once I hid myself in the pull-out larder in the kitchen. Eventually Mum came to get some herbs out and, of course, jumped out of her skin.

Some days I feel like Dad's just hiding. And he's going to jump out at any moment and shout SURPRISE!

He's not done it yet.

Natalie

It's a sign. I know it's a sign. A left luggage ticket? Found so long after he's gone missing? It has to be a sign!

I am standing in the through lounge of 7 Dominic Close with a smattering of neighbours, a glass of orange juice in my hand, watching Harmony and her identical twin Melody kneeling on the floor singing 'Jar of Hearts' in two-part harmony. I say identical. Melody looks like how Harmony would if she didn't have an eating disorder. In terms of entertainment it's not exactly the seven gates of hell, but it comes pretty close. My best mate Lucy is standing next to me and I feel her pinching my arm, tight, which is good as I am trying my hardest not to laugh. The convulsions beside me tell me she's wetting herself as well, but covering valiantly. The 'girls', as they call themselves, are staring straight ahead and one of them, not sure if it's Melody or Harmony, their names confuse me, puts a finger near her ear and presses hard like I've seen pop stars do when they're in the studio.

All the time. All the time I look for signs that he's alive. Or dead. This has to be a sign. This is a part of him we knew nothing about. It should have been discovered ages ago but it wasn't. This . . . is a game-changer.

A harassed-looking woman shuffles over. She has straggly

hair and a baby in a papoose swaddled around her chest. She snaps me out of my reverie.

'Bet you're wishing you'd never moved now,' she whispers, and I like her immediately. I wink at her. 'Tamsin. Number three. And this is Phoebe.'

I do what you're meant to do when meeting someone who can't answer back but to gurgle, and take one of her tiny fingers and gently shake it.

'Aww, like her from *Friends*. The mad one,' I smile. Tamsin looks confused.

'The sitcom? Years ago?' I take a sip of my orange.

She nods, looking rather unnerved. Just then the twins' mum coos over, 'Ladies? Voices down please!'

'Sorry,' I say.

'Don't encourage her,' Tamsin whispers.

As the song ends and the applause ripples round the room I am about to introduce Tamsin to Lucy when Betty Caligary bounds over, seemingly from nowhere. She speaks out of the side of her mouth today, hoping that half the room won't hear.

'Have you seen the size of her now? Skinny Malinx? She'll be back in the psychiatric ward soon being force-fed through a tube. Are you settling in OK there, Natalie?'

She's Scottish. How did I not notice this last time?

'Er, yes thanks, Betty. Still unpacking.'

'Aye well, there's no rush, is there. How was the cake?'

'Absolutely gorgeous. So moist.'

'That'll be the yoghurt. My secret ingredient.'

'Sorry I've not returned your Tupperware.'

'Och, there's no rush. No rush at all.'

'Betty, this is my friend Lucy. And Lucy, this is Tamsin.'

They say hello. Lucy even shakes their hands. I see them staring at Lucy's Senegalese Twists as if she's dared to come to the party with a stuffed cat on her head. I, however, feel proud to have this beautiful woman as my friend.

'Hope you didn't mind me coming, I popped by to see the new place and . . .'

'Oh, you're English.' Betty sounds relieved. I see Lucy's right eyebrow arc up.

Racist cow!

'Anyway, it's not my party,' Betty says curtly, then zooms in on me. 'So. Still no news, then?'

Bloody hell. Talk about direct.

'About . . . ?'

'Your husband.'

I feel like shouting, *Yes. We found him this morning. He's waiting at home to explain where he's been but I thought coming to a neighbour's buffet was more important.*

'No.'

But just you wait. We have found a massive SIGN.

'You poor wee thing. My heart bleeds for you. Were you not getting on?' Without waiting for a response, she turns to Tamsin. 'You've had depression, haven't you, Tamsin?' Then, quickly, she looks to Lucy. 'Shocking disease. The silent killer. They say the true sign of clinical depression is . . .' and then her eyes flit like she's forgotten. 'Something like, if you see a ten-pound note on the lawn. If you're depressed, you won't go and pick it up.'

'I thought that was flu,' says Tamsin.

'No, it's depression. Psychosis is if it's a twenty. Is that your husband smoking in the garden?'

That was directed at Lucy. She nods. 'Yes. Horrible habit.'

'Horrible garden. Have you seen the state of her clematis?' agrees Betty. 'And there's your son, Natalie. Is his partner not here?'

We look into the back garden and see Owen chatting with Dylan. How does she know Owen has a . . . oh yes, she Googled us.

'No, he's working,' I lie.

'Such a shame,' Betty says dreamily.

'Sorry?' I can't help myself sometimes. I should know better. 'Shame he's working?'

'No, dear. Shame he's gay.'

Oh my God. Right first time!

'There's nothing wrong with it, Betty.'

'Now, now, my little Bolshie!' she says, amused, and taps me on the arm. It makes my blood boil. 'I was only meaning it's a shame I can't palm him off on one of my gorgeous granddaughters.'

'He's not a second-hand car, Betty.'

'No, dear.' She's sounding lascivious. 'He's a top-of-the-range Maserati.'

Is she perving over my boy?

'Your husband's very dapper.'

'Thank you,' says Lucy.

'Ah. I see you like to play in the snow.'

Lucy looks horrified. I am confused. I'm about to ask what this means when the twins' mum Margaret comes over, a twin each side. It's like one's a shadow of the other.

'How did you like the impromptu jig?' Margaret sounds desperate to know. Like it's a matter of life or death.

'It's gig, Mother,' says a twin.

'It was lovely,' says a non-twin, me.

'You know they've been on *X Factors* three times?' Margaret again has a tone of urgency.

'I do, yes.'

'And they sang while they were switching the lights on in Bolton. 2006, wasn't it, girls?'

'December the first.' They both reply in unison.

'Now tell me, Natalie. You've been on *This Morning*. Do you have a mobile number for Phillip Schofield?'

I feel Lucy dragging me away, my protector.

'Why don't we go and get some food? Buffet looks lovely.'

As we move away I hear a few sentences spat at each other in lowered voices.

'What did you say that for?'

'She's been on telly.'

'She used to work in nightclubs!'

'So?'

'Well, that's showbiz!'

As we headed into the kitchen I felt like calling out, *See you, girls! Whatever your names are. Now that really* is *showbiz!*

I first met Lucy many moons ago when she was a barmaid at Milk, paying her way through a psychology degree at university. In the Nineties she wore platform trainers, hot pants and a peroxide weave, making her very popular with the boys, who enjoyed seeing her bend over to pull beers out of her fridge. And no, that's not a euphemism. These days she's more at home in a pair of flats, some skinny jeans and a nice cardi and, now that she's in her forties, she is a relationship counsellor. I always rated her because she never showed me anything but respect when she was working for me. Most of the staff treated Danny as the boss and me as his glamorous sidekick, even though I was anything but, but I always felt Lucy admired what I'd achieved when she was still studying. Over the years I've seen so many Milk staff flourish and go on to do so many other wonderful things: some in the music industry, some staying in clubs and promotion, some in hospitality, whilst others have branched, like Lucy, into things completely unrelated. She's taught me a lot over the years, has Lucy, including the fact that at Milk she never liked it if someone described her as half-caste, preferring the term mixed race. And that these days she eschews the likes of mixed race, preferring mixed heritage. Which always makes me think she sounds like a world heritage site. Or something from the National Trust. Which, when you see how gorgeous she is, is so far from the truth. And she is stunning, inside and out. How lucky have I been to have a counsellor as my best friend during the last five years?

She and Dylan are one of those beautiful couples who make everything look effortless. Their house is rarely messy. Everything they wear looks like a stylist chose it for them. They never seem to row. They've read all the books you're meant to have read, seen all the TV programmes everyone raves about but I never have time to watch. It would be quite easy to hate them, but they're so disarmingly kind and involving, they both have a way of making you feel like you're the only person in their universe. You can't help but love them. Sickening, I know. When I grow up I want to be them. Well, I want to be Lucy. I'm not sure I could get away with Dylan's trendy beard.

Lucy and I sit on a canopied swingy banquette thing, even though it's December and we're freezing; anything to escape the house, and the vultures. We pick at our paper plates of brightly coloured E-numbers masquerading as food.

'What did she mean? You like to play in the snow.'

Lucy rolls her eyes as she chews the life out of a Wotsit. 'It's a stupid, sort of racist saying. About black women shagging white men. We like to . . .'

'Play in the snow,' I say with a groan, getting it finally. God, I'm dense today.

'So. You said you wanted to talk about the left luggage thingy.'

I nod solemnly.

'Well, come on. Shoot.'

How American.

'Owen sent me a photo of it this morning, so I checked the date with my old diaries and . . .'

She has stopped eating. I realize I'm making it sound sensational. Like it's gossip when actually it's not. It's eating me up with anxiety.

'What?'

'Remember that time we did Milk in Ibiza, only I couldn't go coz Cally had broken her leg and I didn't want to take her on the plane?'

'Oh yes,' she says, remembering.

'And I didn't want to leave her?'

'Ye-e-es.' She sounds less convinced now.

'So Danny went on his own.'

She's nodding more encouragingly now. I'm finding it hard to speak.

'Well, according to the ticket, Danny put a suitcase in left luggage the day he got back. Why would he do that?'

Lucy looks bewildered, like I'm making a big deal out of it when it really doesn't matter at all. That makes me feel better.

'Maybe he was going for a meeting and just wanted to dump it. Probably picked it up the same day.'

'Possibly.'

'You know, he . . . lands in Manchester Airport. Can't be arsed with a taxi. Takes the train. Has to meet someone, so sticks his luggage there for a few hours.'

I nod, considering this.

'What, you think he's left it there all this time?'

'Well, he's still got the ticket.' Then I correct myself. 'We've still got the ticket. Wouldn't he have had to hand that in to get the case back?'

'You know Danny, always losing things. Maybe he lost the ticket.'

'Well, Owen said it was in the lining of the jacket.'

'And so had a big barney with them and showed them some ID or something and he got the case back. Not knowing that all along the ticket was in the lining of his coat.'

This was plausible. He was always losing things. He's lost himself, hasn't he?

'Well, anyway,' I say, 'there's one way to find out.'

'You're gonna call them?'

'I'm gonna go one better.'

Lucy does that downturned smile thing that conveys confusion. That and a quick judder.

'I'm gonna go there in person.'

'When?'

I drain the last of my orange.

'Now.'

The lips turn up. 'I wondered why you weren't drinking. When you're in staggering distance of home.'

I tip Owen the wink and he comes over quickly, abandoning Dylan near the house, lighting up yet another cigarette. Owen's cheeks are a blushing red. I put it down to the fresh air.

'Ready?' he says.

I look to Lucy. 'Owen's coming with me for moral support.'

'Why don't you just call them? Quote the number on the ticket and . . .'

'Because if the suitcase is there I'll be able to pick it up.'

'And if it's not,' Lucy points out, quite patronizing, 'you've had a wasted journey.'

'She's driving me home anyway. It's on the way.'

Owen is lying, but I appreciate it. It placates Lucy.

'Anyway, she phoned them.' He is quite a good liar – his composure and confidence has to be seen to be believed. 'But she just kept getting the answerphone.'

Lucy groans sympathetically. And I give a 'What can you do?' shrug. Lucy looks to Owen and has to shield her eyes. It might be December, but that cold sun is still bright.

'Is Dylan all right?'

Owen is nonplussed and shrugs. 'Think so. Why?'

'Hasn't spoken to me all afternoon.'

'That's married life, isn't it?'

'Cheek!'

Just then my mobile phone rings. It's a number I don't recognize. I answer it. My heart is in my mouth. I know it's ridiculous after all these years but I see an incoming call from a number I'm unfamiliar with and I think, *It's him. He's swum to safety and he's got a new phone and he's calling me and* . . .

I answer it. 'Yes?'

'Hi, is that the very gorgeous Natalie?' Gosh, whoever this is is very enthusiastic and loud and has an air of 'zany' about them. I think she's going to tell me I've won a free prize. Though I haven't entered any competitions. If she's cold calling, she's a bit OTT about it.

'Sorry?'

'Natalie? Natalie Bioletti?' and then very annoyingly she puts on an Italian accent, 'Natalia Bioletti, Mamma Mia!'

My hackles rise. I don't mind an anonymous phone call. But one that takes the piss?

'Speaking?'

'Oh hi hon, it's Aba? From L'Agence?'

Oh. Well, that figures. Annoying is as annoying does.

'Aba, I can't speak at the moment.'

'Awww, have I caught you at a bad time, hon?'

'Well, yes, or else I'd be able to speak to you.'

For some reason, I already can't bear this woman I've not even met.

'OK, OK . . . look, Nat, I'll call you tomorrow? When's a good time? Or tonight! What you doing tonight?'

Nat? Get lost!

'Call me tomorrow. Morning. Any time.'

'Ah, cool babe.'

As I hear her draw breath to say something else, I kill the call. Filling my daughter's head with nonsense.

'Come on, Owen, let's go.'

It takes a good twenty minutes to leave. Everyone wants to paw us to tell us how brave we are and what a super neighbour-hood it is and how handsome Owen is and what a shame it is, and next time he must bring his partner and I must bring Cally and we must get together for Christmas drinks. Tamsin manages to just say, 'Oh God, I'm leaking,' and I see she has lactated through her blouse, but Owen is dragging me out and Lucy and Dylan are making tracks as well and . . .

All I can think of is that suitcase. It is there. It is there in Manchester, full of his stuff. I can feel it in my waters and even if it is just T-shirts and undies and flip-flops I don't care. It's another bit of him that I've not seen for five years and so it'll be like a bit of him's come back to me. It will smell of him and . . .

Lucy and I hug in the cul-de-sac and she tells me how much she loves my new house. Owen and Dylan do a bit of back-slapping, but if I'm not very much mistaken there seems to be an atmosphere between them. As Lucy and Dylan drive off I ask,

'Is everything OK between you two?'

Owen looks to me quickly. 'Me and Matt?'

'No. You and Dylan. You seemed a bit off with him. He didn't say anything homophobic, did he?'

Owen shakes his head. But he seems distracted.

'Is everything OK with you and Matt?' I worry.

'Course. Come on, Mum. Let's get this over and done with.'

He says he'll drive. I look to my house. No sign of Cally yet. Is it bad that I feel relieved? I'll worry about her later.

But I can't stop worrying as we drive into Manchester. She's sixteen and, despite what she thinks, is not that mature for her age. Truth be told, it's a welcome relief to be worrying about something other than this blessed ticket. But then all roads lead, not just to Manchester, but to Danny. He'd know what to do about Cally. And if he didn't, he'd at least offer words of reassurance, or tell me to cut her some slack. She's just so angry all the time. I expected it when she was thirteen, fourteen; I know a few teachers – ex-Milk regulars – who say that Year 9 students are the worst to teach, because they're all uniformly vile. But that's lingered on for another two years. She's doing her GSCEs in the summer, she needs to buckle down. I can't put it off any more. I am going to have to speak to her.

I call her. She picks up instantly and launches into, 'Mum, I've got a crashing hangover, so make it quick. I can barely speak and Finty's mum's making nachos.'

'I was just wondering when you were coming home.'

'Finty's dad's gonna drive me home this evening. GOD.'

'All right, darling, I was just a bit worried.'

'Aren't you going to even congratulate me on my AMAZ-ING news?'

'Well . . .'

'Has Aba phoned? She said she'd phone. Has she? She's AMAZING.'

'Yes, she did.'

'Oh my God, really?! What did she say?'

'I was busy. I said I'd speak to her tomorrow.'

'You were what? Busy? BUT YOU DON'T EVEN WORK.'

'Cally, I'll speak to you later.'

'You hate me.'

'I don't.'

'You think I'm ugly.'

'Cally, I'm not joining in. I'm your mother, not some stuck-up toff in your playground.'

As I hang up I hear her shouting, 'FINTY GUESS WHAT SHE CALLED YOU.'

Scholarship or no scholarship, we should never have sent her to private school.

And then I think: L'Agence? Who calls a bloody model agency L'Agence?

The man in Left Luggage leans on the counter looking completely bored as I relay the story of the missing ticket. He puts me in mind of Les Dawson doing Cissie and Ada, leaning on the fence to get the gossip, but completely forgetting to act. When I've done my little spiel, I offer him the ticket. He makes no attempt to take it, and just shakes his head.

'I don't know if you recognize my mum,' says Owen. Les looks interested then. 'But my dad, Danny Bioletti, went missing a few years ago . . .'

'Five years ago,' I add, like that explains everything.

'. . . and we've only just found this, and don't know if he collected it or not. Before he went missing.'

'Oh, I remember you,' he says, nonplussed, as if I'd been a contestant on a game show who embarrassed myself. I smile feebly and offer the ticket again. 'But you see, the suitcase won't be here.'

'He collected it?'

'If he did, it won't be here.'

'Yes, I appreciate that,' I say, biting my tongue so I don't add *Because I'm not thick as pig shit.*

'But if he didn't collect it, there's a process.'

'Really?'

'Really.'

And then he goes on to explain. Uncollected luggage is sent to Head Office in Newport, and then a few weeks after that, if it's still unclaimed and they can't trace the owner, it's sent to an auction house. It feels strange, thinking of people bidding for other people's lost luggage. Who on earth would want to do that? It's not exactly my idea of a great night out; or have I been missing a trick all these years? Oh the joy of bidding actual money to win someone else's travel clothes and crusty undercrackers.

'Well, can you at least tell us if the suitcase was picked up?'

Les looks like he's considering it, then clicks his teeth – are they false? Do they *make* yellow false teeth? – and shakes his head.

'Don't keep the records here, see.'

He can see we're deflated. Lucy was right. This has been a wasted journey.

'You could email Newport.'

I've had enough. I snap. 'Do you have an email address,

please? I imagine you're not expecting me to email a whole town?'

'Or we could just get the police to do it,' suggests Owen. Again, Les doesn't look like he gives two hoots.

'I'll write it down for you.'

He disappears into the back office and I look to Owen and shake my head.

'Police'll find out for us,' he says.

'No, it's a wild goose chase.'

'We've had five years of wild goose chases. I think we can bear one more.'

Les returns with a piece of paper. Slowly he licks the nib of his biro and copies down an email address from his computer screen, then hands it over.

As it's a Sunday, Owen has parked in a nearby street on a single yellow. He links me as we head back to the car, knowing I will be fed up. It's pathetic, but it feels like a crushing blow. I suddenly feel a bit wobbly on the old pins, so tell him I want to sit down for a second. We sit on a slate-grey perforated-iron bench and watch the madness around us. People in a rush, people waiting for loved ones, people with too much luggage, the odd pigeon soaring by. People looking up to see information boards, people rowing, people hugging. All of human life is here, and they all have a purpose. They're going somewhere, they're arriving from elsewhere, they're all doing something. And I'm doing nothing, suspended in time. It's an all-too-familiar feeling.

Through the white noise that these normal people are making, a lone voice breaks.

'Natalie?'

I turn to face the voice, but can't see anyone I recognize.

'Natalie? It IS you!'

And suddenly a man is in front of us. Very orange of skin, with wet gelled hair, wearing a uniform. He's tall, but has the pot belly of someone of my age, even if the eyes are of someone younger. Work, perhaps?

'Natalie, I've not seen you for ages!'

He's wearing a name badge. I read it quickly, and then it all slips into place.

'Daffyd!' I shriek and jump to hug him. Wow. I've not seen this guy for . . . ten years? He hugs me, and we do a little 'turning round in a circle' dance.

Daffyd was a regular at Milk for a few years in the nineties. He used to stand on a podium all night doing robotic dancing. We used to call him the Robot. Clever, huh? God, I wouldn't have recognized him if it wasn't for that name badge. I introduce him to Owen, who shifts up the bench to let Daffyd sit between us. He holds my hand and says how sorry he is about Danny, and how he tried to get in touch but didn't have a number for me, and the longer he left it . . . it's a common story. I've heard it so many times before, but it doesn't bother me. He asks what we're doing here, and I tell him. I tell him in minute detail because it's all I can think about at the moment. He looks flabbergasted, and then thrilled.

'What's the smile for?' I ask.

He taps himself, indicating his uniform.

'When you work on the trains, baby, you can find out anything.'

'What? You'll be able to see if he picked the case up?'

'Sure thang.'

Usually I loathe people who say 'thang'. But today I adore it. I hug Daffyd again.

It is a sign. I *knew* it was a sign!

Cally

We're on a train and on the opposite side of the aisle to us this really old woman is writing something in a notepad. She writes REALLY slowly. And stops between each word as if she's thinking about which word to write next.

God, that takes me back.

When we realized Dad was missing all those years ago, I used to leave a note for him on the stairs every time I left the house. Every day, for all those years. It said:

Hey Dad
 Welcome home! So glad you've come back. Don't rush off again! Call me on my mobile NOW. I can't wait to see you. And no you're not in trouble LOL.
 Your loving daughter
 Cally xxxxxxxxxxxxxxxx

And then my mobile number.

This was just in case Dad meandered back in one crazy day and couldn't remember who we were and stuff. Like, if he'd had a bang to the head or been abducted by aliens and interfered with and couldn't remember our names and that. Or if he'd just run away, missed us, had a change of heart and come back, but was scared we might kick off. I just wanted him to know it was all going to be OK.

But of course he never read any of the notes.

And now we've moved, it seems pointless. Unless he's going to knock on every door in the whole of the North West. And how likely is THAT?

I look at Mum. She never left any notes. I am just about to slag her off in my head but then I REMEMBER WHAT SHE HAS DONE FOR ME TODAY AND WHY WE ARE ON THIS BLINKING BLOODING TRAIN N SHIZ.

I don't actually believe this but Mum – God bless her and all who sail in her – has let me have a day off school. A WHOLE DAY to come to London to have a meeting with Aba at L'Agence. Since Sunday night she's been all distracted and weird and checking her phone and teary and like she's not really taking stuff in, but I don't care coz when Aba phoned she was practically like 'Yeah yeah whatever, I'll bring her in on Wednesday.' Like she just wanted to get her off the phone.

Usually I'd be like MUM! YOU CANNOT BE SO RUDE AND STUFF ON THE PHONE YOU BIG FAT NORK.

But coz of the implicationes of what she'd actually said, I let it go.

I like saying implicationes instead of implications. It's like an imp got into the word and is really messing with its head.

Oh God. I can't believe how excited I am.

L'Agence. I think it's such a cooool name. I keep saying it on the train all the way down. Sometimes I say it in a French accent, staring out of the window. Sometimes I go a bit Italian or Scottish. I'm not really that good with accents so the Frenchy version sounds the best. I can see it's getting on Mum's tits and seeing as how she has totally surprised me by being amazing about this London trip I eventually shut the fuck up rather than risk her exploding and insisting we, like, pull the emergency brake cord and jump off and walk back up North, thus totally swerving L'Agence.

I really want to tweet: ON MY WAY TO TOP MODEL AGENCY IN LONDON FOR TEST SHOTS. OMG. #fashion

But Mum has made me promise not to say anything on social media coz she's totally like lying to the school and saying I had 24-hour flu or something. And just this once I thinks she's probably right, coz she says if the school find out they could like fine her or send her to prison which is TOTALLY OUT OF ORD – I mean when you get the chance to go and do test shots at a top London model agency and stuff you DO NOT TURN IT DOWN. Coz if you DARED TO TURN IT DOWN you would be a complete and utter BRAIN DEAD LOONEY CHOON and stuff.

I really wish I could tweet something because I have been perfecting the way models tweet. I looked a few up and . . . now I'm not saying they're all brain dead, but some of them, rather than describing their day like this . . .

Oh hello. Today I am catwalk modelling for Givenchy.

. . . they just do a series of weird hashtags like this:

#modelling #cameras #make-up #catwalk #clothes #designer #Givenchy

Which actually I find totally annoying, but if that's how I have to tweet from now on to make it in this business then so fucking be it and stuff.

I don't know what a model agency is going to look like if I'm like TOTALLY honest but in my head I imagine a building like a castle, perched next to Buckingham Palace and stuff. I see the Queen leaning out of the window of her gaff, having a crafty fag and watching all the comings and goings from next door. And she's like, 'Oh my God, Prince Philip. I just totally saw Cara Delevingne coming out of that modelly place next door and stuff.'

'Who, babe?'

'You know. The Eyebrows and stuff?'

'OMG she is well lush and stuff.'

And the Queen flicks her ash on a passing Pearly King before going back in to watch reruns of *The Face*.

The castley building has turrets and shit, and on each turret there's like a massive flag, and on each flag there's a picture of like Naomi Campbell, and Erin O'Connor. And then the other one from *The Face* with the weird Swedishy voice who, let's be honest, no-one's ever heard of. I'm just wondering whether, if they ever brought it back, I could be her replacement as a mentor on *The Face*, when it's like Mum's reading my mind.

'Cally?'

'Aha?'

'You do know that modelling is full of rejection, don't you?'

'Aha?'

'And that for every Kate Moss there's a million girls who didn't make it.'

God, she just wants to put me down all the time. My life SUCKS. It's like having Rose West sitting opposite me picking at a Caffè Nero fruit salad. But then I remember how nice she has been thus far about letting me come down and do the test shots so I just nod like I'm really taking it in and look out of the window trying to look all winsome and like there's a camera in my face and they're like, 'Come on, Cally. Give us thoughtfulness, sadness, think of all the dying babies in Africa and stuff.'

And I do the face and the photographer has to stop taking pictures because he can't help but give me this amazing round of applause.

L'Agence is beyond amazing. It's not castley-turrety at all, but this incredible out-of-the-way place in somewhere called Marylebone. The front of it's all frosted glass and white wood and in tiny letters at the bottom of the glass, so faint you can barely see it and Mum has to put her special reading glasses on to double-check, it says in swirly writing:

L'Agence

I almost squeal.

When we're waiting in reception I stare at the walls that are covered with row upon row of black-and-white cards with hundreds and hundreds of faces. I get really excited coz I think that one day soon I am going to be up there with them. Mum starts tapping her foot on the floor and checking her phone before moaning to the receptionist, 'Is she going to be much longer?'

So I hiss, 'MUM.' We've already travelled like a zillion miles from Manchester. Ten more minutes never killed anyone. (Unless someone was coming at you with a knife/gun. Ten minutes probs would kill you then.)

'Aba's probably busy and stuff. GOD,' I hiss. Then realize I'm like totally nervous so think if I can just go to the toilet and have a piddle and wash my face or something, I might feel better. So I asks the receptionist if I can go to the loo – Mum gives me this really sarky look coz I'm being UBER POLITE – and the receptionist points me down some stairs.

At the bottom of the iron staircase I am confronted with two stainless-steel doors with KHAZI etched into them. I can't tell if they're engaged or not so I turn the handle on the right-hand one and head in.

But it's totally mortifying coz there's this really old guy bending over the toilet sniffing.

I'm not sure why he'd be doing this at first.

And then it dawns on me.

OH MY GOD HE'S DOING A LINE OF COKE AND STUFF.

He's got a rolled-up twenty in his hand and he takes a long hard snort. He turns and smiles at me, tapping his nose and doing little sniffs.

I think he is going to be embarrassed or shout at me or say WHAT THE FUCK ARE YOU DOING IN HERE YOU BUFFOON CHILD?

But instead he chuckles and says, 'A toot a day keeps the doctor away.' Then does a little giggle.

I giggle back, then hurry out and slam the door and rush into the next 'khazi' and do my business and think, *Oh my god that bloke was about sixty or something. He must be a big cheese here as he's certainly not a model.*

And I think, *Oh my God what world have I entered here?*

And, *Oh my God this is so EXCITING.*

Resisting the urge to tweet *OMG just caught some like PENSIONER doing gak in the bogs #modelling*, I head back upstairs to see if Aba's come and met us yet.

Owen

Who was it said that if you go snooping, you're bound to find something bad?

I really wish I'd not done it now. But then I wasn't snooping, not really. But I did find something bad. I try not to let it pervade my thoughts. I try to focus on the brainstorming session I'm in with Minty and Gerard.

'Whaddabout . . .' says Minty, '"Some people are gay, geddoverit?"'

I stare at her blankly. The pashmina she has slung round her shoulders is an identical hue to the walls of the meeting room. It's like her head is floating in mid-air.

'Well, we can't have that,' tuts Gerard.

'No?'

I say nothing. If only Mum hadn't left her reading glasses in the car. And if only I hadn't tried said glasses on. And then looked at his phone to see how big the apps looked with them on.

'No. That was the logo Stonewall used a few years back.'

Or did I put the glasses on as an excuse to look at his apps? I'm not sure.

Minty shakes her head. I have no idea why she thinks

63

she can disagree. 'That was Get Over It. This is Geddoverit. They're pronounced differently.'

'But they're the same.'

'Tell that to an art director.'

We are meant to be coming up with some gimmicky sayings to put on the website to up our profile. Something catchy to grab a few headlines in the pink press. Usually my heart would be in it. Up until yesterday, I was almost gung-ho about it. Today I feel completely disconnected from my two colleagues, the website, and the task in hand.

'OK, you clearly don't like that,' Minty says.

Minty, real name Araminta, thinks it will really put us on the map. She has a background in PR.

'It's derivative.'

She used to do the PR for Hepatitis B.

'It's an homage. Anyway, I have another. How about . . . "Is that chair really so gay?" with a picture of a chair.'

She quickly draws a chair on her pad, and shows us.

'Obviously it'll look better than that,' she says quickly.

Gerard stares at her, flummoxed.

I've never been sure whether she promoted Hepatitis B – 'Get this, it's a great disease to have!' – or whether she promoted health advice for it. I hope it was the latter.

'Only I was on this, like, train the other day. And these kids got on? And there was this seat? And it had, like, stains on it? And the kids were like "OMG I can't sit there, that chair's so gay?"'

Gerard is looking at me. Dragging my head back into the meeting, I shake it.

'A euphemistic chair doesn't really do it for me.'

'Ah, but is the chair a euphemism? Is it? I don't think so.' Minty is sounding wound up now.

I stand up. It's pretty dramatic. They both look surprised.

'I need some air. I'm taking an early lunch.'

'You do look a bit peaky,' Minty says, full of faux concern, hoping against hope I'm telling the truth and not running as fast as my legs will carry me away from the two most ridiculous ideas in the history of brainstorming. I see Gerard looking punitively at me and I know what he's thinking. *Thanks for leaving me on my own with this loopy bitch.*

But he will never say it. And nor will I. Not here, anyway, at work, as it is a sentence which has the power to offend both fifty per cent of the population (women) and anyone who has ever suffered from problems with mental health.

In that moment I hate how politically correct my life has become, and I head for the door.

'Don't forget you've got that face-to-face with the *Metro* at two-thirty,' Minty calls after me.

'I won't,' I call back. I had forgotten, actually, so it's a good job she's reminded me. More publicity for the website, masquerading as a human-interest piece about 'what it's like five years after your dad goes missing'. I'm dreading it.

I meet Sonia at the Christmas markets and we eat hot dogs as we trudge round the stalls feigning a veneer of caring about Christmas. Sonia's one of my oldest friends. I tell her everything. Ish. If anyone knows where the bodies are buried, it's her.

'Matt's got Grindr on his phone,' I say.

'Since when?' This is what I like about Sonia. Nothing shocks her. Someone else would have shrieked an OMG and been bewildered by this. She puts her level-headedness down to managing a boutique hotel. She says if you can deal with demanding guests and staff day in, day out, nothing fazes you. I couldn't do her job, that's for sure.

'He says it's just been the last few days.'

'He knows you know?'

I nod.

'So. He's getting a bit of extramarital? God, the dirty dog. How do you feel about this?'

'Well, he says he's just got it to chat to mates.'

'Do you believe him?'

'I don't know what to believe. What would you think?'

'It's hard to compare like for like,' she says eventually. 'I don't think there is an app for Josh to find local women for a quick shag.'

'No, there is,' I correct her. 'There's Tinder.'

'Oh yeah. I better check his BlackBerry when I get in.'

'He showed me the messages he's been sending. It was all banter. And on his profile picture thingy it said he was partnered and he was on there for networking.'

'Networking?' She sounds incredulous.

'I know.'

'Come on. Let's go in here. I'm perishing. And I need the loo.'

We head into the theatre, the Royal Exchange. I've not been in for years and had forgotten what an incredible feat of architecture it is. The vast Victorian hall with the Eighties spaceship of a theatre landed in the middle of it. Sonia rushes off to the toilet and I grab us a coffee and a table. I play with my phone. I tag myself and Sonia at the theatre on Facebook. And I know why I'm doing it. I'm doing it so that Matt will see it and be surprised. See, Matt? You're not the only one who does stuff you might not expect. Like go to the theatre in the middle of the day. OK, so it's not up there with sleeping with strange men behind your husband's back, but still. It's as impulsive as I get. When Sonia returns from the toilet it turns out the hall is a completely inappropriate environment for a confidential tête-à-tête between friends of the 'I've just found out my husband is using a quick-shag app on his phone' variety, as every word we say echoes around the cavernous space. We lower our voices when an usherette casts us daggers as she prepares to work the day's matinee performance.

'So it's possible he is just using it for chatting with guys,' she says, noticing on her phone that her lunch hour is quickly coming to an end.

'But why can't he just pick up the phone and chat to his mates?'

'Maybe he's bored.'

That stings. It's what I've already sensed, what I've already felt. Is this phone thing just a manifestation of that? He's bored with me. Why else would he want to chat with other gay men? It's not like Grindr is the best place for swapping ideas and political manifestos. Admittedly the 'banter' he was having in the chats he showed me was pretty mundane. In fact, if he'd been bored before signing up to Grindr, I can't see why he wasn't suicidal by now, such was the banality of the chats, but each to their own, I guess.

But I can't help but think, *What didn't he show me?*

'You two need to do more things together, other than just sitting in every night watching telly and getting wrecked.'

'I don't get wrecked.'

'He does.'

'We're going on the demo against Humphrey Sanderbach next week.'

I can tell she's trying not to roll her eyes. A political sojourn is clearly not her idea of fun.

'How Eighties.' She smiles, tightly. 'Are you going to write a protest song about AZT as well?'

'You have been reading your history books!'

Sonia's brother is much older than her, and the campest thing to ever walk this planet. As a result, Sonia is sometimes better informed on all things lavender than me.

'What was his picture like?' She changes tack suddenly.

'Matt's?'

'Aha.'

'Oh, just a head shot. The one from his Facebook.'

Sonia nods. 'So he didn't have his bits out.' She says this as if it's consolation, proof that nothing is going on. 'Well,' she continues, 'it's as I always say: if you go snooping, you'll definitely find something. The fact that you're suspicious in the first place says it all.'

Ah. So it was her who said it.

'Then you mean I've only got myself to blame?'

'Well . . .'

'I didn't download the fucking app on his phone.'

The usherette narrows her eyes, and looks ready to give me a kung-fu kick.

'So why did you go snooping?'

'I didn't. I swear.'

She looks like she doesn't believe me.

'Mum left her reading glasses in my car. I tried them on to see what they did to my eyes.'

She's laughing. She's laughing because it sounds so far-fetched.

'And you accidentally picked Matt's phone up, entered his passcode and opened one of his apps. I believe you, Owen Bioletti. Thousands, however, would smell a porky.'

'It's true,' I say, defeated.

'I have to go. Sorry. My time's not as flexible as yours.'

I nod, sigh, and get up to hug her. She smells reassuringly as she always does, of Citron Citron by Miller Harris. In fact, I probably bought it for her. And it's nice to know she wears it even when she doesn't realize she's going to be meeting me for an emergency date.

'How's work?' I say as an afterthought, in an 'oh God we talked about me and not about you' kind of way, and she dismisses the question with a shake of her fingerless-mittened hand.

'Another time,' she says. 'New chef. Massive cunt.'

'Literally? Or . . .'

'Is, not has. See you, Sweet Cheeks.'

'See you, Sugar Tits.'

And off she goes. She gathers her poncho around her, bracing herself for the zero temperatures outside. I wouldn't be surprised if it snowed. She stops, turns to look at me and calls back, 'Talk to him.'

It's what she always says. It's what I always know needs doing. I nod to tell her that I will. I turn to grab my coffee and trudge back to the office, something I'm not looking forward to, when I hear a man calling my name. He says it twice before I turn round to locate the face.

It's Dylan. And I'm immediately embarrassed. I saw him only a few days ago at Mum's neighbour's housewarming jaunt. Something happened. It wasn't a biggie in the great scheme of things, but I wish it hadn't. I'm quite a private person, which is a bit of a juxtaposition with that interview I'm doing later, but he'd had a few drinks and was being a bit indiscreet about his and Lucy's sex life. TMI when it's your parents' friends. But then, he'd asked me about my and Matt's sex life. Well, actually, what he'd said was, 'I bet you two are at it like rabbits.' And I'd found myself offloading. I'd not even had a drink and yet I stood there and told him things I'd not even told Sonia. He was really sweet and nodded and touched my arm and made all the right sympathetic noises before saying, 'I'm sure it's just a glitch.' And now here he is, stood in front of me, looking quite funky for his forty-two years in a baggy parka. Matt used to joke that he was a DILF, but I've never really seen it myself. He bounds over, drags me to him for a bear hug and then loudly, ebulliently slaps my back and is full of rather-too-raucous-for-the-theatre bonhomie, asking how I am, what I'm doing here, etc. etc. He was passing and popped in for some greetings cards and he asks if I've time for a drink. I explain I have to get back for an interview, and he says he'll walk part of the way with me as he's heading back to the university where he teaches.

I wonder how my life would have turned out had I gone to university. After Dad went I lost interest in school and bummed around for a few years doing dead-end jobs, just to prove to my mum that I didn't need academia to get me by. Looking back, I think I was running away from Mum, because although I knew she needed my support, I was discovering my sexuality and I didn't want her to. It would probably sound disingenuous to some, but although Mum had always had gay friends and colleagues – as had Dad – I still harboured the suspicion that she would rather her own son wasn't. I was partying a bit too much, drinking a bit too much; thankfully I never got into drugs or anything too wild, but what Mum saw as a reaction to Dad going missing was actually me running away from telling her the truth. She could tell something was up, and I was convinced she had twigged – and when she told me we had to sit down and have a serious talk, I was relieved that I wouldn't have to say it for myself, that she had worked it out and would offer up the simple statement, 'I know you're gay.'

We sat in the kitchen, a brew each. She even put KitKats on a saucer. So this was the recipe for the perfect coming-out tea party, was it?

But instead she said, 'Is there something you're not telling me about your dad?'

She thought that my running around going a bit crazy and coming in at all hours was because I knew some things about Dad's departure and wasn't telling her. That I knew where he was, and was finding the secret hard to keep. When I told her not to be so ridiculous she looked offended. And when I eventually said, 'The thing I'm not telling you is . . . I'm gay,' she actually burst out laughing. Probably with relief.

It must have looked strange to her, her usually sporty son necking vodka and stumbling round the house at two in the morning, bumping into things, breaking things. But I guess I was discovering my identity and readjusting. Throughout my childhood, my dream had been to be a tennis pro. When I messed up the tournament in Eastbourne I had to do a big reality check and realize that maybe that life wasn't for me. It was a staggering feeling, thinking you're on the scrapheap at fourteen years of age. Maybe I just did everything too young.

Or maybe messing up that tournament wasn't completely my fault.

And maybe I did know more about Dad than I'd ever let on.

Oh God.

And then. Something weird happens. It's like I've conjured her up by thinking about Dad and that night and . . .

I see, all of a sudden, my nan walking along on the other

side of the street. I've not seen her for almost a year. It was my birthday. I opened her card. Twenty pounds fell out. But the message read:

> *I'm ashamed of you you great dirty faggot. Oh yes. Stop coming round my house and being all airy fairy and limping your fucking wrists you dirty cock sucker. Oh yes. Fucking Dale Winton features. Your father would be ashamed. Amazed you could even lift a tennis racket with them wrists. Oh yes.*

My nan has a bit of a drink problem. I'd put up with quite a bit over the years. Most of the time she could be quite sweet. But this was the straw that broke the camel's back.

I got straight in my car and drove over to her place. She lives in a little twee street of old cottages. You'd never know what bile lay behind the latticed windows and olde-worlde doors. As I pulled up outside I saw a woman coming out, not Nan, with a shocking pink streak in her hair. Not Nan's age, no idea who she was. I went and banged on the door. No reply. I shouted up at the woman who'd just left, who by now was nearing the end of the street,

'Oi! Pinky Head! Is she in?!'

Pinky Head – I know, SO childish – looked back, looked alarmed to see me, then hurried on her way. I banged on the door again. Inside I heard a noise. She was in.

I banged a few more times, then shouted through the letter box.

'It's me! The cock sucker! I just wanted to say . . .'

And now I put her twenty pounds through the letter box.

'Keep your fucking money, you evil old bitch!'

And then I slammed the letter box. And I got in my car. And I've not seen her since.

Till now. But just as quickly as I see her, she disappears. She's gone. Like I've spirited her away.

I realize that I have been walking alongside Dylan for most of five minutes, saying absolutely nothing.

'I'm sorry,' I say.

'For what?'

'Being so silent.'

'I can do silence,' he says nonchalantly. 'Anyway, you've probably got a lot on your mind.'

I look at him and he smiles sadly. 'By the way, I've not said anything to your mum about . . . what you told me. Not mentioned it to Lucy. What happens between us stays between us.'

I am relieved. But it's odd. I've known this man for years and suddenly there is something approaching intimacy between us. As the sunlight hits his face I notice freckles I've not registered before. If we lived in London he'd be what's known as a Shoreditch hipster. The neatly trimmed beard, oversized glasses, Jesus-long hair tied up in a small ball on top of his head. Skinny jeans, oversized parka – that's got to be pretend fur on the collar, he's too left-wing to wear real – and a battered old satchel slung round his shoulders. His eyes sparkle. Maybe they look bigger because his glasses magnify them.

'A few secrets never did anyone any harm,' he adds with a wink. He holds eye contact for a bit longer than he should and it makes me tingle. I have a physical reaction to a look. I swallow. I feel a tingling in my groin. I catch my breath. We stand staring at each other. It feels like madness. This is my mum's friend's husband. He is a heterosexual man. He is twice my age. There can be nothing between us.

And yet suddenly it feels like there is.

I must be imagining this. But why is he looking at me like that? I make a fumbled excuse about having to rush back, and having to turn right here and he's so cool in the face of my nerves that I know I must be imagining things, I must be. I am just confused because of what I've found out about Matt and I'm looking at my friend here and rewriting the truth. As I rush back to the office I think, it's OK. I hardly ever see him. I can forget that second ever happened. Well, maybe it was longer than a second. But I have shown myself up and read something into a look that clearly wasn't there. But it's OK, as I won't see him again for ages and then it will be forgotten. By me. Over. Kaput.

When I get back to the office I find Minty demolishing a strawberry yoghurt.

'I came up with the best slogan,' she says.

'What's that?' I sound all keen now. The cold air has done me good. I can throw myself into this task and forget what happened at lunchtime.

'Gay is Good.'

Her eyes seek approval. I so want to give it, but I have to be honest.

'I'm pretty sure that's been used before.'

'Really? Shit.'

I nod. Oh, well. Back to the drawing board.

Natalie

Daffyd calls first thing Thursday morning. Well, it's gone eleven when he does, but he apologizes if it's too early and I reassure him that eleven is practically the middle of the day.

'Oh, it's just I associate late nights and lie-ins with you,' he says by way of explanation.

Just get on with it. I've been on pins all week worrying about this.

'Well, even when I ran Milk I was up early to get the kids to school or run the business.'

Why am I encouraging him? JUST BLOODY TELL ME.

'So, any joy?' I blurt.

'Yes. Sorry it's taken a while – my mate had to find the archive folder on the server and it took forever.'

Get on with it.

'So did he take it? Did he collect the case? Was it a case?'

Shut up, Natalie.

'No, he didn't.'

'The case is still there? Somewhere?'

'No, someone else collected the case.'

'Oh. Who?'

'She would've had to show some ID or a letter from Danny granting her permission, etc.'

75

She?

'It was a Miriam Joseph.'

'Miriam Joseph?'

'You don't know her?'

'No. Are you sure they didn't make a mistake?'

'No, he sent me a photo of the entry in the system.'

'Miriam Joseph?'

This is too odd.

'There's an address. D'you want it?'

'Sure. Let me get a pen.'

He dictates it and I write it at the top of the local paper that's lying on the side in the hall.

Miriam Joseph
12 Mayville Road
Chorlton
Manchester
M21 0GY

I stare at the words. Words which make no sense.

'And when was it collected? Does it say?'

'5th August 2008.'

'OK.'

'Could it be someone who worked with him? An employee?'

'Possibly. Does it say what the piece of luggage actually was?'

'Yes. Suitcase. Sorry. Should've said that.'

'For God's sake.' None of this made any sense.

'Well, anyway, I did what I could.'

I realize I am sounding ungrateful so I quickly reassure him he's been amazing and how grateful I am, and minutes later I've hung up and am searching my database of contacts on my main computer for Miriam Joseph, but it keeps coming back blank. I try again with the word Mayville. Again, nothing.

Why would Danny leave a piece of luggage at Piccadilly Station and have it picked up by someone I have never heard of? A woman I have never heard of.

Unless. Unless . . .

Unless it was someone he'd met in Ibiza, and he'd offered to look after it for her.

But why?

Unless. Unless . . .

Unless the reason he was keeping Miriam Joseph secret from me was that he was having an affair with her.

I shake. That idea is so abhorrent. And then it hits me. No wonder he disappeared. He and Miriam have bloody well run off together.

But then I remember that the police went through everything with a fine-tooth comb (cue running gag in our house: why do teeth need to be combed?) and came to the conclusion that he hadn't been having an affair or run off with anyone; which brings me back to my original question.

Who the hell is Miriam fucking Joseph?

I fire off a set of texts. One to Lucy. One to Owen. And one, after several minutes of deliberating, to Danny's mum. Anything is worth a shot.

Does the name Miriam Joseph ring any bells?

I stare at the phone, as if concentration will bring forth replies. Actually, it works, as almost immediately Owen replies.

No. Why? X

So I shoot back:

Oh. Facebook friend request. No worries. Everything good? X
Fine n dandy. X

Lucy pings back:

No babe. Who is she?
Oh just some random friend request on FB. No worries x
Cool. Someone from school? X
Probs x

Then Danny's mum replies.

New phone. Who this? Bar.
Bar it's Nat.
Hi Nat. blast from the past. Never heard of your friend.
She's not my friend Bar.

And then radio silence from his mum.
Owen texts again.

Any joy with the luggage ticket?
Not yet.

Why am I lying? Why can't I just say, *Yes, some bitch called Miriam Joseph went and collected it*?

But I don't want to worry him. I should tell Lucy but again, well, there are no excuses really. But this name feels significant. Call it woman's intuition, call it what you like, but I somehow feel the need to guard this information with my life.

And then I think: Barbara's got a cheek. Blast from the

past?! I saw her recently. Our trolleys passed each other in the freezer aisle of Sainsbury's in Wilmslow. She had several bottles of gin in hers, and a ready-cooked chicken. She said nothing to me. I said nothing to her. I took it from this that she was drunk.

Danny's mum has a split personality. It's all down to her drinking. When she is drunk she is nasty, vitriolic, mean. Sober she is regretful, apologetic, self-hating.

I find it best to just steer clear. So do the kids. So did Danny.

Every now and again I receive a letter from her in which she accuses me of killing Danny. Sometimes it is pre-empted by a phone call.

'I think I sent you a letter yesterday. I can't really remember. Do us a favour and chuck it in the bin. Don't read it.'

I read the first few. Now I don't bother, and they go straight in the flip-lid.

Even when she's sober, she's so adamant that Danny is dead. Some days I am too, and then I can handle her. But when I feel any sense of hope she has the ability to pee on it from a great height. She's never really liked me. I was never really good enough for her brown-eyed boy. And she doesn't have to say it, but even when she doesn't claim I murdered him, I know she thinks he disappeared because of something I did.

It was all so disappointing when I first met her. As my mum had died when I was so young, I had long missed the presence of an older woman in my life. The family I had since fashioned for myself amongst the squats and clubs of Manchester and London comprised people of my own age or slightly older. And even though Danny had little positive to say about Barbara, I had self-important dreams of rescuing their relationship, of making her see sense, of softening her sharp edges. Needless to say, I failed.

Mind you, she was hardly in contention for Mother of the Year. Danny had spent a few years in care when he was younger, and she had done six months inside for shoplifting. But I was never allowed to acknowledge that I knew any of that to her, for fear of upsetting her.

I should call the police. Tell them what I've found out about this Miriam person. But I know they'll think I'm clutching at straws.

Still. They might decide to pay a visit to Ms Joseph. And then at least we'd know why she'd taken Danny's suitcase.

But then, she might not even live in Mayville Road any more. It was six years ago.

But then I think, well, the police don't have the monopoly on home visits. I'm completely within my rights to pay Ms Joseph a visit myself.

And before I've even processed the thought, I have picked up my car key and am heading for the door.

Aba calls as I'm driving across Manchester. I contemplate ignoring the call but, if I'm honest, I'm quite keen to know what she's going to say. Cally was on her best behaviour yesterday, and even I thought the photos they showed us afterwards looked better than average. So I hit the answer button on my steering wheel.

'Hello?'

'Hi, hon, it's me, Aba.'

'Hi, Aba.'

'Wasn't yesterday just THE BEST?'

'Yeah, it was great. Cally really enjoyed herself.'

'Oh, she's such a poppet. And oh my God, she's actually hilarious.'

'She has her moments,' I say, diplomatically.

'How did she think it went?' Oh. A grown-up question

from a woman who frequently screams SOMEONE GIVE ABA HUG BABES!

'Well . . . she wasn't sure, really. I suppose we both thought, it's not about whether she enjoyed it or not, it's about how the pictures look.'

'So right, hon. So right. Hon, can you just hold on a sec . . .'

'Sure.'

'Sorry. For a second there I thought there was a rip in this dress.'

'And is there?'

Why do I even care?

'No.' She's sounding distracted. 'Soooo, Natalia Mamma Mia, I have some innnnnnnnntrusting news.'

'Oh, right?'

'Your daughter is proving very popular with some casting directors, and I'd like to get her in front of a few next week.'

'Oh right. Next week?'

'Yeah, babe.'

'It's just she's got school. How long would she need to be in London for?'

'Well, ideally five days. I just want her to meet as many people as possible.'

'Where would she stay?'

'Babe, we have model flats.'

'What's a model flat?'

'Well, she'd stay with some other young models and they'd have, like, a chaperone. Everyone does it, it's all perfectly legit.'

'I see. What would happen if I said no?'

'Sorry?' her voice went up three octaves there. People rarely contradicted Aba by the sounds of things.

'If I said I'd rather she finished at school next year and then came back to you?'

Aba gives a rather throaty chuckle.

'I'd say we need to strike while the iron's hot, darling.'

Of course she would.

'I'll talk to Cally.'

'One more thing, hon. Is Cally short for anything? Keep meaning to ask.'

'No, it's just . . . Cally.'

'Right. I just keep thinking, "Scally".'

'Sorry?'

'What do you think of the name Calista?'

'For what?'

'For Cally. I'm just thinking marketing. And Calista Bioletti has such a ring to it.'

'But it's not her name.'

'I know.'

'You want to change her name?'

'Everyone changes their name.'

'I haven't.'

'With respect, Natalie. You're not exactly Kate Moss.'

I am so incensed I hang up. She rings back. This time I ignore it. I hear her message afterwards.

'Oh God, hon, you must be in a really shit reception area. Buzz me back once you've had a conflab with Calista. Bye, babe!'

Oh God. The madness has already begun.

The phone rings again. Lucy.

'Hi Luce!'

'Hi Nat. Sorry, are you driving?'

'It's OK, I'm hands free.'

'Ooh, where are you off to?'

'Oh . . . just into town, pick up some bits.'

'Oh right. What time will you be back?'

'I dunno, Luce, why?'

'Oh, it's nothing really, just a silly thing. I've sent you a little housewarming thingy and it's going to be delivered before one.'

'Ah, well, I might be back by then; I hope so.'

'Well, not to worry, if you're not back they can leave it with a neighbour or something.'

Oh God. Please don't make me go and see those neighbours again.

'Thanks, love. I wasn't expecting anything.'

'Oh, it's a silly thing really.'

'Everything OK with you?'

'Yeah. Wonderful. Dylan's been staying over at the Uni last few nights. Finishing this paper he's working on. It's really nice to get the bed to myself.'

I chuckle with recognition.

'And not to hear his snoring.'

'Oh piss off, Luce. Perfect people like you don't suffer shitty little things like snoring and duvet hogging, surely!'

She laughs. She pretends to hate it when I describe her world as idyllic. But I can also tell she really likes it.

'Just you wait till you see what I've sent you as a house-warming.'

'What? What is it?'

'Proof that we're all the same deep down. You'll howl.'

I howl now anyway, desperate to know what it might be.

'Anyway doll, I've got to fly. Got my first client in ten and just need to check I look PERFECT.'

Again we laugh. And hang up.

I can't wait to see what she's sent me. She is the mistress of the funny greetings card and comedy present. For my birth-day she sent me some sparklers that were in the shape of letters. Letters that spelled out a very rude word. A word that rhymes with Hunt. The memory makes me smile.

A thought hits me as I near the delights of Chorlton. What if Danny is living here? At *her* house? What if all along he has assumed a new identity and has been living in Suburbia with Ms Joseph? What if I peer in through her bay window and see them munching lunch for two on trays on their knees, side by side on a cosy couch? What if they have his and hers matching onesies?

But I am getting ahead of myself here. This woman is probably perfectly innocent.

It's a drab road. And I am wrong: it might be Chorlton, home to media types and yummy mummies, but there are no bay windows on this road. Identikit red-brick terraced houses domino past me; I half expect Mr Benn to come out of one of them and head off to a fancy-dress shop. The numbers flit past me, like a countdown to judgement day; I am snailing along like a kerb-crawler. And suddenly it's there. Number 12. As nondescript as every other house, although there are no nets up, and if I was to walk up to the low brick wall and peer in I'd get a pretty good view. I park. I wait. But what am I waiting for? I'm waiting for the courage to arrive, so I can get out of the car and go and knock on the door.

And say what?

Before I can rehearse what I might possibly say, there is movement at the house. The front door opens and a woman comes out. She is about my age. She is wearing quite high-end jogging bottoms, they reek of some unpronounceable label. No make-up, hair scraped back into a cap. She's not bad-looking, and she is taking a small dog for a walk. I do a once-over of her, then look away in case she catches me staring. I hear the clink of her gate swinging shut and then look in my wing mirror to watch her from behind, heading off down the road.

OK, so what do I do now?

Was that Miriam?

There's only one thing for it. I will follow her on her dog walk and start up a conversation with her. I get out of the car and lock it. Pull my coat tight to me and head off in the direction she went.

I have to be careful not to overtake her, as she seems to be stopping at every single lamppost to let the dog – I'm not sure it's any particular breed, just a mongrel – pee on them. At the end of the road she turns out onto the main shopping street. I dawdle, pretending to look in shop windows, but all the time watching her, working out when I might pounce. But now that I'm in touching distance of her my courage has failed me; I don't know where it is today. I was so gung-ho coming over. I practically dived into the car. But now I've come face to face with her . . .

But then, it might not be her. Miriam might have moved from the house years ago.

Miriam might be a lesbian, and this is her lover.

This might be Miriam's dog walker.

Miriam might be the bloody dog!

No. Dogs don't go into left luggage offices and retrieve suitcases.

But what if he's got a bit of retriever in him? Heavens.

So many potentials. So little . . .

Oh. She's gone into the post office. I didn't know you could take dogs into post offices. I walk up to the window. OK, so it's not just a post office, it's a sweet shop of sorts too. I see her chatting with the Asian woman behind the counter. She hands her a small card and then scoots back out. She now seems to be heading back to Mayville Road. I watch her turn back into it. OK, so that was a short dog walk. I will give her a few moments before following her back. I return my gaze to the shopkeeper. She has come out from behind the counter and is heading for the window. I have a worry that she is going to tap on the glass and tell me to keep my nose out of her shop, but instead she comes and slides the card into a display in the window advertising goods for sale or wanted. The card from dog-walking-possibly-Miriam lady reads:

CLEANER / DOG WALKER NEEDED. LOCAL.

And then a mobile number.

I quickly take a photo of the advert and number with my phone. I know what I will do next.

I can't call immediately. I might arouse her suspicions if I ring within seconds of the sign going up.

I return to my car. I have lost sight of her now. There is no sign of life in her house.

I check the photo on my phone and try to memorize the phone number.

It is now ten minutes since the sign went up.

It still feels too soon. But I have to know. So I check the number again. I say it aloud and then quickly dial it.

I hear it ring. Then a woman answers.

'Hello?'

'Hello. I'm calling about the advert in the post office window?'

'Oh right.' She sounds surprised. 'God, I've only just put it up.'

'Oh, really? God, I didn't know that.'

No, I don't suppose I would have done.

'So are you a cleaner?' she asks.

'Yes.' I lie.

'And what's your hourly rate?'

'Ten.' I plucked that from the air.

'And how are you with dogs?'

'Love dogs,' I lie. Well, it's not a lie. I like dogs, but . . .

'Well. Maybe you should come round and meet Snowy, and we can take it from there.'

'Great. Where are you based? I'm assuming somewhere in Chorlton?'

'Yeah, Mayville Road, number twelve. What's your name, by the way?'

'Josie.'

I have no idea where that came from.

'Josie Greengrass. And yours is?'

'Miriam. Miriam Joseph.'

'Great.'

We make an appointment for the next day. I then drive round the corner, park outside the post office and head in. I pretend to look at a display of padded envelopes in front of the window. Then, when the shopkeeper isn't looking, I lean in and slide Miriam's advert out of the display frame. I crumple it up and slide it into my pocket.

Poor Miriam. Just one person applying for the job.

You really can *not* get the staff these days.

I appear to have driven home on autopilot, as when I pull up outside the house I don't recall many details of the journey. But I am here in one piece, and the car is too. I hurry inside and make myself a cup of tea. I look around to see if there is a 'while you were out' card from Lucy's delivery people. There isn't. I hope to God they've not left it with a neighbour. I'm not relishing the prospect of venturing to see any of them again. Even the weird quiet one whose breasts were leaking. Says a lot that she seemed the most normal, yet appeared to be tranquillized up to the eyebrows.

I get my iPad and do something I should have done this morning before my knee-jerk trip to South Manchester: I Google the name Miriam Joseph. I'm not sure what I'm going to find here – not everyone has an existence online, but maybe she's a famous . . . dog groomer, or . . . hand-writer of signs, I don't know, but maybe she's achieved something in her life that has merited a few mentions on some website or other.

Turns out not. There's one Miriam Joseph, who was in fact Sister Miriam Joseph and a bit of a nun who'd written some books about the trivium. I have to then Google the word trivium and discover what it means. My first click tells me it's an American heavy metal band from Orlando, which is an odd thing for a nun to be writing about, and then a further click reveals it's a term from medieval universities, concerning grammar, logic and rhetoric. I stop myself Googling those words, as I kind of know what they mean, and find myself thinking about Lucy. Her Dylan works at the university, and is writing a paper about something. I don't even know what. I know possibly more about Sister Miriam Joseph than I do him right now. I click the screen back a few times and find there's another Miriam Joseph who's a Hollywood film producer, known it says for the movies *Don*, *Rock On* and *Don 2*. I have heard of none of them. Now whereas I would be more than happy to think that a 'top' movie bod could live in a suburban street of red-bricked houses in Chorlton-cum-Hardy, I don't really believe it in my waters.

Miriam Joseph, my Miriam Joseph, appears to have done very little with her life.

Lazy thing, I think. Then catch myself on. I don't know her.

I don't know her connection with Danny, beyond collecting a suitcase on his behalf. This could be perfectly innocent.

Poor Miriam, I think instead, doing so little with her life.

A bit like me.

Yeah, but has she run a few nightclubs? Made enough dosh from them so that she doesn't have to work again?

I'm being bitchy and showy-offy again, and I don't like it.

I'm saved by the bell.

I head to the front door, wondering who it might be. I see the shape of a man through the mottled glass of the porch door. And when I open it, I get a very pleasant surprise.

Cally

Just for the record. And I'm only going to say this once but. My mum is a Class A Disappointment to womankind and all who sail in her.

She's late home from God knows where, she expects me to help her with the tea, and then to top it all, just before I'm going to bed she's like, Oh God, I completely forgot. Aba called.

Wh-a-t?

'Sorry, love. I've had my mind on a million other things.'

Like. Seriously?

You . . . FORGOT?

Hmmmmm.

At first I let my DEEP IRRITATION that she had omitado'd (Spanish) to tell me till the witching hour go, because of course I was totes excited to hear that lovely gorgeous BFF Aba has been touch. But then I couldn't help but get SO ANGRY with her as she wittered on. And if there were an Olympics for wittering my mother would scoop gold, silver and fucking bronze.

What is completely amazing is that Aba thinks my pictures rock and so do loads of amazing modelly-type influential dudes in London who could really take me places. I didn't want to tempt fate when we went to London coz like you just never know what will happen and of course I had Mum in tow, which is like having a massive air raid siren going off non-stop predicting oncoming multiple deaths and gloom, so she'd been saying don't get your hopes up like a fucking MANTRA like she is a Buddhist or something. But I really enjoyed posing for the pictures and when Aba showed us the pics on her laptop I didn't recognize myself and stuff. The girl in the pictures looked really beautiful. Well, she looked really interesting. It was quite a shock, if you must know.

So. Upshot is Aba – who is one of the nicest most genuine people on the planet and has amazing jewellery and shoes and smells like a flower garden in somewhere amazing like Monaco – also she is black, and I don't mean any kind of black, she really IS black, like REALLY black which is SO COOL – wants me to go and stay in London for a week or something and meet some amazing life-changing people so I can have a career in modelling.

And what does Mum want?

The best for her daughter?

Oh no. Remember, this is Mum we're talking about here.

GET THIS, MOFOS.

She wants to say no to Aba, which let's be honest is really unspeakably rude, and tell Aba I have to wait till I've done my exams next summer.

Yes, you heard it right and you heard it here first. Bitch be wantin fe me to say da NO NO. (Patois, babes.)

I mean, seriously. Why take me out of school for the day and treat it like a big exciting adventure if you weren't serious about it in the first place? Er, hello?! Cally calling Sense? Common Sense? Do you hear me?

I can't even talk to her. How do you communicate with

a one hundred per cent numbskull? God. Keesha Lomax's cousin Patsy is cleverer than Mum, and she goes to school on a special bus. Swear down.

I remained a lady at all times. My tiny glimpse into the modelling world and the girls who work at L'Agence showed me they are all super-cool ice maidens who glide about with their heads in the air like nothing ever gets to them, nothing ever pisses them off, so I tried to do this for as long as I could.

Apart from that bloke snorting gak in the bogs. He was a bit weird.

But everyone else was cool.

And actually, cokey bog bloke was kinda reaaaaally cool and stuff?

But like, the girls. They were so aloof and seemed to walk on clouds. So I channelled my inner them.

Oh, don't get me wrong. I did scream at her for about twenty minutes, saying she was ruining my life. Think I might have accused her of killing Dad as well. But mostly it was the usual stuff about how controlling she is and doesn't love me and is thwarting every single thing I choose to do. And what's really bloody annoying is she just stands there, arms folded, staring at me and not REACTING. Like she is an ice queen who works in one of the top London agencies, etc. etc. etc. Yeah right, as if they'd employ her.

She's actually an amoeba.

When I had stopped my pretty amazing speech about the injustices in the world like having had to crawl out of her stinky womb and make my own way in the cosmos with zero help from her, she had the audacity to say, 'Have you quite finished throwing your toys out the pram?'

You know what? Every time she says that to me I reeeaaallly want to get a pram full of toys. Toys with really jagged edges.

AND THROW THEM RIGHT AT HER. SQUARE IN THE CHOPS. GOD!

'I'm going,' I go.

'You're not,' she goes.

'You can't stop me.'

'I'd like to see you try. Now if you don't mind, I've had a busy day and I need my bed. And just for the record, I didn't kill your dad. And it's pretty bloody hurtful when you say I did.'

And then she does this massive queenie strop flounce up the stairs which was SO FUNNY I had to grab hold of the banisters I was peeing my pants that much. I hear her bedroom door slam. She should do stand-up. She's like Jo Brand or something.

I shouldn't have said that. About Dad. But sometimes I feel I have to say something, anything to get her to actually talk about him. Like, when he first went missing, we'd have these things called Dad nights when me and her would curl up on the sofa and watch DVDs of things he liked – *Trigger Happy TV*, *Bottom*, *Red Dwarf* – and eat Mexican food (his favourite) and look through the box of old photos and just talk about him. These days it's as if he never even existed. I've been in her bedroom. At the old house she used to have some photos of him up. Here? None. She has airbrushed him out of history. And yes, OK, she hasn't killed him, but she has DEFO killed his memory. And maybe in a way that's worse. And now I'm bloody CRYING. And I HATE IT when this happens. From nowhere. Bloody great big tears for NO APPARENT REASON. I am such a DUFUS.

Actually I don't really know what a dufus is or does. Maybe it's the name of Rufus De Villeneuve's brother or something.

To cheer myself up I sit on the bottom stair and look at the picture of me and Rufus that Owen took at Clothes Show Live. It's a horrendous shot of me, but what's really cool about it is that Rufus put his like arm around me and it looks a bit like he's indulging in a spot of boob gropage. The pic was greeted with shouts of PAEDO and stuff when I tweeted it and stuck it on Facebook. So much so that Owen said I should take it down as Rufus might catch wind of it and then sue me because apparently if it's on my wall it's like I've written it in the *Times of London* or something and that's a no-go and stuff. Which I did. But it's a shame coz we totally look like boyfriend and girlfriend.

But today it doesn't cheer me up. I'm seriously crying here. What a day I've had. It's been MAJOR. I had to lie to Freya Copeland that her new dip-dye was a huge success which really took it out of me because, even though I love her to bits (not in a lesbo way) she is soooooo needy and kept going on and on about it all day long. I tried to choreograph some Year Sevens in the playground who have decided that Pharrell is STILL a thing. I had the most pathetic litter-picking detention because I was caught cartwheeling in the modern languages corridor. And then I come home to this? The groundbreaking earth-shattering news that I have an opening in the modelling world. One of the most sought-after openings in like the WORLD. And my mother nearly forgets to tell me? Get me that pram full of toys and let me empty it. I've earned the ass out of it.

In my room I get stuff ready for the next day. We've got swimming. I hate swimming. Ever since that day. I was doing swimming with the school when I saw Mum's friend Lucy coming down the side of the pool and talking to the teacher. Then the teacher looked over at me and tilted her head to beckon me over. In the changing room Lucy told me how Dad's car had been found at Beachy Head and what Beachy Head implied. And although I collapsed inside and went to pieces and a million things were shooting through my head. And although all I could see in my imagination's eye was Dad. Facing up. Floating in the water. But below the surface. And although in this image he was actually in the swimming pool I'd just been in and not in the cold, choppy sea. And even though it was a really really hideous image. And even though all I wanted to do was run away, as far from Lucy as possible, and drown myself or scream and scream and scream . . .

I didn't.

I like, looked at her. Sooo calmly.

Like, you wouldn't have known anything of what was going on in my head right then.

And I was like, You dragged me out of swimming to tell me this?

And she looked like I was biggest piece of shit to have ever fallen from the devil himself's anus.

And so she might.

Coz I then just like walked back out of the changing room and got back into the pool.

She came and knelt on the side and told me Mum wanted me to go home. Mum needed me. Mum had sent her.

I just ignored her and carried on with the class.

Imagine that. Mum wanting me. Needing me.

Those were the days.

I don't speak to her over breakfast the next morning. She is not worthy of my words. And I'm sure she makes my porridge taste like wallpaper on purpose to punish for me for 'ranting' last night. I think of something really funny to say but don't say it coz why should I spoil her with my witticisms? Instead I will spoil my followers and make it a twitticism.

> **Maybe the reason I am so skinny is coz you make me shit food Mommie Dearest. #porridgegate**

I wait to see if anyone retweets or favourites it. No-one does.

And then some girl in Year Ten tweets me:

> **I'm sure your mother's food is fine you anorexic freak horse. #haveapastie**

I don't know this girl that well but really LOL at her. I do a 'Quote retweet' and add the comment LOLZ!

She replies again.

> **I wasn't joking you stupid walking rake. Enjoy your mid morning snack of bog roll. #eatingdisorder**

Hahahahahahahahahahaha, mid morning snack of bog roll. Now that really is funny. Some people are just totes jel of my slim physique. I've every mind to tweet about my modelling news but I don't want to ruin anything yet. I don't want to show off about it and then have to own up to the fact that she who passes herself off as my doting mother has actually put a massive great kibosh on it. Nobody knows I even went to London for the day yet, coz loose lips cost lives and I didn't want anyone telling the teachers, coz as far as they're concerned it's fine to miss a day if you're lying on a couch watching Jeremy Kyle and *Loose Women* and feeling a bit headachey. But God forbid you go to the capital city and tout yourself as a model who could make millions and like, buy them a new geography block or theatre wing. Oh no. They want us all to have boring jobs like scientists or politicians or teachers or captains of industry. And wear Alice bands and Barbours. Lily Allen went to boarding school and she doesn't wear that rubbish. At least, she doesn't in public.

But anyway. I don't mind keeping this to myself. Pride comes before a fall. And I don't intend to fall on this one. Oh no.

And besides. I have a plan.

I phone Aba at lunch break. I go right to the other end of the gardens beyond the playground where you sometimes see Mr Meacher having a crafty cig and playing with himself in his nylon trouser pocket. GROSS. Although it was funny that time Jemima Lesser-Beauchamp shouted, 'Don't flick your ash on my bush, Mr Meacher!'

She is so funny. We call her Jemima Lesser-of-two-evils. I came up with that. RANDOM!

Aba picks up on the second ring. She HEARTS ME.

'Babe!'

Awwww.

'Aba, has my mum called you this morning?'

'Yeah babe, and I'm completely gutted.'

'What did she say?'

'I'm a bit upset actually, Cally. It's not every day I get a feeling about someone, and I got that feeling about you.'

'What did she say?'

'Oh, how you're going to put everything on hold till next summer.'

'Did she?'

She is officially the biggest bitch in the universe. No wonder Dad buggered off. Todal Respeck to the Mon. *sucks teeth*

'I understand, babe. It's cool. I did GCSEs too. Not everyone in this business is an airhead.'

I feel like crying.

'I hate her,' I say.

'Babe?'

'She's such a bitch. She knows I want this more than anything in the world and she's insisting I stay on at school and stuff.'

'I know. All I can say is, well, if you can hold off putting any weight on before the summer and we'll see what we can do.'

'I could kill her.'

This actually makes her laugh.

'But until you're sixteen, what she says goes.'

Er, wait on one cotton-pickin' second.

'I am sixteen,' I say, quietly. Why does Aba not know this? I filled in that form when we met at Clothes Show Live.

'Sorry?'

'I am sixteen.' I'm more indignant now.

'But your form says you're not sixteen till next October.'

'No, I was sixteen this October.'

Her voice TOTALLY changes and it is REALLY exciting.

'Are you being honest with me, Cally?'

'Why would I lie?'

I hear her ruffling about with pieces of paper.

'Hang on,' she goes.

I wait. I'm getting excited now. And I'm not sure why. Eventually Aba is like, 'Hon, your form looks like your D.O.B. is 9th October 1999.'

'It's 1998,' I tell her.

'But . . .'

'I was like . . . scribbling when I wrote that. I wasn't leaning on anything. And my handwriting's total pants anyway. I am. I'm sixteen.'

'Straight up?'

'Cross my heart and hope to die, Aba. I wouldn't lie to you. Ever.'

And I'm not lying. For once.

There's this massive silence. Then she goes, 'Look, there's still a problem. Legally she's in charge of you till you're eighteen. It's just that from sixteen it's more of a grey area. I wouldn't feel happy bringing you down here unless I knew she was one hundred per cent on your side.'

And then I hear the pips for the next lesson.

'I'll talk to her tonight.'

'Good luck. And six months isn't that long.'

Isn't it?

I hang up. I look about and suddenly feel like I'm in an amazing adventure movie. The playground is full of girls swirling around, heading back to class. Suddenly they're all the enemy and I have to escape. It's just a matter of when.

A girl jumps out from behind the bushes. She screams ANOREXIC HORSE in my face and then runs off laughing.

Usually I'd find this REALLY FUNNY. Usually I admire girls' cheek and bravado. Today I find myself running after her. She's a bit of a fat bitch so I'm faster than her. I pounce on her and vault her to the ground. She squeals as I sit on her and pull her head back by the ponytail.

'Just you watch, bitch,' I go.

Then I forcibly shove her face into the grass. It makes a totally AMAZING thud noise and I feel her back going weird, as the wind is knocked out of her.

I let go of the ponytail.
I walk away.
I feel INVISIBLE.
Sorry, no.
I feel INVINCIBLE.
During double maths I create a new email address:
NatalieBiolettiMum@hotmail.com
I give myself a password and everything.
As far as the internet's concerned, I am now my mum.
And as far as Aba's concerned, I will be.

From: Natalie Bioletti NatalieBiolettimum@hotmail.com
To: Aba Wilshaw-Smit AbaWSnewfaces@l'agence.com
Subject: Change of Heart

Hey Aba

   This will probably come as a bit of a surprise to you
but having spoken to Cally tonight I have done some more
thinking about your kind offer. I have tried to reason with her
about why I think she should stay on and do her exams in the
summer but she is strong-willed, as you know. I now see I was
probably a bit hasty with that phone call I made to you this
morning.

   On reflection, I'm cool with her coming to London. I just
need your reassurance that she will be taken care of and
looked after. She is a sensitive wee soul at the end of the day,
even if she is amazingly good-looking and got the potential to
be a massive model.

   Do feel free to email me on this email address but don't
bother calling me as my phone is playing up. And anyway I'm
off to stay with some friends abroad tomorrow so I'm going to
be pretty much out of action for a while.

Let me know when you need her to come and I'll make sure she gets down to you, no sweat.

I'm putting a lot of trust in you, Aba. Please don't let me down.

Yours sincerely

Natalie x

God I'm good. And . . . send! Sooo glad I went to a really excellent posh private school and got PROPER English lessons. Coz if I'd been in some scummy comp I probs would've put loads of spelling mistakes in and not known. Also I'd not have known to say shit like *I need your reassurance* and *I'm putting my trust in you* and stuff. Hahahahahaha I'm amazing.

Aba replies almost immediately.

From: Aba Wilshaw-Smith AbaWSnewfaces@l'agence.com
To: Natalie Bioletti NatalieBiolettimum@hotmail.com
Subject: AWESOME SAUCE

Hey Nat-Nat

This is the best email EVER. I've been dancing round the office.

I'll be back in touch with some dates and times and we'll sort C's train tickets and a car from the station.

You won't regret this. I'll look after her like she's one of my own. It's my job.

Laterz

Aba xxxxxx

Looks like I'm going to London, babes!
My mobile rings. It's her! I snap it up.
'Hi Aba!'

'Hi hon, I just had the most AMAZING email from your mother. Is she there? I know her phone's playing up. Just want a quick word.'

'Yeah, she's sat right next to me. We're having a girly evening watching movies and stuff.'

'Sweet.'

'Mum? It's Aba.'

I give the performance of my freaking LIFE. At one point I slip into being Cheryl Cole, but thank FRIG Aba doesn't seem to notice.

Job done.

Owen

If you've ever wondered what working for a 'LGBT' website entails, and I really wouldn't blame you if you hadn't, then it mostly involves sitting around all day staring blankly at a computer screen and pouncing. I pounce in the name of honesty and decency only, but pounce I do, any time I smell a story. The website, called www.gay-mover.co.uk (supposed to sound like 'game over', not sure why) was set up by Gerard a few years ago to report on the latest news affecting LGBT in this country and beyond. We also do some campaigning. Anything to keep Gerard and the website in the black, frankly. I was brought on last year, allegedly because of my profile in the media – something I suppose I have to thank my father for – and Minty is a recent addition, meant to be taking us to 'the next level'. Whatever that is.

I know that since I've joined, Gerard's been pleased with the publicity I have brought the site, mostly down to the interviews I do with various press about my work and my dad and so on. But I don't know if he's really that impressed with the articles I write (he certainly seems happy enough to correct my 'errors'). Matt reckons he keeps me on because he fancies me, which I find incredibly reductive, but actually he might not be far from the truth. Gerard has a funny little face, a myopic runt of the litter who hasn't seen daylight before, and I sometimes catch him staring at me across the office. When I do he shakes his head and goes 'Just thinking . . .'

Matt tells me, *Yeah, just thinking about doing you.*

Why does everything have to be about sex?

And then Matt tells me I am a young fogey.

Well, if I am, so be it.

Sunday I decide to do a few hours from home before heading to the demo. The demo is a little gift from God, right on our doorstep, everything we believe in, bashing a UKIP councillor and his reactionary homophobic views, blah blah blah. It'd be funny if it wasn't so dangerous. I fire my laptop up and hit Twitter. I used to enjoy scrolling through celebrity tweets sniffing out 'an exclusive', as Gerard calls it. Though as it's a celebrity announcing something on here to a million followers, it can hardly be called that. I follow primarily famous gay people, politicians, sportspeople, TV names and pop stars. If anyone refers to anything 'politically' I have to try and turn it into a story for the website. So if, for example, Mariah Carey were to tweet, and admittedly this is highly unlikely, 'God I really don't like Lady Gaga,' I would probably write a one-hundred-word piece called CAREY LAMBASTS GAY ICON. Etc. Though Gerard might contest my use of the word 'lambasts'. Usually we try to be more highbrow than that, naturally, but more often than not we fall short of the mark.

Matt is working this morning. The house is quiet without him. I hear the ticking of the grandfather clock in the hall that, rather appropriately, his granddad left him in his will. I hear the occasional whirr of the washing machine and the pulse of my mobile, but I ignore it. Work must come first for a bit. But as ever, it's hard to work when you're not in an office, distracted by stimuli. My mind wanders and I turn a bit stalkery. I open Matt's Twitter page and am, as ever, disappointed to find he hasn't tweeted for a couple of days; and then it was to some mutual friends, making corny jokes about work.

Why am I disappointed? Do I really want to expose his flirting or setting up some sleazy sex date? As if he's not clever enough to do that behind my back and would do it online in a social media forum for all the world – well, for his 634 followers, self included – to see? It's like I'm willing him to have an affair or be unfaithful just so I can be angry with him. Why is that? Is it just because, post Grindrgate, I have a niggling suspicion that all is not right and therefore I just want proof that my endless worrying is not in vain? Or am I just the opposite of a thrill-seeker, if there is such a thing – a doom-seeker, looking for bad news wherever I can find it? Is this what my job has turned me into? I seek out the contentious online and run with it, while at home I look for a drama that may not even be there?

I shut down Twitter. This is not good for my mental health. I look to the cube of bright sunlight in the window and try and count my blessings.

Matt deactivated his Grindr. He told me the next night. He didn't make a big song and dance about it, he just mentioned it in passing over supper.

'Oh, I shut down my Grindr thing,' he said between mouthfuls of vegetarian lasagne.

'Why?' I'd tried to hide the thrill in my voice.

'Well, I know it was making you uncomfortable. And if I want to gab to people that much I've got Facebook and Whatsapp and loads of other things so . . .'

And we'd said no more about it. I trust him. I have to. So even though I was itching to check his phone and see if he was telling me truth, I did what I should always do in those situations. I took a deep breath and went with it.

I check my phone to see who's been texting. It's Matt.

Sorry bubs. Jen needs me to work till four. Billy off. Gonna miss demo. Soz. Grrr. X

I stare at the screen and feel a rush of anger. Not because Billy is off and Jen is making him cover his shift and therefore he's going to miss the demo. We were looking forward to the demo. At least I thought we were.

I'm angry instead that this could be an elaborate ruse. Billy is not off, Jen has not made him work longer hours, he is heading to a free-for-all in a flat in Rusholme where he will sleep with approximately seventy men, and . . .

I know. Ridiculous. I text him back.

Ah shame. Kill Bill next time you see him LOL x

He replies almost immediately.

Kill Bill LOL x

Sometimes we say so little, but mean such a lot.

I decide to phone Mum as I'm getting ready to go out. I do this a lot, think I can multitask when clearly I can't. So as I'm cleaning my teeth and swapping my top and loading the dishwasher, I battle to keep the phone at my ear and make out like I'm chillaxing on the couch giving her my undivided attention.

'So how did Cally take you telling her she couldn't go to London?'

'Oh, she was furious at first, but remarkably – you'll never believe this – she's been incredibly mature about it for the rest of the week.'

'Oh. Maybe she's finally growing up.'

'Fingers crossed. Are you having a wee?'

'No, I'm running the tap.'

'Oh right. Yeah, she's been sweetness and light these last few days.'

'Well, like you said, you're only asking her to postpone it for six months.'

'I know, but when you're that age, six months is a lifetime.'

'She's probably too scared at the prospect of living on her own and all that.'

'Maybe.'

'So. Any other news?'

'Not really. Not been up to much. Been down to Chorlton a few times.'

'Chorlton? What's in Chorlton?'

'This girl I was at school with. Been chatting a bit on Facebook. Popped round for coffee.'

'Has she changed much?'

'We're both a bit fatter. More wrinkles. Not sure why I bothered, really.' And then her voice changes, brightens. 'Oh, something interesting happened yesterday.'

'Oh aye, what?'

'Lucy sent me a housewarming present. A coffee table book about Martin Parr, the artist?'

'Oh yeah?' Even though I had no idea who he was.

'And she sent it via Amazon, only because she'd booked it to arrive the next day it was delivered by a courier company. Well, it wasn't the Royal Mail, anyway. And the guy who delivered it was the this bloke who used to come to Milk.'

'God, it's been a real trip down Memory Lane this week, hasn't it?'

'It was so weird. He recognized me coz my name was on the package, but we chatted for ages.'

'Mother?!' I gasp faux-dramatically.

'What?'

'Do you fancy him?'

'Owen!'

'Well, it's a simple enough question!'

'How can I fancy him?'

'Because you're a . . .' I want to say single woman. But I can't.

'I don't fancy him,' she says, to cover the obvious. 'But it was really nice to see him.'

'What's his name?'

'Well, I only knew him as Gripper. I never knew why people called him that. Anyway, his name's actually Laurence, and apparently no-one's called him Gripper for years.'

'And why did they call him Gripper? Did you ask?'

'His surname's Stebson, apparently.'

'Is that meant to mean something?'

'He was a character in *Grange Hill*.'

'Who was?'

'Gripper Stebson.'

'Oh, I see.'

And with that, I make my excuses and get ready to head into town.

While I'm having a shave, something in the bathroom mirror catches my eye. Behind me, out on the landing, I can see the corner of the hatch that leads into the loft. My breath shortens. My lungs appear to have shrunk. I flick my leg back and kick the door shut with a slam. If I don't want to look at a loft hatch, I don't have to.

Ain't nothing weird about that.

And as I go out: eyes down, eyes down. Pathetic. But it has to be done.

After getting off the tram I take an elongated stroll towards the university, meandering through St Ann's Square where Mother Hen is. It's busy with its lunchtime service and I see Mother Hen Jen clucking round the bar, filling carafes of red wine. I see Matt, but he doesn't see me. And a further strain of the neck shows no Billy in sight. I slink off quickly, just in case. The smell of their double-baked cheese soufflé stays with me a long time, though, and the resultant rumble in my stomach reminds me I've not eaten much this morning.

Another rumble is more ominous. I've come out without an umbrella in Manchester and this is asking for trouble. True to form, the rumble I hear is thunderous and suddenly there is a torrential downpour. I leap into Waterstones' doorway, yanking my hood up. Why did I wear such a stupidly thin jacket? Why did I assume the weather would remain so bright? I wait for the storm to pass by but it looks like it's here for keeps. Half expecting an ark to float by, I take my courage in both hands and run for my life. It's a long run to the university and I may as well be running through a river. My jeans cling to my legs and I can barely open my eyes. By the time I get to where I need to be I know I am cutting it fine, and I know I look like a drowned rat. And as soon as I get there, sod's law, the rain vanishes as quickly as it came. Within seconds I am bathed in sunlight. Feeling and looking like I've walked through a car wash. And the car wash won. A strong wind builds up. I hope it will blow-dry me warm, but it doesn't. I push against it to find my destination.

Gerard and Minty are waiting outside the lecture hall

when I finally arrive, after getting lost in some concrete wind tunnels behind a gloriously Victorian towery edifice that puts me in mind of Oxford or Cambridge. They look dry. They must have had somewhere to hide. Minty's hair is blowing all over the place, mind you, and Gerard's looking pissed off. They're both wearing www.gay-mover.co.uk T-shirts over their normal clothes, and Minty is holding a megaphone. A pile of sodden placards bearing various anti-homophobia slogans lean neatly against the wall of the lecture hall we're about to protest outside. But the wind is looking like it might send them all scattering any time soon. A frail-looking woman looking a bit like Florence from Florence and the Machine is hovering nearby with an old-fashioned camera. I recognize her as Minty's girlfriend. She never speaks. Nobody else has turned up. And I'm cutting it fine. Oddly, there doesn't appear to be much movement inside the lecture hall building. Usually there'd be some signs of life, lights on, people arriving. But today, nothing.

'Bit of a poor show.'

'I think they've changed the venue,' says Minty.

'Where to?' I venture. And for devilment I direct it at Florence. She shrugs and busies herself with her camera. This was going to be a wonderful photo opportunity for the website. Me, Minty and Gerard haranguing Mr Sanderbach as he made his way in to address the students on UKIP's latest policies. But it looks like no-one's turned up to hear him. A small victory, perhaps?

'Did you not bring an umbrella?' asks Minty.

I roll my eyes. 'Yes. But I decided against putting it up.'

I gestured to show there was nothing in my hands.

'Also, it's invisible.'

She shakes her head. Gerard's not saying anything, but he

110

is scrolling through something on his phone. His face seems to be very pale. And he is chewing his bottom lip.

Minty sighs. 'I'm ringing the uni. Ask them what the hell is going on.'

She starts jabbing a number into her phone.

Just then, we hear a window opening above. We look up. Dylan is leaning out of a window on the second floor, all smiles. Dylan! Looking very dry, it has to be said.

'Owen!'

'Hey Dylan!'

'You here for the Humphrey Sanderbach thing?'

'Yeah. Doesn't seem to be much going on?'

'Well, there wouldn't be!'

'Oh God,' groans Gerard. 'This is a disaster.'

And he starts ripping his T-shirt off.

'Why, what's happened?' I shout back to Dylan.

'He's been dropped by UKIP. And they banned him from coming. They did a press release about an hour ago.'

I look to Minty, who has returned her phone to her pocket. Surely it's her job, as head of PR, to know these things?

'Thought it was quiet,' she bleats.

Gerard is heading for the way out from this concrete courtyard. He spits back at me, 'Get a piece to me ASAP, Owen!'

'It's Sunday!'

'It's NEWS!' And he is gone.

'I wanna go Nando's,' Florence says. And Minty nods. She looks to Dylan and shouts a polite thank you, and the pair of them walk off, leaving me here like a spare part. I look back up to Dylan.

'You look like a drowned rat!'

'I feel like I've wet myself!'

He chuckles. He looks so warm and toasty up there.

'I couldn't use your computer, could I?'

He smirks. 'I'll buzz you up! We can get you out of those wet clothes!'

I laugh and head for the main door. A buzzer sounds and the door clicks on. I realize as I push my way in I don't know how to find him once I'm in there.

His voice calls me up. Warm, excited, as if this has been planned for ages and finally the moment has arrived. When I get a few floors up he's standing there with his study door open. It's an old door, the walls either side red brick. Although the staircase was thoroughly Sixties, I'm obviously stepping into an original part of the building, stepping over the threshold from new to old. He grips my shoulder and pats my back with his other hand and draws me into the room. An electric fire is burning, the walls are covered in bookshelves, a messy desk sits at one side of the room, a battered old sofa at the other. He goes to another door and opens it. Inside are some shelves with a few clothes on. He tells me he sometimes goes running from here and keeps his kit here, and offers it to me. I'm so sodden I think, why not? He pulls out some sweatpants and a T-shirt and hands them to me.

'Come on. We can dry your clothes out. Don't think you'll be too embarrassed to be seen in these.' And as I look for somewhere to change he adds, 'Not that anyone can see.' And emits a warm throaty chuckle. 'Brew?'

I nod and scamper to the fire. I kick off my trainers, then hurriedly peel off my jeans and jacket. Then my shirt. I fold them over a couple of hardback chairs and slide them in front of the fire. I hear the low burbling of a kettle, the clink of mugs and spoons. He's saying nothing. Over the fire there is a mirror. I see him looking at me. Our eyes meet and I smile nervously. I drag my undies down and although I am naked in front of him I'm not embarrassed for some reason. This is not like me. He looks away. I quickly pull on the pants and top. And realize I'm becoming hard. I tuck my cock into the band of the pants to cover it. Why? Why now?

'No-one can see. Pretty much on my own here on a Sunday,' he reiterates. I slide on the parquet flooring to the sofa and sit and grab a cushion to hug. But I know he was looking. And I know what he has seen. I'm shaking.

I must have misread something here. He's my mum's best friend's husband.

He can't have been looking like I think he was looking.

I misinterpret things too much.

He asks me if I take sugar.

Natalie

Miriam Joseph is very particular about how she likes her house cleaned. So much so, she has a clip folder with umpteen sheets in, which she calls the cleaning schedule. There is a spreadsheet of tasks for each room and I have to tick them off and date them as I work my way through them to show they've been done. Some tasks fall into the weekly column and some eight-weekly. And it doesn't stop there. Each task is listed and then has a column next to it called 'instructions and tools'. For instance in the bathroom, a weekly task is 'Bath, taps, surround'. The instructions here read: 'Bathroom sponge, Cif bath cleaner spray, rub, rinse with shower head'.

Who knew cleaning a bath could be so complicated?

'I know it probably seems quite anal,' she said when she first showed me round her mini-palace, 'but experience has taught me it's best to be clear about what exactly I want.'

'You're the boss!' I replied jovially, and that seemed to encourage her.

She has a bright pink streak in her hair. God knows why. It smacks of saying *Look at me, I'm quirky!*, which doesn't seem to fit her personality. I wonder if she has a dyeing schedule that she hands to her colourist, outlining the precise way she wants her locks coloured.

The dog, Snowy, is not always here, she informs me. She shares him with her partner. That's where he is today. But next time she is going to take me on a walk with him. No doubt she has a detailed instruction leaflet about that as well.

'Oh! You have a partner!' I say, overcome with excitement, my subtext being, *So maybe you weren't shagging my husband* . . . She surveys me oddly. Why would it be so exciting that someone was in a relationship? A nod. Then I say, 'How long you been together?'

'Three years,' she says, and she sees the smile straighten at my lips. So she's met someone since Danny went. Great. I almost snarl at her, *Well, come on. Show me your lousy home! Dust, wipe, vac, what else? It can't be that hard, Miriam!*

The one thing I have been amazed by is how trusting people are once you claim to be a cleaner. Miriam asks for no references, she just takes my word that this is what I do, and by my second visit she is happy for me to be in her house alone while she goes off to run errands. I had wanted to rifle through her drawers to see if I could find any clues to her relationship with Danny, but I am so worried about falling behind with the cleaning schedule that I just go full steam ahead. I look on it as a masterclass in how to clean. I now know how to make a set of wooden slatted blinds look brand new, and how to get the best out of a draining board. These are great life skills. I might start making my place look semi-decent! Her living room is wannabe bohemian, all stripped floorboards and Ikea bookshelves. Her books display an interest in modern art, some classics, and the books that Lucy and Dylan talk about but I never get round to reading. Interestingly, she has everything that Jeanette Winterson appears to have ever written.

I remember *Oranges Are Not the Only Fruit* from when it was on TV.

I'm pretty sure this Winterson woman is a lesbian. What if Miriam is too? I really hope she is, because then nothing would ever have gone on between her and Danny.

I have a quick peek in the drawers of a sideboard as I'm cleaning. Nothing untoward in the first one, but I'm not sure exactly what it is I'm looking for.

Oh God. Please let her be a dyke.

We could be friends then. We could be . . .

But I'm getting ahead of myself. Why would I want to be friends with someone who has a *cleaning schedule*?

Oh. Odd. And intriguing. And a link that Miriam is connected to us. In the next drawer are a pile of old tabloid newspapers from years back. Our club Milk was front-page news at the time because a teenage girl died on our premises after taking ecstasy. Why has Miriam got all these? Admittedly it was a massive story at the time, as the girl was white and middle-class and her parents were never off the news trying to highlight how bad drugs were and how kids should just say no. It spelt the beginning of the end for our venue in London, and motivated our move up North. But then beneath those I find more clippings from over the years about other drugs-related deaths. Maybe Miriam is keeping them for some research for work or something. But why would a graphic designer be interested in drug-fuelled deaths? But the Tiffany Keith case was significant to us in so many ways. And there she is. Smiling back at me in her school uniform.

What an odd thing to keep hidden away, I tell myself. And why?

It was also odd the other day when the doorbell rang and the delivery guy kept grinning and saying, 'Nat?' and I was like, 'Yes, that is the name on the parcel.' And it turned out to be Gripper.

But I can't think about that now. I am a woman on a mission. I am doing what the police have failed to do over the years and I am trying to track down my husband. What if he is here? Upstairs in a bedroom and she hasn't told me? Or hiding out in the loft? Or the cellar. What if he can see me now? I dart around the ground floor of her house, listening for signs of life. What if she has a shed at the bottom of the garden? What if she's keeping him locked up in there? I slide across the kitchen floor and unlock the back door. The cold air hits me like a wake-up call. He is, he's out there, I just know it. I hurry into the garden. No shed.

Who the hell doesn't have a shed in their garden? I thought everyone had one in their garden. I thought it was the law!

Miriam Joseph's garden is a bit on the small side. There's room to swing more than a cat, if cat-swinging is your thing, but it's only about as long as two tall people lying end to end. And it's as wide as the house. I realize I am pacing the lawn. This turf looks new. What if he is being held captive in a secret underground chamber and . . .

A man comes out into the next garden. A pensioner with a sun hat on.

'Morning!' he chirrups.

'When was this grass laid? Do you know? This turf. Looks new.'

OK, so I am now behaving like a mad woman. Though he seems to take my urgency in his stride. He leans on the fence dividing his garden from Miriam's, and strokes his chin.

'She had the whole thing dug up and relaid . . . ooh . . . must be a few years ago now?'

'How many? Three? Five?'

He looks at me oddly. 'Sorry, who are you?'

'I'm her cleaner. But I'm really interested in the longevity of different types of grass. I'm . . . I'm actually doing a PhD in it,' I say, with a shrugging sense of completely false modesty.

He looks impressed. It's worked. He settles on five years.

I hurry back inside.

Five years ago Miriam Joseph built a chamber under the ground and Danny is living there. Isn't he? Is he?

I am now thinking like a madwoman.

Don't get ahead of yourself, Natalie.

I steady myself on her bookshelf and take a deep breath to calm down. Which is when I hear the front door go.

Miriam has returned from the shops and seems impressed by what I've achieved.

Yes, I've managed to hold it all together without screaming at you HOW DO YOU KNOW MY HUSBAND?!?!?! IS HE UNDER YOUR BACK GARDEN?!?!?!??!?!

'You're quick,' she says, impressed.

'No beating around the bush with me,' I say. And then worry this might sound a bit lesbophobic, especially as I still have my feather duster hovering close to the Winterson shelf. And I can't remember if I'm supposed to use the feather duster for the books. Isn't that just for high-level dusting, like dado rails and ceiling fans? I'll have to check my schedule . . .

'Tell you what. Why don't you take a break, and we can have a coffee and a natter?' she says, possibly relaxing as she can see this particular cleaner is happy to have a schedule to tick off.

'OK. Why don't I fix us some coffee, then? About time I found my way around the kitchen.'

'Perfect.'

Even though this is my second visit, I've not yet attacked

the kitchen. She asked me to leave it till today, though it looks like she's already cleaned it prior to my arrival. That's what I'd probably do if I had a cleaner.

'I'll just go . . . freshen up. Coffee's in the fridge!' she calls through as I hear her stilettoed feet running up the stairs.

I flip her Philippe Starck kettle on. I used to have one similar, in the Nineties. I get two mugs from the glass-fronted wall unit, then open the fridge.

What I see inside is like a punch to the guts.

Finally. I have seen.

I stand, frozen, staring at it, unable to take my eyes off it. Eventually I hear the footsteps coming down the stairs. I quickly grab a golden packet of coffee out and slide the door shut.

'You'll need the doobry,' says Miriam as she glides into the kitchen, 'the cafetière. Here.' And she pulls it from another glass-fronted cabinet. I go about making coffee for two on autopilot.

'I don't take milk, do you?' she says.

I shake my head. I do take milk, I just don't want to have to see the contents of the fridge again. I realize I am nervous now as I go about performing this most simple of tasks. Coffee in cafetière. Water in cafetière. Leave. Plunge. Pour. I feel her eyes on me and try to snap out of it.

Coffee made, I join her at the kitchen table, where she has fanned a selection of biscuits on a plate because, she tells me, she's feeling naughty. She wonders if I'm feeling naughty. I shake my head.

You have jelly beans in a jar in your fridge.

She's asking if I'm married. I tell her I'm divorced. Well, Josie Greengrass is, I've decided.

This is too much of a coincidence.

It completely wipes out any thoughts I have of asking about the Tiffany Keith drugs clippings.

She's asking if I have kids. I tell her one of each.

No-one keeps jelly beans in the fridge except my husband.

She wants to know their names and ages. Bloody hell, what is this? Twenty questions? I make some up. But then it's time to turn the tables.

Why doesn't she recognize me? Surely she'll have seen the news reports from when he went missing?

'So, come on. Less of me, more of you.'

Oh but my haircut. And glasses. Of course she doesn't recognize me. God! Is she in for a shock. Possibly like the shock I'm feeling now!

'What do you do with yourself, then?'

Apart from nick other people's husbands.

'I'm a graphic designer. Freelance. Work from home.'

You draw pictures. Gosh, now I sit in front of you, you really remind me of Rebekah Brooks. Wow. Someone else I've never trusted.

'Kids?'

'No. Secretly relieved. I'm quite selfish.'

Try very selfish, Rebekah lookalike with your hair that's far too long for a woman of your years. You must be my age, if not older. He must be losing his touch.

'I was tidying up in the front room. And I couldn't help but notice some newspaper clippings.'

She looks confused, like she has no idea what I'm talking about.

'About that girl who died of a drugs overdose down South. Remember?'

'Oh yes. I collect all sorts. I've recently been pitching on a sort of updated Just Say No campaign. Don't know why they're not in my office. I didn't even get the gig.'

Oh. Well, that makes sense, I suppose. It's just a coincidence. Even if it's a pretty freaky coincidence.

'And what does your partner do? Sorry, is it a man?'

'It is. He's a teacher.'

And what the hell does he teach?

'Of what?'

'Maths.'

Liar. Why are you lying to me? I did the books at Milk. Danny was useless. Stop lying.

'But you don't live together?'

'No, we're stupidly independent.'

'What's his name?'

Out with it. Danny. Danny Bioletti. Or have you come up with some preposterous cover name? Enzo? Enya? Hitler?

'Alex.'

Alex? He's calling himself Alex now is he?

'Aww. Have you got a picture? I'd love to see.'

Come on. Then I can slap you. Hard.

Excitement bubbles up inside me as she looks surprised then finds her phone and scrolls through it. She turns it to face me and proudly says,

'There he is. It's not a very good one.'

'No it's not, he looks black.' I say before I can stop myself. The man in this tiny picture is very dark-skinned. Too dark-skinned to be Danny. What an awful picture.

'He is black.' She sounds incredibly offended.

Shit.

That's not Danny.

That's someone called Alex.

He's a teacher.
And now she thinks I'm racist.
How do I get out of this?

'I'm half black,' I say quickly, hoping this will make her like me more. I see her eyes flit across my features. This is the most ridiculous thing I have ever said in my life. And I've said plenty of other ridiculous things. But this is right up there at the top of the winners' podium.

'I know I don't look it,' I add.

'I'd never have guessed.'

'Yeah, my mum was black.'

'Right.'

'Yeah. Her name was Beauty.'

'That's nice. From where?'

'Jamaica.'

And I do actually say it with a slightly Patois twang, hoping this will convince.

'Sorry I said that about . . . I just . . . we got such flack growing up as a mixed-race family. And with me looking white and everything. I sort of thought society felt white people should be with white people and black with black. Awful, I know. Probably some . . . inherent . . . internalized racism.'

She is trying to take this all in.

'A therapist would have a field day!' I say. And she nods.

'No, I can see it now,' she says, giving me a good once-over again. 'If you'd not said, I wouldn't be any the wiser. But yeah.'

All right, love, keep your hair on.

'It's my features,' I say, unsure what I really mean.

What mess have I got myself into now?

'Irie!' I say and hold my fist up to clink knuckles with her. She looks most alarmed and raises her hand slowly.

'Irie!' she replies, politely.

Strangely, very soon after this she decides she has to retreat to her study to work.

No doubt she will fire me at the end of my shift.

Just in case she isn't going to, I run into the living room and tear a sheet of paper from the back of the cleaning folder and quickly write down all the lies I've told.

> *Josie Greengrass*
> *Mixed race*
> *Mum Beauty Jamaica*
> *Divorced*
> *Son Ben 21*
> *Daughter Cate spelt like Cate Blanchette 16*
> *Professional cleaner*
> *Loves dogs*
> *Likes black coffee*

I quickly fold it up and stick it in the back pocket of my jeans. It's time to do the kitchen.

I'm just about to have a go at the fridge when Miriam comes down the stairs again.

'I love coffee but it's so addictive, I just keep wanting more,' she says, and tops herself up from the cafetière.

Amazing. Who knew?! Coffee? Addictive?? Never!

I check the instructions: remove all food. Discard anything out of date. Clean inside and removable shelves with dilute all-purpose detergent and warm water. Dry. Replace food.

I start hoiking stuff out and checking the date.

'Miriam?'

'Aha?'

'Do you really need these jelly beans in here? I don't think keeping them cool will preserve them any longer.'

Jonathan Harvey

She looks at them, deep in thought.

'And they might look nice on display, bring a bit of colour to the room.'

What is she thinking? What are they reminding her of?

'Oh, d'you know, you can chuck those, Josie.'

'Oh?'

'Yeah, I've been meaning to ditch them for ages.'

'Don't you like them?'

'They're years old. Used to belong to . . .' Just then her mobile rings, she retrieves it from her pocket and checks the caller ID.

Say it.

'Sorry. Gotta take this.' And she scampers out of the room.

WHO? WHO DID THEY BELONG TO?

TELL ME ABOUT YOUR GARDEN!

AND NO THAT'S NOT A EUPHEMISM, I MEAN YOUR ACTUAL BACK GARDEN!

I can hear her upstairs in her study. She shuts the door to keep the call private. Probably a work thing.

They belong to him. Or belonged to him. I just know it. And it kills me.

Why has she kept a jar of sweets in her fridge for five years? I'm allowed. I'm the grieving widow. Who does she think she is?

I pull the jar out. I lift off the nipple-like lid. I furtle around, and they're all stuck together. Just like the ones in my old house were. I put the jar carefully on the table and slide into a seat to stare at it. Just then something starts to beep. I look around, unsure what it is. It appears to be coming from the fridge. I lean across and shut the door and it stops. I rest back in the chair and look at the beans. I drag the jar nearer, turning it this way and that, hoping to catch a glimpse of his

124

fingerprints. Was Danny here? Were these his sweets? They must be. This woman collected a suitcase for him. She doesn't know that I know. But I know. And now I discover she has his favourite sweets in his favourite place. That can't be co-incidence, can it? Don't be ridiculous, I tell myself. These are his.

But why did he know this woman? Does he know this woman? I should run upstairs and ask her. Demand answers. I've got nothing to lose. He was my husband, not hers. He was my property to lose, not hers. I should run up there and swipe the phone from her hand, tell her who I am, tell her I'm not leaving until she explains everything.

So why don't I? Am I a coward? Is it a case of what you don't know doesn't hurt you? But it feels like I already know, like I already hurt.

When? When did he have time to have an affair with her? When? I replay images of our time together in my head and try to spot the warning signs. But like I said to the police when he first went missing, he couldn't have been having an affair. He loved me. I was his teenage sweetheart. He wouldn't do that to me, to his kids, he wouldn't throw it all away like that.

But he did throw it away. He threw everything away.

And I'd been lying to the police. I'd been lying then and I'd be lying now if I didn't admit that he did have the time. He did have nights away with the lads and trips abroad and . . . and his background. And . . .

What an idiot I've been.

These beans seem to shout one word at me. *Loser*.

But when I lied to the police, it was only a little white lie. An assumption I'd made. I wasn't lying by missing something out, I was making out he was a decent bloke, the sort who wouldn't do the dirty on his family. Maybe if I'd not been so keen to protect his image I'd have found Miriam sooner, and maybe Danny sooner.

Sooner than what? I've still not found him.

He has been in this house. He has been in this house enough times to keep a stash of his favourite sweets here. The evidence is clear. This woman was significant to him.

I look through the kitchen doors to the hallway, the stairs. And as I do, I hear Miriam open her study door. This is my chance. Now I can call up, *Miriam? Can I have a word?* I'll be polite. I'll be respectful, understanding. She'll feel guilty. She might have grown to like me.

But before I can she shouts down, 'Josie?! It's one o'clock! You can go now! Just finish what you're doing and I'll see you Monday!'

My voice catches in my throat. I can't speak.

'Josie?!' she calls again.

'Great!' I shout back. 'See you Monday!'

'Yeah, we can walk Snowy!'

'Cool!'

And her study door shuts.

I look back at the beans. Evidence. If I was to show this to the police they'd need to see it in situ. I quickly return them to the fridge and take a photo of them in situ on my phone.

I won't throw them away today.

I return the cleaning schedule to the drawer where it lives, grab my coat and car keys, and let myself out.

Next time. Next time I'll confront her. Next time I'll wipe the floor with her.

As I'm leaving, I see a business card in a bowl near the front door. Frog Graphic Design. Must be hers. Has her address and email on it and a cartoon picture of a frog. Original. I imagine stamping on the frog, killing it. And I'm usually very anti-animal cruelty. I cry more at dogs dying on telly than humans.

But cartoon frogs can do one.

As I'm clambering into the car, the mobile rings. I see it's the school calling. I slide my finger across the screen as I fall into my seat.

'Hello?'

'Mrs Bioletti?'

'Speaking.'

'It's Pam Anderson here.'

No. It's not *the* Pamela Anderson. It's Cally's head of year. She just has a rather unfortunate name.

'Oh hi.'

'Just wanted to check how Cally was?'

'Why?'

'Well, she's not come to school today.'

'What?!'

'So we assumed she was poorly.'

'I'm so sorry, Pam. I've been out all morning, I'm just heading home now. She went out this morning in her uniform.'

'Ah. Then this might be what we call a situation.'

'Yes, it might. I'll call you later when I know what's going on.'

'Thanks, Mrs Bioletti.'

En route home, I try Cally's mobile and the landline. Both ring out, then go to answerphone. Maybe she returned home poorly. Maybe she's sleeping it off. Yes, that's what it'll be.

But when I eventually get home, her room is empty. And after many bursts of calling her name politely and then frantically, the resounding silence tells me the house is empty.

And then I see an envelope on the kitchen table. *Mum* is

written on it in her biro'd best. I tear it open and there's a note inside.

Hey Mom.

I hate the way she spells it like that. We're not in Connecticut.

I've decided to go to London and become a model. Aba's cool with it coz you have to be 16 to make your mind up and as I am I have. Or it's a grey area till you're 18. I know you were dead against this but I am a grown-up and it's what Dad would have wanted. He always said I should follow my dreams. And this is what I've wanted all my life and what I was put on the planet for. Well, it is since I went Clothes Show Live.

I'll be in touch again when I know where I'm staying and stuff. Please don't kick off at Aba or anything because I can't bear the idea of you embarrassing me more than you already have done etc. In fact, not calling her would be best.

Remember when we went to Matalan that time? And we were crossing the zebra crossing and all the traffic stopped? And you said, 'It's like being famous'? It was then. Then's when I knew. Thanks for starting this dream off and one day I hope to make you proud, like you are with Owen and all his gay shit.

Take care of yourself
  Cally x

P.S. You supported Owen through the whole tennis thing. Time to support me, yo!

I phone Aba immediately.
I kick off at her.

Midway through my kick-off, the doorbell rings. Please. Not some God-awful neighbours now. I ignore it, but it rings again. I trudge to the door as I continue to berate Aba, and spring the door ajar.

Laurence is standing there. This is a an event of my own making. He is standing there with a parcel I ordered from Amazon yesterday. It's just a book, but by clicking on the bit where it said I wanted it by 1 p.m. today, I knew it would come Special Delivery.

He's grinning.

'Aba, hang on, I'm busy,' I snap, and hold the phone to my shoulder as I grab the parcel from him, a bit brusquely.

'Sorry it's not before one,' he stammers, thinking I'm pissed off with him and not that silly cow in London. 'Called round earlier but you weren't in.'

'No, it's fine. You OK?'

'Yes . . . I . . .'

I indicate that I'm on the phone and can't really speak, even if this is what I wanted, Laurence showing up on my doorstep again.

'Wondered if you fancied a drink sometime.'

'Great. Perfect. Gotta dash.'

And I slam the door shut. I return to calling Aba every name under the sun. As I do, the letter box flips up. I'm not even listening to her bewildered responses. Something about a Hotmail account. Oh do shut up, you child-snatcher.

'I haven't got your number.'

'Aba, can you hang on?'

I kneel in front of the door so I'm eye to eye with him. 'Find me on Facebook. Natalie Milk. There aren't many. My profile pic's Lena Dunham.'

'Who?'

'Off *Girls*.'

'I'll look her up.'

'Brilliant.'

The letter box flips shut.

I have just said yes. Ish. To a date. Am I mad?

Well, I have just found out. Ish. That my husband was having an affair.

Screw you, Danny and Miriam. Time I had some fun.

Then I go back to berating the woman who has forced my daughter to run away from home.

Well, that won't be for long, I can tell you.

When I have had enough I hang up. How dare she say I'd emailed her? How dare she say I'd spoken to her on the phone? How dare she insinuate that I'd forgotten these things and was losing the plot because my husband had gone walkabout? Who does she think she is?

She makes these absurd claims and somehow manages to convince my daughter to move hundreds of miles away on her own when she is barely sixteen?

I'm going to call the police.

I stare at my phone. It would be so easy to dial 999.

Sod it, I will.

But as I stare at the phone it miraculously springs to life. I see that Miriam is calling.

Fuck.

I quickly answer. 'Hello, Josie speaking?'

This seems to throw her. There is a slight pause.

'What's your real name?'

'Sorry?'

'This is Miriam Joseph. Are you a journalist?'

'Miriam, this is Josie. Your cleaner. Who did you think you were ringing?'

'You tell me.'

Why would she think I was a journalist? I instinctively reach for my back jeans pocket.

The piece of paper isn't there. The piece of paper with my notes on Josie on.

Oh God. It must have fallen out in her house.

Oh dear.

A *journalist*?

Cally

'Calista, if you'd like to take a seat, and Aba can shut the door.'

'Yes, Bimbi. Thanks, Bimbi.'

Aba has like brought me to see the massive humoooongous boss of the agency, Bimbi.

(I know. Hashtag amazing name or WHAT?)

Bimbi was like a completely amazing model in the seventies but then she had kids or put loads of weight on or something or maybe she just got old and then she set up L'Agence and now she helps people like me do what she used to do and she's meant to be the best person in the whole wide world though also pretty scary and she can do something called the Death Stare which means she gives you evils and grown men have been known to pee their pants when she does it and I'M NOT EVEN MAKING THAT UP ABA TOLD ME.

Oh, and she's American. I think. Yes, she is. I remember Wikipedia-ing her.

(Her ex-husband Ralph is the guy I caught gakking it up in the toilets on my first visit. He comes and goes but doesn't actually work here.)

I sit opposite her, and she smiles a smile that's so thin it's untrue, like she'd be pleased to see me IF I HADN'T

132

BROUGHT THE PUTRID SMELL OF DOG TURD IN WITH ME.

I immediately like totally have a nervous breakdown coz I know I'm well in trouble now and stuff.

She's stirring something. OMG it could totally be a witch's cauldron. When I look, it's a Müller Fruit Corner.

'Someone's been telling porkies. We don't like porkies at L'Agence.'

She doesn't sound that Yankified.

'Who?' I go. Coz that's really clever. Coz that makes it look like I don't know what she's talking about.

She just stares at me. I hear Aba sitting down and doing loads of really loud sighs like she's not feeling well. After what feels like ages Bimbi goes, 'Why did you pretend you were your mum?'

'I don't know,' I go.

And she slaps her hand on the table. Makes a '*DUH-DUUUUH*' noise like when they get something wrong in *Family Fortunes* and shouts, 'Wrong answer, Missy!' which is scary and funny at the same time, and really American. It certainly makes Aba sit up in her seat. 'Why?' It now sounds like she's barking. What is she? A dog?

I start to cry. Oh God, this is SO embarrassing.

Oh my God, I think I must be morbidly depressed or something. These tears are MASSIVE. I'm half tempted to take my phone out and get a selfie with them in it coz they might actually be the biggest tears in the world or something.

'Calista?' Bimbi goes. (I know. Amazing name or WHAT?)

And I find myself going, 'Coz she didn't want me to come and I did and this is all I've ever dreamed of and Aba's so lovely and I didn't want to let her down and . . .'

'Don't give me that Aba shit,' Bimbi barks again. 'Tell me more about the "this is your dream" stuff, honey.'

Honey. She shouts at me like I've done something wrong but adds a honey on the end like it's all OK?

'Modelling. I really want to do it. So I had to find a way.'

'Why do you want to do it?'

'I don't know.'

'*DUH-DUUUUUH.*' Table slam again. 'Wrong answer, Missy!'

'For the adulation. The acceptance. I don't know, I just . . . I've never been good at anything and to think I could be good at this is totally exciting and even though Aba said I could wait for six months I didn't think I could really coz you should strike while the iron's hot and stuff.'

Bimbi pushes her chair back and stands. It makes an al-mighty fucking screechy noise on the wooden floorboards that really makes me jump. She walks REALLLY SLOWLLLY round to me and stands there looking down on me.

OMG . . . is she going to, like, HIT ME?

She reaches out her hand. It's all gnarled and wrinkly but has THE best rings on it. And I see she's got a tissue in it.

'Blow your nose. Sweet thing,' she says, and now she's all calm and mother-henny.

So I take the tissue. It smells of perfume. Which in itself makes me sneeze when I hold it to my nose to blow it.

She goes on to do this really boring speech about how I have to stop lying to them if they're going to look after me and how they can only look after me if they know that Mum is on our side and how she will only be on our side if the lying stops and we take her seriously and her feelings and how I'm her little girl and she probably finds it really hard to let go and let me come to London and miss a week of school for something that might never lead anywhere and maybe Mum's got a point but we're not playing from a level playing field because now I'm in the wrong and she's in the right because she's been lied to and I've done the lying. Or something. I got a bit lost listening to it if I'm honest coz you know what she sounded like? A BLOODY BUGGERING BOLLOCKING TEACHER. God I thought I'd escaped them FFS. But the plain truth of the matter is if you're sixteen, everyone speaks down to you coz they think you're a kid and that is never EVER going to change.

'Anyway,' she goes. 'We'll have this all sorted out tonight.'

'Why?' I goes.

'Your brother's on his way down.'

'Owen?'

PLEASE DON'T LET THAT MASSIVE WOOFTER COME HERE AND SHOW ME UP. NO. NO. NOOOOO.

AND PLEASE DON'T LET HIM BRING BORING MATTY EITHER HE-E-E-E-E-E-E-E-E-E-E-E-ELP!

Aba pipes up, 'Your mum thought it best if he came as he's more . . .' She can't think of the word, so Bimbi goes, 'Dispassionate. Your mum thinks she'll get too cross with you.'

'She's a total. She's got issues,' I go.

'A total what?' asks Aba.

I shrug. 'Take your pick.'

'You know,' goes Bimbi. And I know we're in for another lecture. She goes and opens a window and lights up a ciggie, which she smokes out of it, 'I'd've killed for that sort of bitchiness at your age.'

'It's not bitchiness, she CARES,' goes Aba. God, she's changed her tune.

'I see girls like you all the time, sweetheart,' Bimbi's going. 'And the spoilt ones, the ones whose parents don't care, they don't have boundaries, you see. So they're a fucking nightmare to work with. What we want are girls with a work ethic. Girls who know right from wrong. Girls who are going to turn up on time and get the job done, and that's usually the girls whose parents have instilled that in them from an early age.'

'Cally's dad went missing a few years ago. Six, was it, hon?' Aba's looking at me.

'Five,' I go.

'Oh, yeah, sorry to hear about that. Press might want to talk about that. Is that OK or is it off limits?'

I just shrug. Coz the idea of anyone wanting to talk to me about anything right now is weird enough, NEVER MIND THE BLOODY PRESS.

Bimbi doesn't sound American any more.

'Why is my brother coming? Is he going to take me home?' I ask.

'I think he's going to rap your knuckles and give you a talking to,' says Aba.

'I had a pretty decent chat with your mum, Calista,' Bimbi's saying. 'And you do need your knuckles rapping a bit; you were out of order. What you need to realize is in life, if you fuck up, there are consequences. Your brother coming here is one of those consequences. Whether he drags you back or lets you stay . . .'

'He's got no power over me.'

She ignores this. 'Whether he drags you back or lets you stay is ultimately down to how you behave when he gets here. Don't you think?'

I shrug. I don't know. But rather than risk the wrath of WRONG ANSWER MISSY I reply, 'Totes 'n' stuff.'

And Bimbi doesn't know what to make of that.

'I hope you stay, Calista. But that's in your hands now. Don't fuck us about and we won't fuck you about. We're all about making money. This is a business. And we could make some out of you, I reckon. Which means you can too. But rearrange the words: lap, Gods, you, up to . . .'

Weirdo or what?

And then with a flourish of the hand, like it's an actual dance move, she dismisses us.

It's like we've been to see the Queen or something, coz Aba walks backwards out of the room doing these little bowy things, all the time saying stuff like, 'Thank you, Bimbi. Much appreciated, Bimbi. Lick me out till I'm panting, Bimbi.'

Or whatever.

Either way it's really annoying.

And either way I just KNOW Owen will make me go home. Well, tough. He'll have to phone the Feds or something. Coz I ain't goin' nowhere wid dat homo homey. *sucks teeth*

I've been doing that a lot lately. Talking all ghetto and sucking my teeth. It really makes Aba laugh. Though she did say I better be careful who I do it in front of. Whatever that means. Like I can choose my audience at all times!

The model flat is amazing. I mean, it's not huge by any stretch of the imagination, and I have to remember that even though we live in a shithole now I have been spoilt living in big amazing houses in the past when Dad was around and he and Mum were coining it in. But this place is, I guess, what they call bijou. Which basically means it's tiny but it's in London, and anywhere in London is worth gazillions of pounds. It's also really dark, but that's coz it's got three bedrooms and there's two sets of bunk beds in each, so it's a bit cramped, and some of the beds are in front of the windows, blocking the light out.

Not all the bunks are being used at the mobo (I'm doing that too. I've started saying mobo instead of moment coz I think it makes me look really ethnic and cultured and street) and stuff. I'm sharing my room with a Brazilian girl called Sabine and this really amazing posh girl called Zaraah who's staying here coz her parents are living in South Africa. I make up LOADS of words in front of them and they just think I'm really cool and quirky and like . . . that's my thing. When actually I just started today, really, coz I'm worried I'm not one hundred per cent hip enough to be a model? Sabina is SO. PRETTY. Like, she has that Brazilian look? (The continent, not the fanny shave.) So her skin is all brown and shiny and her hair is all brown and shiny too, but OH MY GOD you should see her eyes. They are BEYOND.

(Aba says this if she likes something. Everything is BEYOND.)

Coz you'd expect them to be brown or black or dark anyway. But actually they are this piercing sky blue. It looks like she has contacts in but – OMG – she hasn't. I know. BEYOND. And she has these perky little breasts that look like two rum babas on her chest. I don't know this coz I've come over all lesbotic on myself, but actually she hangs around the flat in her skimpety-pimpety undies all the time and usually I'd find that gross and be shouting PUT IT AWAY LOVE but she is the sweetest little thing and just laughs at everything I say, even if I'm being serious.

I didn't understand at first that she just giggles all the time and it's just shyness about not being able to speak the language properly and I was putting a framed photo of Dad on the bedside cabinet and she pointed and giggled and I was like,

'Actually it's not funny? Coz he like . . . went missing? Five years ago? He could actually be dead?'

And she looked at the picture again and then just like PISSED HERSELF.

So I got off the bed and slapped her round the face, which was when Zaraah came in and said, 'Sabine doesn't speak English, babes.'

And I was like, 'Oh God, hon. I'm sorry.' And I opened my arms to Sabine and like went, 'Hug, hon?' (I've decided I'm going to call everyone hon now. It's another of my things.)

But Sabine ran into the bathroom and was crying really loudly.

'Da . . . rama queen!' Zaraah said under her breath. And I just realized in that moment. We're going to be bezzy bezzy mates for forever and a day. Like, even if she made a lezzy bezzy pass at me I'd knock her back and be really forgiving about it. And if she stole my boyfriend off me I know we'd fall out for like, six weeks or something, but eventually we'd be pals again – hashtag, sisters before misters!

Zaraah really rocks a red-haired look. She's like one of those really ginger people that gets away with it? She catches me staring at her arm coz it is so pale it looks see-through and she goes, 'Stop lezzing off on me hon!' and we both REALLY laugh at that.

But then she says red-haired people have one less layer of skin than other people.

And that's how I feel sometimes. And I tell her. And she nods and I just KNOW she can't get over how deep and feelingy and emoshey I am. Like I understand things? Without really having to know them?

She thinks I'm pretty fierce to have lied through my back teeth to get here. Although she has an annoying habit of saying Mum sounds 'cute' when I tell her about her. And even though in the photo by my bed you can see Owen in it and he's about 14 or something, she still reckons he's hot, so I call her a paedo and she REALLY laughs at that.

She looks a bit confused when I explain he 'totally takes it up the pipe' and thinks I'm saying he's on like crack or crystal meth or something so I explain what it means and she nods, then says, 'In South Africa my Uncle Oscar was a gay. But he got shot. Dead. With a gun.'

And I can't tell whether she means he deserved it or whether it was sad and I don't really know what to say so I just go, 'Hashtag gay shooting. Wow.'

And she nods. And then goes, 'Do all Brazilian girls have naked punani?'

And I tell her I don't know. And then I tell her about Bimbi hitting the table and going

'*DUH DUUUUH* – wrong answer Missy!'

And we laugh so much I do actually pee myself a little bit. I tell Zaraah, which makes us laugh even more and . . .

I hear a key in the front door, and then voices in the hall.

Aba is here with Owen.

Owen

It is the most unnerving sight. I pictured many scenarios on the train down, but none of them included walking in on your kid sister and some other skinny teenager, both fuchsia of face and laughing hysterically to the point where it looks painful.

'I had a little accident!' she screams, and then runs into her bedroom.

Aba prepares some Earl Grey in the smallest kitchen in the world – so small I want to call it a kitchenette, but I don't know if that word exists outside of the 1950s – and I wait till Cally is ready to see me. The fact that I've come all this way and she is making me wait starts to make my blood boil. How dare she? How dare she do this to Mum? How dare she do this to herself? Thinking of no one but herself. I want to be angry with Aba, but apparently she phoned Aba and pretended to be Mum, and I know how convincing she can be. Plus when I called in on Aba in L'Agence (HOW pretentious?) she was pretty up-front, and that hard-faced one Bambi, or whatever she's called, held her hands up and said, 'Take her home if you want. Completely up to you.' Like she was washing her hands of her. Like she didn't really care. Although Aba says that's just her manner.

What I find hard to grasp is what they actually see in Cally. I am not being unkind – well, maybe I am, I hate being kept waiting by anyone, never mind your own sister when she's run away from home, but she is, let's just say, unusual looking. As we walked from the agency to the flat I said to Aba,

'Do you guys really think she could be a model?'

And she didn't even take a breath, 'Totally. We meet girls all the time. But we only meet special girls about once a year. Calista's this year's girl.'

'But she's so sort of . . . weird-looking.'

'Photographers want girls who look like pencils. And with slightly goofy teeth. Like this.'

And she stuck her teeth out. And looked ridiculous.

Admittedly Cally does have good hair. Great hair, in fact. She has always taken great care with her locks. When we were growing up, I was the cherubic blonde child with brown eyes and a permanent tan as I was always outside, and passers-by and strangers would often comment about how cute I was (I wish I had the same effect now!) and then they'd look at Cally and feel they had to say something, so she didn't feel left out. And they'd always say, 'And you . . . you have such long hair.'

Of course, I have no intention of taking Cally home. She has made her point, and the tantrums Mum would have to deal with if we forced her to come back now would not be worth it. But I'm not going to let her know that. I can't take her home anyway. I've brought Matt down with me, and we're going to attempt a romantic weekend break in the Big Smoke. Mum is all over the place about this. I've not seen her cry so much in years. Real, guttural sobs when I went round, and lots of, 'It's all such a mess. I don't know what to do. I'm so stupid,' etc. At first I thought she was overreacting, but then

142

Matt pointed out that finding out she'd gone was probably like finding out Dad had gone. Maybe. But at least Cally left a note and explained what she had done. After we'd decided that it was best if I went to London to talk to Cally, Mum said the most odd thing. As she showed me out she said,

'Do you think I need to write down a cleaning schedule?'

I thought about it a while, and asked for clarification.

She shook her head and said, 'I'm being daft.'

And I left.

Matt says she might be having a nervous breakdown and I should watch out for warning signs. I'm not so sure.

I remember Mum opening every drawer in the house, stripping every bed, practically pulling the curtains down in the days after Dad disappeared. Just in case he'd left a note and it had mysteriously vanished. It was like she didn't mind that he'd gone. As long as he told her.

I suppose I have to grant Cally that. She didn't keep Mum in the dark.

I've drunk half my cup of tea by the time Cally's ready for me. She calls, rather grandly, from her room.

'I'm ready for you, Owen!' and I head in.

She is sitting on the bottom bunk of a set of beds and has changed into a thin dressing gown, which is clearly an indicator that she is intending on staying the night. I move and sit next to her.

'I'm sorry I lied,' she says in a tiny voice. 'I know it's a mess.'

On her bedside table she has a framed photo. Only small. I've not seen it for years. It is like a jolt of electricity through my body, and I jump and pick it up.

It's a photo of me and Dad when we came to London, just the two of us, and went to Wimbledon. I've not seen it for so long. It's a bright sunny day and I'm squinting at the camera.

In this picture Dad really looks like I do now. I'd never realized just how similar we looked. Though of course he's a lot
darker than me.

'I know I should have one of Mum, but I just really like that
one of him.'

I swallow. I feel my eyes go hot and tears pricking them.
Embarrassingly, a tear plops onto the glass.

'Do you miss him?' she says.

I look at her. 'Of course.'

'I thought it was just me.'

I shake my head, unable to speak.

'I've got to do this, Owen.'

I don't remember her speaking to me like this in years.
Instead of the ranty shouty service as usual, she is calm.

'It's too good an opportunity. I might never get it again.'

I find myself nodding.

'Life's all about opening yourself up to new opportunities,'
she says. And I immediately think of Dylan.

I don't want to think about Dylan. And his study. Nothing
happened, but everything happened. The world changed as I
sat there talking to him and I felt him really looking at me. I
felt excitement and fear course through my veins, and it was
hard not to become a gibbering wreck.

But I don't want to think about him. I can't afford to think
about him. I've spent too long this past week idly fantasizing
about him. And me. And . . .

'Don't you think?' Cally interrupts my train of thought. A
train that could so easily derail me.

'I hate it when you go all silent and moody.'

'Sorry.'

'Please don't make me go home.' She sounds scared. I know
that feeling. I shake my head. The idea that I could make her

do anything is almost amusing, but the fact that she thinks I might is touching. I see her for what she is, a scared, vulnerable girl who's suddenly found something exciting to cast some daylight into her usually darkened room. She, too, may as well be squinting into the light.

'On one condition,' I say.

She nods.

'No more lies.'

She shakes her head. 'I promise.'

'And I think you owe Mum an apology.'

She nods.

No more lies.

I look back to the photograph. So many memories come flooding back.

As I walk back to the hotel to see Matt, I indulge myself in the memories. I try so hard, usually, to blot them out, but tonight I allow myself to dip my toe in them. Eventually I am swimming.

I think back to a time before our trip to Wimbledon. Me and Dad had gone to Ibiza together. I was thirteen. Milk were doing some nights out there, as they did every summer, but Mum and Cally hadn't come because it was the summer Cally broke her arm. We had a brilliant time: I had tennis coaching every morning with the guy who ran the tennis club in the hills near the old town, and then I'd have lunch on the beach with Dad and whoever he was hanging out with at that time. There was a pop star who'd been in a boy band who'd come most days as he hero-worshipped Dad, and I used to sit and drool over him. He was my first proper crush. He had this skinny girlfriend who I could tell all the men fancied. I found her a bit of a dick, if I'm honest, as she didn't have much to say for herself and referred to me as 'the kid'. 'Isn't the kid cute?' she'd say, and

'Another Diet Coke for the kid.' Looking back I was probably just jealous that she got to spend so much time with the pop star when I didn't, never mind share a bed with him. And I was jealous at all the attention he lavished on her, whereas I just got a cursory nod from him. But that was OK. It was better than nothing. And sometimes, a cursory nod can go a very long way. Dad would go for a lie down later on in the afternoon and I would sit in the villa watching acres of television till he got up. Rosaria the housekeeper would come by to cook dinner, then he would head out to work, and I'd go back to watching telly. Rosaria would stay over and then clean in the morning before having time with her family during the day.

Usually I wouldn't hear Dad getting back from work, but sometimes he'd bring a posse back and they'd party in the living room till lunchtime.

One night I woke when I heard someone diving into the swimming pool. I looked at my digital clock radio. It was five-twenty. I listened out. The house was silent but for the sound of Rosaria's snoring in the next room, but there were giggling noises coming from outside. Maybe Dad was having a party. I tried to get back to sleep.

Then the noises seemed to change. It sounded like some-one was crying, or in pain. They were whimpering. I put my light on, pulled back the curtain, and saw Dad on top of the pop star's girlfriend on one of the sun loungers. Her legs were up over his shoulders and he was fucking her. She had her eyes shut, and his were screwed up too, so neither of them had seen that they were illuminated now by an oblong chunk of light coming from my bedroom. Looking back now, his body was very like mine. Big fat arse, Mum used to say. Although Nan used to say, 'Never trust a man with a fat bum. They're all liars.'

I was bewildered at first. You never expect to see your dad

having sex. And you never expect to see him having sex with someone who isn't your mum.

The pop star's girlfriend opened her eyes as Dad climaxed.

'Pull it out of me! Pull it out of me!' she screamed. And then she screamed again when she saw me looking out of the window.

I ducked down. Heard a few more grunts and then silence.

I lay on my bed, curtains open, light still on, knowing that Dad must know that I'd seen.

But then my bewilderment turned to anger. How could he do that to Mum? And how could he do that to my lovely pop star? After a bit I heard someone dive into the pool. I heard a gate going, and then a car driving off. Five or so minutes later, I heard Dad come in.

I thought he was going to come in and tell me off. For some reason I thought I was in the wrong for seeing him. But he didn't. Eventually I heard his bedroom door shutting.

I switched my light off.

The next morning over breakfast, I could barely look at him. He said he'd been thinking. He felt he didn't spoil me enough. I had no idea what he was talking about.

'I know how much you're into your tennis so I'm gonna look into taking you to some tournaments. Lads' time together, you and me, weekends away. Nice food. See the sights. Go to the tournaments.'

'Like the US Open?' I ventured.

'Exactly. When's the next big one?'

So I told him.

I was so excited that I was going to travel the world and go to these matches that I so loved watching on television. I wrote down all the ones I could think of, and he promised he'd look into it.

Of course, I wasn't stupid. I knew what he was doing. He was buying my silence. He went on about how blokes do things that women don't understand, and I knew he was talking about the incident the night before.

He brought back two more different women during that stay. And I said nothing. And for the next year, me and my dad went on trips to the Australian Open and the US Open. He had bought my silence. And I took the money and ran.

When he went missing, I wondered if he'd run off with the next dumb blonde to cross his path. I couldn't say anything to Mum because it was like Dad and I had a pact, a pact of silence. And I've continued it to this day.

I think back to last Sunday. Dylan. I so wanted to reach out and touch him, discover what he felt like. And in that moment I knew that if I did it, he wouldn't flinch, but touch back. And I stopped myself. And once my clothes were almost dry, I made my excuses and left. But I was tempted. And I wanted to. And I have thought about it all week.

And in a bizarre way, I have enjoyed the thinking and 'what if?' of it all. As it makes me feel closer to my dad.

That doesn't make it right. But it does make it more appealing.

Or maybe I'm the one having the nervous breakdown, not Mum. Imagining that a middle-aged heterosexual man might fancy me. Oh yes, and he's my mother's best friend's husband. Not complicated at all.

Matt's outside the hotel smoking a cigarette when I get back. We're staying right by Seven Dials in Covent Garden. It's eight o'clock and the place is buzzing. I hang back a bit and watch him from the other side of the roundabout. His beauty still, even now, manages to take my breath away. So why am I even thinking about Dylan so much? Matt has his phone out and is tapping away on it. I feel my phone pulse in my pocket. Bless him, he must be texting to see where I am. I smile to myself. I will text back and say there's a guy over the road from you who fancies you. Something nice and romantic. That's what we're here for. A night of romance to rekindle the relationship.

I take my phone out. The text is not from him. It's from Dylan. Oh God. I open it.

If it's ever raining and you happen to be passing, do drop in again x

I stare at the screen. I bite my lip. I look across the road and see that Matt has gone inside. I quickly write back

LOL

and hit send. A second later, he replies.

Hope you're happy kid, whatever or whoever you're doing.

And unlike the pop star's girlfriend, I quite like that he calls me kid. I write back,

Filth.

He replies,

Always.

I put the phone back in my pocket and cross the round-about, dodging a black cab as I go.

Natalie

I wanted to meet Miriam Joseph somewhere public. My instinct was that it might get ugly, and therefore I wanted lots of people around me as witnesses or as deterrents if it was all getting too wayward. I'm not sure how I envisaged it getting ugly – she didn't strike me as a particularly violent person – but I wasn't taking any risks.

My choice of venue for us to meet, however, was not one of my best choices. I had wanted her somewhere where she couldn't easily escape, where if I said something she didn't like, she couldn't do that really annoying thing of just running away.

Public. Hard to escape.

I told her to meet me in the cafe of Ikea.

'The furniture store?' she'd asked.

'Yes,' I'd said, with something approaching conviction.

'On the motorway?'

'That's the one, yes.'

Clearly she thought this a ridiculous suggestion, but she was too intrigued to find out just who I was to disagree. Thus far she'd probably thought the balance of power had swung her way. She'd not pretended to be something she wasn't, like me, so surely she should have called the shots? Now my out-

150

of-the-way choice of meeting place suggested that maybe I was the one in the right and not her.

I get to Ikea early. I've not been for a few years, but I remember it being like a humongous maze, and that the cafe is the final bit you come to just as you think there is no escape and you will never see civilization again, that you will forever be in a halogen-lit universe of flat-pack furniture, line drawings of Audrey Hepburn and lamps that look like lollipops.

I'm glad I got here with plenty of time to spare, as it takes me nearly forty minutes to wind my way to the cafe. I only get lost three times, something of a record for this place, and I'm the recipient of several curious looks as I appear to be the only person not pushing a huge trolley loaded with yucca plants and cardboard. But eventually I am sitting in the cafe by the exit. The tables are shaped like flowers and around me hordes of families sit slurping brightly-coloured drinks or eating meatballs and spaghetti. I'd forgotten the cafe was by the exit – my abiding memory of previous visits was about the claustrophobia of the place – so I am annoyed with myself that I have given Miriam an escape route if my questioning gets too much for her. I check my watch. She's eight minutes late.

To kill some time, I take an envelope from my bag. It's addressed to me but I've not opened it, as it's Barbara's handwriting. You might think my mother-in-law had sent me a housewarming card, but even though I can feel through the lilac envelope that there is a card inside, I know it will be no Hallmark moment with a picture of an overloaded cartoon furniture van. I know this because I got a text yesterday.

Please ignore any cards coming from me. Sorry. Bar.

And another.

PS Hope you and kids well.

I slide my fingernail along one edge and pull out the card. Generic impressionistic flowers in a vase. I flip it over and read:

Dear Slut

    What gets me now is that you've sold his big house and with his money you've moved and are living the life of Riley. Oh yes. Don't think I haven't worked it out.

    I saw a drama on ITV tonight and this bloke was poisoning his wife and then killed her in a car crash. And it brought it all back to me. Oh yes. Before he went missing he was always complaining about headaches. Well I've got your number Slut and I'm going to the police with this one. How did you get back from Beachy Head? Drive down there did you? I bet your shitting yourself now I'm onto you. Oh yes.

    Danny was my pride and joy and to think you poisoned him and then killed him in the car. Words fail me. Oh yes.

    I might come round to your new house and poison all your food and see how you like it Slut.

    You have been warned.

    Barbara. AKA Danny's Mum. My pride and joy. There is a light that has gone out in the world, my Danny.

Even though it is easy for me to dismiss her as completely bonkers, my breathing has become shallow and cold. I return the card and envelope to my bag. How dare she! How dare she accuse me of that? Let her go to the police. Let's see what they have to say for themselves. And hark at her coming over all Mother Teresa when actually she was the worst mother in the world. Why else would Danny end up in care? I try to calm myself, but she definitely knows which buttons to press with me.

Miriam eventually arrives thirteen minutes late, clutching an armful of impulse purchases that are the sole purpose of this store's confusing layout. She places the ceramic owl, quilted cushion and wooden windchime on the floor next to the table, no apologies for keeping me waiting, and informs me she's going to get a coffee. I've finished mine but she doesn't offer me another. She eventually returns and sits. Her cheeks are slightly flushed and there is a rash around her neck. She might be trying to ooze calm and control, but underneath the icy exterior I'd say Miriam Joseph is bricking it. I wait for her to speak.

'So. You're not a journalist.'

I shake my head. 'Why would a journalist be interested in you?'

'Who are you?'

'Don't you know?'

'I've a fair idea.'

'Who am I then?'

Miriam sighs. 'Please. Just . . .'

I bite in. 'I'm Natalie Bioletti. And I want to know how you knew my husband.'

She nods. The rash looks angrier.

'We just . . . knew each other. Did he tell you about me?'

She's not touched her coffee.

'How could he tell me about you? He's been missing for five years.'

Again she nods. I wish she'd tell me something. She's not telling me anything.

'Unless you've seen him during that time?'

She shakes her head.

'How did you find out about me?'

I go in my bag and pull out my phone. I find the recent email I've received from Daffyd. He has forwarded me the photo his pal took of the form where Miriam had signed for the suitcase.

'In 2008 you picked up a suitcase from left luggage at Piccadilly Station. That suitcase was my husband's. There's the proof.'

She looks at the image on my phone.

'Bloody hell,' she mutters.

She really needs to do something about that rash.

'Were you having an affair with him? Please. Just tell me the truth. I can take it.'

She looks straight at me. I see fear in her eyes. And then she gives the tiniest of nods of the head.

I thought I'd be angrier. I thought I'd want to jump across the table and slap her. Give her a nice red welt on her face to match the red splotches on her neck.

Instead I feel an odd sensation of relief. I was right. I had all those negative instincts about who this woman might be and how she fitted into the picture of my life and, instead of me being proved to be a suspicious untrusting nosey parker, I am in fact just . . . well, what? Clever? This doesn't feel like an exercise in vanity for me. Maybe it just makes me a good judge of character and situations.

'Affair's quite a grand term for it.'

'Did you go to Ibiza with him?'

She looks surprised I might have known. She nods again.

'That's where we met. On holiday. He didn't tell me he was married. When we got home I found out and . . . well, I dumped him. End of. Does that make it an affair? On his behalf, possibly. On mine? No.'

'So why have you still got his sweets in the fridge?'

'They're my sweets.' She's sounding crotchety. I feel like giving her a word of advice. When you're meeting your ex-lover's wife, might be a good idea not to come across as a narky cow.

'He had the same jar in my fridge. Our fridge.'

'Maybe he copied me.'

That winds me. I always thought that sweet thing was his thing. Not something he'd picked up from someone else. How dare he! How dare he bring something of hers into our house! The idea makes me wince. But then I remember.

'He always ate those sweets. From when I first met him.'

'He doesn't have the monopoly of keeping sweets in a fridge, you know.'

And she is forceful. Like a politician on *Question Time* who's wanting an end to the discussion because they're inherently right. I change tack.

'So how long did it go on for?'

'A matter of weeks. I don't recall. It was nothing serious.'

'My son was in Ibiza with him. You must've known he was married.'

'He never had me back to his villa, sorry. I don't make a habit of sleeping with married men, you know.'

I pull a face that shows I don't really care. Not sure why I do that.

'And you didn't think to tell the police about this?'

'When? Why?'

'When he went missing. Presumably you knew he'd gone missing.'

'Of course. It was all over the news. Natalie, I think you're blowing this out of proportion.'

'Oh, am I?'

'He was a holiday romance who turned out to be a little shit. Sorry. But that's how it was.'

Fair enough.

'He lied to me. I found out. I dumped him. My heart wasn't broken and it was ages before he went missing. I fail to see how me contacting the police would have helped him get found.'

OK, maybe she has a point.

'All that would've done was hurt you and the kids at a time that was already painful enough for you as it was.'

OK, I believe her.

'Sorry. I need to go to the loo. I was stuck in traffic on the way here and . . . I got lost a few times trying to find the cafe and . . .'

I shrug my shoulders, telling her to be my guest. She scrapes her chair back, then snakes her way through the flower tables to head to the ladies.

I'm starting to feel a bit sorry for her. She goes on holiday. She meets Danny on a night out, probably, has a one-night stand. Sees him a few times on the beach. Maybe dinner one night. Then sees him again back in Manchester and he comes clean. He's married. She tells him to get out. A year later Danny goes missing. Odd for her, but nothing life-changing. Five years later Danny's wife comes round pretending to be a cleaner called Josie. And then gives her a hard time. In a Swedish furniture store on the M62.

Maybe I was piling too much significance onto this woman. When maybe all this sorry episode demonstrates is that my husband was a player, on the playas, put it about a bit, and didn't treat women especially well. Dirty old dog.

I do. I feel sorry for Miriam Joseph.

There's still a question mark hanging over the jelly beans. But for now, I give her the benefit of the doubt.

She's left her purse on her tray. It's small and fat, new, shiny. I want to look in it. I'm not sure why. I am convinced suddenly that she is more significant than she is letting on. That she was seeing Danny for years. And years. Forever. And still is. What if she is lying to me? What if there is something of Danny's in the purse? And I had the chance to see it? And I didn't grab it because she had lulled me into a false sense of security by making me feel sorry for her?

Maybe the key to the underground chamber is in the purse.

I grab it and click it open, furtively looking round the cafe to make sure she's not on her way back. Inside there's thirty-five pounds in cash, several cards, a National Trust card – get her! – and then I see a small photo. It should have been the first thing I saw as I opened it, but instead I was fiddling around at the back. In the front of the purse there's a plastic window and she has a photo in there of a young girl. And I recognize her. It's Tiffany Keith.

I snap the purse shut and return it to the tray, convinced that someone on the next table will shout out, WHY WERE YOU LOOKING IN THE OTHER LADY'S PURSE? WE WILL TELL HER WHEN SHE COMES BACK FROM SPENDING A PENNY!

But they're all too busy with their meatballs to care.

Why would Miriam Joseph have a photograph of Tiffany

Keith in her purse? The girl who died from taking the dodgy ecstasy tablet? And why would she have a photo that looks like it's been cut from the pages of a magazine, not a real photo at all?

She told me she had those clippings because she was re-searching something. What, she got so into the research she needs to keep a photo of the dead girl with her at all times?

But I know I can't ask her about it or she'll know I've been snooping.

Is it so bad to snoop?

Is it worse than passing yourself off as someone's cleaner?

I see her returning from the toilet. And I know that I'm too polite to ask her.

'Oh well,' I say as she sits back down, 'I guess this means you're looking for a new cleaner.'

She gives me a tight smile. I make my excuses and leave. And regret choosing a place so out-of-the-way for our tête-à-tête.

I was never unfaithful to Danny. Working in the club world, I wasn't short of offers, mostly fuelled by lager or chemicals, but I wasn't interested. Why would I be? I had the perfect guy already.

Or at least I thought he was perfect. But now it would appear that he went copping off in Ibiza. And if he did it with Miriam, did he do it with anyone else? If Miriam had been more up for it, could they have ended up having a full-blown affair? Or was he more of a one-night stand kind of a guy? Or was this just a moment of madness? Too much fun in the sun? I tried to think back to that period. How had he been when he came back from the island? How were we getting on? But try as I might, I just can't remember.

He told me he was damaged goods. He told me life had

fucked him up and I was his safety harness. That he'd never hurt me the way life had hurt him. Tosh?

I start thinking about Gripper/Laurence, and how odd it is that he's reappeared in my life now, when I'm discovering this about Danny. Gripper was mates with one of the DJs at Milk, Slim Jim. For ages I thought Gripper was gay. Not because he was particularly camp or fey or banged on about fancying fellas; it was just that he was like Slim's shadow, and I assumed he hero-worshipped him. He was very good-looking, and it was this that caught my assumptions out when I idly said to Lucy one night, 'Why are the best-looking ones always gay?' and indicated Gripper as a case in point. Lucy laughed and pointed out the error of my ways. Gripper was evidently heterosexual and not long out of a long-term relationship with a woman from Finland. The Finn had finished with him, and Gripper's little heart was broken. A few weeks later, Gripper asked if he could have a word. I grabbed us both a drink and took him into the back office. He seemed edgy, nervous, and I asked him what was wrong. I thought he was going to talk about the recent split with the Finnish girl, but instead he very quietly said, 'I think I'm in love with you. And I don't know what to do.'

I was shocked. The thumping bass from the dance floor hammered at the walls. My heart pounded in my chest. What was I meant to say to that? It felt pointless asking him to repeat it. We both left the words hanging in the air.

'You don't really know me,' I pointed out.

'I know.'

'I'm married.'

'I know.'

'Your head's probably mashed from splitting up with that Finnish girl.'

He nodded. But what else could I say? This guy who I hardly knew, who I'd hung out with a few times at work, was proclaiming undying love for me. I looked at him. He looked so vulnerable, like a lost little boy, so fragile that if you touched him he'd break. I mean, on one level it was terribly flattering. In that moment he made me feel movie-star fabulous. Was I really that alluring, that men swooned without me knowing?

I found that very hard to believe.

And then – talk about low self-esteem – I wondered whether Gripper had mental health issues. Maybe he was actually mad, and this was how his problems manifested themselves, by making him proclaim his feelings for random people.

'I know nothing can happen,' he went on, 'but I needed to tell you.'

'Well, I'm flattered, but . . .'

'And I know you and Danny are rock solid.'

'We are.'

'But if anything ever went wrong . . . I'll be there for you after the messy divorce.'

That made me chuckle. And we were both glad of some light relief.

'I can't believe I've said it.'

'It is a bit weird.' I gave a little grimace.

'Can we pretend I never said nothing?'

I nodded. He nodded. Then stood. Looked around the scruffy office, winked, and said, 'I love what you've done with the place.' And then stalked out.

And now he's my delivery driver. And he's asked me out for a drink.

I reach for my phone. I stare at it, then stare out at the Ikea car park. I see Miriam walking from the exit. She's on her phone. It looks like she's crying. Bizarrely, I have a stab of pity for her. Which gives way to anger. Anger at myself that I could even pity her. And then anger at her for sleeping with Danny. Irrational anger, perhaps, as surely it should be he I'm furious with. He knew he was being unfaithful. She didn't. But I can't stem my fury with either of them. I have the urge to wind down the window and scream at her.

Upset, are you? Good. Marriage wrecker!

I imagine starting the car up and driving at her. I see it, clearly, in my mind's eye. I hear the squeal of my tyres. She turns, shocked, as I advance on her, then *smack*! Her blood spits across my window.

This isn't good. I should not be indulging in violent fantasies. I try to turn that anger into something more positive. Anger to love. I write a text to Laurence.

That drink sometime? N x

I wait for him to reply. He doesn't. What was I thinking? Like he's going to reply immediately. That only happens on the telly and in romcoms. Real people are busy, they have work, they have lives.

But then he does reply.

New phone. Who's this?

Oh. Shit. I go to text and explain when he sends another.

ONLY MESSING. Yes. Drink anytime is good.
Tonight?
Fuck it why not. Pick you up at 8?
Cool.
Good work. Agent Bioletti.

My hand's shaking. And I don't know what to say to that. So I just text,

See you later. X

I glance over to Miriam. She is now sitting in her car, still on the phone. I bet she's talking to a girlfriend. If she has any. Meeting your ex's wife isn't something you'd want to chat about with your boyfriend, surely. I can almost hear her.

Oh Jackie it was awful. She'd found the left luggage ticket. I managed to convince her it was a one-off. And she believed me. It was true anyway. Oh, yeah, she was lovely. I know she's been cleaning for me for a bit but . . . today it was like seeing her beauty for the first time.

Actually, I quite like this game.

She was really pretty and . . . dressed really well. I can see why he was with her. And boy, was he lucky to have her. I'd go as far as saying, meeting her was one of the most incredible experiences in my life. And, I might add, she's a really good cleaner. The house has never been so clean. She's like Mary Poppins. But a really sexy one? Yeah, she's a MPILF.

OK, enough of that. I turn my key in the ignition and begin the journey home. I get stuck in traffic, as ever, on the M62. I kill some time by calling Lucy. And like a true friend, she is waiting on the doorstep by the time I get home.

I get her to help me light a bonfire in the back garden. I have decided I want to sacrificially burn something of Danny's, and Lucy thinks it's a good idea. We carry all the files down from the spare room and start to drop them onto the fire.

'And you're sure your accountant said you could get rid of them?' she checks, before dropping a box folder in.

I nod. It feels good. It feels right, doing this. Milk was our baby, but it links me forever with him.

'What was she like?' asks Lucy.

'Bit bland. Clothes a bit too matching, if you know what I mean.'

'And you reckon she's older than you?'

I nod.

'I wonder what her obsession with that Tiffany Keith was all about?' I ask.

'Maybe she knew her. Maybe they were related. You said she hadn't got kids?'

'But it wasn't a proper photo. She'd cut it out of a magazine.'

'Admittedly that is odd.'

'These folders burn well don't they?'

'They do. Is this making you feel better?'

'Not really.'

'How d'you feel?'

'Numb.'

And I did.

'It's just yet another thing I can't ask him about. All these years I've been dying for him to come back, come home, so I can see his face again. Now I want him back so I can have it out with him.'

'That's understandable.'

'But I can't, of course. And anyway, I don't want that Danny back. I want the nice one who adores me and wouldn't step a foot out of line.'

'Basically, you're fucked,' says Lucy, and it makes us both roar with laughter. I have to clutch onto her as my foot slips on the wet grass. I upend the file in my hand and its contents flap around the bonfire. Invoices, printouts of minutes, each slip of paper documenting my life, my work, and I'm saying good bye to it. As I scoop them up to set fire to them, something catches my eye. It's a comp slip. Some writing in biro.

But I've seen the logo on it before. And I know where. My blood runs cold.

'Nat? What is it?'

I show her the slip. It has a cartoon drawn on it of a frog. The name FROG GRAPHIC DESIGN LTD.

'That's her company. That's her writing.'

'What, Miriam?'

'Yes.'

'What, did she do some work for you? When's it from?'

I look. I kneel on the grass and gather some other papers I've dropped to me.

On the comp slip she has written,

> *Good to meet you last week. Hope we can*
> *work together some day. Mim x*

And on the back of the slip, Danny's handwriting says,

> **Not quite right but one to watch.**

My brain whirrs. I can almost hear it spinning like a top inside my skull. Looking at the other papers with it, I piece two and two together, and . . .

'Oh my God. I've met her before, Luce.'

'When?!'

'Oh my GOD.'

I am pacing the garden. Walking round in circles. Smoke billows from the bonfire. Suddenly, from nowhere, it starts to rain. Thick torrential downpour. The smoke from the fire goes blacker than ever as the fire starts to extinguish. I keep pacing the garden, but Lucy pulls me inside.

'I've got to go,' I gasp.

'Go where?'

'See her. Will you drive me? She's been lying to me. She knew he was married a year before he went to Ibiza. I'll fucking kill her.'

Lucy pulls a face. 'Not sure murder's the right idea.'

'OK, I'm probably not going to kill her, but will you give me a lift anyway?'

'I'm not very happy about this. I think you need to . . .'

'Fine, I'll drive myself. I knew I was right about those jelly beans.'

Frog Ltd comp slip still in hand, I head out of the front door. One of the twins is out roller skating. She shrieks a hello at me. I ignore her. She shrieks again as I get back into my car. Just as I sit down, Lucy appears at my side.

'I'll drive. Come on.'

I get out. She gets in. I get in the passenger side. We drive.

'A year before. A year . . . before Danny disappeared, we sold Milk. A year before that, we considered rebranding.'

'I remember.'

'We looked into changing the logo. Complete and utter madness, who changes their logo when they're doing well? Anyway. We interviewed a few graphic designers. Me and Danny. And one of them must have been Miriam.'

'But you don't remember her?'

'Me and Danny were having a massive row that day. I couldn't concentrate on anything other than that.'

'What were you rowing about?'

'I forget. I was really pissed off he was so gung-ho about changing the logo. It was probably that.'

'I'm surprised you didn't recognize her. First time you saw her.'

'It's about seven years ago.'

'I'm surprised she didn't recognize you.'

'I don't understand it. Either way, if she met him on holiday, then she already knew him. And either way she's been lying to me.'

'She might not tell you the truth, you know.'

'I want her to look me in the eye and deny it.'

'She might not be in. Why don't you call her?'

'I want to see her face.'

We drive in silence for a while. Eventually I say, 'Is Dylan faithful to you?'

She looks at me, alarmed, as if the thought had never entered her head.

'Don't you think I might've mentioned it if he wasn't?'

'Sorry.'

Again. Silence. I feel bad for even suggesting it. I feel a pang of jealousy. I want Lucy's life. I want her happiness. Her serenity. Her happy marriage. Her good sex life. Instead I've ended up with a guy who has caused me nothing but heartache for the last five years.

Selfish. Selfish BASTARD.

'Sorry,' I say again.

'Don't be daft. You can say what you like to me.'

And of course, the fact that she's being so reasonable makes me feel even worse.

'She knows where he is,' I say suddenly.

'She might not.'

'She's a liar. If she can lie about how she knew him, she can lie about anything.'

'You might be reading too much into this. She might've been lying coz she didn't want to hurt you any more than she needed to.'

'She lied to save her skin.'

Half an hour later we are in Mayville Road. There is no answer at the door and I can't see her car parked anywhere.

'Call her.'

But I don't want to. As we sit in the car, in the pouring rain, a man walks past us and then turns up her path.

'That's Alex. That's her boyfriend.'

He goes and shelters on her doorstep, trying to duck his head out of the rain.

'He likes to play in the snow,' Lucy murmurs, and we chuckle.

Alex makes a call on his mobile. Looks through the letter box. Rings the doorbell a couple more times. Then angrily storms off.

'Can we follow him?' I ask tentatively.

'What d'you think this is, Nat? *Scott and Bailey*?'

'Please.'

'Why?'

'Well, maybe he's going to meet her.'

Lucy rolls her eyes and starts the car up. Further up Mayville he has got into a black estate car and is driving off. We follow.

We follow for ages. And ages. I've never followed anyone before, and it's quite exciting. And a lot easier than you'd expect. One thing you can say about Alex, he's a very proficient and cautious driver. He eventually pulls over on a suburban row of red-brick semi-detacheds in Crumpsall. Can't say I've spent too much time here either.

He gets out of the car and zaps it shut. He walks up a path. But before he can even get his key in the door, a young black woman opens it. She's stood inside with a baby in her arms. She kisses him. He kisses the baby. The door shuts.

I don't quite know what to make of it.

Lucy breaks the silence.

'She likes her married men, doesn't she?'

I look to her. Maybe she's right.

Cally

'You can see her pain. Look how hurt she looks. It's heart-breaking. She has this aura of melancholy. It's arresting. It's disturbing. It's amazing.'

I pretend I'm not listening to this dude as he leans over my pictures in the next room. I'm on a go-see. A go-see is where you go and see someone from the fashion industry and they check you out and write your name down if they think you're interesting and might be able to work with you in the future. I didn't just happen to know this shit; Aba explained it all to me. So far this week I have been on eight go-sees each day, and this is the third day. That's a lot of bang for your buck in anyone's book.

I don't have a card or a book yet or whatever it's called as I haven't done loads and loads of shoots, but some of the go-sees are with junior photographers who are building up their portfolio and so they do some shots with me and that's been kinda fun. Others I've met have been casting directors. They choose the models to go in various catwalk shows and print stuff (I'm still learning all the words so bear with) and all of them have been really really cool and really really nice. Some of them have even asked about Dad coz I think Aba must have filled them in on the whole going missing thing. She says it's something unique about me and all these guys will want to feel they connect with me on some level so I can use Dad's disappearance as a bit of an icebreaker, and a reason for why they might remember me when they might have met, like, eighty-three models that day. It helps me stand out and stuff. Lots of the peeps I meet make me walk up and down in their offices to see what I'd be like on the runway or whatever it's called. That is the most mortifying thing in the world. I hate even having to walk to the front of the class if the teacher calls me up. But down here, in London, it has a purpose, a better purpose. So I hold my head high, pull a FURIOUS face and then sashay away.

(Yes, I have seen *RuPaul's Drag Race*. And I've been very grateful for it this week.)

If you don't feel it, bitches, fake it.

Actually I made that up. It's quite good. Hashtag almost amazing!

And. I'm not being funny, but I really think I've grown up a lot since coming to London. I feel I'm moving in an adult world and therefore I have to behave more like one.

Maybe where Mum was going wrong all those years was by treating me like A BLOODY KID. So I therefore BEHAVED LIKE A BLOODY KID.

These people treat me like a GROWN-UP. And therefore I AM ONE.

Hardly brain surgery, is it?

I think seeing Owen over the weekend helped a bit actually. It's the first time he's talked to me like I'm not just his mental little sister and AGAIN like I was another human being. I was pretty damned sure he was going to come in all guns blazing and drag me back Up North but instead he actually listened to me and thought about it all and seemed to agree that what I said made actual sense and wasn't the drivelling ramblings of some demented old loon. And what that felt like was . . . was . . . liberating. And when I saw how upset he was about Dad. He NEVER shows me that side of him. EVER. I thought he was just like Mum and had locked his feelings away and it's best not to go there but SHOCK HORROR I was wrong. He was sort of doing what I was doing. Pretending everything's fine just to keep Mommie Dearest happy. (Mind you he reckons we're not that similar coz he still thinks I am a proper little madam who stamps my foot all the time and is incredibly rude. I disagree, I just feel the need to raise my voice sometimes in order to make myself understood with total CRETINS. But there you go.)

After I saw him Friday night he and Matt spent the weekend in London and I totally hung out with them loads. And they took me and Zaraah out for lunch at this amazing place on the Kings Road where they do these INCREDIBLE lobsters and prawns and stuff and they have this REALLY REALLY HOT SAUCE. And they paid for us both. And then took us up the road shopping to this really cool farmer's market and they bought us both these really cute pouches of lavender that you can put in your knicker drawer or in a bag when you go travelling. They're so wonderful and I sleep with mine under my pillow each night, I love it. And we didn't even row. Only a little bit. Mostly when I laughed my head off when Zaraah announced over the deep-fried jalapeños:

'In South Africa my Uncle Oscar was a gay like you. But he got shot. Dead. With a gun.'

And Owen went on about the rise in homophobic hate crimes and how they're not funny and so I felt really bad. But instead of apologizing about it I dug my heels in, just call it my default mode, and demanded to know what the figures were like compared to heterophobic hate crimes. And the lads told me not to be so silly. And even Zaraah was like 'You're totally out of ord.' So I flounced off to the toilets and returned and finished the meal in silence as Owen and Matt asked their new best friend all about apartheid and Mandela and white farmers and the rand, and by the time the bill came I was in a better mood and everyone seemed to have forgotten there'd even been a kick-off.

I'd still like to know the figures on heterophobic hate crimes, mind.

But they hadn't forgotten it, because half an hour later when we were walking down the old Kings Road to the farmer's market Matt started going on about something that had happened at his work. The restaurant he works in is SO not posh. I mean it's OK. I've never been. But it's hardly Nobu n stuff. Anyway like last week? He was serving this table of total twats and they were like taking the piss out of him and one of them called him a fucking queer and the boss – I forget her name but they really like her – had to come over and ask the blokes on this table to pay their bill and leave and the blokes got a bit arsey about the whole thing and smashed a few plates. The owner called the police but the twatty guys had legged it. Matt was all shook up about it and stuff but was fine about it now but I'm sure they brought it up because I'd laughed about homophobic hate crimes. God those two are like elephants. They forget NOTHING.

I shouldn't be so rude. I have of course decided to be all grown up.

Take Monday night when I finally spoke to Mum on the phone. She actually said, 'Well, you know I was dead against this but it sounds like you're really behaving yourself.'

'It won't be a wasted opportunity, Mum.'

'Well, that's good to hear.'

'Mum?'

'Aha? It's just so nice to not hear you screaming at me.'

'I'm sorry I pretended to be you to give Aba permission to have me down here. And I'm sorry I ran away like that. But I did leave a note.'

She didn't say anything. And then I realized. She was crying. And that made me cry a little bit too.

Eventually she went, 'That's really kind of you to say. I do appreciate that, Cally.'

But I know what she really wanted to say.

Why did your dad never say that to me?

I then remembered the thing I know. The thing I know that I'm not meant to know. The thing about Dad that I'm not meant to know. And so I tried REEEAALLLY hard to block it out of my mind.

'I've got to go now, Mum.'

'Did you get the email I forwarded from the school? With the work they want you to do on? It's the only way I could square it with them.'

'God, you pay them enough bloody money. You'd think they could turn a blind eye for one week.'

'It's a good school.'

Yes, it would be. If it didn't have some of those complete and utter bitches in it. I hate them.

'I'm gonna do some homework, Mum.'

And so we said our goodbyes. And for once I actually did do my homework. I have decided to stay true to my promise that I'm not going to fuck this experience up. London is exciting and I love travelling everywhere on the crazy tube system, but they've only sent me a couple of essay things to write.

The guy for this particular go-see is a big cheese. Aba

said he was such a big cheese that he was dangerous for your cholesterol. She then didn't stop laughing for ages. And texted one of her mates to tell her what she'd just said. Then she tweeted it. Then put it on Facebook. I was like, 'Why don't you make a Vine of it?'

And she said, 'Oh I don't really know how to do those.'

Like I was being SERIOUS.

ANYHOO. His name is Seth Barnes and he is a really cool photographer who EVERYONE wants to work with. I looked at his website last night and it has got THE best photos on it. Like, really urban stuff of burning shopping trolleys under fly-overs (I know that sounds shit but believe me. It's not), burnt-out cars in the middle of a gorgeous field, and then others of really stark stunning headshots of models. For once I looked at a load of pictures and thought, 'Oh. I get this.' And couldn't wait to meet the guy who took them. Oh and when he had like pictures of famous people he had made them look completely unrecognizable and I thought that was really clever. So Cara Delevingne was covered in flour and eggs so it took a while to work out who it was. Same with James Franco. He had a pair of tights over his head. And he still managed to look SMOKIN HOT N SHIZ.

In a way I wish I'd not looked at the site now coz I am actually a bag of nerves and so far on my go-sees I've been just dead friendly and nonchalant and like I was just passing and thought I'd pop in and say hey coz Aba's said you were such sweet guys. Now I feel I'm in a job interview. Coz I'd actually LOVE this Josh person to take my pics. I just know it'd be a really exciting thing to experience and be part of . . . seeing how his brain works and how he lines everything up.

I've only met his assistant so far. And she's making me wait in the entrance room to his studio. I can hear the man's voice next door again. It must be him. Going on about how 'beautiful her depression is'. I'm assuming it's Josh and I'm assuming he's talking about me, looking at the pics that Aba had done that day, but I can't be sure. I'm not that morbid-looking, am I?

'OK. Bring her in.'

It is him. It is me. I go in.

I'm not expecting him to be so young. He looks like he can only be a couple of years older than me.

'Seth Barnes,' he says confidently as he holds out his hand to shake mine. Which he does, firmly. 'And you must be Calista?'

'Yes,' I say with a grimace.

Why did I do that? WHY DID I DO THAT.

'Don't put yourself down,' he says playfully, and we both sit on this battered old leather sofa. He introduces his assistant, Leila-Jade.

'Oh, I wasn't putting myself down, it's just that's not my real name.'

'Ah. Cool. So what's your real name?'

'Cally. But Aba at my agency wanted to make it a bit more . . . I dunno . . . fancy. I suppose loads of people in fashion have really zany names. Like . . .'

And oh God. WHY DO I SAY IT?

'Leila-Jade.'

Leila-Jade blushes. But Seth roars. He really laughs.

'Sorry.' I say with a grimace. 'I should really learn to shut up. My mum says I could start a fight in an empty house.'

Seth is still laughing.

'I hate that phrase. It makes me think of ghosts.'

And still he is laughing.

'I don't like ghosts.'

175

Actually. I wish he'd stop, coz this is making me do all the talking. And that's not my strong point. And like Aba said, basically models should be seen and not heard. If at all possible. No-one's hiring you for your brain or filthy sense of humour. They're hiring you for the ability to look good on camera.

'Not that I've . . . ever seen a ghost.'

Leila-Jade is giggling now.

'I've seen *Ghost*. The movie.'

I feel I may as well carry on.

'But I can't really remember what it was about. But thingy was a ghost in it. And she was into making pots. And she had a jukebox in her loft apartment.'

I thought he'd be really serious. His photographs were like NEXT LEVEL serious, oh my God!

'You know,' he eventually gets out, 'for someone who looks so upset in their pics, you don't half crack me up.'

He's got a very cutesy little cockney accent, though something tells me it's a little bit put on, like Madonna's ex-husband's. There's a word for it. I can't remember it. And I don't think it's a good idea to ask this seriously cool-looking dude in front of me, for fear he'll take offence.

I'm in there for a total of about twenty minutes. I think he might be a bit older than I originally thought, coz I could see on his beard stubble there were little bits of grey coming through. But he has a very mod kind of haircut, a bit Paul Weller-ish, and I find I spend the rest of the day thinking of him, and his easy laugh, and the way his lips go funny at the corners like the Joker. Not that he's some deformed hideosity or anything. Far from it. And his voice. I just have to imagine his voice and it's like . . . I dunno. Perfect pitch or something. It just sounds reassuring and . . . nice.

God I sound like a total MORON. SWOON SWOON SWOON and all that shit.

I tell myself to snap out of it.

I don't even know what he was seeing me for.

He didn't even comment on my photos. Well, he did, I suppose. But he didn't do it to my face.

We just sat there being silly and laughing. And at one point I did some impressions of some of the teachers and girls at school.

NOTE TO SELF – NOT COOL – HE'LL THINK YOU'RE A TOTAL INFANT. AND IF HE HAD THE SLIGHTEST FEELING OF FANCYING YOU HE'LL NOW FEEL LIKE A MAHOOSIVE PAEDOPHILE AND STUFF.

So I don't think I'll ever hear from him again.

But it was great to meet him.

And like I said. His photos are great. What an honour and privilege to actually get to meet someone so talented.

Half an hour later Aba rings me.

'So I hear it went well with Seth Barnes!'

'Did it? I don't know.'

'He thought you were great. And he loves your pictures.'

'Wow, that's so cool.' And for a laugh I add, 'Is he going to like put me in all his major shoots and stuff?'

There is silence at the other end. Then . . .

'Actually, Calista. He does want to use you.'

'What for?'

And another pause.

'Babe?'

'Aba?'

'Are you sitting down?'

'No. I'm walking through Soho.'

'Please. Find somewhere and sit down.'

I look around. I see an incredibly low step up to some offices. I go and sit on it.

What is she going to say? Oh my GOD.

Owen

I have this recurring dream. It's that night. I'm back there. I'm standing in this boggy building site. My jeans are ripped because I had to climb the perimeter fence. My knee's muddy and bleeding from where I fell coming down the fence. My heart is pounding as I grip the spade and dig. Dig. Grinding it into the clarty soil. Turning it this way and that. Covering. Hiding.

'What are you burying?' a small voice says beside me.

I turn to locate who it is. It's a small boy. Although it's raining, he's bone dry. He asks again.

'What are you burying?' I realize now that it's me when I was young.

'I'm not burying anything,' I insist, then carry on digging.

'Are you burying a body?'

'No.'

'You are. You're burying a body.'

'I'm not.'

'Are you burying my dad?'

'Fuck off!' and I jab the little boy with the edge of the spade. He screams and falls back and . . .

And that's when I always wake up. This dream comes to me often, when I feel I've done something wrong. I guess

Jonathan Harvey

it's a memory of a guilty secret. One that no-one else knows anything about. I wake and check the clock. It's two a.m. Just after. Matty is snoring by my side, his hands curling over the top of the duvet. He looks so helpless. He looks like a little boy. A child I could never hurt. Yet if he knew what I'd done, it would pain him so much.

I first slept with Dylan after we returned from London at the weekend. I might have been with Matty the whole time, but me and Dylan were in constant contact via text. Our exchanges became more and more loaded as the weekend progressed. I was canny, some might say twisted, enough to change some contacts round in my phone so that it looked like I was getting messages from Gerard at work. I changed Dylan's name to Gerard and Gerard's to Boss, promising myself to revert once I was home. Matty has little time for Gerard and just rolled his eyes when he thought there'd been another text from Gerard coming through.

Will he not let you have a weekend in peace?

Things are tricky at work. One of the advertisers has pulled out and he's bricking it a bit.

Which advertiser?

Oh can we talk about something else? I'm discussing it enough with him.

Was I thrill-seeking? Did I just want an affair for the sake of it? Gone were my assertions that Matty was being unfaithful, or drinking too much, or not communicating properly. Give him his due, he had been the perfect boyfriend during our time away. Attentive to Cally, and her friend, to me. We even had good sex both nights. But maybe that's because when I closed my eyes it wasn't him I was seeing.

I crossed the Rubicon, or whatever you call it, the same day we got back. Matt had to do a shift at the restaurant Sunday evening. I offered to drive him in. Then, heart beating in chest, I texted Dylan and asked if he was at the office. He was. When I got to the top of the stairs and saw him in the doorway he said nothing, just showed me in. I was shaking as he shut the door. We looked at each other and said nothing. We didn't say anything for the next hour. Just once it was over we got into the banal chit-chat of 'How you getting home?' and 'How long you working till?', even 'How was London?' and 'Matty OK?'

I have been back every night this week. Matty has a lot of evening shifts. And I don't know why I'm doing it.

A lot of people stand to get hurt if they find out. Matt. Lucy. My mum. But as Dylan says, they won't. Unless we tell them. And we have both agreed it's just a bit of fun. 'Harmless boysie fun' is what Dylan said. Not sure I agree with that, but at least he's not intending on our secret coming out.

What do I get out of it? He's old enough to be my dad. But I am not seeking some sort of father figure to feel closer to, in some pervy fetishy way. It's sex. It's his body. It's his vigour. It's his excitement. He says there have been a few men over the years, Lucy doesn't know, but he's just experimenting. Well, I am happy to be his case study. He makes me feel alive, cliché or not, because when he looks at me he wants me. He wants something from me. And I have control because I can either give it to him or not. Although physically he can sometimes overpower me, and it's refreshing and exciting when he does, I still feel I retain the control.

'How old is he?' Sonia asks over coffee in the Royal Exchange one lunch time.

'Forty-two, but he's really fit. It's not a dad replacement thing.'

'I'd bloody well hope not, that's disgusting.'

'I know.'

We're keeping our voices down in this cavernous space.

'So you fancy him?'

'Of course I fancy him.'

'Is he gay?'

'He says he's bisexual.'

'So he's still sleeping with the wife?'

I nod.

'Your mum's best mate?'

I nod.

'And Matty's not shagging around?'

I shake my head. She looks bewildered.

'D'you hate me?'

She shakes her head. 'I think you're playing with fire, though.'

'I know. It can't go on forever.'

'You don't sound that convinced.'

'It's not like I love him.'

'Do you love Matty?'

'Yes.' But I sound hesitant.

'Some people would say you can't. If you're prepared to play around behind his back.'

'It's a gay thing. I can differentiate between sex and love.'

'Fuck off. If I said there was a difference between gay people and straight people you'd call me on it.'

'I can.'

'When you thought Matt was fucking around you were devastated.'

'I know. But as I say. It's not gonna go on forever.'

'But if he had been. And you'd found out. And he'd said to you, Oh I can differentiate between love and sex. What would you have said?'

She's right. I know she's right. And I know she's angry with me. And with every right. We sit in silence for a while, and I wish I'd never told her. But I've told her everything. We have no secrets. Well. Apart from the one I dream about when things are going wrong. And even the fact that I'm dreaming about that night proves I know what I'm doing isn't right.

'I wonder if you've not wanted this for years.'

'With Dylan? No. It didn't even cross my mind till . . .'

'No, just . . . a chance to . . . misbehave.'

'I've never been a saint.'

'A chance to feel closer to your dad.'

'How?'

'By behaving like he did. By playing around.'

I'd not thought of it like that. I let the words settle in my brain for a while and feel them taking root. Has she got a point?

'It would make sense,' she adds, sounding a bit holier-than-thou. 'But whatever the reason, Owen, it's all very self-destructive. I think you're being a knob. There. I've said it.'

And I nod. Because I don't disagree with her.

'I don't want to fall out with you.' And from her lips it sounds like a warning.

She does hate me. Of course she does. And it suddenly makes me feel washed with shame. It's like a hot flush rising up me. And she's not even one of the people who stands to get hurt.

'I'll finish it tonight.'

'I hate sounding like Mary Whitehouse.'

'I hate you looking like Mary Whitehouse.'

And that breaks the mood. And she smiles. I hate her hating me. Maybe we all have a desire to be liked. And who wants a best friend who will approve of everything you do? I need people around me who'll call me out when I'm being a fool. And people who'll spur me on to do the right thing.

'So,' she tries to change the theme, 'your Cally's got a big modelling job! Amazing.'

I nod. 'She's off to Mexico for Christmas.'

'Bloody hell, doing what?'

'Oh, some . . . magazine spread on upcoming models.'

'And she has to go to Mexico to do that?'

I nod. 'It's the law.'

What Cally has achieved – or what Cally has been lucky enough to have fall into her lap – is amazing. But I'm in no mood to celebrate her achievement/luck right now.

We say our goodbyes, and I promise to call her when I've done the deed.

I'm meant to be joining Matty at work in an hour or so. They're closing the restaurant for the night and having a party for Mother Hen Jen's 30th. I send him a quick text as I hover on St Ann's Square, hoping he won't see me from the restaurant. I practically glue myself to the side of the theatre, safely ensconced in shadow.

Gonna be an hour late Bubsy. Got to finish off an article for work. Won't be long. See you. Love you. X

He replies immediately. Of course he does. He's not having a sordid affair with a man twice his age.

C u later. Just out for candles for cake. Ran out x

I phone Dylan. He picks up quickly.

'I was hoping you'd call.'

I chuckle. 'Can I come and see you? Can't stop long.'

'Ah, a quickie. It's come to that, has it?'

'Are you at your office?'

'No. Home. Why don't you come here?'

'Is Lucy not with you?'

'No, she's with your mum. Girly night. Or something. Wasn't really listening. She's staying the night. We're perfectly safe.'

'OK.'

I'm nervous as I hail a cab. It starts to rain. Rain. Always reminds me of that night. Sometimes I dream I'm digging with a tennis racquet. Sometimes the pop star's girlfriend is watching. But it always rains.

Dylan and Lucy live in the very chi-chi Hale Barns. Big old brown stone detached houses. Four-by-fours. Bucolic village life for those who don't want to be too far from the city. I've been coming to their house for about ten years. I'm glad I've not slept with Dylan here. Here is the place where we came when I was eleven. Did he notice me then? The thought is so repugnant I almost vomit as the cab bounces over a sleeping policeman. I push the thought from my mind. He is not some sort of paedophile. But even thinking the word makes my heart race with fear. What have I done? What mess have I created? It's time to quash this once and for all.

He opens the door in jogging bottoms and a vest. The muscles in his arm make my groin twitch as he hands me a glass of red wine. I wasn't expecting the drink. But Dutch courage will definitely help. I slurp it greedily.

'You sounded upset.'

'We need to talk.'

'You need to calm down.'

He takes my hand and leads me to the living room. A fire is

burning in the hearth. Now I'm with him, he's not the monster I've painted him in my head. Sometimes. I feel disingenuous for even thinking the worst of him.

'What is it?'

'I can't carry on.'

'With what?'

'With this. I'm having nightmares. I don't know why I'm doing it. I love Matty. I like Lucy. If they find out we're fucked. My mum won't speak to me again. Matty won't speak to me again. I keep panicking about it.'

Owen nods. 'Well, you know I'm not going to tell anyone.'

I nod. He seems so reasonable.

'Why do you panic?'

'When did you first notice me? Sexually?'

He shrugs.

'Since we became Facebook friends, probably. I'd always thought of you as . . . just . . . Nat and Danny's kid. Then one day I was bored. And I saw a post by you. And clicked on it. And saw your pictures. And what a handsome man you'd grown into. And I felt guilty but . . . liked what I saw.'

OK. I think about this. But he continues.

'I've a confession to make.'

I look at him. 'What?'

'The day I bumped into you at the Exchange. It wasn't a coincidence.'

'You what?'

'I saw you'd checked in there on Facebook. I went to see if I could see you. Sorry.'

I shake my head. That's OK. I actually feel flattered.

'So you didn't fancy me when I was eleven?'

He pales. Stands. Stalks to the other side of the room and looks out of the window onto the garden. I suddenly feel terrible. This man is hurt. He's not a monster. I get up. He swings round. There are tears in his eyes.

'How could you even think that?'

'I had to ask.'

'But . . . why?'

'Coz that's how long I've known you!'

'Of course I didn't fucking fancy you back then. Jeez!'

'Sorry.'

And now of course I bitterly regret it. I get up. He looks back out of the window. I approach him and put my arm on his shoulder. He cocks his head to lean it against it. Within minutes we are upstairs. He has the good grace to push me into one of the spare bedrooms. He overpowers me and I surrender and every nerve ending of my body seems to come alive. Afterwards I fall asleep.

I don't know how long I've been asleep but I wake suddenly to the noise of a car engine approaching and the crunch of tyres on the gravel path. Headlights illuminate the room. Dylan wakes too.

'Fuck, she's back.'

We jump out of bed and start scrambling back into clothes.

'We've got five minutes. She takes forever getting the car into the garage.'

And indeed she seems to take longer.

By the time Lucy puts her key in the door, Dylan and I are sat on the sofa, just as we were however long ago I arrived, both sipping on a glass of red.

'Hi love, is that you?' Dylan calls calmly.

Lucy calls back, 'Yeah, bit of an emergency.'

'We've got a visitor!' he calls again.

Lucy comes through. Her face drops. She is astounded to see me.

'Owen, have you not heard your phone? Your mum's been calling you.'

'No, why?'

'He was just in the area and . . .' But Lucy is not listening to Dylan.

'It's Matty. He's been . . . mugged. He's in hospital. They couldn't get hold of you so they called your mum. We better get you to the hospital.'

Adrenalin is coursing through my body as I sit in the back seat of Dylan's car. He and Lucy are up front. I see I have seventeen missed calls on my phone. Some from Matty. Most from Mum. Texts from her, increasingly despondent. I've called her, told her I'm on my way, said I'll explain why I'm an hour late getting back to her when I see her, not that she seems that bothered, she's just relieved I'm finally in contact.

'So what were you doing at ours, Owen?' Lucy says, not like she's trying to catch me out, more like she's been told and can't remember. And now she's asking, I have no idea what to say. I'm panicking too much to think straight. Thank God Dylan jumps in, all calm and reasonable.

'He was in the area, visiting a pal. Called on the off chance.'

'Oh, that's nice. Which pal?'

My mouth is dry as I speak. I have to say Minty twice.

'Minty?'

'From work. She's only round the corner from you.'

'Well, thank God we found you.'

I nod. Yes. Thank God. Though I don't feel very godly right now.

In the hospital car park Lucy gets out before me. I hiss at Dylan.

'It's over. I can't do this any more.'

'Fine,' he says quickly.

'Look what you've made me fucking do.'

I run ahead of Lucy towards the entrance. I don't particularly want my secret lover and his wife witnessing my poor Matty battered and bruised.

Mum has come to reception and guides me through a warren of brightly lit corridors. I feel I have to explain myself.

'I was round at Dylan's. How weird is that? I had to take Minty from work some stuff over and . . . so I called Dylan and . . .'

But Mum is not interested at all. She interrupts, curtly.

'He says it was those guys. Who were rude to him in the restaurant the other week.'

I stop in my tracks. 'They did this coz he was gay?'

'Well, it's not coz he was fucking black, Owen. Come on!'

I can't believe how furious Mum is. She marches off down the corridor and I follow swiftly. At the next door she turns and shakes her head.

'I'm so sorry. I just . . .'

'He is OK, isn't he? He's not going to die?'

'He's going to be fine. He's very scared, though.'

'Why the fuck did I have my phone on silent?'

She touches my arm. Squeezes it. Then pushes through the doors. She tells me he's in a private room.

When I see him it's a shock. He looks like Picasso has painted him. I can tell it's him. But his eye and top lip are swollen. His arm is in a sling. He's been crying. I don't recognize the T-shirt he is wearing.

'I brought that. It's one of your dad's. He didn't want to wear the gown.'

'You all right, Bubsy?' I say, touching his good arm.

'I am now,' he says. And then starts to cry.

I hear footsteps outside as I hug him. Mum retreating to

the corridor. Murmuring voices. Lucy and Dylan. Fortunately they don't come in.

I want the world to go away. I want them to go away.

This is my fault.

This is all my fault.

Natalie

It would appear I've blotted my copybook with Laurence/ Gripper. When I was off on my wild goose chase with Lucy the other day I forgot to take my phone with me. And then I was so caught up in the *what the hell's going on here*? that I forgot he was coming over until it was too late. And by the time I got home, he'd been and left. And also left a few texts that ended with sad faces.

I'm not that keen on grown men who use emoticons on texts. But maybe that's judgemental of me.

Since then I've felt him cooling. Not that, this time any- way, he was that warm to begin with. I called him and tried to explain why I'd stood him up. He sounded hopeful at first, but the more I talked, the more I could hear his voice deflate. And then he said,

'Maybe it's not such a good idea, us going for a drink. Sounds like . . . your life's still all caught up with Danny. And I don't think I can step into his shoes.'

'That's not strictly true,' I countered.

But by the time we finished speaking, I realized he may have had a point. I try not to think about this, though. When I do, I feel crestfallen and slightly panicky. If I can't clear a way for a boyfriend now, five years after Danny went, when will

I ever be ready? Maybe it just feels like Danny's at the fore-front of my mind right now because of what I've discovered. I didn't choose the timing of that.

And what sort of a wife would I be if I didn't try and find out what happened?

Or ex-wife.

Or widow.

Raymond Lee, the detective in charge of the investigation into Danny's disappearance, has a few more grey hairs these days than he did when I first met him all those years ago. He's quite handsome, in a wrong sort of way. Which to my mind means that whenever I'm in his company I always wonder what he'd look like naked. Which isn't so bad now, I suppose, but back in the early days, when the disappear-ance was so fresh, it felt completely inappropriate. He must be about fifty now, and has that sandy brown hair that tells you he was probably a blond child. It's cropped short (whoever saw a policeman with a perm?) and I've never seen eyes that twinkle so much. They're really rather distracting. When I think of the amount of bad news he's given me over the years, it's bizarre that every time it was like there were two bright stars dancing in front of me. As inappropriate as disco lights in a hospice.

And today he's delivering bad news again.

I called him last week and told him about Miriam.

'Well . . . we got her in for questioning,' he says as I pour us both some coffee. I don't know whether to be alarmed or encouraged that he has deigned to visit me at home and not summonsed me to his office.

'You should arrest her for having the gall to have that bloody pink streak in her hair,' I quip nervously.

He chuckles. 'You were right. It wasn't just a one-night stand. It went on for a while.'

'How long is a while?'

'Two years.'

I stir his sugar quite fervently. Two. Years. TWO. YEARS.

'Said she didn't want to tell you the truth because she was trying to protect your feelings.'

I do an involuntary grunt.

'Big of her.' I hand him his coffee.

'She seems to know nothing of his disappearance. Except . . .'

I look at him.

'Except in the run-up to him going, she was putting the pressure on.'

'About what?'

'She wanted him to tell you the truth and leave you.'

'Well, he did one of those things. Nice one, Miriam.'

I take a sip of my coffee. It tastes bitter today. Like my mouth has been coated in iron.

'So what reason did she give for not coming forward when Danny went?'

'She said she was in shock. Didn't feel she had anything interesting to say. And again, didn't see that it would make you feel any better.'

'Knowing he was a two-timing bastard? She might have a point.'

'The interesting thing I discovered. And you might not like this.'

I look at him. What? What is he going to say?

'Danny's mum knew about him and Miriam.'

I discover I am nodding.

'So why didn't she mention it when you talked to her?'

'No doubt wanted to protect the precious reputation of her son.'

Again, I nod. 'Saint Danny of the Dirty Bastards. Sounds about right. He who can do no wrong. Well. She can't have loved him very much if she couldn't be arsed coming forward at the time. I remember you saying, vividly, anyone with any information, no matter how insignificant it may seem. Please come forward.'

'Well . . .'

'So you don't think it's worth digging her garden up?'

Raymond smiles sympathetically. Simpering to my pathetic desperation, probably. 'And why would we want to do that?'

'In case she's killed him and buried him in there.'

'And what makes you think she did that?'

'Because all she's told me so far is a pack of lies.'

'Her story's plausible. Admittedly it's not particularly palatable. But it's believable enough.'

'So why not come forward?'

Something tells me he's not going to budge on this one. My attempts to lay everything at Miriam's feet appear to be fruitless. And maybe he knows more than me, and is more dispassionate.

I look at him. He's not telling me what I want to hear. I wanted him to walk in here and explain everything. Now I just want him gone.

I need to get rid of him, anyway. I need to get to London. I check my watch. It's hours till my train.

Maybe what I really want to do is run away.

Is this how Danny felt? Is this what spurred him on? Things get too much and you just think *screw this, I can't bear to even think about anything any more, I'm offski*. I crave numbness where I don't have to think. I crave the white noise of nothingness.

Cally is going away. She is going to Mexico for ten days with Aba to do a shoot for *Vogue* magazine. I am gobsmacked by this, and I feel she is too. I am at once petrified and proud. Petrified that this is it, she has been swallowed away from me, never to be seen again. Proud that she chose to do something and first indications are that she is doing well. Let's face it, it's hardly bobbing on galoshes for Freeman's catalogue. Some hotshot photographer has been asked to choose his New Faces, the models he think we'll be hearing a lot more of pretty soon, and he is photographing them somewhere in Mexico. I know there is a beach involved. I have to meet Aba and Cally at the flat where she's staying to hand over a suitcase of clothes and toiletries. No doubt I will have got this very wrong and she will throw a hissy fit and I'll leave in tears. But at least I'll have had a go.

On the train down to London I treat myself, even though I shouldn't, to a seat in first class. It's mid-afternoon and I treat myself some more to a small bottle of white wine when the stewardess comes through. I'm really hoping Daffyd isn't working this train. Much as I should really be grateful for what he did for me, I'm not exactly relishing the prospect of seeing him and having to tell him what I've discovered about the woman who collected the luggage.

I don't want to think about it. I don't want to think about her and I don't want to think about what happened. Or didn't happen. No, scrap that, what did happen. It's not a level playing field. I can't trust a word that comes out of her mouth, and I don't have Danny here to ask him if what she says is the truth or a lie.

But of course I can't stop thinking about it, and it's such

a sickening feeling. I actually feel queasy. It's a physical sensation. Like I've eaten a bad prawn. It lingers. This whole sorry business has lingered for five years, and I hate it. I thought it would get better with time. And then Miriam Joseph walks into my life and the old feelings resurface and the pain is there and the sickening feeling, and it's like it only happened bloody yesterday.

And now of course it transpires that Barbara knew all along. She knew Danny was playing away and probably condoned it. Welcomed Miriam with open arms. Of course she did. She never liked me. And Miriam probably played up to her more.

But why? Why hasn't Barbara ever gone to the police? Why hasn't she gone and told them about the affair, that there is another person on this planet who knew Danny and might hold a clue to what happened next? Was it not worth a shot?

All I can keep thinking is this: if Barbara didn't feel the need to go and help the police find her son, maybe she didn't want him found.

Or maybe she didn't need to find him. Because maybe Barbara has known all along what actually happened to Danny. That if he is dead, she knows how it happened. Or that if he is alive, she knows where he is.

And no matter how much I try and argue the point in my head, I keep coming back to this. Barbara didn't tell the police because she didn't need to.

Barbara is in on it. Whatever it is.

The poison pen letters, the angry phone calls, the stand-up rows. What are they?

Red herrings.

Barbara knows what happened to Danny.

And rather than feeling nauseous, I now feel a sudden and transforming exhilaration.

I will pay her a visit very, very soon.

When I get to Cally's flat, it smells of scented candles and bolognese. She has cooked for me. She has never cooked for me before, despite doing well in it at school when she was younger. Whereas in the past she'd get all stroppy and sulky and spit, 'God I can't be BOTHERED. Who needs to EAT?' now she is uncorking me some red wine and telling me to take a seat. I hardly recognize her. I certainly don't recognize her clothes.

'Oh these? Oh, Vincente gave them to me.'

'Vincente?'

'Oh, this designer I did a little show for the other day. I got nine hundred quid and this playsuit.'

And she says it like it's the most normal thing in the world.

Again, pride and petrification. She's here, but I'm losing her.

This girl who only a few weeks ago, if she'd turned round to me and said, 'You know what, Mum? I've given this a lot of thought. I think it's best if you put me into care,' I might have said, 'OK, let me think about it,' I now don't want to lose. She is humbling me.

'You look lovely. It really suits you,' I offer.

'I mean I don't know how much of that nine hundred I'll see. They take a percentage and then some money for rent here. How's Matty?'

'Well, he's home.'

'Oh, that's good.'

'But it's really shaken the pair of them up. None of us are invincible.'

'I've been texting Owen and stuff.'

'Yes, he said.'

'What have school said about me going to Mexico?'

'They're happy about it. On the condition that you keep up with your school work.'

'Which I have.'

'Which you have. They seem rather taken aback.'

'Good. One in the eye for all those twats who said I'd never amount to much.'

'To be fair, Cally, for the last five years you've exuded the aura of a person who thought she wouldn't amount to much.'

'Yeah, but teachers shouldn't say it.'

'No. You're right. They shouldn't. But I've found you hard to manage sometimes; maybe they do too.'

'Hard to manage? What am I? A Renault Espace?'

And she says it with such good humour we both laugh. She hands me the glass of wine she's poured for me.

'Are you going to join me? I'm sure you could have one.'

'I'm not supposed to drink in this flat.'

'Cheers!' I say, lifting my glass, slightly taken aback that someone has set a rule and she is obeying it, possibly because there will be consequences. I'm jealous. She has never shown any enthusiasm for the ground rules I've set down at home.

'I wish my flatmates had been in. They're so cool.'

'Where are they?'

'Oh, they've both got shoots today. I mean, nothing as exciting as my *Vogue* thing. And I've had to play it down a bit with them coz I totally didn't want them to think I was showing off or taking it for granted. But yeah. Everyone's busy.'

I eat her spag bol. It's far too spicy, as it transpires she added a whole jar of harissa paste at some point. But it is of course one of the best meals I've ever eaten in my life because my daughter's made it. For me. For the first time.

After dinner, emboldened by the two glasses of red I've now had, I dare to show her which bits I've packed for her in the suitcase. Though I've been expecting some sulking, stomping and disgusted tutting, she's actually surprisingly docile and, well, you can't by any means say she is gushing in her praise for my choices, but at least she manages to sound vaguely satisfied that she won't look a complete dork in Mexico.

Eventually Aba comes round in a whirl of OMG's and BABEs and hugs and slurps of my red and disorder is restored for a while. She's had a NIGHTMARE sorting the FLIGHTS and the ESTA VISAS – *We're changing at bloody Philadelphia hon. No direct flights left. Huge pisser.* And then she's telling me about what's in store for Cally, and I'm confused by her scattergun approach to passing on information. One minute she's showing me the hotel they'll be staying in, the next she's bringing up pictures by this photographer who's shown so much confidence in Cally's potential. The energy's too much for me and fortunately I realize it's almost time for me to go to get the train back.

Cally walks me to the tube. We hug. I tell her not to let the photographer down. He's given her a massive break, and she shouldn't mess it up. But, not wanting to sound too much like an old crone, I also tell her she should enjoy every second and have the time of her life. I ask her if she needs me to transfer any money to her bank account and she tells me that the agency cover everything. This is a business trip. It's all expenses paid. Plus she will be paid. She drags me in for another hug.

'Text me in the morning. Just before you board.'

'We're going business class.'

'Wow.'

'So we might be able to text from the plane. I think you can tweet.'

'Things have certainly changed since my day.'

And this time I drag her in for a final hug.

'And make sure Aba takes bloody good care of you. She's a nightmare.'

'I'm the grown-up in the relationship,' she says, and we laugh.

'Next time I see you,' she says, 'it'll almost be Christmas.'

'What a year you'll have had,' I say.

She looks so happy.

I cry on the tube back to Euston.

The next morning I lie in bed slightly groggy from last night's red wine. I feel hollow. I should eat something, but I know today it won't touch the sides. This is a hollowness born of the status quo never changing. This ever-present feeling of limbo. I can't move forward, I can't move back. I am stuck up to my waist in mud, not drowning, not being pulled down into it, but it is paralysing me. I want my life change but today, as my daughter jets off to the other side of the world and my son nurses his broken boyfriend, it seems it never will. At what point do I let go? Will I continue to worry away at this sore till the day I die? What will that have achieved? Why can't I just own up to the fact that Danny walked out one day, drove his car to Beachy Head and jumped into the grey, waxy water?

I know why. Because that version of events shows little sympathy for me. I am not important in that story. At no point did he think, 'To save Natalie some pain I will write her a note or at least hint at what I am going to do.' I am not the star of that show.

And even if he ran away, he didn't tell me. I am not the star of that show either.

And why can't I just admit it? He is dead. His car was at a bloody beauty spot popular with suicides. That's a pretty big giveaway.

If he's alive he has not used his passport, or phone, or bank accounts.

He is dead. And the sooner I give in to that, the better. OK, so he had a cloudy past, a few years where he recklessly had an affair with some stupid graphic designer with a daft pink streak in her hair. But maybe that's because he was feeling depressed. And he just couldn't bring himself to tell me.

He's dead. He's always been dead. And I feel pretty damned stupid for not believing it in the first place.

I sit bolt upright.

But Barbara knows something. She knew he was having an affair. And she never told the police. Which means . . .

He told her he was going to kill himself. And she did nothing to stop him.

Maybe that's why she carries on drinking. And why she lashes out at me with all those letters. Maybe she blames me for not stopping him from killing himself. Or for not noticing he was depressed in the first place.

But he wasn't depressed.

I'm going round in circles again. This is helping no-one. Most of all it's not helping me.

Danny is dead. And the sooner I bloody get used to it, the better.

My husband is dead. I am not a woman who's husband went missing. Ish. I am a widow.

Sitting in bed, I hear a slicing noise outside. It comes and goes and I know what it is. I swing my legs round to get out of bed, and as I stand, I draw back the curtains.

Harmony Frayn is roller-skating up and down the cul-de-sac. As I open my curtains she stops and looks up to my window. I'm not sure if she can see me, as the light is hitting the glass. But she stands there, shielding her eyes from the light with a saluting hand, staring at me. It unnerves me. She continues to stand and stare.

I don't know why, but I'm in no mood for weird stuff like this today. To be stared at by some bizarre young woman with pigtails that infantilize her beyond words. I bang on the window and shout a braying FUCK OFF. I stomp off from the window, and hear the slicing of her skates retreating across the street.

Five minutes later, the landline is ringing. I snap it up. Nobody ever calls me on a landline. It feels so Seventies.

'Hello?'

I can't even remember my new number.

'Is that Mrs Bioletti?'

'Speaking?'

'Margaret Frayn here, Melody and Harmony's mum.'

'Oh, hi.' And my heart sinks.

'Did you just swear at my daughter?'

'Yes, I did.'

This silences her. Briefly.

'And if she wants to stare at me twenty-four hours a day when I've just got up, I'm sure I can think of a lot worse things to say to her than "fuck off". Do I make myself clear?'

'My daughter has a very big heart,' Margaret explains.

It's about the only thing that is, I want to say. And then realize I am being bitchy and realize there is more to my mood than Harmony.

'And she cares. She cares about you. And your family. And what you've been through.'

'Well, caring's not going to bring him back. So please tell her to find someone else to worry about. And stare at.'

'Prayers might.'

'Might what?'

'Bring him back.'

'Mrs Frayn. I'm sorry I swore at her. And I'm sorry if my attitude today is rather arsey. But I woke up this morning pretty much convinced – finally – that my husband probably committed suicide and is never coming back. So let's just say this isn't a good day. Now I really must go.'

I hang up. But as I return the phone to its cradle, I hear her say.

'Betty says he's alive.'

But it's too late. I have killed the call. I lift the phone again, as if her voice will magically reappear at the other end.

He's alive? What does she mean? Betty?

I dial 14713. Eventually I hear the phone ring. Margaret answers.

'Hello?'

'What do you mean? He's alive. Betty . . .'

'Melody's been reading up on it all. Online, and . . .'

'Margaret, tell me!'

'Well, she spoke to Betty.'

'Betty?'

'Caligary. Number seven. She like to think she's a psychic.'

'Is she?'

'And Betty's convinced . . . and now she's got Harmony convinced. I'm so sorry.'

'Well, Betty needs to learn to keep her fucking mouth shut!' I snap, and throw the phone down.

I pace. I fume. I decide.

I go to the kitchen and rifle around through the cupboards till I eventually find the Tupperware that Betty gave to me with that hideous cake in when we moved in. I see there's a piece of paper in it. Ah yes, she said she'd written her number down in it for me. I rip the lid off and open out the folded-up piece of notepaper. But there's no number there. Instead I read:

> *Please come and see me when you're ready.*
> *I have news of your husband.*

I march out of the house, across the cul-de-sac, and ring her doorbell. It's musical. It plays the Skye Boat Song. She takes a while to answer, but when she does she seems amused I'm still in my dressing gown.

'Ah. Mrs Bioletti,' she says, all smiley and sing-song. 'I've been expecting you.'

I practically throw the Tupperware at her.

'Well, go on then. If he's alive, where is he?'

'I don't know.'

'Oh, that's handy.'

'All I know is he's not in spirit.'

'Good job you don't do this professionally.'

'He's hot. He's on a beach. He's alive.'

There is so much I want to say. To scream. I want to rant and rave and tell her I hate her glasses. Why? Why is she saying this? Does she not realize this is my life and this is hurtful? I want to hurt her back.

'Your cake was horrific,' I say, and turn and head back towards my house.

At my front door I turn. She is still stood at hers, staring. I look across to the Frayns' house. The twins are in an upstairs bedroom, staring. The world is staring.

A beach. Yeah, right.

'Horrific!' I yell again. And then slam the door shut on them.

Cally

Aba was really facking annoying on the flight over here. Rabbit rabbit rabbit. Really showing off and being SOOOO loud. She was more excited about being on a bloody plane than I was. In the end I had to say,

'Yes, I HAVE travelled business class before, Aba.'

But she was so not listening. 'And see all these films? You can watch ANY of them at ANY time. Isn't that amazeballs slash awesome sauce? CHEERS!'

At which point she thrust her glass of champagne in my face, even though I didn't have a drink by that point to clink with her. And then she started reeling off a list of all the films I could watch. I bit my tongue, stopping myself from saying, *Yes Aba, I can read. I have been to school. I wasn't reared in a derelict house. By APES.*

But instead I stuck my earphones in and listened to some music on my phone.

This trying to be a grown-up at all times malarkey is actually really tiring. So I have got into the habit of, like, to the outside world I am serenity personified, nice to everyone, minding my Ps and Qs, whereas inside I'm just the same as ever. Enjoying being VILE on a minutely basis. Except when Seth's around, and then I revert to 'kooky Northern comedy modelly girl who he met on a go-see' character. Which was basically me as a bag of nerves. And which isn't too much of a stretch to recreate when he's around because he does actually make me feel nervous. Not because he's some dirty great paedo or something, but because I am like TOTALLY IN AWE OF THE PHOTO MONSTER N STUFF.

Everything about him is just so cool. We're all baking in the zillion-degree heat. He walks round without a drop of sweat on him, as if he's lived here all his life. Nothing fazes him, nothing makes him scream OMIGODTHATSAMAZE-BALLS. He's pretty much Zen all the time. He speaks quietly, he's polite, and he speaks Spanish to the locals like a native. (Of Spain.) (Well, actually of Mejicocococo.) (Actually I must remember not to say that out loud. Mejicocococo is quite annoying. NOTE TO SELF KLAXON)

There are six of us models in total.

(I CAN'T BELIEVE I NOW ACTUALLY REFER TO MY-SELF AS A MODEL. HOW PRETENSH AM I?!?!?!?!)

And four of them are complete jerks. They really do think they're too cool for school, so I just ignore them. The other one is really sweet and is just in a constant state of panic all the time. She's from a council estate in Dewsbury and just freaks out at everything she sees and everything they ask her to do.

Oh my God what's that?! you'll hear her shrieking on the beach.

And Aba's like that: *Hon. Chill. It's just a pelican.*
I thought that was like a zebra crossing.
No it's a bird.
Why does it keep diving into the sea like that? Is it like Jaws?
It won't come near you, it's fishing in the water.
For what? SHARKS?

No, for tiny little fish. Fishettes.

Right. OK.

Her name is Nancy. Which her agent made up. Her real name is Kylie, but she was told it was too chavvy.

Nancy, she goes. *That's what my nan calls her minge.*

In fact, I'm the only model to have my agent here. Aba says this is because the staff at L'Agence go above and beyond. I reckon she's only here for the cocktails. Honest to God, she's always on them. She looks at her watch after breakfast and she's like,

Mmm. Mohito time!

By mid-morning she's just dancing everywhere and asking for the 'sounds' to be turned up coz she just can't help but 'get her groove on'. No one seems to mind, though. And she never gets lairy or aggressive. She's more an aul lush than anything else. And the minute she needs to get worky, say Bimbi calls from London or the stylist needs something or one of the girls is upset or stroppy, she's really good at snapping out of it and channelling into 'business bitch'. Even if it is slightly annoying that the rest of the time she's always gyrating and booty bouncing and twerking like she's the first person to ever do it in the whole wide world.

Still, it seems to keep the other models amused. She can get a smile out of anyone. Including the severe lesbian-y one from the Isle of Mull. She reads books all the time and says shit like, 'That sky's very foreboding, is it not?' like she's in an arthouse movie and is possessed by Jesus or something.

The hotel we're staying in is pretty amazing. It's meant to be the best in Tulum. I can't judge that coz we've so far only been either at the hotel or the bit of beach where we shoot the pictures, but of all the places round the world where I've stayed – and thanks to my mum and dad's work I've stayed in a fair few posh places – this is the best. My room isn't the biggest in the world, but it's got everything you need. And the best thing is it's at ground level and it opens . . . STRAIGHT OUT ONTO THE BEACH. In front of my French windows a palm tree stands either side, a hammock linking the two, and then there's just a twenty-footstep walk into the sea.

AMAZE SLASH PARADISE KLAXON!

The food in the hotel is SO TASTY. And it's not even that Mexican coz the guy who owns it is Italian and so it's all pastas and pizzas for tea which I LOVE. And breakfast is all fresh fruits decorating your plate in the shape of a smiley face and stuff and they do this GORGEOUS spinachy-type juice which looks HORRENDOUS but is actually YUMMY.

We're under strict instructions not to sunbathe and if we are going to lie out we practically have to wear a sleeping bag and beekeeper's hat coz Seth wants us looking pale in the bright sunlight. Most days it's too hot for me anyway so I am more than happy to lie in my room watching programmes in Mexican. No idea what they're talking about but I'm quite addicted to some sort of fashion police programme where they show someone on a red carpet wearing something HIDEOUS and then the guys back in the studio talk ten to the dozen about it, CLEARLY hating everything they see and getting quite MURDEROUS, which is hilarious to watch when said in Mexican. Which I think is Spanish. I do Spanish at school, but this is a different type of Spanish, and I only catch about three words out of ten, because they all speak like they're on speed. Honest to God, they all say approximately eighty-three words per second.

The most HILARIOSA thing is that in the hotel lobby

there is a man with no legs who sits in white robes playing the sitar. Don't ask me why. He may also be blind. But he plays all these (trying to be) trendy choons on his sitar like 'Get Lucky' by Daft Punk. It really is BEYOND.

Aba keeps throwing coins at him and saying, 'Take it to the bridge, baby!' before closing her eyes and dancing round him like she's walking over hot coals in some spiritual ritual. Admittedly, she usually only does this in the evenings, after lots of heat and lots of after lunch piña coladas.

Actually, maybe he's not blind, coz when she does that he always looks a bit mortified and seems to look around as if saying, *I wish there was security in this hotel. This woman should be sectioned. By Arlene Frigging Phillips.*

There is one person here who really messes with my head. Like, really, does my swede in. And that's the stylist. She's called Iris and she's from Primrose Hill ('But like, the working-class bit') and she ALWAYS wears these platform trainers which have fairy lights round them. I have met girls like her at school. Poshest private school in the area, chauffeurs driving them hither and thither, nannies, trust funds, relatives called Jocasta and STILL they claim to be 'like, really working-class and stuff'? Imbeciles.

Well, that's what Iris is like.

Her hair. MAN ALIVE, her hair! She describes 'the story' of her look as 'prom queen on her way home who's stopped off to get fucked in some bushes by her boyfriend'. Which basically means it is lacquered to high heaven, almost in a beehive, but then one bit is REALLY MESSY. Once she explains 'the story of her hair', it kind of makes sense. But if you don't know, you just see loads of Mexican people and guests in the hotel giving her a double-take and thinking, WHAT THE HELL DID THIS MOFO COME AS? SHEEEZ!

Actually, I did hear one American woman whispering to her husband as Iris walked past once, 'Oh God, Bud. Is it a costume party? Let's stay in the room.'

And even I know that in Yankee-land, a costume party is a fancy dress party.

Silly bitch. (Iris, not Bud's wife.) I think she thinks she's a little like Lily Allen. I say to Nancy, 'She's more like Alan buggery Carr.' And Nancy really laughs her head off.

Iris is prone to bursting out crying every five minutes. Also, at the moment she has her 'Big P' – which is what she calls her period. And ON MY LIFE I SWEAR you would think she was the first person in the history of the world AND menstruation to ever have had a period. She keeps telling everyone. Like it's something none of us have ever heard of.

I do actually say one time, *A period? What's that?*

And she actually starts explaining. Before seeing everyone laughing.

I then realize that was a bad move. She hates me now.

She also hates that a couple of times I have called her Irish instead of Iris. That didn't go down too well. Whoops.

Oh, and another time I was saying to Aba, 'D'you reckon without those hideous trainers on she's three foot two?' only I didn't realize Iris was walking past behind me. I just saw Aba's eyes widen in horror as she took a MAHOOSIVE slurp of her piña colada.

Never piss the stylist off. She will make you look shit.

Oh, well. It's not like I wanted her to be my best friend or anything.

The other thing that really pisses me off is that she keeps saying to Seth, 'What's the journey here?'

At first I thought she was asking for directions to guide one of her mates to the hotel or the location, but no, she's asking how he wants the pictures to look.

At first I thought Seth thought the sun shone out of her arse. Aba seemed impressed that the wonderful Iris was doing this shoot, but as the days have drawn on I can see her becoming exasperated with the girl with the weird hair. And I can see Seth's eyes glazing over whenever she questions the journey of the clothes.

OK. So here's the journey. Or, in normalspeak, here's what I think Seth wants the pictures to look like:

Each model stripped bare. Almost a photograph that hasn't been properly developed. The background in sharp focus, the model fading away. With each picture she becomes more focussed, stronger or something.

I just stand where I'm told to.

Though I do make Seth laugh at breakfast one day when I go, 'What's the journey of this kumquat?' while I'm having my fruit salad.

One day we shoot in the sea. One day we shoot on the sand. One day lying round a pool. One day on a jetty, walking into the water. One day hanging upside down from a palm tree. Between photos, hair and make-up poke and prod and backcomb and do all manner of things.

One time, when I'm not hanging bat-like from a palm branch, one of the vile models sidles up to me.

'Heard about your dad.'

Her name is Angel. Devil would be more appropriate. She grunts at everyone on set and has NO manners. She once handed Aba a bottle of water before a take and went, *Hold that. Quickly.*

Which I think is totally out of order.

She's not a fucking slave, I shouted.

And everyone looked really uncomfortable because of *12 Years a Slave* and because Aba's black. But that's how Angel was treating her and it really got ON MY TITS.

Aba diffused the atmosphere by calling, *Turn the choons up, guy!* And carried on swaying to the music.

I shrug. So what if she's heard about my dad?

'Bare bad times, babe.'

I roll my eyes. She has a Brummie accent. She better learn to keep that grid shut if she wants to get on.

'D'you ever worry that . . . people will hire you because they sort of have a morbid fascination?'

I look at her.

'I just tell it how it is, babe.'

I hate it when people say that. I mean, I've been known to say it sometimes. Well. Quite a bit actually.

But when other people say it, I now realize it's really FACKING annoying.

'Sorry?' I say. Coz I'm actually flabbergasted. My flabbers are well and truly gasted.

She repeats herself. 'D'you ever worry that . . . people will hire you because, they sort of have a morbid fascination?'

So I reply, 'D'you ever worry that people won't hire you coz you're a massive cunt?' At which point Seth overhears, and calls me back up the tree.

On a couple of nights we have all piled into a stream of taxis and headed to this GORGEOUS restaurant in a different part of Tulum. It's on this narrow lane of hotels and restaurants and it serves modern Mexican cuisine. It's weird. I thought I knew all about Mexican food coz it's what my dad used to make if Mum asked him to cook. He was actually really good at it and could cook up a feast of fajitas and burritos and chillies and . . . it was all gorgeous. But this restaurant, El Paisano, is BEYOND.

For a start, it's so hot here that the restaurant is OUTSIDE.

And secondly, the food is SOME OF THE BEST I HAVE EVER TASTED IN MY ENTIRE LIFE.

And don't just take my word for it because OH MY GOD. The first night we went, REESE WITHERSPOON was in there.

And the second night, DEMI MOORE was eating there.

Exactly. BEYOND.

Admittedly I didn't see either of them. The bad thing about the restaurant place is that it is EXTREMELY dark and atmospheric and candle-y. And if you're sitting more than a table away from me, I won't be able to tell if you've keeled over dead into your soup and stuff. But everyone was saying they were there.

And it's totally feasabilidido. Because . . .You see, what I didn't know before I came to Tulum is that Mexico is really easy for Americans to get to (unlike us Brits) and so they all come here non-stop. And the other thing is, the place they have brought us to, Tulum, is a real hangout for celebs and the fashion world.

But anyway. The food. The menu hangs on two mahoosive blackboards overlooking the bar. It is chock full of stuff like stuffed jalapeño pepper, lavender prawns, seafood in almond cream.

Exactly. TOP NOSH KLAXON.

The atmosphere here is amazing. Though on the second night I notice that it's only really me, Aba and the other models who are eating. Everyone else is just knocking back the drinks at our ginormous table. The place must feed about sixty people at a time, has live music and a very long bar, which is rammed. The toilets are near the bar and I see Iris going there non-bloody-stop. Each time she comes back she is more and more enlivened and annoying. It's quite clear she's on coke. And if I, as a sixteen-year-old, can tell that, then surely everyone else can.

But then I remember my first encounter with Bimbi's husband.

A toot a day keeps the doctor away.

Maybe they're all on it. Oh God. WHAT IF THEY'RE ALL TOTAL GAK HEADS, GUY?!

After I've eaten we're all sitting round drinking wine (Aba has lifted her no booze ban now that we're abroad and I'm earning money), when Iris sidles up next to me and goes on and on and on about how we've got off on the wrong foot and she sees a lot of herself in me.

Lesbian! I joke. But she doesn't get it.

And then she takes my hand and says some more coked-up bollocks about the pain in my eyes painting an interesting landscape of distrust.

Exactly. OFF HER MONG BOX KLAXON.

And when she takes her hand away I realize she's left something in the palm of my hand. I look. It's a small rolled-up ball of cling film. And inside is some white powder.

'Go to the loo, babe,' she whispers. 'Want me to come with you?'

I freeze. But then find myself standing. And heading towards the loos next to the bar. I realize she is behind me because as well as telling me what an amazing model I am, she keeps saying hello to all the fashion bitches she knows on her way over.

There's a row of four loos to the side of the bar which look all rustic and wooden, like the doors have been made from driftwood from the beach or something. At the moment they're all in use.

When one of the loos comes free I head in and she comes in with me, shutting the door behind us. I am instantly nervous. Surely this is illegal and someone must have seen us come in together. One of the bar staff, one of the waiters. But she grabs the coke off me and flips the loo seat down and in a matter of seconds has a credit card out and is chopping out two fat lines. I stand watching, mesmerized. She then quickly uncoils a note from her pocket.

A memory hits me.

I've always tried to forget it, wipe it out. But it's here again.

I'm about ten.

Mum's at Aunty Lucy's.

Dad's in his office doing some accounts.

I decide to go and surprise him with a picture I've drawn of the club. I've drawn three people dancing and him and Mum flying above them.

But when I push the door open he is bent over his desk. He is sniffing. Has he got a cold? He stand up, throws his head back, then rubs the bridge of his nose. He bends again. And this time as he sniffs I see a white line magically disappear.

I gasp.

Magic.

He turns. He looks angry.

He comes to me. Kneels. And says, 'You must never tell anyone you saw me do this. Not even Mum.'

I nod.

I am jolted back to reality by the toilet door being burst open. The manager comes in and starts pulling me and Iris out, shouting 83 words per second in Spanish. I can see Aba running over like a bomb has gone off. Seth is following. He has some sort of urgent discussion with the manager. But as they do, we are very brusquely manhandled out of the restaurant.

The SHAME.

Everyone is looking.

Iris is screaming.

I didn't even get to do any coke.

Owen

From www.gay-mover.co.uk:

Coming Out Poster Boy Has Face Pummelled in Homophobic Attack

by Gerard Woolerton

A waiter from Manchester suffered damage to his face, teeth and arm in an assault which he claims was fuelled by homophobia. Manchester police say they are treating their investigation as a homophobic hate crime. Matthew Warburton, aged 22, from Bolton, partner of gay-mover journalist Owen Bioletti . . .

I can't read any more. I click off the website and hear the post plopping through the letter box. I hate that our personal life has become cheap tabloid fodder. That because of my actions, my man has ended up on the very pages of the website I work for. Oh the irony.

Can't live with him, can't live without him? No. Wasn't there to protect him, can't stop him appearing online. Typical.

I instinctively go to play with my chain. I've never taken it off since Mum gave it to me years ago. Whenever I'm anxious

218

I twiddle it round between my fingers till it gets too tight and constricts on my neck. It has D N O C engraved on it – each of our initials. But then I remember I've not been able to find it these last few days.

It's not worth much and I could easily get a replacement, but it's the sentimental value. Mum gave us each one. When Dad was still around. And now I can't find mine anywhere.

At first I had a panic on, as I thought I'd lost it at Dylan's. I didn't particularly relish the prospect of calling him and asking him to look for it but when I did he was so sweet and concerned about Matty I realized I didn't have to lay any 'it's over' ground rules down. He looked in his car, the bedroom, the living room, everywhere I'd been, no joy. But then he said he couldn't remember seeing it round my neck while we were . . . while we were in bed, so it sounds like I'd lost it already, before I went to his house. Not that that gives me much pleasure. The necklace is still gone.

I hear footsteps crunching the ceiling. The muffled strains of Matty on the phone, probably to his mum. Looking up at the Artex, the sounds are almost sinister. Like he's gagged and groaning for help. Then I realize he is laughing. Then he really does groan. I know it hurts him to laugh at the moment.

Good job he's living with me, then. I'm hardly a laugh a minute at the moment.

I check Cally's Instagram. Another bleach-white beach, emerald sea, diamond sun.

At least something's going right for someone in this family.

Mum's been a bit distant lately. I wonder if it's anything to do with this delivery guy she met. She's not said anything since he asked her out, but my instinct is that she's started seeing him and doesn't know how to tell me. Personally I'd be thrilled if she started seeing someone; it would be the much-hoped-for sign that she'd moved on. But maybe she's worried about broaching the subject with me in case I get upset.

Personally I wish she'd met someone else years ago. Before everything with Dad happened, frankly.

Maybe I should give her a call and see how she is and casually mention him, saying I hope it's going well.

Or maybe I should order her something online and ask for it to be delivered by his company. Except I can't remember which company he works for.

I will call.

The phone rings for ages, and then goes to voicemail. I'm not sure why but this wrong-foots me and I find myself hanging up instead of leaving a message. She always answers! I try the landline and she picks up almost immediately, but sounds groggy.

'Oh sorry, did I wake you?'

'Oh, I was just having a lie-in.'

'Oh, sorry.'

'No, it's all right. Everything OK? Bit early for you, isn't?'

'I'm sorry, I'll call back later.'

'No, I'm awake now, go on.'

'No, I was just . . . ringing for a catch-up.'

'At half-eight in the morning?'

'Well . . . I was just wondering. If you'd seen any more of that fella.'

'Which fella?'

'The delivery guy.'

'Laurence?'

'Aha.'

'No.'

'Oh.'

Well, that's answered that then.

'He thinks I'm still too obsessed with your dad.'

'And are you?'

'A little bit. And not in a good way.'

'I wish you'd move on, Mum.'

'So do I. But . . . it's not easy. Though I did decide this week that he's defo killed himself.'

'Oh, right.'

'Sorry if that's harsh.'

Actually, I feel relieved.

'No, it's . . . what's brought this on?'

'Not helped by her over the road turning all psychic on me and saying she'd got a message from him and he's living the life of Riley somewhere on a beach.'

'Imagine,' I say, with a laugh.

'And. Well. I've been debating whether to tell you this or not, but . . .'

'What?'

'I found out he was having an affair.'

Gulp. I feel as if someone has whipped the sofa out from under me and I've crashed onto the carpet.

'You what?'

'That left luggage ticket. It was collected by a woman. And it turns out she was seeing him.'

My mouth has gone dry.

'And does she know anything about . . .'

'No, the police have questioned her and they're quite confident she's as much in the dark as we are.'

'Bloody hell. How d'you feel about all that?'

'Still processing it, really. It's hard, though. Coz he's not here to have a go at.'

'Right.'

'Oh, and your nan knew.'

'Knew what?'

'About the affair.'

'Who is this woman?'

'She's called Miriam.'

'Didn't you ask me about her ages back?'

'Yeah.'

'Have you known for ages?'

'It's . . . been complicated. And I didn't want to bother you till I knew everything.'

'Suppose.'

'And now I know everything. It feels like I know even less than I ever did before.'

'Sure.'

It just feels so weird. The main thing I've been trying to protect my mum from all these years, she now has an inkling of.

'D'you wanna meet for a coffee?' I suggest.

'I'm meant to be seeing Lucy. Why don't you join us?'

Because I've been knocking off her husband.

'Er, no. I best get on with my work anyway, really.'

'How's Matty today? Sorry, I should've . . .'

'He's getting there.'

I hear the post arriving. I head out to the hall. Pick it up.

'Oh well, give him my love. Have you heard from Cally?'

The top envelope makes my blood freeze. Nan's handwriting.

'Mum, I've had a card from Nan.'

'Chuck it in the bin. Don't read it. She sent me one the other day.'

'Yeah, you're right.'

But I don't.

'Mum, I better go. Give my love to Lucy.'

You hypocrite, Owen.

We say goodbye. I head to the kitchen and top up my coffee from the cafetière.

The card, when I read it, is straight to the point. And although she doesn't sign it, I know it's from her.

I know you killed my Danny. Oh yes. Mickey Joe Hart says you had a gun in your house. We all knew you had a motive. And if your mum can't see that she is one stupid bitch. He was the brightest light in my world and you have snuffed him out. Is it any wonder I drink? The shame. Oh yes. Your father never liked you never took to you and I'm the same. Maybe its because he realized you were MURDERING BASTARD SCUM. Oh yes. I hope no one kills you one dark night when your out getting fucked in the arse. DIE. SOON.

My hand's shaking.

Mickey Joe Hart. No idea who that is.

'Anything interesting in the post?' goes Matty as he comes through eating Coco Pops from a bowl. I slide Nan's card between a pizza delivery card and a locksmith's flyer. I didn't even hear him coming down the stairs.

'Oh, nothing. Just freebie crap. I'm tempted to get one of those signs. No junk mail, or whatever they say. Those poor rainforests.'

And I take the mail to the bin in the kitchen and get rid of the flyers. And fold the card and slip it into my back pocket. I can't risk Matty finding it. Even though it's highly unlikely he might upend the bin and go through its contents today, I still can't take that chance.

'Who were you on the phone to?' Matty follows me into the kitchen.

'Mum. You?'

'Jen. She's pregnant.'

'Oh, that's wonderful. Mother Hen really will be a mother finally.'

Matty beams. 'She's already said she wants me to be god-father.'

'Well, she's got great taste.'

'And she's not even religious.'

'I know. Fancy.'

I head back to the lounge. I don't want him looking at me. I feel I'm shaking so much I must look epileptic.

'Are you OK, bubs? You look really pale,' he says, following me again.

'Yeah, I just . . . didn't sleep very well.'

Plus this card is burning a hole in my back pocket.

'Aww, was I snoring?'

'A bit.'

'Sorry.'

I check in the mirror above the fireplace. And he's right. I really do look like I've seen a ghost.

Or maybe I've been picturing one.

'What you doing today? Oh, you're working from home, aren't you?'

'Actually . . . I need to nip out for a bit. Just a few things I've got to check with Minty.'

'Why don't you just call her?'

'I need to give her some books back she lent me. Drive'll do me good, got a few articles I need to think about.'

'Bubs?'

'Aha?'

'I've been thinking. My arm's a lot better now. And I'm feeling so useless round here.'

'Aha?'

If he's going to suggest going back to work he's got another thing coming. There's no way Jen will let him serve the paying public with a swollen lip and a black eye.

'I think I might put some of this stuff in the loft.'

I freeze.

'Owen. I don't know why you're scared of going in lofts. And I know you won't seek help about it. But I'm not scared. And I'm sick of all this shit lying around everywhere . . .'

'I keep it tidy!'

'In piles . . . and if I can just put a lot of it up in the loft. Well. Think of how much more space we'll have.'

'Not that much more.'

'I'm bored, Owen.'

'Then read a fucking book!'

'It's not normal, Owen!'

'Oh, do what you fucking like!'

I storm out. I slam the door. I rush down the path and practically hurl myself into my car. I know better than to drive when I'm so angry. And I know better than to shout at Matty when he's not in the wrong. I am.

It's just. When I think of the loft. I think of that loft. And what was up there. And what I had to bury. I feel the familiar sensations of a panic attack. Heat rising through me like a geyser. Sweaty palms, shortness of breath. I want to get out of the car and run.

I ran that night. I ran in the pouring rain. I ran so fast I skidded, my trainers unable to grip on the paving stones. That was the first time I had a panic attack.

When I found what I found, I panicked. And ran. I ran all the way to where they were building the Oaktree Estate, scaled a perimeter fence, and went in.

I start the car up. I head for the Oaktree. The place where my mum now lives. How weird is that? The place of my worst nightmares. Now the respectable housing estate.

But back then. What was it? A shallow grave?

We call it the estate; the residents like to call it a gated community. When I watch *Question Time* they always talk of the country's housing crisis. Sometimes it feels like the only place built in the last ten years was Oaktree. And it shows. It still looks shiny as a new pin, like it's had a fresh fall of rain, but the dry ground betrays this illusion. I drive around the edges of the estate, trying to work out where I was that night. I stop where I think it was. It's the entrance to a street, not unlike my mum's. But really it could be anywhere in this maze of branch-like roads and houses. I sit in the car and stare.

A knock at the window. I jump out of my skin.

I half expect it to be a ghost.

WELCOME BACK, OWEN!

But instead I see a bespectacled woman smiling down on me.

I wind the window down. The woman speaks.

'Owen? I'm a friend of your mother's. Betty Caligary. We met briefly at that dreadful housewarming. What are you doing round these parts?'

Do people use that phrase? Round these parts? *Really?*

She clearly sees me hesitate. 'Are you lost? Do you want your mum?'

What am I, nine?

'No, I . . . was just finishing off a phone call. Pulled over.'

'Oh. Modern technology.' I see her eyes dart about the car, looking for the non-existent phone. I left in such a rush, I didn't pick it up.

Suddenly her nosiness angers me.

'Are you the psychic one, Betty?'

'Aye. I have been known to . . . have the gift. When Margaret Frayn's pussy went missing, let's just say. I was very hands-on in getting her back. She spoke to me.'

'The cat?'

'Yes.'

'Cats can't speak, Betty.'

'They can send messages. All animals can. And she showed me a mural of the Manchester tram system. There's only one person round here with that on their splashbacks.'

'You're talking bollocks, Betty.'

'I took them straight to Enid Duncan's. She was away for the fortnight. Silly woman had gone and left her cat flap switched to 'in only'. Poor pussy was trapped inside.'

'Listen to me, Betty, and listen good.'

Oh dear, I was starting to sound like I was in *West Side Story*.

'My dad is not lying on some beach in the heat, and you know it. Stop filling me mam's head with shite. Do I make myself clear?'

'Sorry?'

I don't answer. I switch the ignition on, zap the window up and pull off. I don't even look to see her face. Charlatans, liars, fraudsters – the world is full of them, and they circle like flies round dung when someone goes missing.

I know what I have to do. I know the way to go. I drive

away from the estate, straight to my nan's house. The street's full. The problem with these tiny little terraced cottages is that people now have cars, big cars, and you only have to put three Land Rovers on her street and the place is packed. I zoom round to a parallel street and park up there. My back wheel's on a double yellow, but as my anger hasn't abated, I don't particularly care.

I lift my arse off the seat and slip the card out of my back pocket. I unfold it and read it again.

This time it doesn't make me angry. It makes me scared. What if she goes round saying this to people? Telling them I had a gun in my house. Any fool can see these are the ramblings of a madwoman when they're written down like this, but a word in the wrong ear . . . maybe she'll be taken seriously. And aren't grandmothers supposed to know their grandkids inside out? Love them? Always see the good in them?

I've never told Mum the truth about what happened when Dad went missing. What I did. What I hid. But maybe I should tell Nan to keep her mouth shut. If she was pissed when she wrote this bile, maybe she'll be hung over today. Maybe she'll listen.

I get out of the car and walk round. As I approach her cottage the sun is high in the sky and dazzling all the windows. But I hear the telly is on. She always has it so loud. So she must be in. I decide the friendliest approach is best, as if nothing is wrong.

I lean in to the window, cupping my hand above my eyes, readying to tap on the glass and call, 'Only me!'

But I don't tap.

I freeze.

I don't see Nan sat on the settee watching daytime telly.

I see a man.

He looks a bit different. The years haven't been kind to him. His hair's all long and straggly like never before. He doesn't see me. I stare. It's definitely him.

It's my dad.

PART TWO

Danny, 2014

I need to explain, to myself more than anyone else, why I did what I did. I might go off at tangents sometimes but that's the way my mind works. I've never been good at writing stuff down so I've always kept stuff in my head all these years, a jumble of information. But the problem is, as you get older, the more and more stuff you wanna keep in there. And there's just not the room. So where does it all go?

My life feels like a mass of memories. Some brief and fleeting. Others lingering longer. They're all bubbling around. Some crystal-clear. Others tired and jaded, coz I don't remember so good, or I've remembered them too much and worn them out.

But they're there, somewhere.

And if I can string these memories together I might get a sense of why I did these mad things. Coz sometimes I get so wrapped up in the here and now that I can't remember why I had to make the change.

And it was a pretty big fucking change all right.

And why I'm about to make the even bigger change. The final change.

Danny: The Eighties

Class

I was born and bred in St Helens, it's an industrial town in the North West, keep up. Equidistant between Liverpool and Manchester, it's like their bastard child. And the accent, a mish-mash of the two, is hardly poetry in motion so, you know, forgive me and all that.

Manchester people are all right about folk from St Helens. But Scousers, folk from Liverpool, they call us 'woolly backs'. I've no idea why this is; someone at school said it was coz in the olden days everyone in St Helens wore sheepskin coats and they saw us all as sheepshaggers, but I don't know.

What I do know is the Scousers had a song about us (to the tune of 'Tavern in the Town'. I thank you):

There's a woolly over there, over there
Baggy kecks and feathered hair, feathered hair
With a three-star jumper halfway up his back
There's a woolly over there. Woolly back.

The biggest employer when I was growing up was the local double glazing factory, St Helens Glass. Whenever the advert came on the radio or the telly we would stop whatever we were doing and join in with the jingle.

'St Helens Glass . . . BOOM BOOM . . . has the class!'

The BOOM BOOM bits were like big bass drum beats, and I used to whack whatever was nearest in time with them. We liked that song. We liked that glass. It was the reason there was food on the table.

Sometimes my dad would do a stupid voice and sing it posh, so it went 'St Helens Glarse . . . BOOM BOOM . . . has the clarse!' and then he'd add out the corner of his mouth, just for my benefit, 'Stick it up yer arse.' Which could reduce me to hysterics. It's the one of the few times I remember him having a sense of humour, actually.

But that makes it sound like we were an all-singing, all-dancing happy-go-lucky family that smiled a lot and had a soundtrack to our lives.

We weren't.

We lived in a tiny two-up, two-down terraced house on a street called Perseverance Street. Me, my mum, my dad, and my gerbil called Pig.

I did think I was very clever and very funny to call my gerbil Pig.

My dad was from Italian stock but had a Birmingham accent you could break your teeth on. If that sounds contradictory, don't worry, he was a stereotypical bloke in other ways. Friday night was boozer night. And whether Mammy liked it or not, and of course she didn't, he'd come home after and knock ten bells out of her.

Ah, the stereotypical working class of yesteryear. Don't you just love 'em?

He must've loved her at some point, the Brummie bastard, but evidence was pretty thin on the ground by the time I was out of Pampers. She'd come over from Ireland when she was seventeen and met him in a bar, and they were married within the month.

'Worst mistake of my life,' she'd always say.

'You wanna try looking at it from where I'm standing,' he'd always snap back, like it was banter, but the menace was constantly there.

Although her name was Barbara and I called her Mum, he always referred to her as 'Mammy', as though because she was Irish that's what she should be called. Again, there was an element of threat in his use of the name, like it was ironic, like he didn't think much of her as a mother. Maybe she wasn't brilliant. She was useless round the house, the place was a shithole, and her idea of cooking was sticking a tin of soup in the oven and switching on. But looking back it's coz she was Mogadonned up to the eyeballs, probably as a result of having to live with him. She could spend countless hours staring at the wallpaper or looking out the window, her eyes glassy, like there were tears there but they were frozen and couldn't come. She'd had a job at the glass factory before I was born, but she'd given it up when she found out she was pregnant with twins. My twin brother died when we were born. And I just knew that my dad thought the one that went to heaven would have been a better son than I was making out to be.

He rarely called me by my name either. I was always 'the lad'. 'The lad's a Mammy's boy,' he'd always say, even though I wasn't. It's just I preferred her company to his. There wasn't much competition. I knew where I stood with her; he was more unpredictable, and even though he'd never hit me, you never knew when that sort of stuff might start. So best to avoid in the first place.

Oh yeah, there was my method in my madness back then, all right. Or so I thought.

Some of the kids at school called me Bio. Or Eye-Tie (that was my nickname, short for Italian). But most of them called me 'the nip'. On account of the fact that with my jet-black hair I also had eyes that they reckoned made me look Japanese or Chinese or something.

Here he comes, the nip.

Hey. Nippy. Fuck off.

Or they'd slant their eyes with their hands and go, *Sweet and sour prawn balls please.*

It was quite frustrating, really.

My happiest time back then was lying on the living room floor looking up at the Artexed ceiling, radio going full pelt. For no-one in particular I used to mimic all the voices on it. Sometimes Mum would hear me and laugh. Other times Dad'd hear me and go, 'The lad's a basket case.'

'Yeah, but he's good though,' Mum'd counter.

And both of them agreed, I'd give Mike Yarwood a run for his money.

I learned a lot listening to that wireless. I remember hearing the word Nefertiti for the first time and thinking it was the most amazing word in the English language. Not realizing, like, that it wasn't actually English. I didn't really know what it meant. But just lying there. And saying it.

Nefertiti.

That could make me happy, too. And I could say it like a proper posh person!

There was one night when I was about ten when my mum sent me the pub to get my dad and bring him home. I forget the reason why. My dad was quite far gone by the time I got there, and in one of those moods where the drink turns you happy and back-slappy. And he started telling the barmaid, and then the other punters, about all the impressions I could do. Except I didn't really do anyone famous, I just did the people I heard on the radio, the DJs, the adverts, stuff like that. For some reason I preferred the radio to the telly. Probably coz I could just lie there staring at the ceiling and the radio was like a voice in my head. Anyway, he made me do all these different voices for people and I noticed as I was doing it he was passing round his empty pint pot and folk were sticking coins in it. And coz he was being so friendly and warm and chuckly, I carried on till the glass was half full. Then he bought himself a pint of bitter and told me to run home and tell the Mammy he'd be ten minutes.

Oh yeah. I remember now. The Mammy was boiling a ham. And she'd had her hair 'done nice'. It was their wedding anniversary.

He rolled in at midnight.

The skill

Another skill I had from an early age was to be able to walk into a room, or any sort of space, and assess everyone in it quickly. Mum said it was because her aunty was a psychic but I don't believe in all that. She also said my eyes never stopped moving – well, that much was true. But say she sent me to get my dad from the boozer: I could walk into the Feathers and within seconds, work out who was having a pleasant evening and who was about to kick off. Call it instinct or whatever, I've always been able to read a room like that. I could even tell which members of the bar staff were likely to have their hand in the till and who was likely to be knocking off the landlord. When she wasn't blaming her distant relatives, Mum also said it was probably because I'd had to get used to reading Dad's varying moods.

'The only thing predictable about that bastard is his un-predictability,' she'd say.

Virgin. Whore

When my mum was a little girl she'd played the Virgin Mary in the church nativity play. It was her proudest moment and her eyes lit up whenever she talked about it. They'd had a real-life donkey and she'd had to ride down the aisle on its back while she and the bloke playing Joseph sang, 'How far is it to Bethlehem?', which was hard to imagine as Mum was a bit tone-deaf. And that's putting it kindly.

Like, she always based her look on Dusty Springfield. The peroxide, the panda eyes. Dad loved telling the story of her going to a party and people thinking she was Dusty and Mum going along with it. Anyway, they asked her to sing a song, so she started singing 'Son of a Preacher Man', only she was so shit someone threw a trifle at her and she had to get off.

One day Dad said we were going to Manchester. In the car. We never went anywhere in the car, it just used to sit outside the house, always clean but usually redundant, so this felt like a Special Occasion. Mum was away at the time, she'd gone to Lincoln to see a cousin who'd not long given birth. I wasn't particularly relishing the prospect of an evening in the company of my father; who bloody would? But the decision to go for a run out to Manchester was better than stopping in. I'd been 13 the week before and they'd bought me a BMX bike. I'd done nothing since – when I wasn't in school – but ride around on it, thinking I looked like the coolest thing in Christendom. Driving down the motorway, I wondered what it'd be like to ride my bike down the hard shoulder. I reckoned I'd be able to do St Helens to Manchester in half an hour tops.

'What we gonna do in Manchester?' I asked my dad as he drove.

He thought for a while then went, 'Probably go for something to eat.'

Eating. I liked the sound of that. And maybe we'd go to a restaurant rather than a pub as Dad was driving. At least I knew he wouldn't get bladdered and therefore handy with his fists. And maybe we'd have prawn cocktail. I'd been to a restaurant for one of Dad's brother's birthdays once and we'd had that as a starter and it was like heaven on a plate. Prawn cocktail, and maybe I'd be allowed a glass of Mateus Rosé. You never knew.

After parking in a multistorey above the coach station we went to a hotel on Piccadilly Gardens called the Britannia. Inside was all chandeliers and thick carpets, and Dad insisted we sat in the foyer and had afternoon tea.

Four receptionists. Three in their twenties. One about fifty. All women. The fifty one had too much make-up. The twenty one fancied the bellboy guy who was hanging round dying to take your bags to your rooms, tip-hungry bastard. Small queue checking in. Checked shorts. White socks with sandals. Loud. Yanks. Of course. Couples having afternoon tea. Airs and graces. Fur coat and no knickers, the lot of them. Lipstick-stained teeth. False teeth, no less. A wonky wig.

Please believe me when I say neither me nor my dad had ever had afternoon tea in our lives before. And I think it showed. I'm sat there in my Sergio Tacchini trackie top. He's in a puffa jacket. We must've looked like we were casing the joint rather than having cake and butties. In fact, I can't honestly say, hand on heart, that I'd ever been in a hotel before. Our family never went to hotels. We hardly ever went on holiday. The idea of Mum and Dad trapped in a caravan on the North Wales coast for two weeks was all of our ideas of hell. Best avoided, if you ask me.

The tea was hot and sweet. It came with a tiered tray of cakes and butties that had the crusts cut off.

'I'm gonna eat the cake *then* the butties,' I told Dad. Pure mental!

But he wasn't looking at me. He was staring at the door.

Some of the butties had cucumber in, nowt else. Which back then I thought was a major swizz and – not that I was paranoid or anything – wondered if the waiter had done on purpose coz he thought we didn't deserve to be here.

Well, we were paying our money, weren't we? And my dad always said, *Money opens doors.*

Open Sesame! Abracadabra!

Not that money opened these hotel doors. You just had to walk up to them and *swish*! They opened magically.

After cramming these tiny cakes into my gob and then shovelling in the cucumber sandwich, the cucumber was sticking to the roof of my mouth. I was just trying to dislodge it with a hot blast of tea when I saw my dad was smiling. Not at me. And not in a nice way. I looked to where he was looking.

A woman with her hair done was at the reception desk. Big blonde backcombed hair. The panda eyes. Someone who hadn't really changed their look from the Sixties.

That woman was my mum.

It looked like she was checking in.

I felt a surge of excitement. Was this all an elaborate surprise? A wind-up? Were we actually all going to stay at the hotel, like a holiday for the night or something? I could probably cope with that. If I got my own room. And I could have as many baths as I like and watch whatever telly I wanted to watch and order stuff from room service, money no object. They might even have a radio.

The money no object thing was a bit far-fetched.

And when I looked to the floor to the right of where Mum was standing, I saw she only had a small vanity case. She'd never have fitted three people's stuff into that, even if it was for one night. I looked to my dad, about to ask him what was going on.

The smile had gone from his face and he had a look of rage now instead.

The next bit happened in slow motion.

Or maybe that's just how I remember it.

Mum turns from reception desk.

Mum has key in hand.

Mum walks towards lift.

To do this she has to walk past us.

She doesn't see us.

As she passes us I go, 'Mum!'

And as she turns to look Dad jumps up and grabs her.

She looks shit scared.

As he pulls her this way and that, shouting his head off, her case falls open.

A negligee and sexy knickers and bra fall out onto the carpet.

Mum's in tears.

Dad's shouting, You fucking whore.

The receptionist's running over. And the bellboy.

Dyslexic

Looks like I couldn't read everyone as well as I thought. I'd not read the fact that Mum had been having an affair with some bloke from the glass factory for the past few months. Not that I blamed her, even then. You've got to take your pleasures where you can. And she was married to that Brummie Bastard. No pleasure there.

R.I.P. Pig

The morning after the hotel incident, I discovered that Dad had killed the gerbil. He had forced him into a milk bottle, so he'd probably crushed him to death then. But just to make sure, Dad had covered the top of the bottle with tin foil so he could suffocate to death too. This was probably because I'd called him a cunt after what he did to Mum. He left me and her in Manchester and we had to make our own way back to St Helens on the train. Mum cried the whole way.

She didn't want to stay at our house that night so we stopped with some mate of hers who she used to work with. When we eventually returned home the next morning we found good news and bad news.

The bad news was that Pig was dead.

The good news was that Dad had left for good.

I gave Pig a burial at sea. I flushed him down the lav. But it got blocked, and Mum had to call a plumber out.

Friendly with the plumber

Mum was quite drunk by the time the plumber came. And it was Ronnie Wolfe from Inkerman Street, round the back of us. Ronnie was the go-to guy if anything went wrong in anyone's house. All the women fussed over him coz his lovely wife had not long passed away and he'd been left to bring up his son Declan on his own. Declan was a lot older than me and everyone said he was highly strung. I didn't know what highly strung meant but it made me think of Mam's Wimbledon and the tennis racquets. He was a nervous boy, I knew that much, and even though he must have been sixteen, he had got all anxious since his mum died and didn't like to be on his own or away from his dad. So when Ronnie came to sort the toilet out, Declan came too. Mum made us sit in the front parlour and drink milk. I didn't really have much of a stomach for milk as it reminded me of Pig squeezed in the bottle, so I gave mine to Declan. He didn't even say thank you. In fact, he didn't really say much. He just sat there, all gangly and awkward in school trousers that were too short for his long legs – his socks didn't match – and neither of us knew what to say. After a while I said,

'Is your mam dead?'

He nodded. 'Yeah. She died of the cancers.'

I nodded. 'My gerbil's dead.'

And he nodded, but showed me no sympathy.

Mind you, I'd not shown him any. But I'd thought it might bond us. It hadn't. Looking back, I'm not surprised.

Bored, and unable to hear any noises from upstairs and the bathroom, I went up to investigate.

I pushed the door open and something didn't look right. Ronnie wasn't doing anything with the toilet. He was sat on the side of the bath. Mum was kneeling in front of him and her head was in his lap.

'Is the bog mended?' I asked. Mum fell back and was sprawled on the floor, shocked at the sound of my voice. Ronnie was doing his flies up.

'Nearly,' he said.

Later, Mum said he was upset about his wife and she'd been giving him a cuddle. To make him feel better.

'What was Declan like?' she asked, changing the subject.

'He had odd socks on,' I said.

And she nodded. Like that was to be expected when your mum had died.

244

On ice

After Dad left, Mum started drinking quite heavily. She had a massive jug in the kitchen and she would make what she called her Long Island Iced Tea. She had met a Yank once before she met my dad and he had made it for her, God only knows why. She could never remember what you were meant to put in it so she just put what she could afford, and as much of it as possible, into the jug. In would go vodka, gin, Tia Maria, Blue Bols, peach schnapps, lager, and then a big bottle of Coke and a few cubes of ice. She'd mix it all up and then be blotto for the rest of the day. She would have three jugs a day and then sleep from teatime onwards. I'd hear her getting up in the night and having a ciggie. Then I'd hear the unscrewing of a tablet jar. Then she'd go back to sleep. Next day, new jugs. Oblivion.

Was she missing my dad? Was she missing Ireland? Was she missing my brother and what might have been if both twins had remained? Who knew? Maybe even she didn't. Or maybe it was that she didn't want to think. And the iced tea helped that.

I certainly often used to wonder how my life would be different if my twinny had survived. I'd've had a best mate to share everything with. The other half of me who'd understand. I'd've had safety in numbers from the mad ways of the world, and power in numbers in the face of Mum's withdrawal. Well, all the power and safety you can muster from being two instead of one. But it would've been company. Someone to make me laugh, cheer me up, piss me off, get on my tits.

Maybe fate had done this for a reason, though. Maybe I was just best on my own. It certainly felt that way.

It was during this period that I stopped going to school.

I stopped a lot, actually: washing, changing my clothes that much, speaking. What I really stopped was caring. And what I learned to do, pretty succinctly, was disappear. Blend in. Become invisible. I'd always been slightly built for my age, so the sight of me wandering round central St Helens during the day when I should have been at school should have caused a certain amount of alarm to the education officers who'd roam the town looking for truants, or saggers as we called them then. But somehow I managed to hide from them, even in plain sight. I developed the new skill of camouflaging myself to my surroundings. I started to feel invincible, like no-one could touch me.

I now know this is a very dangerous feeling to have.

I was often hungry back then. Mum rarely put food on the table as all her money went on her 'tea'. So I hung round the back of the baker's at closing time and waited for them to chuck out the empty stock into the big bins. Sometimes I'd take a plastic bag so I could stock up for twenty-four hours.

Other times, I threw caution to the wind and just nicked food from various shops. It was easy enough to do. After all, I'd made myself more or less invisible.

It was an odd feeling during that time. Like everything had stopped. Like I couldn't see anything ahead of me. Like nothing was changing, whereas everything had. My dad had buggered off. My mum had retreated behind a wall of glass. And I had made the streets my friend. But it felt like I was treading water, not knowing what was going to happen next.

My life was like Mum's Long Island Iced Tea. On ice.

Assessment

It wasn't uncommon for me to go home of a night and find Mum face down on the floor, having taken a tumble in her pissed-up state. But this night was different. There was a small pool of blood beside her head, so I called an ambulance.

I remember sitting there watching her, waiting for it to come. And realizing I didn't really care if she lived or died. That sounds so bad, I know, but that's honestly how I felt. Says a lot, really.

I remember lying to the ambulance man and the doctors when we got to the hospital and they said she'd have to stay in that yes, I did have my dad at home, and that I'd be fine.

But I didn't have any money on me and I had to walk home, which was a bit of a pisser as it was pouring with rain.

The next day I nicked a sausage roll from the baker's and got caught and they called the police. And when the police took me in and I had to eventually admit that there was no-one to come and get me, that's how I ended up in the assessment centre.

I still, to this day, don't know what an assessment centre's meant to do. While I was there I have no recollection of being assessed for anything. It just seemed to be the dumping ground where they sent problem lads, or orphans, or lads who'd been taken off their parents, or lads who'd run away from home, or lads who'd never lived anywhere else. Some people referred to it as a Boy's Home, or a Children's Home. Not quite a borstal – we weren't locked up – most people just called it by its name, Hansbury Vale.

Hansbury Vale was this big mausoleum of a country house sitting in acre upon acre of hilly parkland. In the grounds new buildings had sprung up as classrooms: Portakabins, prefabs, caravans. Privately run – but answering to the local council, I imagine – Hansbury Vale liked to describe itself as a community. Running that community was eccentric owner Hugh Arthur. Or as we called him, Huge Arthur, coz he really was

HUGE. A mountain of a man, he'd bought the estate in the sixties and slowly built and built over the years, charging the local authorities a fortune to keep us in his care. I later found out he had no qualifications to do this, and you didn't need them, and at first glance if he was in the business of caring, then he definitely cared for the lads in the Community.

For most of us, arriving at Hansbury Vale was like landing on another planet. The green fields and smell of manure from neighbouring farms were as alien to us as the red rocks of Mars. The big house was divided into four houses, one of which we all belonged to – I was in Crosby House – and the regime seemed to be strict on discipline in the day, when you worked hard to earn points for your team, but pretty lax in the evenings.

If Huge Arthur was coining it in by squeezing as many lads as possible into the big house, then he was also spending a fortune on treats for the lads. Especially if you were one of his favourites. Bikes, stereos, clothes – you name it, mate. Money seemed no object with some of the gifts, and believe you me, they were lapped up gratefully.

Guinness

My best mate at the home was a lad they called Guinness. Why? Not very politically correct and you'd be slaughtered for it today, but when he arrived he was this mixed-race lad with bleached hair, so they said he looked like a pint of it. He didn't seem to mind his nickname; from the look of him, he was probably relieved that they didn't think of something more derogatory. My instinct told me he was different. Bright, sharp as a tack, and a keeper of secrets. He'd been sent to Hansbury coz he'd set fire to his school. At first this made him a bit of a hero, but his propensity to enjoy his own company and keep himself to himself meant that people soon lost interest in him. Guinness later told me he only started hanging out with me coz he thought I was half Chinese and therefore he thought we'd have our dual heritage thing in common.

Jeez.

One person who took a great deal of interest in Guinness was Huge. And when he did, it all suddenly clicked into place. With his big green eyes and his coffee skin, already surprisingly muscular for a thirteen-year-old lad, Huge couldn't stop looking at him. I now knew Huge's game. And lo and behold, Guinness started getting gifts from him.

In any other school, Guinness's fey demeanour and girly walk would have earned him catcalls of *fruit*, or *queer*, or *poofter*. Not so here. The words were occasionally spat when there were no adults about, and I found this odd, but gradually kind of got my head round it.

Guinness's real name was Sam Korniskey. He didn't talk about his family much, but I learned slowly that his mum had died when he was little and his dad had been a bit too handy with his fists for Guinness's liking. Reading between the lines, his dad wanted Sam to stand up and be more of a man, but Sam didn't see the point in toeing the line. He'd had a run-in with one of his teachers at school, and he'd been kicked out. Bored, he'd sought revenge by going back and torching the place. Fair dos, like. The one person he did talk about with some frequency was his big sister Linda. It was Our Linda this, Our Linda that. Our Linda was a hairdresser and she'd moved to London when Sam was a toddler. She was the one who'd done all right for herself and escaped their dad's tyrannical reign. He was adamant that one day he'd move to London and Our Linda would look after him, and everything would finally be all right in the world.

Huh – little did he know. But that's another story.

I'd never hung out with anyone like Guinness before and I'm not sure why I was so drawn to him. Part of me wanted to protect him, probably, as he was more like a girl than the other lads; but his banter was good, once you'd gained his trust. His sharp tongue and skewed view of all the people in there made me laugh. But sometimes I worried about how compliant he could be for the grown-ups. Even though he'd been sent here for challenging and upsetting authority, once in here, if they said *jump*, he said *how high, and how camp? And can I wear a tutu while I do it?*

How I won Guinness's trust

The Falklands War had been rumbling on for a couple of months, and it held no interest to me whatsoever. The notion of 'abroad' was something I couldn't get my head round. I could just about get France and Spain and stuff, as they were so close to home, but a set of islands so far away? Not arsed, mate, sorry. And as for seeing endless shots of Maggie Thatcher riding around in a tank and waving and wearing a headscarf and goggles, kicking the arse out of Up the British. No thanks.

Huge, on the other hand, saw it as a great excuse to hang posters of the Iron Lady everywhere and have us all singing the national anthem in assembly each morning and flying Union Jack flags from every building, even the Portakabins. Lots of the lads got into the jingoistic spirit, but it all got a bit National Front for my liking. Many's the time Guinness got a smack in the face coz he looked Argentinian – he looked nothing of the sort of course, he just didn't look like those knobs.

'Are you from the junta?' they'd say. 'Are you a massive

junta?' – admittedly I quite liked that one. 'Is your mam on the *Belgrano*?'

When word got back to Huge that this was kicking off with Guinness, he had a word with us all in assembly. I'll never forget it. Even though I was only a kid, I knew what he was saying was bang out of order. Not the first bit, mind, the last bit.

'And we'll have no more bullying of Samuel Korniskey, thank you. He does not look Argentinian and is not Argentinian. He is half-caste. That dusky mix of black and white that, despite what a lot think, some people find very appealing in a person. Many half-caste ladies have gone on to win beauty pageants, for example. So think on.' He seemed to be getting a bit carried away now. 'No, if you want to know what Argentinian people look like, they're more along the lines of Gurprit Singh here,' and he pointed to an Asian lad on the front row, and everyone turned to stare. Gurprit was a fat lump who never joined in with anything. With all eyes on him, Gurprit looked like he was shitting himself. And well he might. I knew his life was going to be hell from then on in, poor sod.

To give Guinness a treat for having been picked on, Huge said he could have a night in the caravan. The caravan was a tiny thing with two small beds underneath some trees, and it was usually set aside for the older lads as a treat if they were doing well in their studies. Basically, and God knows why it was a treat, but it was, two lads at a time were allowed to go and sleep there for the night, like they were on holiday. There was a record player to play records (though only a Rod Stewart LP and one by the Wurzels; hardly *Pick of the Pops*) and fizzy pop and crisps. etc. But the most exciting thing was, there was a portable telly. Guinness was allowed to pick one other lad to share the caravan with him, and he chose me. There was a flinch from Huge, and a dart of the eyes that told me he was disappointed in Guinness's choice. Immediately I was suspicious.

We had a pleasant enough evening in the caravan watching *Knight Rider* on the telly. Looking back, it was a bit shit, as the screen was so tiny and the black and white contrast not great – but at the time we lapped it up, even though Guinness admitted that usually he had no time for the talking car. Later on in the evening there was a knock at the door, and Huge called through, 'Are you decent?'

And we were, so we told him to come in.

He had a tin tray with a picture of Prince Charles and Lady Di on it. And sat on the tray were two mugs of hot milk which, he said, would help us sleep. He kept going on about how we should be changing into our pyjamas soon and be getting comfortable. He wanted to know who was going to have which bed, so we told him. After a bit he left. It was then I noticed that there were no curtains on any of the windows. I didn't say anything to Guinness about it, but I did suggest that maybe it'd be warmer if we slept in our normal clothes.

I took one sip of the hot milk, and realized it was off.

'Don't drink it,' I told Guinness. 'There's something wrong with it.'

I took both mugs and poured them down the little sink.

When we were knackered we got into bed, but not before I suggested we swapped beds coz I'd decided I didn't like sleeping on the left side of the caravan. Guinness wasn't arsed. See? Compliant.

Lights off, and soon I could hear the gentle snoring that told me my mate was spark out.

I woke about an hour later to the noise of someone trying to come in through the door. I'd locked it, so that was pointless. Guinness didn't stir. A moment later I heard someone trying to climb through the window next to my bed. I jumped up and as he tried to get through I instinctively lashed out and punched him one in the face. Whoever it was fell back, and Guinness woke up. He put the light on and went outside and, of course, found Huge lying there clasping his face.

'I was checking you were OK!' he cried. *Of course you flaming were*, I was thinking.

Guinness pretended to be bothered, I pretended to be apologetic. Huge pretended to be professional.

The next day Huge had a black eye in assembly. Served him bloody right.

Guinness and me never spoke about that night again. But I'm pretty sure he understood what had happened.

It was that night I decided I had to get the hell out of there.

Swatting flies

Folk often said later in life, God, wasn't it scary living in that place, with all that went on? But when you don't know any different, you just get used to it. I was lucky on the whole. Coz I was a bit gobby and handy with my fists, or coz I could blend into the background when required, I was, for the most part, left alone. But if there ever was any hassle, it was irritating more than scary, and you just got used to it. A bit like being in the country and there's loads of shit about. You just get used to swatting flies.

Running away

I'd made the odd phone call to Mum while I'd been at Hansbury, but she rarely made contact with me; it wasn't really encouraged. One thing Huge was into was putting on shows and recitals. This year he was putting on a no-holds-barred production of a thing called *Her Benny*. It was a bit like *Oliver Twist*, he said, but set in the North West. Guinness was cast as Benny's sister, Nelly the match girl, and I was a street urchin (no lines, not arsed). It was a story about poverty-stricken street kids in Liverpool in the 1800s who found redemption in hard work and Jesus. On the instructions of Huge, those of us who still had contact with our families wrote letters inviting them. To this day, I remember the wording he made us use.

> Dear Mother
>   On the evenings of Thursday 19th – Saturday 21st August I shall be playing the part of Street Urchin in Mr Arthur's new production of Her Benny: A Victorian Tragedy. It would please me greatly if you could attend. Please contact the Community office to arrange your tickets.
>   Your loving son,
>   Danny.

I remember thinking as I handed it in, there's no way she'll come, she'll think I've been brainwashed. And the description hardly bigs the thing up.

I really wanted to add:

> P.S. I haven't got any lines despite being the best at accents in the whole place. But Mr Arthur says I blend in too much.

Huge had actually said that. I told him I'd be good playing the posh judge fella in the play. I even did the posh accent for him.

'I can't fault your dialect, Eye-Tie,' he said, 'but for me, you're not a front-of-stage type person. You blend in too much.'

'To what, Sir?'

'The scenery.'

I just assumed it was payback for me blacking his eye that time.

Needless to say, she didn't come.

Life at Hansbury changed considerably in the weeks following the production of *Her Benny*. The local remand centre, Risley, had become overcrowded and so to make some more money, prisoners were housed at Hansbury for a short while. It was never really going to work. Some of us had to be moved out of the main hall and into some new prefabs because the prisoners needed to be locked in of a night, and this could only be done in the old building. But it was odd having the old lags rubbing shoulders with kids. And I'm sure, looking back, Huge didn't enjoy having guys his own age breathing down his neck and seeing the way things were run.

So behind our backs, talks were under way to get the prisoners moved on. But we didn't know that, and it just seemed like all the fun had gone out of living here.

So I decided to run away. They might have locked the old fuckers up, but they didn't lock us up. I don't know why more lads didn't do it, to be honest. The gates were open – you just had to walk through them. I did it after dusk one night. One of the benefits of, as Huge put it, blending into the scenery was that nobody seemed to notice or care. No alarms when whirring out, no spotlights chasing me down the path and onto the country lane.

By the time I'd thumbed a lift to St Helens and then bunked on a bus and got home, it was gone nine o'clock. There was nobody in, and the curtains were drawn. There were new curtains up in the front room, I noticed. I didn't have a key any more, but that didn't worry me: Mum always kept a spare behind a loose brick in the back yard wall. She was either out, or lying in a puddle of her own humiliation.

Long Island Iced Tea, anyone?

The key was there, but Mum wasn't. And as I looked around I saw that everything had changed.

It wasn't just the curtains that were different. She had new carpets down, a new three-piece suite. A new telly, new pictures on the wall. And then I saw she had framed pictures of schoolkids in uniforms on the wall. Kids that weren't me. Asian kids. There was a statue of an elephant God with loads of waggly arms on the mantelpiece.

That's when I realized. Mum didn't live here any more.

I checked the bedrooms out: yup, all my stuff had gone. I nicked a bit of money from the sideboard downstairs and locked the place up as I'd found it. Though admittedly thirty quid lighter.

My mum had moved house. A new family had moved in. My mum had gone off, and she hadn't bothered to tell me.

Huge had taken some of his special boys into Manchester that night to 'catch a show', as he put it. When they got back, he had them in his quarters listening to music. I hitched a lift back and got there just after midnight.

None of the officials had even noticed I'd gone missing.

Guinness saw me coming in, though. The light from the moon peeking in through the too-thin curtains hit his eyes and I could see him staring at me. I got undressed and said nothing. When I got into my bed I looked back at him. He was asleep then.

A week or so later, Huge had these security lights installed along the drive. They lit up if they sensed movement; they were forever going off if a wild animal ran across the grounds. I realized if I ever wanted to run away again, I'd have to re-think my tactics.

Benefactor

Special guest of honour when we'd been doing *Her Benny*, and a person Huge got his right royal knickers in a twist over, was local Tory MP Benedict Bishop. Or Hairy Benny, as Guinness referred to him, what with his hirsute appearance. He was Old School. Dead posh accent, shiny old suit, crumbs in his beard, shiny shoes. Thick Coke-bottle glasses. As your mam would say, a real catch.

The community play was the first time I'd laid eyes on him in my time there, but I'd heard a lot about him from the lads who'd been in longer than me. He was a great supporter and benefactor of the centre, taking groups of boys out for meals, paying for much-needed building work. Like Huge, really, but with more money and class. He arrived at Hansbury in an actual Rolls-Royce with a chauffeur. Me and Guinness had never seen the like before. In the months after the show, Hairy Benny was a regular visitor to Hansbury.

One day he turned up unannounced and walked into the refectory, where me and Guinness were both having a milk-shake. Well, we were drinking milk and we'd dropped a Pink Panther biscuit in it and tried to stir it up, so it was as good as.

'Delia Smith, eat your fucking heart out,' went Guinness, which really made me laugh.

He stood beside us watching us drink, passing the time of

day, asking us why we were in there. He asked if we did much sport. Despite outward appearances with Guinness, he didn't. I just looked like a skinny runt, so said, 'Do I look like I do much sport?'

'Indeed. But when you get to my age, it's hard to differentiate between the litheness of youth and the litheness of the athlete.'

'Or the skinniness of the undernourished,' I said. And then wished I hadn't. Coz it made him more interested in me.

A lesson I was learning during my time in that place was, keep a low profile. Blend into the background like you did on stage. Raise your head above the parapet, and suddenly people are interested in you. You're a target, for good or for bad – and I was, right there, right then.

Benedict Bishop was staring down at me like an archaeologist inspecting a pile of old bones.

'Are you an orphan?'

'No, sir.'

'Any contact with your family?'

'No, sir.'

This seemed to impress him.

'On the lowest rung of society. What little hope there is for you, young man.'

This made me want to punch him.

'We shall go for a run in the Rolls. Bring your friend.'

And with that, he turned round and walked out of the refectory.

I knew the minute we got in the car it was a mistake. I wasn't daft, I'd heard rumours of what happened on these runs out into the countryside. And it wasn't pretty.

The good news was, he had his chauffeur with him, and for some reason that made me feel more safe.

The way I saw it was, I had to make myself less attractive to him. And the only way I knew how to do that was, *blend in.* Gold star for Bioletti!

So if he asked me a question, I shrugged or gave one-word answers, and soon my ploy worked. He grew disinterested in me. The spark, the cheek he'd seen at Hansbury had evaporated. I knew he was beginning to regret inviting me. He'd've got more craic out of Helen frigging Keller.

It was easy to keep silent because I don't know what was going on with our Guinness there, but Jesus, he was singing like someone had given him fucking canary seed. Answering every question with the flourish of a pop star on *Wogan.* Why use three words when thirty-three would do? The old man was entertained. I say old; I discovered that day that he was thirty-nine. I discovered this because Guinness asked him outright. And then answered like he was a saloon-bar hostess:

Oh, you don't look it, Mr Bishop. Honest to God, is it genetic? My mam always said she had good skin on her mam's side. She said if you've got bad skin that's it, you're fucked. Oh sorry, Mr Bishop. My mouth. I'm like a navvy sometimes. Worse than a navvy, some might say. D'you know what I mean?

And then this irritating little chuckle. Shirley Temple on speed.

I just looked at him, incredulous. What the frig was he playing at?

I wondered if he thought by talking so much it would put the old man off him, but it seemed a risky strategy, especially as Guinness could make you laugh till it hurt. But something worked. We drove round the countryside, Bishop pointed a few things out on the landscape, and an hour or so later he dropped us back at Hansbury.

After he'd gone I said to Guinness, 'What was all that about?'

'All what?'

'The gossip. The gift of the gab. You was all over him.'

'I wasn't.'

'You was!'

'Oh, who gives a fuck, Danny?'

'You do know what they all say about him?'

'Yeah. That if you do what he wants, he gives you money.'

I was gobsmacked.

'You want money off him?'

'No, knobhead. I want him to ask me to marry him.'

And with that, Guinness did a massive flounce back to the house. The sarcasm, man. The brass neck and the sarcasm! I watched him go. Don't get me wrong, I liked the lad, but sometimes, just sometimes, I wanted to punch his face in.

I didn't speak to Guinness much after that. I tried giving him the old silent treatment for a bit. I thought he'd be devastated. I thought he'd come crying to me, going, 'What have I done, Danny? What have I said?'

But he never. He just kept his distance back. I thought he'd be all lonely, but maybe he was taking himself off somewhere to think, coz half the time I couldn't find him anywhere.

And then one of the other lads filled me in. They'd seen him getting into Bishop's Rolls. On more than one occasion.

Spanner

One of the old lags on the overspill from Risley told me he knew my dad. His name was Spanner and he reckoned he'd been to school with him, and then they'd worked together briefly at the glassworks before Spanner was found nicking

260

stuff and was given his marching orders. He'd not had much luck since and only had one kidney, but he was decent enough. God knows why, but there was an old banger knocking about one of the yards at Hansbury for the lads to mess about with once they were seventeen, and Spanner offered to give me driving lessons (of sorts) in it. You couldn't go far in the car, which was probably a blessing for Huge, as this particular yard was more of a courtyard, blocked either side by either prefabs or barns. It was an automatic car, so there wasn't much to learn; but I still lapped up everything he told me, thinking I was really mature for my years.

And it was in that car that Spanner taught me a thing or two about life. Well, life as he knew it. I lapped that up too, even if it was all mostly about how to behave if I ever got stopped by the police. Looking back, I'm amazed I took him seriously. If he was that good at handling himself with the filth and being the slippery snake he claimed to be, how come he was in and out of the nick all his life?

His main piece of advice to me was this – when being stopped by the police, do the following:

Be polite.

Act dumb.

Then stutter.

'You stutter, Danny, they panic. They don't want to be seen to be making a young lad anxious. Looks bad on them if they arrest you.'

'Oh, the homespun words of wisdom from me Grandma's knee,' I'd say. Which made him piss himself. Even though I didn't really know what it meant and it sounded a bit showy-offy. But it was something my dad used to say to my mum if she nagged him about something. And it didn't half used to wind her up.

Sometimes I'd see Huge looking at us through one of the prefab windows as we'd sit in the car gabbing. God alone knows what he was thinking. Was he fearful for me? Was he worried? Envious? Did he think Spanner was doing the sort of things he did? He didn't stare for long. Especially if Spanner gave him the old evils. Then he'd duck away like a nosy suburban neighbour caught twitching the nets.

'He's a weirdo, him, isn't he?' Spanner'd say.

'He's all right,' I'd say. 'He's harmless.'

A whistle between his teeth told me Spanner definitely thought otherwise. 'He's a nonce, Danny. It's not right, what he does.'

Right? Right? It was hard to get your head round right and wrong in there. It just *was*. There were pros and cons to Huge's behaviour, of course there were; but it's just what went on, and there didn't seem anything odd about it, it was just the nature of the beast. Shit happens, etc. And at the end of the day, everyone got something out of it. Huge got his end away, the lads got their perks. 'Right' was a concept I couldn't fathom.

I can now, don't you worry.

Well. You'd think, wouldn't you?

'Can you find out where my mum is, Spanner? I asked Huge, and he's not had any luck. She's moved, only she's not told me where it is she's gone.'

He looked at me a while. And then went, 'I'll have a go, son. I'll have a go.'

I liked it when he called me son.

I'd always thought what I was missing was my twin brother.

But actually, in that moment, I realized what I'd really, really wanted was a proper dad.

Night lad

On my fourteenth birthday Huge summonsed me to his office. It wasn't a place I'd been to much, and I assumed he wanted to wish me a happy day.

Wrong.

He had his poker face on the minute I went in and I, wrongly, thought I was in the shit.

He was stirring a cup of tea in a bone china cup. There was a saucer. There was even a matching teapot.

'I'm afraid I have bad news, Danny.' He avoided any eye contact with me, preferring now to keep his gaze firmly on his tea. 'Your father is in hospital and it looks like he hasn't got long left.'

Truth be told, I was gutted. I'd much rather he'd just wished me a happy birthday.

'I will take you there shortly to say your goodbyes.'

'Sir?'

'Danny?'

'What if I don't want to go?'

'What you want is of little consequence. We're going. I'm sure you'll regret it one day if you don't.'

'But I can't stick him, sir.'

'Bit of a disciplinarian, was he?'

I shook my head. No point telling him anything. Already he was referring to the Brummie Bastard in the past tense. And I kinda liked it.

Huge drove to the hospital in his Bentley. He let me sit up front with him but he put some classical music on the radio, which sent out the warning: no conversation. Didn't bother me. I sometimes wondered if he was a little bit scared of me since the caravan incident. The favoured boys were the pretty but putty ones who lapped up his attention, and laughed at his jokes.

The hospital was red brick, Victorian. Its windows were long and narrow, and the floors polished like mirrors. I remember thinking I wished I still had my BMX bike so I could ride down them dead fast. The nurses wore starchy white hats and all looked furious. Good. Hopefully a few of them were knocking him about a bit like he used to do to my mum. Payback time.

He wasn't like a shadow of his former self; I recognized him immediately. He was still built like a brick shithouse, it's just that now his skin was yellow and his brow as shiny as the floor with sweat. There were tubes. His breathing rattled like Mum's twin-tub. Huge hung back in the corridor. A nurse touched Dad's arm.

'Mr Bioletti? Your son's here.'

His eyes opened. Closed again. Then opened.

'All right, lad?'

I nodded. 'All right, Dad?'

'I've not got long.'

'I know.'

'Sit down.'

I shook my head. I didn't want to stay. I wanted this to last for as brief a time as possible.

'Sit down,' he said with more menace, and so I did.

Then he closed his eyes again, and I thought he'd fallen asleep. I looked out of the ward to the corridor and saw that Huge was staring in, observing. What was he worried about? That I was going to smash a window and jump out and run away?

Dad opened his eyes. He motioned me to him. I sighed and

leaned forward in my chair. When he spoke, it was hardly a whisper.

'Lad?'

'What?'

'There's something you need to know before I go coz your mammy'll never tell you.'

I don't even know where my mammy is, I wanted to say, but I didn't.

'Your brother didn't die.'

He took a deep breath.

'Your Mam give him away.'

He took another deep one. My head span. Jesus.

'She was cleaning for Mrs Albright and she give him to her. Gone to Canada. Your brother's alive.'

I stared at him. And the effort in him talking to me and spilling his beans must have taken it out of him, coz he fell asleep then. So deep, in fact, that I thought he'd died.

I got up and went into the corridor.

'Ready?' asked Huge.

I nodded and we left.

In the car on the way back to Hansbury, Huge was like, 'What did he say?'

'Not a lot.'

Low profile. Under the radar. Don't give too much away. Clearly that was becoming my motto.

Years later, our Owen got into that musical *Blood Brothers*. He was always going on at me to take him to London to see it. When we went, I was in for a shock. Seeing my mother's story on the stage, set to music, screwed my head a little.

But the thing is, I never knew whether or not to believe my old man. He was a cruel git sometimes. But why would he make something like this up? It made complete sense that

Mum might have done that and regretted it. I know they struggled financially having just me to feed, so God knows what it would have been like with the two of us. It would make sense of their rowing, his disapproval of her, her subsequent drinking. It made sense that they'd never taken me to my brother's grave, or told me where he was buried.

Was my brother going by the name of Albright and living out in Toronto or somewhere? My doppelganger, walking this planet with a Canadian accent?

And with that information, what was my dad trying to do? Twist my melon? Help me? Make me hate my mother for lying to me?

On the journey back to Hansbury, with the strings of Handel (I asked) playing in the car, I buried that information somewhere deep inside me. By the time I got out of the Bentley it was as if the day had not even happened.

I was an only child. I had a dead brother.

I was very good at burying things.

I still am.

All good things must come to an end

I honestly thought I was doing the right thing, you see. There was this bird, and she'd come to Hansbury Vale to have a look round. She was from the local council and she was a social worker or something. She had a clipboard anyway, and dead long red hair like her off of *Carrie*, and skin equally as pale. Like a ghost. But this look on her face, deadpan, honest to God, you could've told her the funniest joke in the world and she'd've still looked like she was bored shitless at a funeral. She slithered round the different buildings and outhouses and stared blankly at what was going on – we were being shown a film about a mouse being dissected, God knows why – and then she'd be gone from the room and you'd see her half an hour later during break, standing near the bogs and the like.

She was an outsider.

She was checking us out to see how the set-up worked.

For some reason, I felt she had power. All day long I was working up the courage to speak to her. Lads kept going from class to have informal chats with her about how they were getting on, and what the teachers were like. It was all the soft lads, Huge's favourites, the compliant ones.

Lads that weren't me, basically.

I could picture them with her. Drinking tea out of Huge's bone china bollocks and going, *Oh yes, Carrie, this place runs smooth as clockwork, nothing to see here. Huge is fantastic and we're like one big happy family.*

And Carrie sat there, noting it all down, thinking, *Aren't we the clever ones giving Huge his licence? Let me just write him another cheque for ten gazillion pounds.*

Lads stopped slipping out. Next time I looked out of the window I saw her in the car park. Next time the teacher wasn't looking, I slipped quietly out of class. The class was so bloody noisy, no one noticed anyway. And I legged it to the car park. She was driving off. It must have been summer, coz her wheels were blowing dust up from the ground. I legged it after her and caught up with her, she can't have been going that fast, and I banged on her window. She stopped, and looked like she was shitting herself – first bit of emotion she'd displayed all day – and wound her window down.

'Stuff goes on here. Stuff no one talks about.' I was gasping, out of breath from my quick sprint now. 'My mate Guinness goes off on day trips with that MP Bishop. Hugh's the same. It's going on all over. He won't do it to me coz I decked him and give him a black eye, Miss.'

Now she was back to the default mode face. The poker face. The one with no emotion.

I'd blurted. I'd splurged. I'd said what I'd come to say. And as she wasn't saying anything back, I thought I'd blown it. So without waiting for a reaction I legged it back to the classroom. Once back inside, I returned to my desk. Still the teacher hadn't noticed I'd been and come back. But a minute or so later, I saw Carrie's car reversing back into the car park. And she parked up. A few minutes later she was getting out of her car with the clipboard. Then she went inside. And I started bricking it.

That night I was called to Huge's office. He was all on his own, Carrie had long gone, and he was completely furious. It was like he had smoke coming out of his ears.

He wasn't drinking tea now. He had a whiskey on the go.

Not good.

'How dare you? How dare you go around casting slanderous accusations about our kindest benefactor? Who comes to visit us out of the goodness of his own heart. Who offers only kindness and the civil hand of friendship. And you have to besmirch that generosity with your repugnant vulgarity? Claiming that he . . . I can barely say the words . . .'

I said nothing. Just sat there. Like a gravestone.

'I explained to Mrs Eastern that if what you infer is true, you should not be telling her but informing the police.'

At this he shoved his phone across my desk.

'Phone them. If you dare.'

I stared at the phone.

'If you have irrefutable proof. That things . . . untoward . . . have occurred. Phone them. Make yourself a laughing stock. Is this what Sam Korniskey has told you?'

I remained silent.

'Well?'

I continued with the silent treatment.

'What's the matter, lad? Cat got your tongue?'

I shook my head.

'Is this or is this not what Sam Korniskey has told you?'

I shook my head.

'What has he told you?'

Gravestone again.

'Can't hear you, lad!'

'He never told us nothing.'

'Ah, I see. Now we are trying a man and hanging him on the basis of what? Chinese Whispers?'

I couldn't bear to look at him.

'I tell you what, though, Danny. Phone them anyway. Let's see what happens. A wimpy little bastard like you, the runt of a very unfortunate litter. So wayward was he, indeed, that he was sent to live in council-approved care. Oh yes, Danny, very impressive, I'm sure the boys in blue would lap your story up. But let's see how they rate your word compared to that of a Member of Parliament such as Sir Benedict Bishop!'

'You're all right, sir,' I whispered.

He almost choked on his laughter.

'Oh, there's really no need to point that out, boy. Really no need at all. You see – you are the plankton of the pecking order. Shout what you like, from the highest rooftop in the land. You will never be believed. None of you will.'

I nodded. I knew he was right, actually. You had to hand it to him. Fair play and all that.

'But just to be on the safe side. And to avoid any re-occurrence of this sort of embarrassment. I think we can safely say we'll bring to an end Sir Benedict's trips out in the

Rolls with young Master Korniskey. You can explain to him why this has happened. Leave. Now.'

I got up to leave. As I got to the door, he was off on one again.

'And just in case I didn't make myself clear . . .'

I looked round. He was smiling. He was – he was actually enjoying this.

'You will never be believed, Danny Bioletti. Ever.'

He pointed to the door. I left.

The next time the Rolls came, it drove off with another lad. It drove off with a lad someone said was a Vietnamese boat child, whose parents had died in the boat on the way over to wherever they were going, and only he'd survived. It gave him a bit of cachet amongst the residents of Hansbury. Most of us were in there coz we'd screwed up, or our parents had, or they just plain didn't want us or know what to do with us. His reason had an air of the swashbuckle to it – adventure on the high seas, and all that. I found him a bit of a knob, if I'm honest. He had violin lessons and, God forgive me, I hated him for it. So actually, that night I was quite pleased when I saw him getting in the Rolls and Guinness stomping round the car park like the disgruntled ex-wife. Through a broken window – I forget where I was – I then saw Huge coming out and taking Guinness by the shoulder and leading him inside.

I knew then it was only a matter of time.

I went back to my dorm. Lay on my bed, arms tucked behind my head, whistling silently to myself.

Minutes later, the door burst open and Guinness bounded in, calling me for everything. I was the biggest knob on this planet, the most interfering twat he'd ever had the bad luck to bump into, the misfortune to live with. It was quite the performance. You had to give it to him: when he was on form he was very, very good. In the end, I jumped off the bed and rugby-tackled him onto his bed to shut him up. There's nothing I disliked more than attention being brought to my door. And the sooner he shut his face, the better. But he just kept kicking and screaming and calling me this and calling me that. In the end I clamped my hand over his mouth, and for a fleeting second I realized what it must be like to kill somebody. In that second, I wished I could. In that second I found him so ungrateful, after everything I had tried to do for him, and the thanks, the hatred I was getting in return, well, why didn't I?

Oh, I didn't, of course. I don't think I've got it in me. I certainly didn't have then.

Also. The minute I put my hand over his mouth, the little fucker bit me.

Like I said: when he was on form, there was no getting near him.

And it was such a shock, I jumped back and left him to it. But at least he wasn't shouting and screaming like a demented loon any more.

I shifted myself back to my own bed, quick smart. Checked my hand. No blood. But that bastard had nicked my finger in two places on the inside of the knuckles, indentations like paper cuts.

Guinness was up off his bed, and pulling his mattress up.

Look. Come on, look. See all this?

He was beckoning me over to look under the mattress. I half-heartedly peered towards his bed. There under the mattress was a plastic bag. He yanked it out. The mattress thumped back down and he slid across the floor on his knees, presenting me with the open bag, telling me to look inside. I did. It was just full of tenners. Tenners and tenners and tenners and tenners.

Where am I gonna get money like that now, eh? he was going. *He never laid a finger on me. He just gave me pocket money. Thirty quid each time. Next week he was gonna let me stay overnight. And now . . .*

He was gonna LET you?

It was my money. My escape money. With this money I was gonna get on a train and fuck off to London and see our Linda and live there and . . .

He burst out crying.

He was saving it. All the money he got, the handouts from Bishop. They'd been leading to something, but he was saving it to go and see his Linda.

You've got loads there, Guinness.

I know, but I wanted more. What if our Linda doesn't wanna know me? What if I've got to fend for meself?

And again he broke down in sobs. He looked so pathetic. Waterfalls cascading from his eyes.

And from realizing how easy it would've been to finish him off, I now felt how easy it was to make him feel better. And that's all I wanted to do, right there, right then.

Guinness, stop it. I'll make it up to you, I swear. I'll get you to London. By hook or by crook.

I was starting to sound like a frigging nursery rhyme.

He looked up at me. Them big daft Bambi eyes. Almost double their size from the tears.

You wanna go to London? We'll go. The pair of us. There's nothing down here for me now. My dad's a goner. My mum's done a runner. Huge hates us coz I knocked him sparko. And now I've told him what Bishop gets up to and he's fuming with me. My days are numbered here, kid, I swear. Sooner I get out of here the better. You in?

Guinness nodded. He was in.

Nothing keeping me here now, is there?

And of course there was the possibility that Bishop might come looking for him.

London, eh, Guin. You and me. Can't wait.

And for the first time since he'd come skidding into that dorm, Guinness smiled.

And I will runaway (runaway) (runaway) with you

Although the atmosphere could be quite lax at times at Hansbury, the knobs at the top weren't idiots. Two lads couldn't just walk out of the gates without anyone noticing, as the drive from the Hall to the main gates was about half a mile long, and by now of course they had those buggering security lights installed. You'd soon get noticed. Guinness started trusting me again after my promise to get him to London. Though God knows why he really needed me in the first place. He was the one with the bag full of dosh, not me. He started knocking about with me like he had in the old days, and our favourite pastime became planning the Great Escape.

My suggestions were, on the whole, quite practical: climbing the fence round the back of the caravan, traversing the woods till we got down to the main road and then thumbing a lift. His smacked of the decidedly outrageous: disguise ourselves as milkmaids searching the fields for cows (don't ask), dress up as scarecrows and run through the fields (too much *Wizard of Oz*) or steal a hot air balloon and fly away. Because hot air balloons are so easy to steal – no-brainer!

In the end, I asked Spanner what he'd do if he was me and he wanted to run away.

The good thing about Spanner was, he always took you seriously. He said he'd get back to me.

He got back to me the next day. He said we were going

for a walk. I thought he was going to do the paternal chit-chat thing of saying, 'What's wrong? Why do you need to run away?' before gently advising me to stop here and not get into any trouble. Especially when he walked me round the front of the Hall and to outside the entrance. There was a garden bench out front, and he motioned towards that. Here it came, I thought, the big chat.

Instead, he sat there in silence. And then went, 'We're just gonna wait here a bit. And then all will become obvious.'

So we did.

And it did.

And soon, me and Guinness had our plan.

It wasn't a foolproof plan, and there was some danger involved. But once I'd explained it all to Guinness, he was defo up for it. And no doubt with the naivety, bravery and down-right foolhardery of youth – if there is such a word – we threw ourselves into it like rats down a sewer.

This was the plan. Since the arrival of the cons at the Hall there was a lot of to-ing and fro-ing of said prisoners from this, their overspill remand centre, either to prison or to court. Spanner reckoned there were on average two prison vans coming in and out each day. On Wednesday night there was going to be a van in the evening, after sunset – he actually used those words, which made it sound even more like we were in a movie – and it would be taking one of the prisoners to prison, as he was some sort of special case who'd then be going the following morning to court. Spanner reckoned the van would be outside the Hall for half an hour, tops. And that in the darkness, me and Guinness would be able to climb on top of the van, lie down and then drive away, out of the grounds and into Manchester, where we could, at some point, jump off. Initially I was worried, as was Guinness, about how we would manage to hang on, on top of the van. But Spanner said there were this duct sticking out the top of the van, slap bang in the middle, for air conditioning. If we lay either side of that we could hang onto it. No doubt for dear life.

To prepare for the Great Escape, I made Guinness sit with me on the bench and watch as the vans came in and out a few times. The biggest challenge was going to be scaling the side of the van to get on top of it without the aid of a ladder. And doing it deftly enough so as not to raise suspicion from the driver or anyone else inside. The way I saw it, we had two choices – we both scaled the side of the van at the same time, or one at a time – but I was worried that even with our slight builds, we'd still draw attention to ourselves with a clattering of feet. The other option would be that Guinness gave me a leg up, and then I pulled him up. I didn't trust us to do it the other way round; I couldn't see him dragging me up, somehow.

We practised on the caravan. We got it down to a slick twelve seconds. Guinness holds out his hands. I step on. Bounce up. Drag myself onto the top. Lower my hands, pull him up. Twelve seconds. We were proud of ourselves. We were invincible.

Wednesday came, and with it a storm. That gave us good news and bad news. The good news was that the rain was pelting so heavily on the metal roof of the van that it made it less likely that the people inside would be as aware of us climbing up. The bad news was that that rain was heavy, man. As we crept round the side of the Hall in our puffa jackets, we were pretty soon soaked to the skin. This was going to make staying on top of the van challenging at best. Also, I was worried about Guinness's tenners, which were currently stuffed down his front in a plastic bag. What if that let the rain in and they got soaked, and we ended up with no money?

As we turned the corner we saw the van coming up the drive. Its stark yellow headlights looked like they were pumping smoke out as they battled through the rain, finally parking up some twenty feet or so from us. We heard the slam of metal doors swinging back. The tread of Doc Martens on gravel. We ran lightly. As rehearsed, Guinness faced me, his hands cupped towards me. I held his shoulders and jumped up. We were fucking poetry in motion as he yanked his hands high like a volleyball player and I grabbed the roof of the van before scrambling on. The roof was cold and hard and very very wet, like lying in a metal paddling pool. I swivelled round and held my hands over the side, then pulled Guinness up. We were on.

Now for the bit we'd not been able to rehearse. I located the air-con vent in the middle and drew Guinness's hands to it. We swivelled round on opposite sides. This didn't feel good. The vent was circular, wet and hard to grip. So I grabbed Guinness's hands and tried to interlock his fingers with mine, like a cat's cradle. I didn't dare look at him in case he was freaking out. Instead I crooked my head to the left, looking at the Hall, a black cube against the pitch sky. Gashes of bright yellow light where curtains hung open at the windows.

Footsteps. Voices. I tried to block it all out and just grip. Eventually a slam and the van shook. I felt Guinness tighten his grip. And then, slowly, we were off. I didn't dare look up. Head down. Eyes tight shut. Focus. Stay calm. Stay fucking on. Under that radar.

The van drove slowly down the drive and picked up speed as it turned out of the gates.

My feet found a wedge somewhere. I could only imagine

it was a ridge at the front of the van above the windscreen. It gave me a bit more security. I jammed both feet against it and suddenly felt more confident. As long as I kept hold of Guinness's hands, we were going to do this. After five minutes I looked up. We'd agreed that we couldn't stay on the roof for too long in case we drew attention to ourselves. Even with our dark clothes it would only take one bright spark at some traffic lights to clock us and beep their horn and tell the driver. Even under the cloak of darkness. Street lights were bound to reflect off our clothes, our skin.

It was my job to decide when to jump. When I tapped Guinness's hand three times, it would be time.

What felt like hours later, though it could only have been about five or so minutes in reality, we were driving through a council estate. I cricked my neck and saw some traffic lights ahead. They were changing to red. I tapped Guinness three times. As we slowed down, approaching the lights, we let go of each other and gently slid to the side and then down the sides of the van. And then ran. Ran as fast as our legs could carry us.

A promise on the bus

Eventually we came to a chippy. Got fish and chips, which gave us change from a tenner (all dry). With the change, we got a bus into Manchester (didn't want to risk a taxi as it might've looked odd, two young lads hailing a cab in the dark) and then we bunked onto a train. On the bus we hardly spoke, convinced that everyone else on the bus was going to turn round at any point, rip off their mask like in *Scooby Doo* and reveal they'd been following us and we had to go back. I saw Guinness was shaking. I had to make him feel better. I couldn't risk him freaking out and making a show and drawing attention to us. I nudged him, he looked at me.

We're in this together, Sam, you and me.

He nodded.

I'm never gonna let you down, you know. Leave your side. Whatever happens. I've got your back.

He nodded.

Wherever we end up. Whatever we end up doing. You have a problem? It's me you turn to.

Sam nodded. A few moments later, I noticed he'd stopped shaking and was looking calmer.

Trains were different in them days. There weren't all the computerized barriers – I mean, blimey, what was a computer back then? – and if you were as deft and nimble as we were, free train travel was your oyster. Once on the train, we set up camp in a toilet and settled down. On the journey to our new life.

Seven Sisters Road

I thought it was so apt that the area in London we had to get to was called the Seven Sisters Road. It put me in mind of the old movies Mum used to watch of a Sunday afternoon, or up the picture house. *Seven Brides for Seven Brothers.* Your singing nun with her seven punchworthy kids. The number seven loomed large in families in the olden days, clearly, and this road was no exception. All the way there in the taxi from Euston I kept seeing big ghostly women looming large over the top of the shops and flats, looking down on us, all mixed race like Guinness. His seven sisters, not sure what to make of us. Would we get a warm welcome? Would Linda still be living at the address that Guinness had for her? What if she'd done a runner like my mum?

I remember 'Baker Street' was playing on the radio in the black cab. Even though it was years old and I'd heard it so many times before, it was like hearing it for the first time. Again it was like it was welcoming us to London as we sped jerkily through the hazy neon midnight streets. Now whenever I think of London, I see it accompanied with a saxophone solo, and it's that. And whichever street I'm on – the Embankment, Piccadilly, an underpass – in my head it's 'Baker Street' that's the soundtrack. Cheesy, I know, but it's stuck with me.

At first when we got to the flats on Remington Road I was crushed. This boring old council block could've been anywhere in the country. I wanted something to make it distinctive, make it London. And then when this white woman opened the door on the second floor I thought we'd got the wrong place, or that Guinness's sister had moved on.

But this scrawny bird with the red hair and the dressing gown looked gobsmacked and gave Guinness such a hug and yes, this was Linda. Linda seemed genuinely thrown to have two young lads on her doorstep in the early hours, and who could blame her? She'd not seen Guinness for years, he'd given her no warning he was coming, and she said she no longer had any contact with anyone else in his family. We squeezed past towering piles of shopping bags in her hall – ''Scuse the mess, lads' – and then she turned the couch in her living room into a double bed. I'd never seen a sofa bed, and it struck me as the height of sophistication. Now I really did feel like I was in That London. She made us tea and crumpets and said we could stay 'till we worked out what to do'.

I didn't know what that meant either. But there was something that struck me as not quite right about her.

Before too long, I'd learn what that was.

Rolling, rolling, rolling

Linda, it turned out, was a fence (that's not the dodgy thing, that'll come later) for a small gang of shoplifters in the West End. This turned out to be a bit of a touch.

On our first night in Remington Road me and Guinness lay on that sofa bed like it was the comfiest thing in the world, full to the brim and bumper with buttery crumpets and hot tea and I made him laugh by pretending to be Huge discovering we'd gone missing. I did the big booming snooty voice and Guinness lay beside me pissing himself. I could hear Linda pottering in the kitchen. And then our door creaked open and she looked in.

'Who's doing that voice?' she went.

'He was,' Guinness went.

And I thought no more of it.

The next day Linda said she might have a job for me. You see? That was the touch. If she'd worked in an office or a factory there'd've been nothing down for me. But she didn't. And there was.

Mid-morning, she pulled various garments of clothing out of the designer bags in the hall and told us to get togged up. Once we were in our new clothes – I didn't then quite understand why she might have teenage lads' clothes to hand, though I was soon to find out – there was a ring at the doorbell and a man in a peaked cap and smart suit said he was ready for us.

The driver took us in a spotless car, all white leather interiors, to an address in somewhere called Little Venice, and although it sounded like we were going to Italy when we got there, finally I felt like we'd arrived in London. Tall white houses with pillars, trees, a canal. We climbed some steps and Linda rang one of many bells.

The woman she'd brought us to see looked like Joan Collins or something. Even indoors she was wearing a power suit and a hat that half covered her face. She sat staring at us while sucking on the skinniest cigarette I'd ever seen, and every now and then taking a dainty sip of tea. She asked me to say something in my posh accent, so I said, 'What d'you want me to say?' and the poshness pleased her. She told me to tell her how we'd managed to get out of the home and down to London, so I explained, keeping the posh accent up.

'D'you want me to say anything?' Guinness interrupted eventually. 'I can do funny voices. I was Little Nell in *Her Benny*.'

The woman in the hat smiled politely and said 'No. You won't do.' As if that explained something. Though we were none the wiser.

The woman's name was Gretchen Tate. A cockney by birth, she'd grown up to become one of the best female criminals in the East End, before taking up residence in the West End and becoming a dreaded nuisance to the balance sheets of the boutiques and department stores. She now ran a small gang of women and girls who stole only the best from the best and made a small fortune out of it. She disappeared into a bedroom and then returned with a school uniform for me. I'd never seen the likes before. Striped blazer, piping on the collar and cuffs – there was even a bleeding cap! Imagine! She invited me to try them on. Still a bit bewildered as to what was going on, I obliged. And she seemed to like what she saw.

'You don't think he looks a bit too Chinese-ified?' Linda said, a note of caution in her voice.

Gretchen just shook her head. 'He looks perfect.'

The next day I started working for her.

I had to dress up in the school uniform and the driver drove me, Gretchen and two other women into the West End. He parked on double yellows and basically it was all about convincing the shopworkers you were posh, and therefore not going to arouse suspicion. This is why they weren't interested in Guinness; God love him, but because he was black they didn't want to risk some racist shopgirl thinking, 'He looks dodgy, I'll call security.' Whereas I, with my posh accent and my practically Eton schoolboy outfit, would impress them and slot right in.

I worked with Gretchen for two weeks and those days were complete eye-openers. In more ways than one . . .

I had never seen department stores so swanky in my life. The gleaming glass, the escalators, the chrome rails, the lobster bars, the champagne bars. It was 1983 and business was booming. And so was Gretchen Tate.

Gretchen and her cohorts really did look like princesses when they went to work. They'd walk into those shops in their fancy coats and glide through the fashion sections like they were used to having, rather than having nowt.

My job was to wander in with an empty holdall, which was identical to one being filled by one of these good-looking girls. When the time was right I'd idly pass said girl and quickly, deftly swap the bags. No drama.

Gretchen liked me because not only did I look the part, I never drew attention to myself. And she was really impressed with how smooth my swaps were. And because she was happy, I was too. And on the odd occasion where I saw that a shop assistant might have thought something untoward was going on in that corner where the woman was holding the frock up as if asking her pal what she thought, I would slide over and – in my best plummy voice – ask a tricky question. And ask it so loud I alerted the others to my diversionary tactics, giving them the green light to get out of the shop as fast as they could.

Whatever money was eventually made from the contents of the holdalls, I got 10% of it. Not bad at the age of fourteen.

I liked my new job. Right then, I'd've been happy to think that was me for life. Or for the foreseeable.

That is, till I realized how dodgy Linda was. And it had nothing to do with being a fence.

The white one can stay

It was the middle of the night. I woke and felt dead thirsty. Heading to the kitchen for a glass of water, I stopped in the hall, coz I could hear Gretchen talking in the kitchen. The door was ajar; they didn't know I was there. Or listening in.

'I can find Danny lodgings,' Gretchen was saying.

'And the darkie?'

That was Linda's voice. Linda was calling her own brother a darkie? I wanted to go in there and slap her cheeky face. But I didn't. I thought it best to wait and hear what the outcome was.

'I can't do anything for him. Is that a problem, Linda?'

'No, don't be daft.'

'But you said yourself, he can't stay here forever.'

Oh, couldn't he?

'I'll call 999. He's on the run from a children's home. Surprised they haven't been knocking the doors down already.'

'Send him back up North?'

'Or down here. Makes no odds to me. Silly little queer.'

And I heard both women laughing. It was only a little laugh. But it was cold as ice.

I didn't bother with a drink. I returned to the sofa bed and lay there, staring at the ceiling. Guinness lay beside me, snoring lightly.

I had to make a decision. I could go off with Gretchen and get somewhere else to live while Guinness went back to Hansbury.

But I'd never seen him so happy since getting out of Hansbury. Even if his sister hated him, the racist bitch, she'd done a first-class impression of someone who was glad to see him and take him in. But at the end of the day, she was greedy. She liked the money she made from being a fence. She'd told me, she liked living in her little council flat and drinking champagne and wearing designer gear. She liked her life. Why would she then want her half-brother moving in and spoiling her peace?

But before I told Guinness what she'd said and what she had planned, I needed to work out a plan of my own. I worried away at it for an hour or so, till sleep overcame me. But when I woke the next morning, the plan was crystal-clear in my head.

Uncle Benedict

'How do I know you're not making it up?'

'Why would I make it up? I was on a cushy number back there.'

'Yeah, but . . .'

'But nothing, Guin.'

'She never said any of that to me. How do I know you're . . .'

'Oh, all right then, Guin. You get back there and ask her. And see how long it is before the rozzers arrive, eh?'

We walked in silence for a while.

'I can't believe you nicked all her money,' he said, only this time there was a giggle in his voice. Like he was believing me. Like she had it coming.

'Yeah, well. Sure she'll earn a load more again soon.'

'For her fucking champagne.'

'I know. Silly bitch.'

We were at a place called Parliament Square. The Houses of Parliament lay before us; Big Ben loomed high, blocking the sun. The square was busy, and I had to stop myself from taking Guinness's hand when we crossed the road. I had to stop treating him like a kid.

Eventually we found the entrance. A security guard looked horrified as we approached. He didn't say anything. Just gave us daggers.

Which is when I said in my plummiest tones.

'Hello. We're here to see our uncle, Sir Benedict Bishop?'

The guard looked us up and down, and then folded his arms.

'He's not here,' he said.

'Don't lie!' Guinness practically screamed. 'He's an MP. He works here. And WE wanna see him.'

The security guy looked, how to put it nicely, taken aback.

Before he could say anything, I grabbed Guinness and yanked him away.

'You're all right, mate,' I went. 'We'll give him a bell. Come back another time.' And I frog-marched Guinness down the road.

'It's the summer recess!' the guard called after us. As if he was about to add, 'You pair of bloody knobheads.'

'That gob of yours is gonna get you in trouble one day,' I

warned Guinness, but he shook me off and walked despond-
ently to the corner.

'What the fuck's a summer recess anyway?' Guinness was
practically tapping his feet in the shadow of Big Ben.

'I don't know.'

'So much for this big plan of yours.'

I didn't dignify that with a response. Cheeky git.

'So what do we do now?' Guinness had folded his arms.

And that was the million-dollar question.

Under the radar

You might think we had it made. Two lads in London with
money to burn. We had the best part of three hundred quid
in our pockets – well, in Guinness's plastic bag – which was
a lot in those days. But with no contacts and nowhere to stay,
we were screwed. Guinness wanted to stay in a hotel, but I
knew this was a non-starter. We couldn't afford to ring any
alarm bells, and two teenage lads checking into even the
scuzziest B & B might prompt a call to the authorities. And
quiet words on the sly meant tracing us back to Hansbury.
And that meant a one-way ticket back up North. We had to
stay under the radar.

In the countryside you could sleep under trees and in
barns, I figured, but where could you sleep in the centre of the
biggest city in the country? The streets might have been my
friend back in St Helens, but I didn't know this place – only
the bits I'd seen from the comfort of Gretchen Tate's motor.
We'd need cover, we'd need shelter, we'd need warmth. I know
it sounds mental now, but I took us both in a cab to Harrods,
one of the few shops I knew, and spent some dosh on sleeping
bags. Truth be told we were going to try and nick them, but
with no holdalls and no hoisting drawers we were stymied.

And so we paid for them with cold hard cash. Had sleeping bags, I reckoned, could travel. We still had no idea where we were going to lay our heads down, but with sleeping bags we stood a chance of a few hours' comfortable sleep. We wandered the streets, trying not to look too conspicuous walking round with sleeping bags in plastic bags, and as night fell it became obvious that in central London every street corner, every alleyway, was someone's bedroom. Maybe this wouldn't be as difficult as I'd first feared.

We spent the next few days on a hamster wheel of kipping in back alleys, walking round in the daytimes and exploring our still-new city, hanging round on corners watching the world go by, then moving on each time we saw a copper coming. We'd even do some begging, and we'd make a few coppers, nothing substantial, and each hour we'd move on and keep going. I had no idea where we were heading. But I hoped and prayed something good was round the corner.

I didn't know what that something good might be. But hopefully we'd find it.

One day another lad told us we were hanging round in the wrong places. He said we were too near Bayswater to make any money. We'd strayed north from Knightsbridge, apparently, and we needed to 'get our arses down to Piccadilly'.

So we followed his directions, and we did.

Snow in the summer

I don't know what month it was, but I remember the sweltering heat. As we hit Piccadilly, Guinness wandered into a souvenir shop and spent ages looking at all the snowglobes in there. They came in all different sizes, from little miniature ones to ones the size of a loaf of bread. The London skyline, St Paul's, Nelson's Column. At the flick of your wrist they'd be lost in a blizzard. Guinness loved them. He loved working his way along the row of them, one by one; then just as the snow was settling he'd start again, eyes ablaze, chuckling like a kid in a Christmas card.

You gonna get one? I went.

He looked at me, surprised. Then shook his head.

As we left the shop he said, *Nowhere to put it, have I?*

And he was bang on. When you sleep in a sleeping bag, when all you have is the stuff you stand up in and a bag of tenners, you can't have things. Yet people say things make them happy. The shops are full of things. Things we really don't need, but that make us chuckle like Guinness did.

One day, not sure how, I determined that I'd have somewhere to amass loads and loads of things.

One day you will, I went. And Guinness shrugged like it didn't matter.

But I thought it did.

The Meat Rack

When I caught my first glimpse of Piccadilly Circus, I knew I'd come home. It was early evening, the lights were on and this was a futuristic city all of its own, basking in neon. The look and feel of the place excited me, like the electricity from the hoardings and signage was rippling through me. This didn't feel like home as in, this was where I wanted to live or a place where I felt comfortable; but it felt like a place I instinctively knew how to work.

And instinct, as you know, has always been a gift that was important to me.

I looked around the place and almost instantly knew what to do.

The furtive glances of younger lads and older men were practically sending off beeping radar signals to me. Five minutes of checking the swirling crowd out around Eros and the islands of pavement opposite had my pulse racing. I knew what to do. The lads were alien to me, but as familiar as my brothers. It was like I'd stepped into the Hansbury end-of-term disco and the dirty bastard teachers were swooping. But no-one was making the first move. The odd transaction happened, I clocked that; but I wanted to put a rocket up their lazy arses. I told Guinness to mind the bags, and got to work.

A guy in a duffel coat and briefcase was checking out a blond skinny lad leaning against a railing, but he didn't have the bottle to go up to him, not yet. I approached the duffel.

You want him? Twenty quid.

He looked panicked.

I'm not Old Bill, mate. Look at me.

He nodded. That was all the info I needed.

I approached blondie.

Bloke in the duffel coat. Twenty quid. You give me five.

Now he looked alarmed.

Or I'll fucking go with him.

Blondie nodded. Tipped Duffel the wink.

Off they went.

Ten minutes later Blondie was back. And I was a fiver up. Word got around. By the end of the night I was a hundred quid up.

But Guinness was nowhere to be seen. Looked like I'd need a new sleeping bag.

I didn't realize it then, but I wouldn't see Guinness again for five years.

Loyalty

The lads on the Meat Rack liked me. I got them work. I got them more work than they would've got on their own. They could be a lily-livered bunch, as could the fellas pussyfooting round them. What they were all doing was illegal, of course it was, so they were all bricking it about making the first move. So where they might've taken anything up to half an hour to work up the courage to make a negotiation, I stuck me foot on the accelerator pedal and got the ball rolling. Soon the lads learned they could trust me. And the fellas. I'd earned their loyalty, their trust. And I was earning a crust.

The million-dollar question

But how does a lad from nowhere – on the run, allegedly, from the police – end up owning one of the best clubs of the 1990s? A lad who slept in a (this time stolen) Harrods sleeping bag in an alley round the back of the Dominion Theatre: how does he go from that to millionaire in the space of ten years? What's the career ladder for that? Two things, really. Drive. And the man in the orang-utan coat.

Hello, Danny

The first thing you need to know to really get this is that in Piccadilly and Soho I went by the name of Jimmy. Don't ask me why I chose that particular name; I guess I wanted something neutral that couldn't be linked to Bioletti, and instinct told me when those first lads asked me what I was called it was best to keep a bit back. So Jimmy I was. Also, if anyone asked, I was seventeen. Whether folk believed it's another thing, but it lessened anyone's interest in me. 'See him there?

He's only fifteen.' At seventeen the world was your oyster, and besides, what's a couple of years here and there?

I bought myself the BMX I'd been missing all those years and stored it in the flat of a kindly hooker called Framboise (I think that was about as real a name as mine was Jimmy, and for a French lass she had one heck of a Doncaster accent on her). She was based in a side street called Tisbury Court, which was a tiny hiccup of a walkway between Wardour Street and Rupert Street. I'd pick it up first thing in the morning, and drop it off at hers last thing at night. She let me keep my sleeping bag there too, though sometimes she'd invite me in for a drink and I'd kip on her couch, though I didn't make too much of a habit of it. She even let me keep some stuff in an old locker she had there. I think she thought I kept toiletries in it. In fact it's where I stashed my hard-earned cash. The new bike gave me freedom if I spotted the Old Bill hanging around. It also earned me the nickname of Jimmy the Bike.

It was the middle of the morning and not much was going down on the Dilly, so I decided to go for a bike ride and grab myself my latest favourite meal, homity pie, in a vegetarian place called Cranks on Marshall Street. Get me, vegetarian food, I know. London hadn't just opened my eyes to a brave new world, it'd opened my taste buds and palate too.

I was dawdling up Wardour Street on the pavement, feet off the pedals, pushing myself along with my feet, when I saw a weird car parked outside the little church garden there. It was a convertible Mini, something I'd never seen before and haven't seen since – baby blue, and the roof was down. And leaning against it was this fella. He was as odd-looking as his motor. He was tall, like a beanpole. His skin was pock-marked, but he'd tried to hide that by too many sunbeds or too many holidays (I later found out it was the former). He had big New Romantic hair, three different shades of blonde. His eyes were covered in mirrored shades and he was wearing what looked like a dead orang-utan around him, though on closer inspection it was some horrendous fun-fur coat with red feathers hanging off it. Quite an arresting sight, I think you'll agree.

And this dude was looking straight at me.

Of course, I was used to men looking at me: this was Soho, anyone could be easy meat. But there was something else about this look that told me he was no ordinary punter, and I couldn't help but stare back. I found myself slowing the bike down as I got nearer him, and he nodded, like this was what he expected me to do.

What did he want? A lad? Nothing doing there for now. Maybe I could tell him to give me half an hour or so.

But he was on a double yellow, and I wouldn't have time to sort anything without him getting a ticket or clamped – they were ruthless round here.

As I stopped in front of him, he smiled. And then he said something that was like a punch to the guts.

'Danny Bioletti.' He spoke quite posh. Like it was put on. Like he'd taken his words and ironed them flat. And he took this dramatic pause while I registered that he knew my name, my real name. My full name. 'I was so sorry to hear about your dad.'

I knew I had to get away. I didn't know who this geezer was, but he wasn't good news. I rammed my foot on the pedal, fighting the urge to throw up, and pedalled as hard and fast down the street as I could. Fight or flight reaction. And I flew.

He couldn't be Old Bill, could he? Old Bill wouldn't dress like some freaky Boy George wannabe?

But he had to be Old Bill. In plain clothes? Or whatever

the opposite of plain clothes was? How did he know my name otherwise? Was he after me? Did he want to send me back to Hansbury? But why do it with the barmy car and mirrored shades routine? And if he was plain clothes then I'm sorry, those clothes weren't plain. Halfway up Wardour Street, swerving for my life to avoid pedestrians, I saw he was still idly leaning against the car, watching me go.

I got the hell out of Dodge.

And he was dodge. Well dodgy.

But if he was Old Bill why didn't he come after me?

And why was I so shaken up by the brief encounter?

Coz he'd known my name. My real name. And I'd never seen him before.

I wanted to speak to Guinness. I'd not seen him for the best part of a month. I went to a phone box and called the number I had for his Linda. She told me he no longer lived there. When I asked her where he was she said she didn't know. I asked did the police take him. She gave a curt *Yeah, they mighta done*. I hung up.

Anger coursed through my veins. I snapped the receiver up again and redialled the number, shoving a 10p in the slot.

'D'you know another thing? I think it's bang out of order calling Guinness a darkie, you racist twat.'

And I hung up. I stood there, staring at the phone, furious. The fear triggered by the man in the suit, the fear of the unknown, the new, was making me the angriest I'd been in a long time.

Suddenly the phone rang. I picked it up. No-one rang phone boxes, did they?

It was Linda. 'Racist I might be,' she snapped. 'But you're the one that calls him fucking Guinness.'

And now it was her turn to hang up.

As she did it was like I'd been slapped in the face. And the sharpness of it had slapped some sense into me. And I could see she had a point.

His name wasn't Guinness, it was Sam. Guinness was a piss-take because of the colour of his skin.

I felt bad. I'd used the name so much, I'd forgotten what it meant. So had he.

But it in no way made it right.

Fancy his Linda, the old trout, teaching me a lesson.

From that second on I vowed only to ever think about him as, or call him by, his real name.

As I stood in the phone box, my BMX leaning up against it outside, I became aware of a car slowing down on the street outside. I looked. It was him. He was looking at me.

OK, so this was it. He was going to arrest me. *Sod it. I've had enough. I can't cope with this. Slap the handcuffs on, mate, and take me now.*

I thought he'd stop the car and get out.

He didn't. He did a thumbs-up sign at me. Then he sped off up the street.

The Green Lady

There's a painting by this Russian artist guy called *The Chinese Girl*, but you might know it by its more common name, *The Green Lady*. It's a really well-known painting, and it's distinctive because the artist fella painted this Chinese woman and used green paint for her face. She's wearing this brown dress with yellow bits at the top and she's got this black hair. If you can't picture it, look it up online. It's the sort of thing that was over every other fireplace in St Helens when I was growing up.

Around this time I was cycling round Piccadilly when I saw a queue outside the Café de Paris. I stopped the bike coz I'd never seen a more amazing, more motley crew waiting to go into a club. There were fellas in drag, but not just any old drag, really over-the-top drag; one had lightbulbs flashing round his face – God knows how. There were women in PVC bodysuits. I couldn't take my eyes off them.

I knew the bouncers at the Café by sight so I asked one of them, an Irish guy, what was going on. He answered with a grin, 'Kinky Gelinky.'

And that's when the door opened, and that's when I saw her.

The girl doing the door, the sort they called in those days the 'door bitch', was a sight for sore eyes. And I knew in a heartbeat that she was significant – not just because she was the most mesmerizing creature I'd never laid eyes on, but because the thump of my heart told me she was. Instinct, again, was speaking to me.

And this was no ordinary door bitch. She was completely done up as the Green Lady. Her face was coated in green make-up, her eyes painted to look Chinese. She had a black wig on. The brown dress, the yellow bit at the top. And, this actually made me laugh out loud, she had a picture frame attached to her which went all the way around her upper body and face. She ignored my laugh and clasped a clipboard to her chest and shouted, 'Guest list!'

I recognized the accent as Mancunian.

I asked the Irish guy what her name was.

He said, 'Natalie.'

I took one last look at her, then cycled on.

I wanted to see her again, of course, so I was a bit lax with the old pimping duties at the Rack that night and kept swanning away to go past the Café and glimpse the Green Lady. She never noticed me; she was too busy working for that, but each sighting of her made me want her more. I'd never felt like this before. I'd never been in the company of girls my own age before. And I wanted to know more.

The last time I went to look, there was another woman on the door. Bit boringly dressed, truth be told, in a sort of ballet outfit and bald head. I asked when the club was on again, and the bouncer told me it was a monthly thing. I hoped and prayed that the Green Lady would make a comeback next month.

Another plan

Instinct told me Natalie was going to be part of my life. Up until then I'd sometimes worried I was asexual. I fancied so few people. Maybe it was a result of being so self-reliant all this time, but the idea of copping off, or having a girlfriend, or settling down and having kids – it was anathema to me. Maybe it was this that made me so at ease amongst the fellas I worked with. Maybe it was because I didn't need anyone else by my side dragging me down like Guinness, sorry, *Sam*, had. Look after number one. With someone else at your side, that's harder to do. Eventually you'll be caught out. But those glimpses of Natalie changed all that. I planned that next time, I'd speak to her. It was going to be so straightforward. I'd charm the birds from the trees. I'd be sweetness itself. She'd recognize my St Helens accent. She'd feel like I was a piece of home. And she'd be drawn to me. Simple.

But then what?

I was fifteen, with no sexual experience at all beyond the odd solitary wank. What did I have to offer a woman who was so worldly wise as to be working the door at that freakishly bang-on-trend place?

So I took myself to a prostitute in a side street in Soho – not my Framboise, no point shitting on your own doorstep – and basically told her to teach me everything.

And on a musty single bed with a framed *Beverly Hills Cop* poster looking down on me – 'I just love Eddie,' the hooker told me – she did.

I was now officially a man of the world. I was ready to meet the Green Lady again in a month's time. Bring it on, baby!

A surprise on Framboise's couch

I went in to get my bike one morning as usual. Well, a bit unusually, I was running late, as I'd seen a woman being knocked down by a car. I'd stopped to give a witness statement to the police, upstanding citizen that I was. I'd given a false name and date of birth, but they'd not radioed in to check I was the real deal. Anyway, that made me late, and when Framboise opened the door she was looking a bit flustered.

'Can you come upstairs?'

As I followed her up the rickety staircase, she added, 'There's someone to see you.'

She was sounding apologetic. I felt a surge of excitement as I wondered if it'd be Sam. But when she pushed open the door to her living room, there, sat on the couch, was Him.

The man in the fun-fur coat. The shades were off now, and his eyes were like pinpricks. He was on something. And he was chewing gum like it was going out of fashion.

'I'm sorry,' she said. And I turned to run back down the stairs.

'What you so fucking scared of?' he called after me.

His voice didn't sound so posh this time. And the 'u' of

fucking sounded definitely Northern. Was the posh bit just an act?

I looked back. 'Who are you?'

'Don't you remember me, Danny?'

Framboise pushed past me. 'I'll leave you to it.' And she went onto the landing and closed the door, shutting us in.

'I just wanted to see you, Danny.'

'Who are you?'

'I'm Declan. Declan Wolfe.'

Declan Wolfe. The name rang a bell.

Declan WOLFE? The lad from the street behind us whose mam had died and whose dad had come round to sort the broken toilet out (amongst other things)?

I looked at him again. Could it be? Could it really?

'What d'you want?'

It was like he'd forgotten. He just sat there chewing, staring at me.

'I'm not rent,' I said.

'I know. Little straight lad like you? I'm not fucking stupid, Danny. How's your mam?'

'I haven't got a clue, Declan.'

He nodded. Like he understood. He stood up and went and looked out of the window, down onto the back of Wardour Street.

'I hardly ever go back now. Dad can't accept . . .' and with a flourish of the hand he indicated what he was wearing and his hair and . . . his life, no doubt. He fell back onto the sofa. His energy was all over the place. Probably the drugs.

My, Declan Wolfe! How you've changed!

He patted the sofa next to him. The sofa I sometimes slept on. I shook my head. I was fine standing.

'I know Soho. You were a new face. And then I placed it.'

'What d'you do with yourself now?'

'Promotion.'

I had no idea what that meant.

'Club promotion.'

'It's not Kinky Gerlinky, is it?'

He shook his head.

'How old are you now, Danny?'

I shrugged.

'Oh, come on. You and I both know you're too young to be down here. Where are you living?'

Again, I shrugged.

'What's the matter, Danny? Cat got your tongue?'

I shrugged again, just to wind him up. He stood up again and moved closer to me. I backed to the wall.

'You don't take the piss out of me, Danny Bioletti. I run Soho. If I want you out, I'll get you out.'

He owned Soho? What was he on?

'You don't believe me?' He sounded threatening.

'I'm not really that arsed, Declan.'

'I'll prove it.'

'You what? How?'

'Tomorrow. Get yourself into trouble.'

'What d'you mean?'

'Oh, I don't know. But you will. Create a situation where a policeman stops you. When he asks for your details, give your name. Your proper name. Date of birth, everything. And you'll see.'

'See what?'

'That it is indeed possible to be bigger than Old Bill.'

I said nothing. He was off his head, clearly.

'It's my way of showing you I'm a man of my word.'

He was losing me. I was confused. I wasn't sure what he

wanted from me, or why he felt the need to prove himself to a fifteen-year-old lad.

'And what if I give my name? And date of birth? And they send me back home? I don't wanna go home.'

'Well, you can't go home. Your mam's inside.'

Wow. Well, that was news to me. It made sense. But it was still news.

'Is she?'

'Do you like games?'

I shook my head.

'Well, you'll like this one.'

'What's she inside for?'

'Nothing too serious.' He looked surprised. 'You didn't know?'

I shook my head.

'I can't remember what she's inside for, but I'll know by Monday.'

Was it me he wanted?

'When I said I'm not rent. I'm not . . . I'm not bent, or gay, or . . .'

'I don't want sex with you, Danny. Put me to the test. See if I'm trustworthy. And touch wood . . .' He tapped the door-frame. 'We can do business together.'

He took a biro from the pocket of the fun-fur coat. He ripped a piece of wallpaper off the wall (the room wasn't in the best of states). He wrote a number on it.

'And when I pass the test – call me.'

I looked at the paper. His long O1 number, and DEC scrawled above it. He opened the door and went out of the room. I stood there for a while, heard the front door slam, then heard Framboise coming up the stairs.

'What did he want?' she asked, lighting a cigarette.

'Well, you tell me. He was sat on your couch, love.'

'He paid me two hundred quid. Then said he'd wait for you. Said he knew you.'

Under the radar. Not too many questions.

'Not really,' I said. 'Disgruntled punter. All sorted.'

She looked disappointed.

'I'll get my bike.'

She nodded.

Blimey, two hundred quid?

A crushing disappointment and a kerfuffle on the tube

Meeting him had unnerved me. I'd wanted to spend the weekend getting ready, mentally and fashionably, to attend the club on Monday, but I found I couldn't settle. Even though I didn't see Declan, I felt at all times like I was being watched. Was I? Did he have contacts, watching my every move? I was shit on the Meat Rack. Every bloke who approached me, I was convinced they were a mate of his, and it put me off my stride.

Saturday night I cycled past the Café and there was a queue of goths waiting to go in. I high-fived the Irish bouncer – quite out of character, but I knew how to play the game – and I said with a laugh, 'Is it that Kinky Gerlinky this Monday?'

A nod told me it was.

'Thinking of coming myself,' I said, like he was going to be blessed by a royal visit.

'Can't wait to see what you'll have on.'

'Oh, I think I've got a few things up my sleeve.'

Truth be told I'd not, but I still had a couple of days' grace to get something suitably ridiculous. The ends would justify the means.

'Is that Natalie gonna be working the door again, is she?'

'Hey, she's spoken for, mate.'

301

Another stomach punch. The possibility that Natalie, despite being the most gorgeous girl in Soho, might even have a boyfriend hadn't entered my tiny mind.

'You're joking.'

He could see how gutted I was. He nodded sympathetically.

'Yeah, she goes out with one of the DJs.'

'Oh, right.'

'Well, listen. We'll see you Monday, mate.'

'Yeah, looking forward to it.'

And I cycled off.

I never drank. Didn't see the point. Having my wits about me was how I got by in Soho. I couldn't think of the last time a drop had passed my lips. If ever.

But right then, I jibbed off the Rack and went to the Coach and Horses on Greek Street. With uncharacteristic abandon I left my bike outside and went and ordered a pint and a whiskey chaser. And downed them. And ordered some more. And some more.

An hour later, I staggered outside. Some bastard had nicked my bike. My own stupid fault, of course, but still, it didn't stop me swearing my head off at all the people drinking on the pavement.

I was a bit unsteady on my feet, being unused to sinking so much booze, and couldn't decide what to do.

In that moment, I happened upon what I took to be a genius idea. I would go for a ride on the tube and sleep this off.

I went into Leicester Square tube. Down the steps. I didn't understand the tube system as I was so used to my bike by then, and before that I'd relied on walking and cabs. I stared at the ticket barrier. And I decided to jump over it.

As I did – another genius idea, or so I thought – I caught my leg on the barrier, and fell in a heap on the other side.

I felt a hand on my shoulder and looked up to see a tube worker giving me daggers. He was radioing into a walkie-talkie. Five minutes later, I was outside on the pavement with him and a policeman.

The policeman was asking me my name.

I'd lost Natalie. I had nothing else to lose. And possibly something to gain.

I told him the truth.

I remember him radioing through. 'Can I get a C.R.O. on Danny Bioletti.' Then he gave my date of birth.

I was too pissed to be scared. I heard a crackle on his radio. And I remember him going 'What?!' in real disbelief.

The rest of it was a bit of a blur. But a minute or so later, I was a free man.

Swerving my way up Charing Cross Road, I couldn't really take it in. The Old Bill had stopped me. I'd committed a crime. And they'd let me go.

The last thing I remember from that night is standing in the middle of traffic at Cambridge Circus, and bellowing at the top of my voice:

'Declan! You beaut!!!'

Next thing I knew, I was waking up on Framboise's couch. I didn't have any clothes on. I think I'd slept with her.

The Wolfe of Great Queen Street

Who was I trying to kid, you know? Me. The runt of the litter. The lad who blended in with the frigging wallpaper. How on earth would I have walked into Kinky Gerlinky anyway? And how would I have impressed the fair damsel Natalie in the first place? What would I have worn? A telly on my head?

Naked but for a fig leaf? Everyone in the queue, as I watched them going in that Monday, wore 'look at me' outfits. And I could see that if they weren't dolled up to look like they'd just landed from another planet, Natalie was turning them away.

She couldn't see me, of course. No way. How would the siren of Soho see the Invisible Man staring at her from across the street, huddled next to the statue of horses on the corner? She had downplayed the outfit a bit this month, but she still looked breathtaking. Without the green slap on her mush, I could see she was more beautiful than ever. She wore this gold sequinned bomber jacket, and a pair of those weird bondage trousers that even I knew were made by Vivienne Westwood. But of course, this being the hippest destination in London, her one concession to the madness was that she was wearing roller skates.

I wanted to run across the street and drag her by the arm, roll her away and . . .

It was pointless having these fantasies. She was spoken for. As soon as I'd dragged her away, the pair of us now magically, in my mind, both on roller skates, we'd be chased by her bloody DJ boyfriend. Who'd batter me. And she'd think I was mental.

And maybe I was.

Coz look at me. Stood there. On a Monday night. Staring at the unobtainable.

Unobtainable. I liked that word. It jolted back a memory of my mammy.

We'd been shopping for a new carpet for her bedroom. We'd been in a place in St Helens, and the woman serving was right up her own arse.

I remember her saying, *When I look at this carpet, Mrs Bioletti, I think movie star. I think unobtainable.*

And then she must have remembered she was trying to flog it, coz she continued, *And yet . . . it is obtainable. Because you can actually buy it for a very reasonable price.*

Mammy had got the carpet. But from the looks of it, I was never going to get Natalie.

I took out the scrap of wallpaper and found a phone box.

I called Declan.

He told me to go over to his flat in Great Queen Street.

The deal with Declan

God only knows why Declan had done the big song and dance to win me over. He had strutted about like a peacock – *look at all this power I have* – when actually, what he wanted from me was very simple. Something that needed no wowing to get me on board. It was a straightforward enough deal: he wanted me to hand out flyers for his new nightclub. For every flyer that got a punter through his doors, I would get a pound.

I give Joe Bloggs a flyer on the street.

Joe Bloggs goes in Declan's club.

Joe Bloggs shows the flyer.

Declan knows he's one of mine.

I get myself a nice quid.

I said yes to Declan's deal.

It worked out well. It suited me. In a few months, I had several of the lads from the Meat Rack working for me, whizzing round town on their BMXs handing out the flyers. Every month I was earning thousands and thousands of pounds. But I was still heading back to the Dominion to sleep.

The deal with me

I got all the clubs buying in the end. Declan didn't have sole use of my skills. When people go clubbing, they want to have a good time. In order to have a good time they often want drugs. More often than not, when I was giving out the flyers, folk would be asking me if I knew anywhere they could get decent pills. When you work the streets you do, so I'd point them in the right direction.

After a while I got thinking: *that's where the money's at*. So I decided to cut out the middleman. Once I worked out where the dealers were getting their pills from, I went to them and starting doing my own dealing.

There was a lot of money to be made from selling pills. I could buy them from my contact at three or four quid each, and then sell them on at fifteen quid each. That's how much they went for, back in the day. And you don't have to be Alan Sugar to work out that's a pretty good markup, and profits were huge.

So if I was buying, say, in the space of a year, 100,000 ecstasy tablets – you're looking at a profit of 125k.

I often wonder how my life would've turned out if I'd not seen Declan that day on the street. Dealing had never been a goal of mine; it was something that had never crossed my mind. I never used the stuff I was selling. I hardly ever drank. It was only years later, when I went through a bit of a dark patch, that I took. And took. And took. But back then, I was clean and serene.

But the dealing was only ever meant to be a stopgap. A quick money-earner to enable me to do the things I wanted to do in my life.

I'd just have to work out what those were.

I was the kid who'd always had nothing. And I was stock-piling money till I decided what I wanted to have.

I'd always shied away from banks and bank accounts, but it

was becoming increasingly hard to keep an eye on bucketloads of money when I didn't have a roof over my head. One of my BMX lads, Fridgehead – no idea why he was called that, he just was – it was his job to keep an eye on the money all the time, and it kind of messed with his head. So one day when the figures were getting ridiculous, I decided action needed to be taken.

I realized it was best not to arouse suspicions, so using Framboise's address, I opened five different Abbey National accounts in different local branches in suburbs of London that were easy to get to on the tube. And I started depositing the cash we were earning in them each day.

Sometimes I'd think that all I wanted to do was splurge the money on travelling the world. The idea of eking out the rest of my days on some sun-drenched beach really appealed to me. Not that I'd ever experienced that before. But the freedom of not having to live on your wits, one eye behind your back – that seemed to be summed up in the fantasy of a hot beach where you couldn't keep either eye open, as you dozed in the sun.

The other fantasy I had was: buy a massive fuck-off mansion in the countryside, and just ride around it all day on my BMX. I'd have shiny floors, roaring fires, loads of land. And it would all be mine, every last inch of it.

It was these fantasies that kept me warm at night. All day long, my mind would be racing. On the go. Looking here and there. Looking for any sign of danger. At night, the stars above me, wrapped like a worm in my sleeping bag, I'd fend off nightmares, or anything that might make me anxious, with the dreams of where I'd one day be.

The marathon begins

The Green Lady, my Kinky Gerlinky girl, came back into my life one night when I went to a party put on by a mate of Declan's.

Life was so different in the eighties. You didn't have mobile phones. There was no such thing as the internet, never mind social networking. So it was really hard to stalk your prey if you fancied someone. You just had to take pot luck, and hope incredibly hard that one day you'd bump into the woman of your dreams again. Coincidence was the name of the game. And it was a very welcome coincidence that Natalie and I found ourselves in the same room on the same night. An even more welcome bit of news was that she had recently split up with her DJ boyfriend.

I don't remember everything about that evening. I've had a few haircuts since then. But these are the bits I do recall – I want to say like it was yesterday, but it doesn't feel like that at all. It feels centuries ago. Like I'm looking at the memory through an upside-down telescope. It's locked away in a glass cabinet. I can't touch it. But it's there. Maybe the glass needs cleaning, but it's there. Somewhere.

I remember her hair. Long and brown. Shiny. Good hair. Poker-straight. A fringe. Right across the eyes. Smoky eyes. At the time women used to have massive hair, blow-dried to fuck. Her bucking of that trend made me think she was cool.

I remember her clothes. She was wearing this weirdly patterned black and white stretchy catsuit thing that had holes cut out in it – on the knees, side of the chest. It showed off her figure brilliantly – also a good thing, I decided – and one of her mates said it was a Bodymap outfit. I had no idea what this meant, but I knew I was meant to be impressed, so practically gave it a round of applause.

When she smoked she twirled the cigarette round between her fingers deftly and quickly, like a mini baton being twirled by a cheerleader. I thought this was achingly beautiful.

I was too embarrassed to speak to her. I just watched from a distance, like it was the school play and she wasn't just living, she was performing. She'd see me looking, and I'd smile. But I never ventured to the stage and joined her. Everyone else was on it. Or getting off it. I, for some reason, had brought a bag of my favourite sweets with me. She probably thought I was chewing coz I was off my tits on pills. Instead the only E's I was on were E numbers.

I liked her laugh. She would tell me later that she'd been exaggerating her laugh to try and get my attention. I knew she'd seen me, but I guessed, wrongly, that I'd been dismissed: the lad who blended into the background. But when she laughed, she threw her head back and grabbed the arm of the girl next to her.

Look at me. I'm having a great time. I'm having such a laugh.

At one point her and her mates were walking out of the room. I stepped aside to let them out of the door. As she passed she flashed me a smile, so I held out my bag of sweets. She peered inside, all quizzical, but didn't take one. She said, *We're going on the roof. Wanna come?*

I did. On the way up, she took a sweet.

We were in a block of flats in Westbourne Park. I want to call it Herpes Point, but I think it was Hermes. The outside of the flats was white. I remember the windows were like the windows you get on a train. Probably someone's idea of cool in the sixties, when they were probably built, but they made you feel like you were travelling somewhere. Wouldn't have done for me. If you're going to live in a flat, isn't that where you want to chill out? Rather than feeling like you're always on the move.

We went up in a silver lift and Natalie explained that her and her mates all lived in this block. Apparently they'd been on the news recently coz the place had been found to have been built with asbestos. She also told me she'd had her car parked outside the flats one night, and when she woke up the next morning the council had painted double yellow lines round the block and she'd looked out of the window to see her motor being towed away.

We got to the top floor and then one of them used a key to a door which led to a small staircase, and the next thing I knew, we were on the roof.

I remember the view. The image has never left me. The streetlamps lighting the local streets gave the impression they were on fire: they were streams of molten lava out of which the black block buildings rose, trying to escape the danger. The Westway was a scribble of red and white lines, the cars zooming up and down it. In the distance was the skyline of London. I knew this city from the bottom looking up – to see it from the opposite angle blew me away.

As did she.

We talked. And talked. I only had eyes for the view, and ears for Natalie. After a while I realized her mates had left us, gone back down. Did they say goodbye and I didn't hear?

I didn't care.

All I kept thinking was, *I'm so glad she's not a twat.*

She was funny. And sarcastic. But she really listened when I spoke. And really smiled, and really . . . oh, she was just

310

heaven on earth. I might've been homeless, but that night it felt like I'd come home. I saw forever in her eyes. My instinct screamed at me, *this is it. This is what and who you've been waiting for.*

We talked for ages up there on the roof.

As we did, it started to rain.

As we headed inside, I told her *You're the kinda girl I could fall in love with.*

It was so unlike me. Mr Cautious. Mr Keep-it-all-in. Mr Stay-under-the-radar.

And she'd laughed. And she was like, *It's a marathon, Danny, not a sprint. Get back to me in a few years.*

When we got back to the party it became clear that Declan was off his tits. He was rabbiting away to no one in particular about the future of clubs. He kept going on about how he was 'in the know'. About his contacts. Making out he was on first-name terms with some very powerful people. Natalie said what this boiled down to was that he was in a long-term affair with a policeman who was quite high up in the Met. The bloke was still married, but shared enough pillow talk with Declan to substantiate his claims. Thinking about it, this was probably how he'd stopped me from being arrested that time. He'd had a word with someone so that when my name was flagged up in the system I was deemed untouchable, or something. A great quality to have!

He was going on about the government. And how Thatcher didn't want the West End full of people staggering round at night, off their faces. She wanted to close all the clubs in Soho and make Vauxhall a leisure destination, send the clubs there. The bars. That's the future, he said, and we thought he was nuts.

The future

I kept on seeing Natalie, hanging out as mates. After two years
– the longest wait and marathon of my life – she said she was
ready. She also issued me an ultimatum:

Stop selling the drugs and we've got a future. Keep on, and
we haven't.

I stopped overnight. I'd saved enough to pay off the lads
who'd helped me with some severance pay and still have
enough dosh to live on for a couple of years or so. I was glad
of the change, actually. I was glad I didn't have to keep watching my back.

I moved in with her. It was weird sleeping under a roof
again and not the stars, or in squats or on a series of mates'
sofas. She was starting to get fed up with being a door bitch
and fancied a new adventure. She reckoned she could have a
go at running her own club night. With the money I'd saved
from dealing, I reckoned we should go for it. So far in my
career I'd sold sex, and I'd sold drugs – now I was gonna sell
parties.

Sam, Sam, the piper's son

I'd often wondered what had happened to Sam since I'd
seen him last. I used to lie in that sleeping bag, staring up
at the black sky, and think of a rhyme we learned at nursery
school. My mammy had called our nursery 'play school'. So
when she'd said I was going to play school, I'd got confused.
There was a kids' TV programme on called *Play School*, so I
assumed I was going to be on the telly. I wasn't.

Anyway, at play school we learned this rhyme:

Tom, Tom, the piper's son,
Stole a pig, and away did run;
The pig was eat
And Tom was beat,
And Tom went howling down the street.

In my head, I don't know why, but that always came into my head when I tried to picture him. I'd change the words to *Sam, Sam* and hear the rhyme, picturing him running down the street with a pig under his arms. Don't ask me why.

And then I'd think . . . I hope he isn't running. I hope he hasn't nicked a pig. I hope wherever he is, he's safe. And happy. And doing all right for himself. I hope he's back at Hansbury, getting on with his shit, being left alone by the weirdos.

But the longer I kept hanging out with Natalie, the more everything else faded away. And with it, too, my thoughts of Sam. I'd not seen him in so long. I wanted him to know I was thinking of him. It felt like a real need that was building up in me. So one day I went down to Piccadilly and went in the souvenir shop we'd both gone into, after we'd stopped staying at his sister's. I bought a small snowglobe. It had a little model of St Paul's in it. I then put it in a padded envelope and wrote on the front, *Sam Korniskey, Hansbury Vale, Mustard Lane, Culcheth, Warrington.*

Stuck a stamp on it.

Wrote on the envelope, PLEASE FORWARD TO WHEREVER HE IS.

Bam. Over the counter at the post office. It was like saying goodbye. I just assumed I'd never see him again. I just assumed he'd never get it, that I may as well have been sending it on a rocket into the ether.

How wrong I was.

Natalie, 2014

Well, I wasn't expecting this. Here I am, sitting minding my own business, feeling cut off from the world in an empty house, again. Eating myself up with bitterness about what a mess I've made of my life, again. Sat in a house that's too big for me. Alone. Scared. Not even sure what I'm scared of. Fighting off a rising sense of panic. Again.

My phone keeps ringing. I ignore it. Again.

I don't want to speak to anyone today. Again.

There are too many agains in my life for my liking.

I look in the fridge. It's full. There's far too much in there for one person. Another thing I'm crap at. Half of it will be put out for the birds, or thrown away. I toy with ripping the wrapper off a chicken and mushroom pie and eating it cold, but there is too much bile in my stomach to digest. I shut the fridge door.

Stupid pie!

I feel sick.

I can't stop thinking about the neighbours. Cally was right. We should never have moved here.

I keep hating them for their crass insensitivity, wishing I was more vindictive, wishing I could target them all on social media with cutting observations about their tawdry little lives. You see people in the papers, online, ugly trolls in woolly hats who've made people's lives a misery with their online hate campaigns. And suddenly I empathize with them. I'm wondering whether to fashion dolls of each of my neighbours from soap and then spend the day sporadically sticking pins in them.

To try and cheer myself up, distract myself, I read the postcard that has arrived from Cally this morning.

Dear Mum

I miss you. It's really weird being so far away. Sure I'll Skype or Facetime before you get this but just wanted you to get something through the post. All good here. Ish. The modelling is going well if a bit boring. Hotel lush. Got telly in bathroom. Result.

Love you
C xx

Lush. Her hotel is lush. I wouldn't mind a bit of lush at the moment.

But hang on. The modelling is going well. Does that mean other stuff isn't?

Before I have too much time to think about this, my doorbell rings. Sensing it's one of *them* – come to, what? Apologize? Antagonize me even more? – I rush to the front door and yank it open, ready for battle. Bring it on! Natalie Bioletti is ready for battle!

But before I can say anything or see who it is, a hand darts in, faster than lightning, and slaps me round the face.

It doesn't hurt at first. It's not even a very good hit.

But as the hand retreats, I see for the first time who has hit me.

Lucy.

'What the . . .'

'How COULD YOU?!' she screams, and pushes past me into the house. 'Is he here now? Where is he?! I'll kill him! He said he was off to a conference, but you can't fool me! Said he was delivering a paper! I bet he fucking is!'

'Lucy, what the fuck's going on?!'

'Don't you fucking swear at me!'

'You've just fucking hit me! Lucy, what is it?'

She's prowling the rooms downstairs. Whatever she's looking for clearly isn't here. She pushes past me again to go up the stairs, so I grab her arm and scream,

'What's going on? Who? Who you looking for?'

'DYLAN! Duh!'

What?! I stand there, agog, as she pushes me away then runs up the stairs. I make to follow her, then decide against it. Why the hell would Dylan be here?

What does she think?

She is exhibiting the behaviour of a woman scorned.

She thinks me and Dylan have . . .

What on earth would make her think that?

I hear the heavy thud of doors slamming and pacing about as she satisfies herself that her blessed husband isn't there.

Her. With her perfect marriage.

Her. With her couples' counselling.

Her. The epitome of calm, rational understanding.

She's lost it.

I go in the kitchen and get my phone. I take a photograph of myself, then check it to see how my cheek is looking, as it's stinging now. It is disappointingly unimpressive. It just looks like I've put some blusher on in the dark. I sit at the kitchen table when I realize I am shaking. I have no idea what is going on, but she is bound to calm down sooner or later and explain.

If I felt sick before, I feel even sicker now. And I've not even done anything wrong.

I hear her hurtling down the stairs. She bounds into the kitchen and hurls something at me.

It misses. It goes skidding across the floor, making a tiny, tinny, scratchy noise. I look at the floor.

It's a necklace.

I pick it up.

It's one of the necklaces I had made for the millennium. I have one, the kids have one, Danny . . .

'I found it . . .' she spits, '. . . when I was changing the sheets in the spare room. It was all caught up in the bedding. How could you?!'

I turn and look at her, feeling myself starting to boil with rage.

'You think I've been having an affair? With Dylan?!'

'Well, it all makes sense doesn't it?'

The sanctimony in her voice is incredibly bloody annoying. She may as well be sticking to a story that . . . that . . . the world is flat.

'Does it?!'

'You've been all het up about Danny doing the dirty . . .'

'What, so I go and bang your husband? That's really my style? And, what, Dylan's confirmed this?!'

'And he's working all the hours God sends. How could you, Natalie?'

'And he's confirmed this?!' I repeat, exasperated.

'He's claiming innocence! Says he's no idea how it got there! Says I must be mad!'

'This makes absolutely no sense whatsoever!'

'Oh, it's always the woman who's mad, isn't it? Well, I'm not daft, Natalie!'

'Well, you must be!'

'It's your bloody necklace!'

I pull the neckline down on my jumper, and practically snap my own chain from my neck.

'That's mine! There! Round my bloody neck, where it always is! Or what? There's a spare? I've got two? One for each of my two faces?!'

Now she looks bewildered. She leans against the draining board like the life is draining out of her.

I place the necklace carefully on the table, like it's an exhibit in a museum, a precious piece of evidence in a trial. A thought is pushing into my head, but I push it away.

Dylan's right. It's just coincidence. It could have got there a million different ways.

Or could it?

And then. Oh God. I hear the front door open, and Owen and Matty coming in.

Alarm drills inside me. I just know that this is incredibly bad timing.

It's all a bit of a blur now. Owen's shouting through from the hallway about not answering my phone, and how he needs to talk, and Matty's urging caution, and they both come in like something's playing on their minds.

And it's like he doesn't even see her there. He just walks in, clocks the necklace, picks it up and slips it on.

'Oh God, is this mine? I've been looking for it everywhere.'

And then carries on talking about this thing he wants to tell me. He's been to visit his nan. He's got the shock of his life. Matty's telling him to calm down, he's warbling.

Then he notices Lucy stood there, drained of colour. He stops talking.

'Oh sorry, Lucy. Didn't see you there. You OK?'

She just stares at him.

'You all right, Lucy?'

She just says, 'How long?'

Oh, shit. The bad thing I imagined. She's imagined it now too. Which means she considers Dylan capable of it. Which isn't a good sign.

'Sorry?'

'How long has it been going on?'

She is less combative now. The fight has evaporated from her along with the colour. But her tone seems even more threatening than before.

Before, when she was angry at me. Now she is angry with him.

I see Owen's eyes dart towards Matty.

He has hesitated.

'What you on about, Lucy?' Matty says.

She fold her arms and does a an outraged shriek to the heavens. Then a big long shake of the head. Then . . .

'Let your boyfriend tell you.'

Owen speaks. 'I . . .' but then appears to forget what he was going to say. He looks at his necklace. 'Shit.'

'What's going on?' Matty is genuinely bemused. He looks to me. 'Do you know?'

I shake my head.

'While you were getting beaten up, Matthew,' Lucy says, her tone now more like a petulant schoolteacher, 'your boy-friend was in bed with my husband.'

Matty actually laughs. He does, he giggles. Then apologetically raises his hand to his mouth.

Owen is staring at the necklace.

The smile freezes on Matty's face. 'Bubsy?' he says. His voice is small. He sounds scared.

I honestly can't believe this is happening.

'It was only a couple of times. A few. It didn't go on very long.'

I want to be sick. I am going to be sick. I run to the back door and into the garden and throw up into wet soil. Back inside, I can hear the noise of a chair sliding. I think Matty has hit Owen. I hear him crying, 'I'm so sorry!' Owen's voice is high, girly, unlike him.

I hear footsteps behind me. I know it's Lucy before she speaks.

'You wanna sort your family out. No wonder Danny fucking left.'

I feel the anger erupt in me. I'm a volcano.

'Get out of my house!'

'Like Danny did?'

'No wonder Dylan had to go looking elsewhere!'

'Like Danny did?'

Her voice is so annoying. Thinks she's clever. Maybe she is. But in that moment, I am too caught up in my anger. She is walking towards the front door. I follow. I'm not sure why. Am I going to push her?

'Yeah, well, at least my husband's not gay!' I add. She spins round.

'Neither was mine! Till he met your slut of a son!'

'Don't shout at me, you aggressive bitch! Go and take it out on Dylan! None of this is my fault!'

'You gave birth to it!'

And she opens the front door. I see a skinny girl skating past, but I don't care. I'm not thinking of the potential audience when I scream, 'He's old enough to be his father! He must've groomed him!'

But she's not listening. She heads straight to her car and gets in. The skinny skater skids past again, not wanting to miss a thing. Lucy bangs her foot on the accelerator as she revs up and the car bunny-hops forward, almost onto the pavement. Then she realizes her mistake and smoothly reverses, does a three-point turn, and is gone.

Here's Skinny Skater again.

'Everything all right, Natalie?'

I give her an evil look.

'Fine.'

'You don't look it.'

'Neither do you.'

She just stares at me. I've heard this about people with eating disorders. They're in denial about the extent of their problems. I have an idea. In that instant, it is genius.

'Wait there!'

She looks surprised. I run inside. I go to the fridge. I catch Matty out of the corner of my eye, in the garden, smoking. Owen is sitting, crying, at the kitchen table.

'Mum? I'm so sorry.'

'Oh, piss off.'

I appear to be channelling common or garden fishwife today. So sue me!

I grab the chicken and mushroom pie, and zoom back outside again.

'Have this!' I call as I run towards Harmony. She backs off – slowly, she's not quite mastered reversing on skates – but I'm practically jumping on her, forcing the pie into her hands. 'Go on. Have a pie. Chicken and mushroom. You must be starving . . .'

'What are you . . .'

'I don't want it. You have it. You need feeding up. What's the matter with you?'

'But . . .'

'Have the bloody pie, Harmony!'

'I don't want it!'

'You need it!'

'I can't eat too much!'

'Eat it!'

'I'm dying!'

'Well, you will, if you don't fucking eat!'

'No, I've got cancer!'

My breath catches. And freeze. I can't breathe. She stands before me. So thin she could break. And in that instant I see every mistake I've ever made sweep past me like train windows. And I realize that this is the biggest mistake I've ever made. She's unsteady on her skates. She looks like she might topple backwards. I grab her to steady her. The pie falls to the ground. But instead, I find that I am falling. To my knees. Still holding onto her. She's coming down too. We fall to the pavement in a mess of limbs and skates and I think I might have broken her. I am crying.

'I'm so sorry.'

She doesn't say anything.

'I'm so sorry.'

I hear her mum coming across the cul-de-sac. I hear her panicked screams.

'Harmony? Harmony! What's the matter? Natalie, what have you done now?'

But by the time she gets to us and sees me sobbing my heart out, she is instantly sympathetic.

'Is it your husband?'

I shake my head. Margaret just looks from me to her daughter. Harmony says quietly, like it makes perfect sense, like it's something people do all the time, 'She had a fight with her friend. And then tried to give me a pie.'

Margaret nods, though I can see she is as wrong-footed as any rational person would be.

'Would you like to come over for some tea?'

I nod. I don't know why, but I nod. Possibly because I can't face going back indoors yet. I'm pathetic. A woman I barely know, and her dying daughter on skates, help me stagger across the road. For a cup of tea. They carry me like the walking wounded, even though their suffering is surely greater than mine.

'How old are you, Harmony?' I ask, sipping sweet tea in their through lounge. Suddenly their world feels welcoming, cosy, warm. A grandfather clock ticks away, and I can't help but hear it as a countdown to her passing. This is no longer a home, but a very comfortable waiting room.

'Seventeen,' she says cheerfully, like this is an achievement.

'And what sort of cancer do you have?'

'Pancreatic.'

'I'm so sorry.'

'That's OK. You didn't give it to me!'

And she laughs. Like this is funny. And even though I want to cry for her, I laugh along too. After a while she gets bored and says she's going for a lie down.

'What's it like losing someone you love?' Margaret asks when she is safely ensconced upstairs.

I feel guilty. I originally put her scraggy hair and tired eyes down to lack of vanity. Now I realize there are other reasons. Her question stings me. Not because I don't want to go there.

But because I can't compare my loss with what she might be going through. She can.

'Is there no hope? There's all sorts of treatments these days.'

'The prognosis for pancreatic cancer hasn't changed in forty years. It gets the least amount of research, and . . .' she sighs, 'I could go on. It's my bandwagon. But no. We have hope, but we also have sense.'

'My husband disappeared. He went out one day and never came back.'

'And in a way, one day she'll do the same.' She chuckles ironically. 'I know what you're thinking. Thank God you had twins, a matching pair, at least you'll have one of them left.'

'No, I'd never think like that.'

'Sorry. You develop quite a dark sense of humour.'

'I know.'

She looks at me like she is with a kindred spirit.

'But Margaret – someone walking out. A grown adult. That's very different from losing a child. I can't begin to imagine what that feels like.'

'It's the worst feeling in the world.'

I nod.

'Magnified by about a million. Some days I don't want to get up. But as long as she's here, I have to.'

'Margaret, I've said some terrible things to you recently. To her . . .'

'Grief, I guess.'

Her pragmatism humbles me.

'How's Melody taking it all?'

'Denial. Buries herself in her music. The neighbours have no idea. They've never bothered to ask. They even know she's been in hospital. But that idiot Betty Caligary just assumed she'd been sectioned, and d'you know what? I couldn't be bothered to disabuse her of it. Let them think what they like. And when we take her out of here in her wooden box, I hope they feel guilty.'

'Are you a Christian?' I ask, remembering her words to me the other day about prayers maybe bringing back Danny.

'I am,' she says falteringly. 'But I have good days and bad days. I'm a yo-yo believer.'

And again she makes me smile.

'I want to run away, Margaret.'

I didn't even know I thought it till I said it.

'Join the club.'

We sit in silence for a while. It's a comforting silence, with no pressure to fill it, even though this woman is more or less a stranger. She's probably a similar age to me. And today, somehow, we have found each other. And it might only just be for today. For now. But there is nothing wrong with that.

'I always think,' she continues, 'that I can walk out and never come back. And that when I'm gone . . . an illustrator from Walt Disney will come along and work his magic with . . . some pastel crayons. Paint everyone happy. Cartoon birds in the trees. Rainbows. Healthy happy kids.'

'Disney does death these days,' I correct her. '*The Fault in Our Stars.*'

Margaret rolls her eyebrows. 'I didn't last five minutes in that film. Couldn't stop crying.'

Again, silence.

'Actually,' I say, embarrassed, 'I'm not sure that was a Disney film.'

'Oh well. I mostly talk rubbish. But said with conviction, you can get away with murder. What would you be running away from?'

And I tell her. I tell her about the necklace. And Lucy. And how she's one of my oldest friends. And how I've just found out that her husband and my son . . . blah blah blah. How I just don't know how to react right now.

'You've had a shock. I'm sure you'll make sense of it soon.'

'But what if Owen's fractured my friendship?'

'Then you'll just have to find a way to cope.'

'I thought she had it all.'

'Nobody has it all.'

Again, silence. I notice a framed photo on a low shelf next to the fireplace. Melody and Harmony when they were about twelve. A school photo. Before one of them lost weight because she was ill. They're the double of each other; they could literally swap heads. Bright as buttons. Hair in bunches. Smiles. Hand-knitted cardis.

'Did you hear about Tamsin from across the way?'

I shake my head. 'The one with the baby?'

'Yes. She's left her husband. Walked out one day with the baby and left him a note in the fridge. On top of a cheese salad.'

'Why did she do that?'

'I have absolutely no idea. Husband's devastated.'

'Poor thing. Does he know where she is?'

'On a round-the-world cruise.' And then she adds, like this explains why anyone would want to go on a cruise, 'She has a history of depression.'

'Maybe I should go round.' I, more than anyone, know a little of how he feels.

'Just don't take an apple pie. Apparently there's been a steady succession of women from the estate going round, batting their eyelids at him, getting coquettish over an apple pie they've made him, or a midweek lasagne.'

I smile.

'You have cheered me up, Margaret. When you threw me that party I thought you were a fame-hungry showbiz mum.'

'It was Harmony's wish to go on *X Factors* one more time before . . .' and she stops herself. 'But I don't think she's up to it.'

It's X Factor, I want to say. But you can't say that to a woman whose child is dying.

Just then the doorbell rings. I hear Harmony coming down the stairs, slowly.

'She likes to answer the door,' Margaret says quietly, 'and I like to let her. Usually she takes so long they've gone by the time she gets there.'

And we share a conspiratorial grin. I hear voices in the hall, and then Harmony comes in with Matty.

'You have a visitor,' she says, and then positions herself carefully in an armchair. She picks up a magazine, but we all know she's only here to eavesdrop.

'Hi, Matty. This is Margaret.'

They say a polite hello to each other, then Matty turns to me.

'Nat, can Owen stay with you for a bit? I don't want him around.' He looks like Margaret. Tired. Sick of everything.

A good mother might beg him to take Owen back. A good mother might fight her son's corner.

'Don't you worry about Owen. You just concentrate on getting yourself better.'

'Did you know?' His eyes go glassy with imminent tears.

I get up and hug him. And tell him I didn't. This lovely boy who my son has treated so badly. I feel his body vibrate like he's crying, but he makes no sound. I see Harmony peering over the top of her magazine. When she sees me looking she lifts the magazine higher so she disappears from view. Embarrassed, Matty makes his excuses and leaves.

Harmony's looking again. And disappearing from view again. I look to Margaret.

'I better get back. Face the music.'

She nods. 'Well, I'm here if you need me.'

'Thank you.'

As I leave, she gives me a comforting hug. I let it go on a bit longer than I usually would. Since Danny left there has been a paucity of physical contact, and now that I have some I relish it.

As I cross the road I see Matty heading off in a taxi. Owen's car is outside the house. I go in, and then I remember the chicken and mushroom pie that's still on the pavement. I go back and get it. It's all squashed from where we fell on top of it, and gunk oozes out of its polythene wrapper. I head inside.

Owen's in the living room. He's staring out of the back window, so he's not seen my return. He's on the phone. I stand. Watch. Listen.

'Yeah, well, she knows, and she's absolutely furious about it, and now Matthew's kicked me out, so yeah. Nice one. I wish I'd never fucking met you.'

He hangs up. He turns. He's wearing that Barbour coat of his father's.

'Take that off,' I say.

He looks to the coat. 'This?'

I nod. He visibly relaxes. He looks younger. He smiles.

'I can stay? Oh Mum, I thought . . . well, I don't know what I thought . . .'

'You don't deserve to wear it.'

He keeps the coat on. 'My dad wasn't all that, you know.'

His voice is steely. Like a put-upon villain in a period drama.

'Get out of my house.'

His eyes widen with incredulity. He is affronted. If he had pearls, he'd clutch them.

'I've got nowhere to go.'

'That's not my problem.'

I head into the kitchen. He follows me. 'Whatever it is I've done . . .'

'Oh, you know what you've done, Owen!'

I chuck the pie in the bin. What a waste of money.

'It doesn't make my father a saint.'

'We're not having this discussion.' I've got some of the mushroom-sauce gunk on my hand, so I run it under the tap.

'I'm sorry, Mum. I'm really sorry. Me and Matthew have been going through a hard time and . . . Dylan reached out to me.'

'Yeah, that's not all he did.'

'I was so wracked with guilt, I finished it.'

I dry my hands on a tea towel. It has a map of the Lake District. Owen made me buy it when we were on holiday there. He said it would encourage him to help with the washing and drying up. It didn't.

'What were you doing at Lucy's house when Matty was beaten up, then?'

'Finishing it!'

'In his bed?!'

'I went round there with the best of intentions!'

'Oh, you're your father's son, all right! Couldn't keep it in your pants. Don't care about anyone else's feelings, and guess what? The whole thing goes off in your face! And you get hurt. And I get hurt. And Lucy gets hurt. And as for Matthew!'

'I am not like my dad,' he says softly, almost menacingly.

'Get out, Owen.'

'Where will I go?'

'I'm sure you'll think of something.'

'I thought I saw Dad today.'

I don't want to hear. Another pathetic sighting. We've all had so many over the years.

'I went to Nan's. Had another letter from her. I'd had enough. Went round, and he's sat there on her couch.'

My stomach flips over. I fear I am going to be sick again. My heart races. What on earth is he saying?

'What?!'

'It wasn't him. It was so weird.' He starts to cry.

The little drama queen! Dangling the carrot like that! Making me think . . .

'Of course it wasn't him, your father's dead.'

'It was his identical twin. You never told me he had a twin.'

'Are you making this up?'

He shakes his head. 'Nan gave him up for adoption when they were born. He was brought up in Canada. Recently got in touch.'

'A twin?!'

Owen nods. 'I think I'm going mad. I freaked out. I am freaking out. I don't know what's wrong with me. He was really nice. Bit shell-shocked by Nan. I am, I'm going mad. Why did Dad keep so many secrets?'

That gets me. I feel sorry for him. I might be heartless. He might be seriously pissing me off. He might have just thoughtlessly wrecked everything in my life, and his. But he is still my son. My first-born. My little boy. And right now he looks so helpless.

His phone rings. He takes it out of his coat pocket. He

330

sighs. I look. The caller ID tells me Dylan is calling. I snatch the phone from him and answer. I say nothing. Then I hear Dylan's voice.

'Sweetheart, can you meet me tonight? Usual place.'

I pause. As I hear his intake of breath to say something else, I speak.

'Listen, you dirty old pervert. Keep away from my son. And this family. Forever. Got that?'

I hang up. I hand the phone back to Owen.

'What did he say?'

'Why?' Suddenly the volcano has erupted again. 'Why is important what he said?'

'I dunno, it just is.'

'Well, it's not!'

'And he's not a pervert. It was a two-way street.'

'You disgust me.'

He laughs. A short, shrill shriek of affrontery.

'God, everyone needs to lighten up round here.' He is so bloody dismissive as he passes me and opens the fridge door.

'Did I say you could stay?'

He looks round, incredulous. 'You're really kicking me out?'

'Owen, do you not have any concept of the upset you've caused?'

He fold his arms. And suddenly he's his father. His father in a business meeting where things aren't going his way and he has to be really patronizing to get his pathetic or ill-conceived point across, because everyone has to listen to him, because at the end of the day he's the bloody boss. Well, Owen is not the boss in my house.

'I know it's a fucking nightmare, Mum. But we'll work our way through it. Me and Matty'll sort it out. And I'm sure Lucy and Dylan will.'

'And what about me?'

'Well . . .'

'You all work it out. But say it's my birthday. And I want to go to Pizza Express. What do we do? All sit round playing happy families? You just didn't think, did you?'

'Yeah, but . . .'

'You lot might be all right, but what about me? What about me and my best friend?'

He looks incredulous again. I reach out and slap him hard across the face. I know it's hurt him, because it certainly hurts me.

'Out of my fucking house now, you heartless little brat!'

And he doesn't like that. I have crossed a line, just like him, and he is offended that I'm encroaching on his territory.

'And take your dad's coat off.'

He tears the coat away from him and drops it onto the table. 'If you knew the truth about Dad.'

'I know everything. He had affairs.' And then, pointedly indicating him, I add, 'Everyone does, apparently.'

'Oh, there's worse things than that, mother.' He leans into me. He scares me. 'And if you knew them, you'd burn that coat and everything that smells of him.'

He heads for the door. I call after him, following him to the hall. 'Owen? Owen, what d'you mean? You're making stuff up now, and it's not funny.'

At the front door he turns to look at me. He's crying.

'I'm not a liar, Mum.'

And he goes. The door swings shut and he's vanished. Like Harmony behind her magazine. Like Danny off the cliff. Like Cally to Mexico. Like my lovely mum.

Everyone. Everyone in my life vanishes eventually.

Danny: The Nineties

The world at my feet

By the mid-nineties, it felt like I had the world at my feet. We started our first club, China Crisis, in 1993 after a few years of running one-off nights in other clubs. With the money I'd saved from You Know What we managed to secure a long-term lease on two disused warehouses by the old flower market in Vauxhall for forty grand, and before you could say Top Night Out we were running the latest destination venue for London clubbers.

I'd wanted to call the club Milk from the off. Instinctively I knew it had legs. But Natalie thought my byline – 'the white stuff's good for you' – was too druggy, and so she persuaded me to go with China Crisis. Neither of us were particularly interested in China, it's just that the first slow dance we ever had, all those years before, had been to 'Wishful Thinking' by China Crisis. It was our song. And we both agreed China Crisis sounded like a decent name for a club.

Also, it made me feel like I was turning the tables on all those racist twats at school who used to say I looked Chinese. I'll take that insult and run, thank you.

I knew our good fortune wouldn't last forever. All clubs have a shelf life. They're there for you right now. And that's it. I just didn't know what would bring us to any sort of close, or when that would be. Everyone knows that in clubland you can be blown away in the next breeze as somewhere younger and cooler opens. But for now, we were the new kids on the block – or the new kids on Vauxhall Cross, anyway. Me and Natalie had got married with some strangers we'd met on the street at Marylebone Registry Office as witnesses, and we had a loft apartment in Shoreditch, which was yet to get trendy. Owen had been born in late '93, and we really did feel like we were living the dream. I had a roof over my head, I had money rolling in, and I had what felt like my first ever proper family.

Mini-me

Owen didn't half look like me at that age. Poor sod. I mean, I didn't have anyone in my life who could verify this. And it's not like I had any photos of me from that age – or any age, really. But I knew, looking at him, it was like stepping back in time. And because of that I was determined to make sure this little fella, who could make my heart leap with joy better than any ecstasy tablet, was not going to end up feeling anything like I did as a kid, and not end up in the sort of places I had. If there was one thing I could do, I told myself, it would be this. And it was to that end that I kept on striving to keep my nose clean, and the club buoyant, and the punters happy, and my wife like she didn't have to want for anything. Whatever she wanted, I'd try and make it happen. I had people to do it for now, and I knew that I would. No matter what.

Honour amongst thieves

There were some girls in one night celebrating a birthday party. They were on the DJ's guest list and therefore allowed in the VIP area, which was a cordoned-off area up some stairs to a balcony which overlooked the dance floor. Each night I would go and do a meet and greet with everyone up there and get them some free champagne (Pomagne in a ponced-up bottle, always already open – how did that happen?) and when I got talking to these girls, one of them turned out to be called Honour. She was beautifully spoken, and when she said she was brought up in Little Venice, I told her I used to know someone from there. When I told her it was Gretchen Tate she nearly keeled over. She was Gretchen's daughter. She said she was going to put me in touch with her mum. I couldn't help laughing to myself. Gretchen, bringing a kid up amongst all those robbers, thieves. And look what she'd called her. Genius.

A lady who lunched

'I got out of the lifting game years back. I grew tired of it. Too old. And every store detective in London knew the face. And gone were the days where I had the get up and go to actually get up and go further afield to other cities. The criminal world's changed. The gentlemen have gone. There's no place for women any more. It's all about drugs. IRA. Guns. I can't be doing with it.'

Gretchen had had work. I could see that. I'd never seen plastic surgery close up. Why would I? It hadn't really come into fashion yet, and I didn't know the first thing about it, but you'd have had to be Stevie Wonder not to work out she'd now got lips like undercooked sausages.

'I liked you, Danny. You had instinct. Everyone thinks they've got it. They haven't. It's a rare few. Still. You got out and done well for yourself. I'm proud.'

She'd taken me for lunch at the Ritz. I had to wear a jacket.

I'd borrowed one off my accountant. It was like acting in a play on the poshest stage set in the world. It made me think: so much of life is a performance. Putting on an act. Seeing it through with conviction. When are any of us ever just ourselves? Hardly ever.

'You ever need any help, you come to me.'

'Help?'

'One day you might. You never know.'

'I'll bear that in mind, Gretchen. But it's my aim to be able to stand on my own two feet now. Do you . . . d'you still see Linda? My mate's sister?'

She shook her head and tapped her cigarette holder, an inch of ash falling into an ashtray.

'She bad-mouthed me. She ripped me off. I'm good to people, Danny. I expect the same in return; shame, really.'

I remembered another time when I'd come for afternoon tea in a posh hotel. I was a child. We had the same tower of cucumber sandwiches and cakes. Same pot of tea. But it hadn't gone so well.

I wondered how my life might've been different with Gretchen as my old girl. Thinking of Honour, and her plummy voice, and her good skin and fine clothes. I pictured the childhood: leaves on trees that weren't in parks; chauffeurs taking me to private school; success, and belonging, and . . .

And I had to remind myself I'd not done too badly, all things considered.

She'd asked to see photographs of Owen, so I'd taken a packet. She leafed through them, placing them on the table in front of her like she was reading my fortune.

'He's adorable, Danny. And I can see you in him. Would you like any more?'

I shook my head. It was hard to explain. Instinct had taught me everything I knew. How to sell sex. How to own every E in Soho. Actually, how to sell E when I'd never even taken it myself. How to succeed in business. But it hadn't taught me parenting. And it scared me. Owen scared me. I'd had to keep an eye on so many people in the past, but this was a whole new ball game.

'Well. Natalie wants another, but I'm not sure.'

'And what Natalie wants, Natalie gets?'

'Usually.'

Owen brought me so much happiness. And so much fear. What if I got it wrong? What if I messed his head up, the way my folks had mine? I'd been in scary situations in the past, but none felt scarier than this. Why double that up with another kid to fret about? It felt like too much for me to handle.

As I was walking down Piccadilly afterwards, I saw the rent boys gathering. I saw the men circling. I saw other things, naturally, but I always had that instinct for a transaction. And I thought about how my life had changed. I found the spot where I last saw Sam. The world had changed – well, my world had, the Circus itself had. And it made me think of what led me there. And seeing Gretchen again had got me thinking:

I wonder what ever happened to my mum?

Bouncer

One of the bouncers at China Crisis was an ex-copper who'd been kicked out of the force for doing something dodgy, passing on information to a gangster or something. He liked to think of himself as something of a part-time private dick, so I set him a challenge. He'd do anything for money, this one. I told him to find my mum, and if he did, I'd bung him five hundred nice ones. Good lad – he found her in three days.

I didn't ask how. But I spoke to him on the Tuesday night, and by the Friday morning I had an address and a telephone number. The rest was gonna be up to me.

But as soon as I had the details, I went cold on the idea.

Natalie tried to be the voice of reason. But I just saw it as the voice of treason.

'She might've changed. Prison might've reformed her. She might go to AA. You never know.'

In my heart, maybe I did. Instinct.

'And we might be denying Owen a grandparent.'

Or making matters ten times worse.

A lady of letters

I wrote a letter to her. It was the Nineties, you did that in those days. Email was just arriving but not everyone had a computer, let alone electronic mail. When we first got the internet, me and Natalie shared an email address for ages.

I enclosed some photos of Owen for her to see, and said the ball was in her court. I had heard over the years that she had been to prison and I knew she'd have no way of finding me, as I'd run away from Hansbury but was now settled in London. If she wanted to get in touch, drop us a line, sort of thing. Another thing people did in the Nineties.

The lady at Victoria Coach Station

She was smaller than I'd remembered. But then, I'd not seen her for about twelve, thirteen years. And I didn't remember the Northern Irish accent being quite so strong. She looked lost amidst the chaos of the coach station but she looked smart, with her hair freshly set and her winter coat all buttoned up against London's icy chill. I didn't know whether or not to hug her so I opted for shaking her hand, which she looked relieved about. We'd decided she'd stay at a cheap B & B near the coach station on Ebury Street.

As we walked along she talked ten to the dozen, and I realized that in the past the alcohol must have muted her. As a child I remembered the vast acres of silence, the staring into space; I could go days without her speaking to me. All those words she'd never said, it was like she was saying them all now, to make up for lost time. She put me in mind of the club kids off their tits who talked shite if you engaged with them while you were going about doing your job.

But I could tell she was sober. I just knew. And she assured me she'd knocked that on the head years back, ever since coming out of prison. I settled her in her room, and then we took a cab over to the loft to meet Natalie and Owen, and she was sweetness personified. She'd brought some cheap perfume for Natalie, which Natalie received like she was being given a bar of gold bullion. And she brought some clothes for Owen that were far too small for him. It was clear even to her, and I felt for her embarrassment; it was as if we'd just seen a physical example of how shit she'd been as a mother. She then kept saying, 'Shall we go for a walk to the local park?' only Natalie had made us some tea, but Mammy was insistent on it. 'No, we'll go for a walk to a nice park. That's what families do. Come on, where's your nearest park?' So we got a bus up to Shoreditch Park and walked around for a bit, but you could see that Mammy was freezing her tits off, so I suggested we go and grab a coffee somewhere, and we went and found a cafe. She was edgy, nervous now, as if she might be running out of things to say. And that if she did that would be a bad thing, because in the silences, one of us might be tempted to say, *So. You were a pretty shit mother. Do we hear an apology springing from your lips?*

Or, *And what were you inside for, Mammy?*

Or, *Do I have a twin?*

Although I'd never told Natalie that personally. Mostly coz I didn't want to believe it was true. Even though there was the possibility that my twinny might walk into the club one night and go, 'Surprise, surprise!' You never knew. Stranger things had happened. And if something like that did happen, I'd just feign innocence. Nobody else knew that Dad had told me. Make it up as you go along. Usually worked for me.

Natalie mentioned that I had a mobile phone and Mammy was all inquisitive, and so I showed her it, and then she started acting like I'd handed her a ticking bomb. 'Fancy London use-lessness', I think was the phrase she used.

She said she was working back at the glass factory, only this time she was cleaning, and she described it as 'a beautiful job'.

'The girls are lovely. I mean, I'm the only white one, but some of them have immaculate personal hygiene.'

Yeah. I thought. *You didn't have much of that when you were lying face down in a puddle of your own piss, did you, Mam?*

She didn't ask me once about my time at Hansbury, or running away, or what my childhood had been like. She be-haved, nerves aside, as if we'd not seen each other for a couple of weeks and she'd always been this fine upstanding pillar of the community. It was at once unsettling and a relief. I didn't really want to think about Hansbury these days. When I did, I got anxious. And she was the reason I'd been there.

So, fine. We could all draw a veil over it and pretend it hadn't happened. That was completely fine by me.

I told her I'd been to see Dad before he'd passed on, and she shifted uncomfortably in her seat.

'He made my life hell, Natalie. I can't say I'm sad to see the back of him.'

And then she said she had a new man in her life. She'd met him at Alcoholics Anonymous – at this point me and Nat shot each other a look; it was the first time she'd mentioned anything of this nature – and they were very happy together. He was a mechanic at a 'beautiful' garage a few miles from where she now lived. And he was a good man. And a family man. The only problem was, his family were no longer talking to him, which was 'a great big shame'. She hoped we'd come up to visit soon.

She then kept going on and on about how she was going to take the clothes she'd brought for Owen back to the 'beautiful market stall' and ask the woman to swap them for bigger items, and then she'd send them down next week.

After our coffee I took her back to her hotel. Then in the evening I took her to see *Phantom of the Opera*, which did my head in, but she said she liked, as 'it was obvious they'd all put a lot of work into it.' I took her back to the B & B in a cab and said good night. No kiss. No hug. Just another shake of the hand.

Bad vibes

The next day she was taking a midday coach back to Liverpool. And then her nice mechanic was picking her up and driving her back to St Helens. She said that before she went she'd like to see the club. I picked her up after she'd had her breakfast and took her down there.

Empty clubs are strange places. The smoke and mirrors aren't there, and all there is is potential. It felt like walking round a shipwreck. The cleaners were in, but nothing could get rid of the smell of impregnated smoke, spilt beer, sweat. Ain't no joss stick gonna fix that. It was clear Mammy wasn't impressed. And being a cleaner herself, she had a few choice comments about the standard of cleanliness behind the cleaners' backs. In the office she ran a finger along my desk and checked it for dust, giving a disgusted grimace at what she saw.

'You must be very proud of what you've achieved, son,' she said. 'But I get a bad vibe off this place. Like it's cursed.'

Gee, thanks, Mum.

I took her to Victoria. She said the taxis in London were too bumpy.

'It's like someone's playing my ribcage like a xylophone.'

Some folk were never happy. I was glad we'd not arranged for her to stay any longer. Or with us, come to think of it.

Baby steps.

The snowglobe returns

I'd done a few magazine interviews, on the advice of my accountant, to make sure everyone knew about China Crisis. I didn't like seeing my face in print. Not because I found myself an ugly pig, but more because, as you know, I liked to keep my head down and fly under the radar. I was worried someone might clock the trendy new club owner and write to the magazine going, *Oh, he was a drug dealer.*

Oh, he was a pimp.

He ran away from our school.

You just didn't know who or what was gonna come crawling out of the woodwork.

I was working in the office one night when one of the bouncers came through with a face on him.

'There's someone in the queue, says he's guest list, but he's not. Says he knows you.'

This was always happening. I sighed, put down the pile of twenties I was counting.

'Name?'

'Said he didn't need to give a name. Said to give you this.'

He pulled something out of his pocket and slammed it on the table. It was a snowglobe. As the plastic snow inside it bobbed around and then settled, I saw it was the one I'd sent to Sam all those years ago.

'Bring him in here.'

'He's off his face.'

'Just do it.'

'Yes, Boss.'

I didn't like it when he called me Boss. It always sounded insincere. Like when my dad called my mum Mammy and there was that vague threat to it, that tinge of sarcasm, like she was anything but. But I wasn't going to show him how I really felt. Right now I had bigger fish to fry.

Sam. In the flesh. After all these years. I was so excited. I shoved the money in the safe and went about fixing him a brandy. I didn't know if he liked brandy, but there was a bottle and glass to hand, so I poured him some. I was nervous. First-date butterflies. I was more excited to see him again than I had been my own mother. With her, it was more a case of 'best get this out of the way in case I'm denying my son something'. But this was something I'd hoped would happen one day, but didn't really think it would.

I heard him before I saw him. I heard raucous laughter and screaming and general camp rambunctiousness. And then the door was flung open, and there he was. He raised one arm in the air, bent the other to his waist and shouted,

'HERE SHE IS!!!!'

Then did what I can only describe as a jagged catwalk flounce over, and gave me the biggest hug I'd ever had in my life.

Mammy/Sam = polar opposites.

And there were no baby steps here.

Once he'd said his hellos he went back into the corridor, and then dragged a massive holdall in with him. Eventually, the inevitable happened: I said he could stay at ours.

Room at the inn

There wasn't really any room at the inn. But we made some. One of the problems of loft living is the lack of privacy, and it was magnified with Sam staying with us. The loft was basic-ally a very large room. On one side there was a bathroom, for all the world to see. A bath and a sink on a raised platform. If you wanted privacy you could pull a curtain round the plat-form, which we started doing when he moved in. There was a door off to the loo and a utility room, so at least some things weren't shared. And the bedrooms were in these little pods that you had to climb a ladder to get to. Basically the space above the loo and utility room had been hollowed out and separated into two bedrooms, which only just fitted a mat-tress and a wardrobe in. Owen came and slept with us. Sam got his own pod. Nat was so kind letting him stay – admittedly he didn't think he'd be there long, but he'd moved to London and wanted to see what was what before deciding what to do.

Whenever I thought I might broach the subject of *What are you planning to do next?*, he'd trot out the line,

'Ah, d'you remember that night when you said . . . if you're ever in trouble, come to me? I've never forgotten that.'

Well, here he was.

Owen was fascinated by him, couldn't take his eyes off him. He was so loud, brash, camp, funny. The loft was all industrial polished cement and exposed brickwork, metal pipes and strip lights. He brought a much-needed dash of colour to it.

'He's so unlike you,' Natalie always said.

'Thank fuck,' I'd say back, and she'd do that playful slap that was Natalie sign language for *You've got to believe in yourself more.*

Sam had commandeered his pod and marked his territory with a swathe of scarves and wraps and throws – God knows why he felt the need to carry all them around with him – and he had all sorts of lotions and potions spread out on his duvet, as if he was constantly trying stuff out in a beauty parlour. Propped up to the side of his pillows was his holdall. Even that looked like it had been placed there by a dresser or art director. But he'd just shoved it there on arrival.

The chaos

It wasn't just his pod that was chaotic. He was, too. His personality. His life. I mean, I felt for him, but God, he was hard work. From the night I brought him back, off his tits, every day he rabbited on about himself. It was so draining.

He'd grown into a thick-set bloke. The muscles of his youth had given way to late-onset puppy fat. And I wasn't surprised when I saw the sort of food he put away: takeaways, burgers, everything on the hop. He was amazed that Natalie cooked proper meals, said it wasn't something he'd really had since Hansbury.

Ah, Hansbury. Whenever I asked him about it, his demeanour changed.

'That place. That fucking place, Danny. I could bring down the government with what happened. And I've got evidence.'

'What evidence?'

'That's for me to know and you to find out.'

He'd talk about Benedict Bishop like he was the devil incarnate.

And look at him now. Lording it over the country, and look at me. Fucked.

Natalie gave him help sorting out his benefits. He'd not worked since leaving Hansbury – too busy, always on the go. To my mind, he was a hustler. He wasn't the prettiest lad on the block, but blokes will pay for anything in the early hours. And back then, of course, I thought that at twenty-six, twenty-seven he was past it. Now I realize he still had youth on his side. Sometimes he'd disappear for days, then reappear off his nut with pockets full of cash.

'You never look in there,' he had said the first night, pointing to his holdall. 'Promise?'

I promised. And I never did.

The longer he came and went, the more Natalie got pissed off with him. Looking back, it was only for about a month, but it felt like a lifetime, and he never had a key. Since having Owen, one of us was usually there. Natalie had taken more of a back seat with the club, so she had to cope with him more than me, and it was starting to grate. She never dared leave him in charge of Owen for any period of time, as she felt his chaos wasn't to be trusted. She once nipped to the shops for a few bits and came back to find Owen in tears because Sam had painted some of her make-up on his face. He didn't like it, and nor did she. Words were exchanged and Sam went walk-about again.

The fridge

No, not the nightclub in Brixton. This was the Nineties. Fridges with pictures on them were all the rage. Me and Nat got one from John Lewis – I know, cutting-edge – that was bright blue, with a massive photo of a bright yellow lemon on it. It shone like a beacon against all the stainless steel of the rest of the kitchen in the corner of the loft. But after we'd had it a few weeks, it stopped working. So they said they'd exchange it for another. When the new one arrived it had a different photo on it. This one was blue on the sides, but the front showed a photo of a tropical beach. White sands, turquoise sea. We both decided we preferred it to the lemons one, so it stayed. I could spend hours staring at that view, making out I was there. I found it so calming. Whenever I was worried about anything, I could sit on the couch and stare at my fridge. Nat used to laugh that it was cheaper than therapy for me.

Actually, a few times she suggested I go for therapy. I hadn't told her half the things I'd seen in my life. I'd told her a few, and even that tiny amount made her think that a bit of counselling might help. I know you're supposed to be honest in relationships and share everything, and not be scared of being judged. But you know me: I like to keep a bit back. And blimey, if she thought I needed help after all she'd heard, imagine if she'd heard the lot! She'd have me down as a basket case.

No shortage of offers

Women were always coming on to me in the club. The odd fella, too. But I'd never really been driven by my dick. I didn't find it that hard to stay faithful. I mean, don't get me wrong, some of these birds were beautiful. Real stunners. But I'd promised myself, hadn't I? I'd never do anything to screw up what I had at home. Some of the blokes in the office thought I was mental. They reckoned what Natalie didn't know didn't hurt her. But that was mostly their booze and lines talking. To do their heads in, sometimes I wiped baby oil on my desk where they'd do their lines. I'd try not to laugh as they upended their wraps of coke onto the surface and then not be able to work out why it wasn't being hoovered up through their tenners when they went in for a snort. Got them every time with that one.

My favourite times

It may have been a throwback to what I did when I was a kid, but the happiest times back then were not when I was working, but when I was back in the loft, lying on this massive inflatable armchair we had, Owen sprawled over my chest, with the telly on in the background. And I'd do silly impressions of whoever was on the box. And Owen would lie there, chortling. And when I stopped he'd go, 'Again.' Or just poke me in the arm. Or poke his knee into my chest. And I'd do some more. He smelt of fresh sheets. They were the best times.

Just another manic Monday

I woke to the sound of Sam kicking off. Natalie was shouting at him, and Owen was crying.

'For fuck's sake!' I shouted. 'Do you know what time I got in? Jesus!'

'Danny? Tell him!' – Natalie's voice.

I dragged myself off the mattress and started clambering down the ladder. Sam was still screeching.

'Sam, will you pack it in?'

'I've told you! No-one goes in my bag!'

'Who went in your bag?'

'Owen went in his bag! He's two! He doesn't understand!'

'Yeah, well, he does now! Don't you, you little twat!' The tone in his voice was murderous.

'Right that's it. Take your things and get out of my house.' I really had had enough.

'It's not a house, it's a loft. As you keep on telling everyone. It's hardly Buckingham Palace, dear!'

'I want you out, Sam. You don't speak to my son or my wife like that.'

'You said. You said any time I was in trouble. Come to you. Liar!'

'You came! And now you're going! You've outstayed your welcome, lad!'

He was walking round the loft picking up his things, grabbing his holdall to him for dear life. He was only half dressed as he stumbled to the door, shoving things into the bag. At the door he looked back, lifting the bag aloft.

'I could bring down a fucking government with this!'

And that was it. He was gone. Now bloody Natalie was crying as well, hugging Owen to her, rocking him on the sofa, telling him the nasty man was gone.

Then it was, 'Nice one, Danny. Bringing that into our house. I told you he was dodgy.'

'I was trying to do the right thing, love.'

'Well, next time, don't bother.'

'Oh, don't worry, love. There won't be a next time.'

I tried to join them on the couch, to put an arm round Owen and tell him everything was OK. But she sort of pulled him into her more, like it was me he was scared of.

'It's not me he's scared of,' I went.

And she gave me this look. Incredulous. As if to say, *Oh, isn't it?*

Down in the street below there was some sort of commotion going on. A car horn was beeping and someone was shouting. I went to the window. Sam was stood in the street, in the middle of the road. Traffic had stopped each side of him and he was staggering round, swinging his bag, shouting either up to us or out to the world. I pulled the blind down to block him out. I turned to Natalie. Owen was calming now.

'We have never, ever spoken to Owen like that,' she said softly to me. 'I don't want my son raised in that kind of environment. I don't want to replicate your childhood.'

'You don't know the first thing about my childhood.'

'I don't wanna know.'

'Don't worry. I only tell people I'm arsed about,' I said. Arsey. And then clambered back up the ladder to go back to sleep.

I regretted it instantly, of course. The promise I'd made to myself. To keep her happy. And now I was saying things to hurt her. Is this what happened when you'd been together so long?

I buried my head in the pillow, hating myself. Then looked up at the ceiling, turning on my back.

'Sorry!' I shouted out. 'I'm a tit.'

But instead of a response, I just heard the front door going. Ah, well. Served me right.

A crisis in China

It was just a normal night in China Crisis. The place was heaving. It was a hot summer's night, and Natalie wasn't in coz she'd just found out she was pregnant. Although I'd been wary of taking the plunge and having another, the news had thrilled me, and I was bouncing round the gaff with a spring most definitely in my step. Life was good. Profits were up. Every banging DJ in London, the world probably, wanted to play a set at CC. Life was sweet.

The only dark cloud on the horizon was that our licence was up for renewal, and word on the street was that the council were looking for any excuse these days to shut down the clubs that had sprung up in the area. Not that the attendees were a nuisance to the locals, per se; Vauxhall Cross was just a massive roundabout and a couple of train stations. But MI6 had not long opened their new headquarters there, and there was surveillance everywhere. And they didn't miss a thing. No doubt the council didn't want to go showing themselves up in the eyes of the spies. So I was paranoid about getting any sort of bad reputation. The slightest fracas in the club, I was on it: cops were called, the kids detained. I couldn't afford to have any trouble at my door. Or outside it.

I was giving it large on the VIP floor, coked up to the eyeballs as per – with Diet Coke, naturally – when Jimmy the bouncer came up the stairs and gave a flick of his eyes for me to follow him. I knew immediately there was trouble.

That trouble was a girl lying dead in a corridor out the back of the club. God knows who she was. And God knows what she was doing in the back corridor, which hardly anyone ever used. There was a fire escape there, and her head was up against it. She must have been trying to get out.

'She's dead, Danny.'

I could see that. For a moment I froze, staring at her. Somebody's daughter. She could only have been about fifteen.

'Who the fuck let a kid in?'

He shrugged.

'Fuckinell. Has she got a pulse?'

He shook his head.

I opened the fire door. Looked up the lane behind. Nobody about. I panicked. I'm not proud of what I did next, but I couldn't think what else to do.

'Get her in your car. Drive her to St Thomas's. Drop her off at A and E. Leave her there. It's only what an ambulance'd do.'

He looked at me like I was mad.

'I'll give you an 'and. Got your keys?'

He nodded.

And God alone knows if those surveillance cameras all suddenly spun round to watch two grown men carry a young girl out of a club, but something happened, because as soon as we were getting into Jimmy's car there was a flashing blue light in our faces.

I turned in the performance of my lifetime. I was so convincing, even Jimmy seemed to buy it. As they radioed through for an ambulance, I insisted we were just about to drive her to the hospital. Look, I had my phone, I was just about to call the cops myself. We'd literally just found her. We'd get her to hospital just as quick as any ambulance. We were a stone's throw away.

The girl's name was Tiffany Keith. She was from a good middle-class family in a leafy suburb of London. Her dad was a copper. Her mum was a teacher. She'd been to a friend's birthday party and taken E for the first time. For a while after her death, she became the poster girl for the anti-drugs brigade. She'd only had one tablet, but had drunk so much water (as she'd heard the drug made you dehydrated) that it caused some sort of overload in the brain. It was her caution that killed her. Well, if she'd not taken the drug, of course she'd have still been alive.

The only saving grace for China Crisis was that her friends were adamant they'd taken the drugs at the party and not at the club, where they'd gone on afterwards. She was on the cover of every newspaper, our logo spread-eagled across it too. And even though some of the press were quite lenient on us – I was coming across as the bewildered boss who was so upset he tried to drive her to hospital himself; some papers even printed a map showing how close the club was to the hospital – instinct told me, in a very loud voice, that our days were numbered.

I never told Natalie what had actually happened. I gave Jimmy a pay rise, but he was too messed up about it to ever come clean about what we were really doing.

If anything, the girl's parents were the ones pilloried for letting their young daughter attend the sort of party where there might be drugs. The general consensus was that Tiffany and her pals looked well over eighteen, and this was in the days before we asked for ID on the doors of clubs. If you looked the part, you got in. So in a bizarre twist of fate, her mum and dad were being seen as the devils and me and Jimmy as the saints.

And although this sat as uncomfortably on me as a bull mastiff on a stool, what could I do? The die was cast. I had a little lad, and a baby on the way. I needed to keep that club open.

Remarkably, we kept our licence. But it was a black mark against us, and we were warned that if there were any further incidents we'd be in serious trouble. We didn't even face prosecution, as it was deemed that we hadn't exercised undue negligence. We were in the clear. We couldn't believe our luck.

We lucked out legally, but word gets around. And from then on, China Crisis was seen as the killer club. The place where that girl had died. After a few weeks of ambulance chasers parting with their hard-earned cash to see what the fuss was all about, to visit the almost-grave of Tiffany Keith, the numbers started dwindling. The kids wanted to go where they were safe. And let's be honest, the human rights record in China has never been that great. Talk about a crisis!

Sinking

It's pointless running a club when no-one wants to come. It's better to shut down and rebrand or move on. I knew we had to do it, it was just deciding when. The better DJs didn't want to come any more, even the ones we'd given their first breaks to. There's no loyalty in clubland.

Natalie was five months pregnant and was now saying she didn't want to bring both kids up in London. She'd taken against the grime and pollution, the crowded streets, tubes, buses, the fact that no-one ever spoke to you in public without risk of being sectioned. Since Thatcher had introduced the care in the community lark, honestly, everyone assumed anyone who opened their mouth in public had just been let out of the local asylum. But with our savings disappearing, the only thing we had going for us was our loft. The mortgage was paid off. Maybe we could sell that and use the money to buy somewhere up North. A contact passed on some advance news of some railway arches in Manchester that Railtrack were going to be selling off, but the purchase price was sixty grand. Sixty grand we didn't currently have.

Salvation

I'll never forget where I was when that initial phone call came through. I was walking down Shoreditch High Street holding Owen's hand, taking him to a soft play games session in a converted church. We always attracted looks and glances whenever we were out. I looked too young for my years and Natalie always dressed the kid in über-cool clothes that she got from designer friends who frequented China Crisis. Or used to, before the rot set in. I can still picture what he was wearing. This sort of woollen beanie hat, an oversized cardigan coat thing, and baggy jeans. My mobile rang, and a posh voice said,

'Hello, is that Daniel Bioletti?'

'It is.'

'Oh, hello, Mr Bioletti. Sorry to disturb you. Do you have two minutes to talk?'

'Possibly. Who is this?'

Instinct told me to be wary.

'I'm calling with regard to a friend of yours. Samuel Korniskey.'

'Oh, shit. What's he done now?'

Owen looked up at me. He knew 'shit' was a bad word. I pulled a 'sorry' face, and he looked away.

'I was wondering whether we might meet to discuss that. It really could prove quite advantageous for you.'

He'd piqued my interest. Anyone using the word advantageous did.

It was only when I hung up that I realized I'd arranged to meet a fella without even getting his name.

Disadvantageous. But I was still going to go.

We met on the South Bank, by the Royal Festival Hall, next to the steps up to Charing Cross Bridge. The man was in his mid to late forties, and had the air of a civil servant who'd done a trolley dash in Burton's Menswear to try and look like a normal man on the street. It was like he was in fancy dress. Mr Normal. He walked up to me confidently and held out his hand.

'Danny? Alastair Carmichael. Let's walk and talk. Today I will be speaking completely off the record.'

He said he was representing an anonymous third party. He said he wanted to sound me out about something, no strings attached.

Except when he got to the end of his little discourse, there weren't just strings, there were frigging guy ropes attached.

It turned out Sam had been a busy boy since I got rid of him that day. He had been making a bit of a nuisance of himself up the Houses of Parliament, turning up on the gate and waving his bag in the air, shouting, 'HERE SHE IS!' and claiming he could bring the whole place down with what he knew. And he claimed to have evidence.

When this had proved fruitless, he'd gone to the police. He'd made an accusation against Sir Benedict Bishop – that over the course of many years, Sir Benedict had sexually abused him at his home on days out from his assessment centre. He said he had proof in the form of letters that Benedict had written to him over the years, but he wasn't prepared to show them until he had some sort of financial compensation from the MP for messing up his life. When the police explained that wasn't how it worked, Sam asked how it did work. They said that they would need to see evidence and decide whether to press charges. Sam said he'd think about it. He then returned a week or so later saying his flat had been burgled and the evidence stolen. But he was adamant he now wanted to press charges, as he felt 'the powers that be' had got wind of this and had it in for him, which is why they'd robbed the evidence from him.

As this was now an investigation that stretched back a good few years, there was no physical evidence. This was just going to be Sam's word against Sir Benedict's. But Sam was also adamant that his best friend from the assessment centre would back him up and tell them the abuse had happened. That friend was, of course, me.

Oh, God. This was not something I wanted to get into. I felt a pang of fear in my guts. Did I really want to take on the establishment when things were already going so badly for me?

But it appeared I had a Get Out of Jail Free card.

'What we are proposing is this. We are friends of Sir Benedict. He is a man of good character, at the peak of his career. It will be your word against his. Mr Korniskey is clearly an unstable individual.'

Yeah, you got that right, mate. But maybe you need to ask yourself why?

'And were you to corroborate his story, this could ruin your character on the stand in a court of law. It would be a very hard case to prove, and a decent barrister would make mincemeat out of two boys who'd been in care.'

OK.

'I believe you are in the process of trying to secure a loan to purchase new business premises in the North West?'

How? How did he know that?

'Unsuccessfully.'

My eyes narrowed. This was like talking to God. He knew everything.

'If you were to deny Mr Korniskey's claims, this would be looked upon very favourably. And you would discover that you had several successful financial backers to help you in your transition.'

Jesus. He was offering me some sort of deal?

'So, what? I say that Sam's lying, and miraculously I get money for my new club?'

'You wouldn't even have to accuse your friend of lying. You could just claim innocence. That you don't actually know.'

We'd stopped. We were leaning on railings looking out onto the Thames. Today it looked like gravy.

They wanted me to sell Sam down the Swannee – whoever *they* were. Which, the more I thought about it, meant this person was probably Benedict's right-hand man.

'I need time to think,' I said. And I did.

'I hear there are great things afoot in the North West. Liverpool, Manchester, all going to get complete makeovers.'

'How much time have I got?'

'If I were you, I'd expect to be hearing from the police in a matter of days.'

Ah, the ticking bomb.

'Give me half an hour.' He looked taken aback that I might resolve this so quickly. 'Meet me back at the steps to the bridge in half an hour.'

He nodded, unsure whether this was promising or not; after all, I'd given nothing away.

My heart was pounding in my chest. I ran. I ran through the side alleys of the South Bank, away from him, past stretches of grass, across streets, under barriers, till I found myself in Cardboard City. It's not there any more, but it used to be this crucible of a shanty town: fires burning, makeshift boxes covered in old curtains, the smell of piss, the sound of groaning. I kicked a can. Some grey-looking fella with a nicotine beard looked up. I ignored him. I went and leaned against one of the concrete pillars that seemed to be holding up the roundabout above. One of the busiest intersections in London, and the homeless had used it as their umbrella. And I thought. And I thought.

I had accused Benedict Bishop of this before. And I'd not been believed. And why?

Two things. Firstly, I'd told a social worker who'd gone and repeated my accusations to a fellow abuser.

Secondly, I'd had no evidence.

All I had ever seen was Sam chatting with this fella. All I'd then seen was him clambering into his Rolls-Royce. And back then, Sam had told me he hadn't laid a finger on him. Since then, the only things I knew were the hints that Sam had dropped when he'd reappeared in my life.

But I couldn't go back to this Alastair bloke and tell him it didn't matter coz I didn't know anything for FACT. There was nothing I'd witnessed, in terms of Bishop, with my own two eyes.

But he didn't know that.

They were assuming Sam was telling the truth.

If I went and told him, 'OK, I'll say nothing,' I'd stand to make a lot of money here.

Sixty K was a lot in those days. It still is, of course. But no-one else was going to get me that money right now.

They wouldn't know I was hiding an untruth. Or was it a truth? I was even confusing myself. Should I just step up to the plate and defend Sam?

The bottom line was, I'd be a useless witness. I'd not seen anything; I'd be laughed out of the police station, never mind the court.

But maybe I should talk to the police. Tell them what I'd told the social worker that day. Stand up against all the shit that went on that must have messed up so many lives.

I was torn. The idea of the sixty grand kept spinning round my head like a boil wash.

I looked around me at the squalor. I certainly didn't want me or my wife or my kids to end up anywhere like this. And for what? To defend a lad who'd kicked off at my toddler? Sam? Off-his-face, talking-shite Sam?

I looked back to the concrete buildings barring me from the steps to the bridge.

I'd decide on my way to meet the bloke.

I started to walk.

Cally, 2014

Aba says she's going to call Mum about what happened at El Paisano.

That is SO . . . UNFAIR!

Why? Well, several reasons actually:

One: I didn't really do anything wrong.

Two: I didn't do any drugs – the staff at the restaurant put paid to that.

And three: well, all of the above, really. Plus it was that stupid insect Iris who practically forced me into the toilets. If it was the sort of place that had CCTV cameras in it they'd have seen that, et ceterata n shiz. I was practically frog-marched to the loos, like something out of World War Two n shiz. Completely ridonculous. But oh no! I'm now officially the big bad wolf or something. When really I should be Little Miss Red Riding Hood, et ceteratalala.

I quite like that. Et ceteratalala. Might start saying it. Might make it a thing.

'I don't know why you're bothering, you know, Aba,' I say, like it really wasn't a big deal.

'Because, like Bimbi said, you need to learn that your actions have consequences.'

God, she's changed her tune. She's come over all holier-than-thou. Whereas up until the 'incident' occurred she was half-cut on piña coladas ninety per cent of the time and getting on everyone's tits with her non-stop twerking. Jeez! Talk about double standards!

THIS WHOLE TRIP IS TWISTING MY MELON, GUY!

Aba says everyone is really pissed off because the restaurant have banned us from going back and that's seriously bad news as El Paisano was the only place Seth wanted to eat. Last time he was here he got food poisoning from a crab shack on the beach, and that's put him off it for life. He's now insisting the magazine provide him with his own personal chef while we either eat in the hotel or down on one of the salmonella stalls on said beach. Well, I'm more than happy with pizza, thank you.

I seem to have gained some new-found respeck from those haughty knoblets that are the other models on the shoot – Angel and the severe lesbiany one – not Nancy, she's always thought I was coolio inglesiarse. They give me the time of day now. And the severe lesbiany one even said she really liked my hair over breakfast this morning. Well, I say that; what she actually said was, 'I covet your hair. It's so . . .'

'It's a wig,' I butted in. 'I went prematurely bald because of the stress about my dad going.'

'Really?!'

'No.' And then I tutted – which, when I think about it, is a bit rude – she was only being nice. So I take her a bottle of water later, when she's shooting on the beach, and say something about her looking hot.

Only as I walk away I think, ERMIGERDDDDD – hope she doesn't think I meant *hot* as in sex on legs. So I turn round and call back, 'As in temperature?'

And she's like, 'Sorry?'

So I explain, 'Just in case you thought I was a total lez pants?'

She looks back to Seth. Iris prods at her grass skirt.

Every time I see Aba, I'm like, 'Have you called her yet?'

And she's like, 'I'm just about to,' or 'My phone's dead,' or 'Mind your own, nosey Joan.' No, I have no idea what that means either and it's incredibly irritatingado.

I think I might be depressed. I'm choosing to stay in my room more, rather than hang out on the beach with the others. Depression is no laughing matter, I've seen documentaries about it. And Stephen Fry's got it. Oh my God. Maybe it only happens to super-brainy intelligent intellectuals like me and him. Maybe I'm like . . . a genius child. I'm sure there's a word for it, only I can't think of it.

Oh God, I should really know that word. Especially if I'm so intelligent now.

I go online on my iPad and do an IQ test to double check. But four questions in I know I'm doing really shit at it, so I switch it off. I think I got the IQ test for, like, forty-year-olds. I don't understand half the things they're asking me. And I'm fracking brainy! Imagine if thick people were doing it. They might take it really seriously and have no chance and be like, 'Oh God, I'm really stupid.' Whereas everyone knows it's really cruel to let stupid people know they are stupid. We did it at school. In a lesson about tolerance. I remember turning to Keesha Lomax and saying, 'I just want you to know I will never refer to your cousin as stupid.'

And then the ungrateful haystack went on Twitter saying I had issues with people with learning difficulties. She hasn't even got learning difficulties, she's got Down's Syndrome! God! Some people need to read a few books! I tweeted that back to her and did that full stop before the tweet so that THE WORLD gets to see it and join in. She tweeted back that I was digging myself a hole and then blocked me. Bitch.

Aba eventually calls Mum. And calls her again. But each time, she can't get hold of her. I hear that she doesn't leave any messages and I twig that Aba's as embarrassed as me. I'm meant to be in her care and a 'bad thing' happened. I say this to her. I do think it's worth pointing out.

'Aba?'

'Yes, hon?'

'Are you worried about telling Mum because she'll go really ape and blame you rather than me coz you're like a grown-up and I've not even left school and stuff?'

She gives me a Bimbi-esque death stare.

'I'm not going to play your mind games, Calista.'

And I wander off, muttering under my breath, 'Thanks for the heads up, babe.'

She is. She's totally pooeroonying her La Perla panties. It's like every time I see her she's probs doing these tiny smell-less ladyfarts. Bet you any money.

Oh God! Major scandal!

Angel has put the fear of God in all of us. Some guy from the restaurant we are now longer persona non grassy-arse at (or maybe it's the other way around?), called Chino, named after the pants presumably, has been off sick from work since we were there (how she knows this I don't know, but severe lesbiany one reckons Angel is giving blowjobs to one of the waiters in return for takeaway starters which she then eats in her room). And now Angel reckons she's seen him in the bushes at the hotel, staring up at her balcony. She says she keeps seeing him, watching her. She gets quite hysterical one day and makes Aba get the hotel to call the police, who come and talk to her, with the receptionist from the hotel acting as an interpreter. I can just imagine what they're saying.

ANGEL: There's a man in the bushes. I think it's Chino from the restaurant.

RECEPTIONIST (in Spanish): Take no notice. This one's a Brummie dingbat. Thinks some random fancies her. Just talk any old shite back to me, thick bitch'll believe anything.

POLICEMAN (in Spanish): God! Dense wench or what?!

RECEPTIONIST (in Spanish): Totes!

And they more or less pat Angel on the head and then get off. None of us are any the wiser.

But d'you know? I don't ACTUALLY care about all or any of the above because . . . guess what?!

O.M. Actual G.

I've totally met a really nice guy.

I know. And he's not even a gayer. Not that all gayers are nice. Look at my loathsome jobsworthy brother.

Although he was quite sweet about letting me stay in London.

Oh, who cares?

So. This guy.

So there's this family staying at the hotel and they've been here since before we got here and they're like really cool and they're from London and they like always come here for the Christmas break. Daddy's in banking and Mummy wears really vile culottes, but she's quite sweet really, and very fond of a straw hat. The oldest daughter has a little toddler only her husband can't be here because he's got to keep an eye on a hedge fund or something. And then there's these two slightly potty younger sisters, and then the baby of the family, Luke.

I know. Luke. Isn't that a, like, totally gorgeous name?

And their surname is Fenton-Mace.

Fenton-Mace. I know. Amazing. Cally Fenton-Mace has a bit of a ring to it. Don't you think?

So anyway, he has this totally awesome fit body, he totally looks like he's a porn star or something coz that's the absolute best bit of holidays, everyone walks round practically naked, like there's nothing wrong with it. (This doesn't really work in somewhere honking like, I dunno, Skegness.) (Unless you're in a nudist camp, natch.) (Does natch mean naturally? I really hope so.)

And each morning I've seen him like paddling on a surfing board along the coast. It's a really MESSED UP IMAGE actch. Coz it looks like he's just floating past on water, like he's walking on water, without moving his legs. I could tell Nancy fancied him coz she was really vile about him.

'Oh, here he is. Poca-flaming-hontas.'

Though that did actually make me laugh.

Then on the day I wasn't shooting I made sure I was nice and early for lunch and scooted around, sitting myself at the table where his family always sits. To make myself appear interesting and really high-IQ-y, I took a book from one of the shelves in the hotel drawing room and sat there doing pretend reading when his family came and took over the next table.

And JOY OF JOYS OH YES THERE IS A GOD AND HE OR SHE IS TOTALLY INTO MAKING ROMANCE HAPPEN he sat at the chair nearest mine. Eventually he caught my eye as his family were ordering. He pointed to the book.

'Any good?'

I shrugged. And then said what I thought sounded really clever. 'Really intriguing denouement.'

To which he pissed himself.

'What language is that?' he asks.

Which is the first time I realize I am pretending to read a book IN A FOREIGN LANGUAGE.

I have no idea what language. So I hazard a guess. 'German.'

Which garners more laughs from his table, and his sister pipes up with, 'That's Swedish.'

'I always get the two confused.'

And the boy winks at me.

Over lunch he asks what I'm doing here, and I really enjoy showing off that I'm on a shoot for *Vogue*, and you can tell he's really impressed.

And by dessert, he's asked if I want to go snorkelling with him that afternoon.

I hate snorkelling, but I say yes.

And snorkel we do. And we've pretty much been inseparable since.

So anyway . . . tonight he's coming round to my room to watch *The Grand Budapest Hotel* – or whatever it's called – with me coz they've got it live-streaming on the hotel telly and I'm like . . . SO nervous. Coz although we've had the odd snog in the sea and at the door to my room at the end of an evening – when you're alone indoors together, stuff happens.

I've never really done stuff.

Well, I've done bits.

Here's what I've done:

1. Seen an actual real penis when Phoebe Scarfe's big brother did that thing at the school Christmas Fayre last year where he came to our stall with a plastic cup and was like 'Does anyone want this tea?' and I said 'I'll have it' – but when I looked in it, he had cut a hole in the bottom of the beaker and his actual penis was inside the cup. Gross.

2. I gave Michaela Warburton a love bite once, but that doesn't make me a lesbian because she gave me one too and we were just practising for when we have to do it on lads.

3. I've read *Fifty Shades of Grey*. Filthy.

4. Snogged four lads. I can't even be BOTHERED to give their names as none of them were that memorable.

5. Although one groped my left boob so hard he bruised it. But he was really apologetic afterwards, and he's gay now anyway.

So I am feeling a bit ill prepared for Luke coming round tonight, truth be told.

Maybe I should watch some porn online or something. But Mum says that will give me totally unrealistic expectations of sex. And of how long it takes for a plumber to come out. So I decide instead to just . . . play it by ear.

He comes round about seven. He looks really handsome in these totally cool cut-off denims, some less cool Adidas flip-flops, and an orange shirt that he hasn't bothered to button up. I can smell that he's cleaned his teeth when he quickly pecks me on the cheek on arrival. We order some room service and then watch the movie, but get bored about ten minutes in, and Luke suggests we go for a swim.

I look out of my room and see that no-one is about. It's dark. The sun has fallen into the sea. And so I say yes. We rush to the black water's edge. And then he surprises me. He rips his shorts off, drops his shirt, and throws himself in naked. I find myself following suit and soon we are both paddling around. COMPLETELY STARKERS. We're splashing each other and chatting and giggling and holding hands every now and then when suddenly he grabs me to him so that I'm like totally sitting on his lap, facing him. And OH MY GOD he has the most massive erection I have ever felt in my life.

OK, so it's the first one I've felt.

And I didn't expect to feel it for the first time riding up the back of my bum crack.

'I don't really want to do anal?' I say.

And he's like 'Fuck, sorry.' And he lifts me up and schlops it to the front of me, so it's grazing my belly button.

And then he kisses me. And we float about for a bit, necking. Like teenagers. Well, we are teenagers. But you know, like this is IT. And it feels special. And beautiful. And the moonlight's making the sea look like it's littered with glitter and stars. And I reach down and put my hand round his doodah. And it feels hard and soft at the same time. Like . . . like . . . like nothing else I've ever touched before, actually. But that's probably a good thing. Coz imagine if loads of things in life felt like penises. It'd be really disconcerting. Like, I dunno, like an Evian bottle. That'd be really off-putting if every time you picked up an Evian bottle it totally felt like you were bringing someone off. GROSS.

I've literally only had it in my hand for about ten seconds when I feel Luke tense up, and whimper in my ear, 'God, you dirty bitch,' and then he lets out this yelp.

Which is when I realize he's thingied. Ejaculatado'd. Come.

I really don't like that word. Come.

I don't mind it so much when you have to say 'come here.' But, you know, when it's referring to what Luke just did. It leaves a really funny taste in my mouth.

I'm just crouching there in the sea, bouncing up and down on his knees thinking that 'God, you dirty bitch,' isn't exactly the sort of thing you could imagine Katherine Jenkins' boyfriend saying, when he suddenly goes a bit limp and pushes me away from him. I'm just thinking it's all a bit aggressive when he starts giggling and says, 'Race you to the beach, Cal!' and we have a swimming race back to shore.

Oh God. Imagine if anyone was watching from their hotel rooms. The shame!

But wait. There is more shame when we hit the beach.

'Where's my . . . ?'

Where we left our clothes . . . mine are there . . . but his aren't. We look everywhere. Which is a bit embarrassing because I'm dressed now and he's staggering about completely naked. His penis is limp and tiny now, possibly because he's starting to feel the cold. He starts getting quite ratty with me.

'Have you moved my bloody clothes?!'

'Luke, you know I haven't! I was with you the whole time!'

'For fuck's sake! I'm gonna have to put your dressing gown on or something.'

At which point we hear some glass breaking. And then, a few seconds later, some raised voices.

'That sounds like my mum,' he says, and hurries into my room to put my dressing gown on. He hurries out without saying anything. The film is still playing.

I don't know how I feel about the evening, really. Except it was all over very quickly. And I don't know what to make of a guy who calls you a 'dirty bitch' on your first sexy time.

Maybe it's OK. Maybe he felt comfortable enough with me to be living out some kind of fantasy like in *Fifty Shades*.

Or maybe he's a bit of a twat. One of the two.

I decide to give him the benefit of the doubt coz he's just so dreamy. And up until the skinny dipping, it was all going so sweetly.

I step outside onto the sandy bit outside my room. Which is when I hear him shouting at the top of his voice, 'Oh, I do not BELIEVE this, Mother!'

And I venture back inside. I think I might have had enough of him for one night.

The next morning at breakfast his family have clearly been up late rowing, as you could cut the atmosphere with a knife. Angel informs me that Luke had his room broken into last night and some of his stuff taken. I go over to tell him I'm really sorry. But he's all monosyllabic and shruggy, so I just let him be.

I decide to go to a yoga class on the beach with Nancy for a laugh.

I tell her what happened with Luke last night, and what he said when he was you-know-what-ing, and she looks horrified and then throws her head back and laughs, before saying, 'Oh my God, he's Rapey Luke!' Only she says it really loudly, and the yoga teacher's like, 'I have asked for silence, girls.'

So I was like, 'Sorry, Jaschinta.'

Halfway into our yoga lesson, we're just starting to get into it. I'm feeling quite perky as I do a thing called the pigeon. Or something. And the combination of the gentle music Jaschinta is playing, and the view of the ocean . . . it just makes me feel so relaxed.

But then our peace is shattered by the sound of a man yelping in pain. He yelps and yelps and yelps some more. And then shouts: 'CAN SOMEONE GET ME A FUCKING AMBULANCE?!'

And that's when I realize it's Luke.

I'm too scared to go and look right now, coz Jaschinta's a bit of a bully. But minutes later we hear a siren. And then a commotion. Then, 'THAT FUCKING HURTS, MATEY BOY!'

And a further, 'I'M GOING TO SUE THE ASS OFF THIS SHITHOLE!'

And then, 'YOUR HOTEL! THAT'S THE SHITHOLE TO WHICH I'M REFERRING, MY FRIEND!'

The aggression in his voice scares me, actually. And really puts me off my yoga.

Later, Aba informs me that Luke had gone down to get his surfboard as he does every day. Same place. Same time. Same old same old. Only he didn't see that someone had put a trap out to kill a wild animal. And basically he got his leg clamped by these big metal teeth. He'll live, and he'll walk, but he will have these big metal teeth-mark things on his leg. He's back from hospital. With, like, a zillion stitches.

No-one has any idea who would have left it there. Or for what purpose.

I'm just pondering how he hasn't had much luck in the last twenty-four hours when my mobile rings. It's Mum. Has Aba told her? Oh GOD.

I answer. 'Hi, Mum.'

'Hi, love. How's Mehico?'

'Mehico is great, thanks, Mum.'

'Listen, I've been thinking.'

'Aha?'

'How d'you fancy staying on for a few more days when you finish?'

'What?'

'Why don't I come and join you for Christmas?'

'Serious?'

'Yep. Just spoke to the hotel and they've had a cancellation. I could come and join you on Saturday.'

Blimey. Life. My mum. Everything and everyone is full of surprises.

'Well . . .'

'I thought you'd jump at the chance.'

'It's just . . .'

'What, darling?'

'I've got something to tell you. I said I wouldn't keep any more secrets from you . . .'

'Cally?'

In for a penny. In for a gram of coke I never toke (past tense for take) (somewhere).

Oh GOD. SHE'S GONNA HATE ME.

HELP!!!!!!!!!!!!!!!!!

I tell her. The line goes silent.

What she says next really, REALLY surprises me.

Danny: The Noughties

Whingeing grid

'I can't go on like this.'

  'Like what?'

  'Us two. Seeing each other.'

  'That's not fair, Danny.'

  'No, Mims. What's not fair is you putting pressure on me. I've always told you, Natalie comes first.'

  'You don't love her.'

  'I do.'

  'If you loved her, what you doing here?'

  'Tryina finish it with you, you daft mare.'

  'That's mental abuse.'

  'Fucking hell, man, you'd test the patience of a saint.'

  'I don't want it to finish, Danny.'

  'You might not have much choice in the matter, love.'

  'I'll go to Natalie and tell her.'

  'Well, then it'll defo be over.'

  'OK, then, I won't.'

  'I don't *want* to hurt you, Mims. I just don't see any other way.'

  'I'm more than happy to be the other woman, Danny.'

  'I know, and that's not fair.'

'OK then, leave her. Come to me.'

'You're doing me head in, Mims.'

'You used to say you liked me doing your head in.'

'Wearing a bit thin now, love.'

'Your mum thinks we're good together.'

'Not being funny. But my mam doesn't know which way up she is half the time.'

'She gets me. I get her. And she thinks I'm better for you than Natalie.'

And so it went. On and on. Round and round in circles. The same conversation, week in, week out. Why did I let her have this hold over me? And why could I never end it? Me, who had no problem lashing off a dodgy barman at the club, back in the day. Me, who'd have a barney in the street if someone was getting on my tits. Reduced to rubble by Miriam frigging Joseph.

'What time's your flight tomorrow?'

I was off to the States. Taking our Owen to see another tournament. I was looking forward to it this time, if I was honest; anything to get away from her whingeing grid.

I told her. Well, I lied. I made it earlier, so she wouldn't expect a phone call or a visit or anything daft like that.

'Only, I was thinking.'

'What?' And then I realized what was coming.

'I could come over and surprise you.'

'I think our Owen'd get the bigger surprise, love.'

Although would he? Really? Bearing in mind the reason we had to go to those tournaments in the first place?

'He wouldn't need to know.'

'No, Mims. This is father and son time. Anyway, we share a room.'

She looked like she didn't believe me. As well she might. But my message was clear: no fucking way.

She made moussaka that night. From scratch. Funny the things you remember.

The biggest loser in Loserville goes thrill-seeking

Why, you might ask yourself, was I prepared to lose everything by dipping my ink with the most bonkersest woman in Manchester? Well. Coz I was clearly the biggest loser in Loserville. And she hadn't seemed that bleeding bonkers when I met her. Every time I accused her of being bonkers, she reckoned it was me that had sent her over the edge. And maybe she had a point. But the truth of it was, she hunted me down and found me. I didn't know that at the time. But she did.

We'd opened our new place in Manchester, Milk. We'd had some very generous funding from a very polite man in a suit who was cautious but ultimately helpful. We hit the crest of a wave up North, as the Hacienda was in its heyday, and it politely squeezed up and made room for another similar spot. And with the buzz of us being from the infamous China Crisis, our railway arches round the back of Deansgate soon became a destination venue. We kept it small, but soon there was interest from other venues round the country wanting in on the name. With some careful planning from our accountants and contacts, and our nice suited man, Milk started to leak round England, hitting Bristol, Brighton and even London. We were a franchise, baby, and six or seven years later, the money was rolling in.

Me and Nat were nightclub stars.

We had it all.

Two beautiful kids, Owen and Cally. And what felt like a million and one party palaces all over the world.

Even if it was only Manchester, Bristol, Brighton, London and Ibiza in the summer.

My ugly mug was on the cover of magazines. The *Big Issue* loved me – homeless boy makes good. What's not to love? And that's how Miriam Joseph found me, I guess.

I just thought she was some nice piece who crossed my path and tipped me the wink at a time when I wanted to take a few risks in my life, and that was that. But the truth was weirder than any kind of fiction. When I found out, a million alarm bells should've rung, only they didn't. Coz her obsession with me appealed to my vanity. I'm not afraid to say it now, but she had some sort of Messiah complex about me, and she was Mary whatsername, wanting to wash my feet. And instead of going, *Hang on a sec love, that's a bit of a weird one*, I was like . . . *Yeah, go 'ed, babe. I'll just kick me trainers off. Sorry about the smell.*

We met in a business meeting originally. Natalie was even there for some of it. We were toying with rebranding Milk prior to the franchising business, and she'd come in to pitch for the new logo. Looking back, I've sometimes wondered whether she'd invented the graphic design company just to get to meet me. But she always insisted it was just a happy coincidence. And she was a good designer. Mad bitch or not.

Then we bumped into each other in Ibiza.

I was being a bit of a bad lad back then and knocking off all sorts, coz Natalie had got into this habit of not coming out there, and I arrogantly thought that gave me a free pass to do what the hell I wanted. Coz I soon discovered, blokes who are on your payroll are pretty good at keeping that zipped when they see stuff they're not meant to. Then we kept on seeing each other when we got back. Casually, like, on and off. Then it just petered out.

Lords and ladies

A club at more than one venue is a headache for anyone. It's a brand, and it stops being yours. You can fight tooth and nail to hang onto your identity, make the experience identical in whichever venue you go to; but you can't do it alone. Two become three become blah blah blah, and soon there's a whole army of faces and you're the figureheads and it stops being fun. And when fun is what you're selling, it needs to feel like it at the top. And it wasn't. And we'd had enough. And we wanted out. So we got out. We got out rich. But Milk was no longer ours. Our Milk had curdled.

We were lords and ladies of leisure. That's when the rot really set in for me. Gone were the adrenalin rushes. Gone were the challenges. Gone was everything. And all that was left were the boring shitty bits.

Yes, we had the big posh house in the country. Yes, we had our kids in private school. But when you've lived your life upside down for as long as you can remember . . . out at night, sleeping all day, the cash rolling in . . . well, sometimes, when that's gone . . . well, I didn't half feel hollow.

And that's when I started being a really bad lad.

I hooked up with Miriam again. And she was more than happy to come along for the ride. Shameful now when I think of it, but then, I was a cocky fucker. From being the lad who had nothing to being the bloke who if he wanted something, he got it – I didn't think twice about digging my claws in. Entitlement, that's what I felt. Selfishness is another way of looking at it.

I used to tell Natalie I was off out meeting mates. Playing golf. Playing footy. Blimey, she must've thought I was training for the frigging Olympics, the amount of 'sport' I was doing.

But I wasn't. I was round at Mim's house. I was down the bookies, wasting my hard-earned cash. I even started caning it for the first time in my life. Looking back, I was bored and just thrill-seeking. And slowly but surely, the reserves we'd put aside were chipped away at.

I didn't love her. The sex was dirty and the company was easy, back then.

And then I found her stash of cuttings from newspapers about Tiffany Keith. And that's when I should've run a mile.

But I didn't. Coz that's when she came clean and told me she'd practically been stalking me. And coz I was a knobhead who was chasing them thrills, I lapped it up and stayed with it.

Like I said. The biggest loser in Loserville.

The baby she gave away

Not long after I first met her, Mim had told me that she'd had a baby when she was fifteen. She also said she'd never found her, and didn't know what had happened to her. This turned out to be a bit of a white lie. Coz now that I'd seen the Tiffany Keith stuff, she came clean. She had tried to find her baby – and when she did, she had recently died of a drug overdose in some crack house down South. Obviously Mim was full of remorse and shame and guilt that she'd given the baby away, and felt she'd had a part in the poor girl's downfall, yadda yadda yadda. Then when she read about Tiffany Keith dying, it brought it all back to her. And when she read that I had been trying to get the poor girl to hospital . . . she became obsessed by my kindness, because she wished she had been able to do that for her daughter.

I never had the heart, or the honesty, to tell her that this was all complete bollocks.

She had a Messiah complex about me. What was I supposed to do? Shatter her illusions?

Yeah, I know, I know. All along, I was the Bad Samaritan. Well, if the cap fits . . .

Framboise lives on

People used to think we'd made Cally's name up. We hadn't. Framboise – the brass who'd been kind to me when I needed it –she once had her mum down, and I overheard her calling her by her real name, Cally. Framboise was murdered in the mid-nineties. Cut up by some pimp, they said, in a Soho back alley. I know it sounds odd naming your daughter after a brass and that, but she was good to me, old Framboise, and I wanted part of her to live on.

I was never very good with kids. I can't really say I was much cop with my own kids. Natalie was a natural. I was putting on an act. When Owen was a baby, I was useless with him. Whenever I picked him up he'd start mewling and skriking. As he got older, he got easier. He was eager to please, and he was easily pleased. He looked a bit like me, but with everything put right. And as long as he thought you weren't hacked off with him, he'd do anything for you.

Cally was a different kettle of fish altogether. I remember Mammy looking down on her when she'd got back from the hospital. Natalie was asleep. Thank God she couldn't hear. Coz Mammy said, 'The alien has landed.'

I remember the smell of Pernod on her breath as she said it, and I wanted to hit her. But Cally was an odd-looking baby. Otherworldly. She seemed to flinch when Mammy went near her, and bawled her eyes out when she picked her up. But when she passed her to me: silent. Comfort. I knew this one'd be OK. She had instinct, just like me. The apple doesn't fall far from the tree.

And as she got older I liked her weirdness, her complete lack of desire to conform. It petered out a bit before I left, but the otherworldliness never went. Natalie saw it as sweetness. I saw it as if she had higher powers. Or maybe that was my arrogance, projecting onto her something I thought I'd always had.

It's all about me. Jeez.

Mashed

How d'you want your spuds doing, Danny? Natalie used to say. And I'd always say, *Mashed, like me head.*

Now you might think that for me to be carrying on like a complete bastard behind Natalie's back meant that I'd fallen out of love with her. And maybe I had. Maybe I'd never been in love with her. But I thought I had, and I thought I was. Like Prince Charles once said, 'whatever love means'. But in my sphere of experience, Natalie was the love of my life. And nothing had changed between us, really, in all the years of being together. OK, the sex was a bit pedestrian, but there ain't nothing wrong with walking on the pavement all your life – at least you're not gonna get run over. In films and telly when someone has an affair it's always coz everything's gone tits up at home. And that's the stupid thing about me. None of that had happened. We were just sailing along, as per. It was just me. And me mashed head. My skewed view of the world that meant I was greedy. Or maybe that's how it always is for fellas. And they get it wrong on the silver screen.

Though they do get one thing right. Usually the hero, if he plays away, he ends up choosing a loose fucking cannon. Yeah.

Dodged a bullet there, lad? No. Took the full force of it. And I may as well have pulled the trigger.

And that other little lad

Not so little now, no doubt. But did I ever stop and think about Sam Korniskey? Truth be told, I didn't really. Not that often. I'd done my bad thing and pushed him to the back of my mind. Taken the money and run a club with it. The police had come knocking at my door all those years ago. Could I back his story? Had I seen anything? Maybe a decent mate would've made something up, embellished the truth. But I looked them in the eye and told them the truth. I'd seen nothing, knew nothing. I did it with enough alarm in the voice so that they knew. Subtext was – Sam Korniskey's a bit mental. Weeks later, Sam came to see me. All rage and accusations. I lied point-blank and said the coppers hadn't seen me. That shut him up. And then sent him into a rant about how everyone was out to get him, the system was out to get him, he was a walking, talking conspiracy theory waiting to happen. And I'd lit the touch paper.

I did try and finish it . . .

I did try and finish it with Mim a few times. Once it even worked. But the next time I went round to my mum's, who did I find sitting in her front room? Bleeding Mim! Jesus! And she's sat there practically feeding my old girl vodka. And Mum's eyes were all glassy, and she was all, 'She's told me everything. I think the way you've treated her is something shocking.'

And again, it trapped me. She was inveigling her way into every part of my life. I had to put a stop to it. I just couldn't work out how.

Me, the canny one, who could come up with a solution to everything. I couldn't work out how to jib the bit on the side. Sounds daft now, I know, but I didn't want to risk her telling Natalie. Once that little cat was out of the bag, I'd lose everything.

But what was everything? Everything wasn't fine, not really. So what was I scared of?

Chi-chi

Big posh house in the country. Kids at private school. Electric gates. A swimming pool. A gardener. Well, a gardener once a week, but it was still a gardener. Cleaner. Our life had gone ever so, ever so . . . chi-chi, that's how I saw it. Natalie hated it when I called it that – she was so protective of her new life. Even though we were sinking money faster than an alkie with the beers. Oh, and then there was Lucy and Dylan, who she thought the sun shone out of. Look, don't get me wrong, Lucy was all right, if a bit right-on since her days at Milk: wandering around in her hot pants, loving all the lads trying to get a glimpse up her jaxie every time she bent over. But him? Never took to him. Always had to be wearing the latest fashion, always had to have the latest gadget. It was all surface with him, and despite that, I always felt him looking down his nose at me while pretending to blow smoke up my arse. Yeah, a contortionist. And a bit of a prick. But I smiled and nodded and laughed at his crap jokes every time they came over for dinner, and every time we went over to theirs and 'just had to try this latest cheese', and all that shite. Dylan was in a cheese club. They met once a fortnight and tried different cheeses and, I dunno, wanked over them or something. Natalie even suggested I join at one point. I told her where to get off. Right there, mate!

It dawned on me that I'd been a bit of an adrenalin junkie all my life, though not through choice. Living on my wits on the streets of St Helens, making ends meet while Mammy was busy with her tea. Punching the boss at Hansbury. Escaping. The Meat Rack. The streets. Then the dealing. The promoting. The clubs. Then nothing. Electric gates and wall-to-wall leisure. No adrenalin. It's like I'd had the gland removed. I know it's daft, but I missed those days. I missed the buzz. That's probably why I indulged in so many mad things. I was starting to feel more and more cut off from everything around me, craving something from the past, even though the past was far from perfect. Biggest loser, indeed. Never happy. Maybe I'd never been happy. Whatever happy was, or is.

Mammy was back on the sauce

'Nuff said, really. She was an effing nightmare. And now she had her new best friend. Mim. And every time she saw me she'd tap her nose and go, *Nat'll never know. Stuck-up bitch.*

Bye-bye, Benedict Bishop

It was New Year's Day 2009 – I'll never forget it – when I opened up the paper and saw the words MP and SUICIDE in the headline. It was Sir Benedict Bishop, and he'd killed himself, throwing himself from some cliffs on the coastline of North Wales. My stomach flipped. It felt like a jellyfish, squeezing itself in and up inside me. There was a picture of him. Same as I'd remembered him, but balder and uglier; and, of course, twenty years older. Reading down the article, it said several allegations of historical child abuse were about to be revealed and he had been wanted for questioning.

I felt so many things, all at the same time. I felt a tiny bee-sting of triumph that he had gone, that whatever evil things he'd done in the past could never be done again and there'd been some sort of retribution. But the major feeling that consumed me was guilt.

Several allegations.

Several.

That meant . . . not just Sam. Maybe Sam wasn't even one of them.

Shit.

Had me not standing up for Sam all those years ago meant that he'd got away scot-free to carry on doing what he'd always done? Had the money he'd bought my silence with ultimately been blood money? The blood of all the lads he'd interfered with? I looked around the kitchen I was sat in. The stainless-steel units. The Fired Earth floor tiles. The coffee machine the size of a bungalow. Had they all been paid for by his abuse?

I'd never told Natalie at the time how I'd met the contact in the suit who was so eager to offer advice and hand over sixty thousand quid in investment. Admittedly we'd paid him back within the year, so obviously our success was our own doing. But without it, where would we be now?

I couldn't sit still. I got up and grabbed my coat. Shoved on Owen's bobble hat and shouted, to no-one in particular, 'I'm going for a walk!'

And no-one in particular called back.

Our house – if you could call it that, it was more like frigging Southfork, I swear, every corner I turned I expected to see Sue-Ellen shaking with a G and T in her sweaty mitts – was in the middle of nowhere, in Cheshire. A county I now hated with a vengeance. Whoever invented snooty, they must've been from Cheshire. The neighbours – if you could call them that, the nearest house was half a mile away – hated us with a passion. New money. No class. Cheeky fuckers. They were the epitome of snoot. Yeah, they were impressed by the Range Rover Sport, the schools the kids went to, where Nat got her hair done. Yes, they were impressed that we could afford to live there. But you could see it in their dead eyes every time they looked at us. Disdain. Disgust. De nada.

And the bad thing about the area, and them – we were near a little village called Swettenham – was that if you went for a walk and just walked across fields, those fields were owned by one of the snooty bastards, and the next thing you knew you'd have some old sap in a hat shouting, GET OFF MY LAND. Or worse, they'd send a bull after you. It made just walking out and going for a stroll a bit of a bugger really, coz you were in the middle of all this really beautiful English countryside, fields, fields, rape as far as your eye could see, in the summer, bluebell woods; but you had to walk down the lanes, not in the middle of the beauty. So walk down the lanes I did. All the time thinking, all the time hating. Hating what I'd done.

I'd contributed in some way. I knew I had. I couldn't quite articulate how but I had. The words weren't there, the description wasn't, but it was just on the tip of my tongue, patched onto the next bit of brain and I couldn't get to it.

A four-by-four drove past as if it didn't see me, the wheels sluicing up a spray of mud that hit me like bullets. And as it did, a new revelation hit me.

What if he didn't kill himself? What if Sam actually pushed him off that cliff?

Right there, right then, it seemed completely plausible. Sam, denied his moment in court, denied the chance to see the man who abused him punished for what he did, eats himself up with bitterness, tracks him down, sweet-talks him into a cliff-top walk, pushes him off. QED. Whatever QED meant.

Oh yeah. Quite easily done.

Well, not that easily. But doable.

I passed the opening to the track that led down to the courtyard of barn conversions. A family were in their garden having a barbecue. A barbecue. At ten in the morning on New Year's Day. A breakfast barbie? If that was plausible – and there it was, right before my eyes – then so was the situation with Sam.

I carried on walking towards the village, soaked to the skin. Another realization. All those years, all that time, the memories. I remembered being in the car with Bishop and Sam, Sam chattering away. The months after, when Sam defended him, liked him, wanted to spend time with him. Part of me always hated Sam because I thought he was flirting with Bishop, complicit in whatever was about to happen. Sam wanted to spend time with him. And then, after he returned to Hansbury after the London days, it happened. And part of me assumed Sam had seduced him.

Again I felt nauseous. Sam had been younger than Owen was now. Sam didn't seduce him. And if he felt he did, or I felt he did, it was because the bastard had bloody well groomed him. I'd seen it with my own eyes. Seen how all those bastards at Hansbury did it. The gifts. The treats. The compliments. The privileges. Grooming. It was going on right before my eyes, but I'd not been able to give it a name. Just thought the lads were playing along, Sam was playing along, and enjoying it. Part of it. All of it. And now I was a grown-up, it was crystal clear.

And I could have done something about it. But I didn't. In fact, I did the opposite. I chose to actively condone it, in a way.

When I got to the village, it was like a ghost town. Like those villages you see that were abandoned in the Second

World War, then no-one returned. The places armies practise their killing sprees on. The pub was shut. The shop was shut. The world was shut. The place felt like it was rotting.

I felt stupid. I felt humiliated. I felt angry. Not even angry with Bishop – I felt angry with myself.

That was when the rot truly set in. And really, there was no coming back.

But what d'you do when you're consumed with terror? Terror that your whole life is built upon someone else's pain? Even if there's an outside chance that you're just bigging your part up; making out you were the centre of the drama when actually you weren't, you were just a bit-part player. What do you do with all those feelings? When you know you've shat on someone from a great height, someone you promised you'd always be there for? Even if that was a promise from childhood. I still made the promise, and I thought I was a man of my word. What d'you do when you've been so selfish that you thought you'd stopped to think how your actions might affect others – when all along, all you'd cared about was yourself?

I didn't have a clue, mate. But I knew I'd have to do something. And something fucking drastic.

Help.

But I was about to find out.

Three magic words

It was something Miriam said when I was round at hers one night. Three words. Three short words. That's where the idea came from.

Let's run away.

Never had three words spoken to me so acutely before. They fizzed round my body like a really good pill.

Yes. Run away!

And before I could stop myself saying it, I said it.

Brilliant.

Her eyes lit up. And so began Project Mim. I got carried along with it at first. The two of us. Running away. Going abroad, and just sacking off our lives.

I couldn't bear to be in the house since Bishop's death. Everything I owned reminded me of him and what he'd done. I'd see him peering down at me in the refectory that day, and what might have been. I saw Sam clutching his bag of 'evidence' – God knows what he had in there. I'd started to look at the family as if through glass, like they were exhibitions at an art gallery and I couldn't touch them or get through to them; as if they too were products of what had happened, of what I'd done. And here was a solution: get out. Stay out. Never come back. And all these emotions I was feeling would disappear. I hoped.

My life had become staid. A life I'd thought I'd wanted, but now I had it, it provided me with no solace or contentment. The longer I skimmed along in it, with its middle-class pretensions and its Lucys and Dylans and online grocery deliveries and farm shops and prize days in cathedrals, the more I hated it. Pile onto that the ugly poison of what I'd done for Bishop, and . . . I think the American phrase was 'enough already'.

Yet here was a get-out clause. Here was a way of leaving everything behind and starting again. I missed the adrenalin rushes of the early days and wanted them back. The days when I looked over my shoulder. The days when I only had to think of number one. Yes, that's selfish, but it's honest.

But if I wasn't benefiting from Bishop's money – if it was just the kids and Natalie, who knew frig all about it – maybe that was a good thing, an altruistic thing, for me to let them live that life and for me to escape it.

I know it sounds mad, but that made such sense to me right then.

The kids. I bet they would say, 'He wasn't much cop as a dad.' Natalie was the natural. I was the one doing things as if I was a dad. Not *as* a dad. I know most parents think they're useless at parenting; I was different. I knew. I had instinct and nous – I just didn't have the patriarch gene. I'd see the confusion in their eyes when they looked at me. When I mentioned it to Natalie she'd say I was imagining it, that I wasn't used to intimacy, that I wasn't used to love. But still, when I looked at them, they'd look back with the subtext . . . *no, you're doing this all wrong.*

Basically, they'd be better off without me. Owen was sixteen now, Cally eleven. They'd manage just fine with their mum. Good Mum. Steady Mum. She was no Mim, that's for sure.

Sixteen and eleven! How did they get that old? It seemed only yesterday I was watching Nat outside the club. How did I go from that to this?

And the worst bit of it was that I'd given them the world, but it was all based on two things. Drug dealing and child abuse. Yeah. Great dad I was.

We set a date for the 15th of June. Slap bang in the middle of the year. It was four months off, and felt like enough time to get everything in place. Mim was full of big ideas, and I let her chunder away with them. It was a train to France. Across France in a hire car. Then a gorgeous little village she knew in the south of France. From there I could ring Natalie and say I'd had enough. It all kind of made sense; but the longer she planned and pored over maps, the colder my feet got. But the instinct to run was still there.

You are going to leave her, aren't you?
Of course.
You're not going to let me down?
Of course not.
If I don't think your heart's in this . . .
It is.
Then I . . .
What?
I'll phone her now and tell her what we've got planned.
My heart's in it. Shut up and plan.

But the longer we went on, the stronger I felt.

I was going to do this one alone. And if I was going to do that there'd be no goodbyes and no 'let's keep in touch, yeah?' In order for my family to get on with their lives they'd have to think that was it. The end. Finito. They'd have to think I was dead. They'd have to think Danny Bioletti was no more. They could mourn, heal, move on. Natalie could marry some snobby git from the village, and . . .

Hey, Mrs! Turned out nice again!

But how?

Benedict Bishop died falling off cliffs.

Bingo. So would I.

RIP Declan Wolfe

I read about Declan's death online and told Natalie I thought I'd better go down South for the funeral, which was at Golder's Green Crem. Truth be told, I wasn't that cut up about it, although as you get older it does make you contemplate your own mortality when your peers or childhood friends start dropping off their perches. And as you know, I was very much into contemplating my own mortality at that point, even making preparations for it. So there was an ulterior motive to my decision to visit and pay my respects. At one point Natalie was all for coming too; she reckoned if it hadn't been for Declan we might never have met. But I managed to convince her that she was better off staying put and keeping an eye on things at the ranch. I might even stay overnight . . .

Going back to London put my head in a spin. The funeral wasn't till the afternoon, so I spent a happy hour or two walking the streets of my youth. So much had changed, so much had stayed the same. The Meat Rack I'd once seen as something of a spiritual home now felt like an old flame who'd put on a bit of weight but had some better clothes on. The whiff of vice had gone and in its place, consumerism of another kind. More than ever before it felt like the anodyne central fountain in a shopping mall. Sell, sell, fucking sell. Not a rent boy in sight, unless my skills were deserting me. It was like the ex was looking good, doing all right for herself, but had lost all of her personality with the makeover. You couldn't see the steps up to the statue of Eros for the Eastern European tourists and their cameras and their shopping bags. On every bag a designer label. Or maybe they weren't tourists; maybe they were living here now. I'd heard stories of Polish kids coming here to work and doing the shittiest of jobs for about 2p an hour, the sort our own kids wouldn't do: maybe this was them, having a well-earned day out.

I walked up to the Dominion Theatre, checked out my old bedroom. Someone from the council was round with a power hose, drenching the place with H_2O. How would I have survived that? I shuddered to think. I even traipsed down to the South Bank, where I'd had my fateful meeting about Sam. Headed through to Cardboard City. All gone. In its place a sanitized bullring of white-tiled walkways; it was like walking through a massive urinal. Where had all the homeless people gone? Their fires, their ramshackle houses, their spirit? It saddened me that it was no longer here, part of the swarming fabric of life under the bridges and roundabouts. But hey, I guess that was progress.

I took the tube up to Golders Green. It felt less familiar than the rest of the city, but that would be down to the fact I'd always walked or cycled anywhere when I was working. And then, when I'd made some money in the China Crisis days, it was cabs all the way for me.

The crem was fit to bursting. I recognized many faces from back in the day, but they didn't recognize me. I kept my sunglasses on the whole way through, and I slipped away quietly at the end. There were plenty I didn't recognize, mind. But then it'd be hard to place everyone from a youth where the kids in clubs caked themselves in make-up, the more extravagant the better, everyone their own little work of art. And now: grey, decaying bodies that hadn't seen enough daylight to flourish. Declan had died from a problem with his heart. Yeah, we had problems with that, mate. Nobody said it, but my guess was his health finally caught up with him after years of caning it.

On leaving the crem we were encouraged to say our goodbyes and touch the coffin, which looked like a picnic basket, on our way out. As we left, some Sinatra played. I listened to the lyrics. It was an uplifting tune. And listening to it, I knew where I was going to run to.

South of the border. Down Mexico way.

I came out into the bright sunlight and headed into town to meet an old friend for dinner. But first, I had to see a man about a dog.

Jonathan Harvey

Woof, woof

I met my ex-bouncer, the one who used to be a copper and liked to think he knew a thing or two back in the day, outside Liberty's. His choice, not mine. I wasn't that keen; when I saw the place, I clocked a cottage nearby. The whole place must've been swarming with plain clothes. We walked down towards Soho and fair play to him, this time he'd come up trumps. Down a back alley near Dean Street I handed him an envelope stuffed with twenties and he handed me a slim envelope, which I stuck in my inside pocket.

'Don't you wanna check it, Boss?'

I shook my head. 'I trust you. Don't you wanna check mine?'

He shook his head. 'Snap.'

I left him on Old Compton Street. Neither of us said goodbye. Just drifted apart like we'd never been together. Nothing bad had happened. I found the little side street where Framboise used to ply her trade. There was a new girl's name on her doorbell. It made me glad. Not all of London had become gentrified.

It was here I chose to look in the envelope. I ripped it open with my fingernail, being careful not to give myself a paper cut.

Inside was a smart new passport. A flick to the back, and there was my ugly mug staring back at me. Quick check of the name. Excellent.

Martin Swann.

Nefarious goings-on underground

I learned a word once, and I really liked it. Nefarious. It reminded me of my childhood favourite, Nefertiti. And maybe that's why I liked Nefertiti back then, coz it sounded like it could be a bit nefarious.

Nefarious: wicked, criminal.

And there were some nefarious goings-on that night, I can tell you.

Gretchen looked incredible. The age of her, mind, but she'd had her tits done. Either that or she'd been hiding her light under a bushel these past twenty years. Her lips looked bigger too, and I had this overwhelming urge to touch them. It was so bizarre. This woman who was old enough to be my mother, who I'd known for so long, and suddenly, out of nowhere, I fancy her? I realized I was staring at her tits. I looked back at my menu.

She'd booked this amazing underground place on Berwick Street market. Posh dim sum, she called it, not that I really knew what dim sum were. I let her order. We drank this odd hot sweet wine, and eventually I got round to picking her brains.

'Last time I saw you, you said if I ever needed your help, to ask.'

She nodded. No flies on her.

'If you wanted to disappear, Gretchen, what would you do?'

She took a bite of her king crab dumpling, and as she chewed I could practically hear the cogs turning in her brain. The restaurant was dark. The seats were low. The lighting seemed to flicker like candles. It was a good job she'd had everything made bigger on her face. It made her easier to see. I liked that she was taking me seriously.

After a bit she said, 'Get on a boat. Sail away. Land on a desert island.'

'I can't sail.'

'You wouldn't necessarily need to.'

'I don't know the first thing about boats.'

'You wouldn't have to. Boats are good because they're . . . more private.'

'Could you sail to, say, Mexico?'

'Bit of an epic journey. But I don't see why not.'

And then she went on to tell me about mates of hers on the south coast who lived in this big posh house. And how the back of their house had a jetty into this river. And their idea of going on holiday was walking to the bottom of their garden, getting in their boat and just sailing and sailing and ending up in Greece. They didn't even have to fork out on a hotel.

'Are you serious about disappearing?'

I nodded.

'I'll make some enquiries.'

I went back to my hotel.

She phoned me the next week. 'You're in luck.'

'I am?'

'Friends of friends. Sailing round the world. Happy to take you to Mexico.'

My heart danced.

'When?'

'They're leaving May the twentieth.'

'How much do they want?'

'Five grand. No questions asked. Cash.'

'I'll take it.'

Standing. Alone. On the platform

I wanted to ask Mim if we could bring the date forward from June to May. I liked the idea of me zooming off in a boat down South somewhere and Mim being stood there, alone, on the platform at the railway station, completely stood up.

Where is he? He said he'd be here.

She could go and phone Natalie then.

Then Natalie would think I'd topped myself. The guilt of the affair.

Ah, if only it was that straightforward.

Actually, this was good, keeping it from Miriam. Having our secret, and then my secret. And with any luck she'd get in touch with Natalie anyway and expose the affair, and bingo. Natalie buys the story.

The people I'd be sailing with were an actual lord and lady. Danny Bioletti certainly had come up in the world. As far as they were concerned, they'd be doing their mate Gretchen's mate Martin Swann a favour, and they had five grand to put towards the upkeep of the boat and fuel, etc. They'd be setting off mid-morning on the arranged day. I'd go and put my clothes at Beachy Head, leave my car there, and Gretchen would then drive me along the coast to a place called Hamble, where the lord and lady, Rick and Caroline, lived. Walk down the bottom of their garden. Get in the boat. Off we pop.

The final push

Some days I thought the plan was lousy and I'd never go through with it. Other times I wanted nothing more, and felt it a genius idea. If I'd been in two minds at all, the final nail in the coffin was when I got a phone call from Sam. He was up in Manchester visiting family. Could he see me? I said he could.

I got a hell of a shock when I saw him. We met at Piccadilly station and went for a stroll round town. Ended up in some pub near St Anne's Square where they do a good roast, and I made sure I fed him up.

He looked like he'd not eaten for a week. A month. His

cheeks were sallow and he was a bag of bones. He clutched his holdall to him all the time, only resting it in his lap when we sat in the pub.

At a guess, I'd say he'd been doing smack. But his speech was quite slow, and his eyes lifeless. His reactions were kind of on mute as well. Had an appetite though, I'll give him that. He told me he was about to be made homeless and needed me to look after his bag. It contained his evidence, and one day he was still convinced he would bring down the government with it. It was the only time he seemed to come alive. Benedict Bishop might be dead, but he wasn't the only one to have got his mucky paws on our Sam, and he would prove it. One day. But he couldn't risk losing his evidence, and that's where I came in. I took the bag and told him I'd guard it with my life. And for good measure I added,

'And if anything ever happens to me. Like I die or something. It'll be in the loft in my house. OK?'

He nodded, slowly. And then started to cry.

'They fucked me up, Danny. You're so lucky. They fucked me up.'

I took a swig of my pint. Never very good around emotion, me. He wiped the tears with an unkempt sleeve.

'Come on, Sam. Try and eat your meal.'

That bag. That bloody bag. D'you know? I never even looked in it. For all I knew it was bloody empty. Such was the madness in Sam's eyes. But if that's what it took to keep him off my back, help him through this rough patch, fine. I'd take his empty bag full of paranoia and blank conspiracies and hold it safe for him. Play along. Keep him sweet.

I've got something to tell you

Such a knob. Such a knob. The night before I went, I remember I almost told Natalie what was going on. It overwhelmed me, the enormity of what I was about to do. She was peeling spuds in the kitchen, must've been getting the tea on. The ordinariness of it got to me. I was about to do something major, and she was just peeling potatoes.

'Nat?'

'Mm?'

'I've got something to tell you.'

She swung round. Potato in one hand, peeler in the other. Panic in her eyes. My voice caught in my throat. I didn't want that to be my last memory of her. I had to make this moment right.

'Ha! Got you!' I laughed and she looked so relieved, shaking her head.

Scratch. Scratch. Scrape. Back to the spuds. Back to me.

That night I got up in the middle of the night and went and looked in on Owen, then Cally, as they were sleeping. I sat on Owen's bed and whispered, 'Look after them for me. Won't you, lad? Look after them.'

The next day I waited till Nat was having a bath, and I made out I was nipping out for milk.

She didn't even reply, didn't even say goodbye.

I drove down to Eastbourne. Stayed in a B & B.

The next morning – Danny Bioletti's last on earth – I got up early.

My final piece of theatre was to throw my necklace into the sea.

Owen, 2014

I should never have said that to Mum. Now she'll be asking for explanations. And I know full well I will never tell her what I know, what I saw. Ever. I've never told anyone. I couldn't. I wouldn't.

It's one thing being the son of a famous missing person. But to be known as the son of . . . no. Doesn't even bear thinking about.

She said she was going away. She said I could move in and mind the house while she was on holiday. She thinks she's being all clever, saying she's not sure where she's going, but I know she's going to see Cally. Judging by the amount of times Cally's been using the hashtag *#lovemymummysomuchnstuff* on Twitter, she's clearly done something bad and Mum needs to go out to Mexico and sort it out. Probably just pissed the whole country off or something. Anything's a possibility where Cally's concerned.

Matty is completely furious with me and milking it for all the sympathy he can get. Our friends have had to take sides, and naturally they've mostly sided with him. He's the injured party, I'm the out and out bastard.

He sent me a text saying I miss my dad so much, I have tried to recreate the age gap thing by finding a 'daddy' to sleep with. This is preposterous. The thing with Dylan took me completely by surprise. I didn't go looking for an older man, it just happened.

Didn't it?

Or does he have a point? Is that what I was seeking with Dylan? A father figure?

I push these thoughts to the back of my mind.

Instinct tells me he will forgive me and make overtures to me in a few weeks' time. He is angry and hurting now, but that will pass eventually. Something bad will happen. Someone will die, or he'll lose his job, something awful – and it'll be me he wants to see. And slowly he'll remember what he saw in me, and realize the Dylan thing was a moment of madness. And I don't want that to happen. I have to remind myself why I ended up in bed with someone else. It wasn't just because I was seeking an older man. It was that I was starting to feel bored and unsatisfied in my relationship. I am not blaming Matty for that, but that was the status quo and that's why I was so badly behaved. This sorry affair has given me the excuse to break free from a relationship that felt like it was going no-where.

Maybe I'll keep up the pretence that I'm devastated, that I feel so awful for trashing Matty's feelings like that and that I really want him back but it's just not happening. Might not be too good an idea to say, 'I wanted out, so I had an affair. Whoops!'

Maybe this *is* to do with my dad. Maybe I was so upset by his disappearance that I threw myself into this particular relationship to try and make myself feel better – like it was a balm, like I needed the distraction – when really I was too young, and should've shopped around a bit longer. I am only twenty-one. There are plenty more fish in the sea. And plenty more seas I've not even glimpsed, let alone swum in.

Twenty-one. And yet I feel about ninety. No wonder Matty described me as a young fogey.

Lucy has kicked Dylan out. I know this because Dylan has been hassling me to see him. It's all quite distasteful because instead of seeming rudderless and ashamed, he seems to be enjoying his taste of freedom. For a while he barraged me day and night with increasingly filthy texts. In the end I just ignored them, and it feels like he's gone away.

Instinct tells me they will make it up. They will counsel themselves and therapy themselves to within an inch of their lives, and they'll get back on track. Mum will be the collateral damage. That's what I feel worst about. None of this is her fault. As if she hasn't suffered enough already.

Enough already. That's how I feel about my life right now.

Is that how Dad felt all those years ago? *Enough already? I want out?*

Every time I look out of the window, I see that skinny girl opposite looking out of *her* bedroom window. *Rear Window* in reverse. Tonight an ambulance was outside. She's not looking out of the window any more. Maybe she's been taken in to hospital so they can get some food in her; it's so sad. I've never understood eating disorders before, but maybe she felt her life was falling out of control and the one thing she could control was what went in her mouth. I can see the sense in that. Poor girl.

I go and lie in the hall. It feels as good a place as any. I'm not staying here for days on end to surprise Mum when she gets back, but I enjoy seeing the stars through the glass above the front door. I feel peaceful. The house is new enough to not make any strange creaking noises that will unnerve me. All quiet on the Oaktree Estate.

I was lying down that day. I'd gone for a lie down in the loft. I thought it'd be a great way of surprising Dad. The trap door was open to the loft, and I climbed up and nestled myself away amongst the boxes of Christmas decorations and old books. He'd obviously been planning on coming up, or else the ladder wouldn't have been down. It's not long before I hear the ladder creak and I see Dad coming up. But he stops and waits before lifting himself up at the top of the ladder. He waits and listens. And instantly I know I shouldn't be here. He is checking no-one has heard him coming up. I try to breathe quietly. This was a stupid idea. But if I just lie still. If I just lie still he won't hear me.

He comes into the loft and fortunately doesn't come near me. He has a battered brown leather bag. He squeezes it down the back of some shelving which is housing some old books. Then he deftly returns to the hatch and disappears from view. The ladder is then slid back into the loft, and I hear the door being shut from the outside.

What could be in the bag?

I give it five minutes, then kneel up from my lying position.

Dad was hiding that bag. Why else would he shove it down the back of that bookcase? It's not a bag I've seen before.

I nudge my way over to the shelving on my knees. I manage to drag the bag out and lie it in front of me. I slowly unzip it.

And then wish I hadn't.

Because what I see in the bag changes my opinion of my father irrevocably.

Inside is an old video tape. And a packet of photographs.

Black and white photographs showing a mixed race lad. He can only be about fourteen. I feel sick. I put the photos and then the bag back.

Where did he get the pictures from? I dread to think what might be on the video. Is this what my dad is into?

He didn't stay round long enough for me to ask him.

But when he went missing I knew the police would be sniffing round the house. And that's when I decided to bury the bag. The last thing we needed was the papers finding out about the photos. Maybe he didn't know what was in the bag. Maybe it wasn't his bag.

I was trying to protect him. Or maybe I was trying to protect myself. But either way I disposed of the crap. I didn't dare light a bonfire, would've created too much interest. But there was that new estate being built down the road.

Who was I trying to protect?

I was trying to protect him, I decide. God knows why.

And that's why I can never tell Mum what I know. It would destroy her.

Nan got it into her head that he'd been hiding a gun in the loft. I don't know how she knew he'd been hiding anything in the loft. I put her right the day I went round and met Dad's brother. He was so like him to look at. But he had a Canadian accent. And was a bit dull. I think he'd bored Nan, actually. She kept saying, 'I feel like taking something.'

'It wasn't a gun, Nan.'

'How the fuck would you know?'

'I'd've known. And the police would've found it.'

She'd looked nonplussed. If she'd only known the truth!

Some days I think Dad must have been . . . it's so hard to say that word, or think it. It's the worst thing in a world where there's stiff competition for vile, evil things. Some days I put everything that has gone wrong in my life down to Dad's unhealthy interests.

And other days I think . . . well . . . I never saw any other evidence of him being like that. He never touched me inappropriately. And then it's easy to pretend I never saw the bag, or buried it underneath the houses where we're now living.

I stare up at the stars. And know.

I'll take that secret to the grave.

Sometimes you have to.

A shadow crosses me. There's someone outside. The doorbell rings. I haul myself up and go to the door.

'Who is it?' I say, anxious, through the glass, not looking.

'Is this Natalie's house?' a man calls back.

I open the door. A bloke in his forties stands there. Mixed race. He looks familiar.

'She's away,' I say.

'You're never baby Owen,' he says.

I nod.

'My name's Sam. I was a friend of your dad's. I gave him something to mind. Years ago. Can I come in?'

My heart leaps, and I let him in.

Danny

Chino

The less said about the journey over, the better. We were sailing for six weeks and it's safe to say I never really found my sea legs. In retrospect it would have been easier, quicker and less problematic, especially with my new passport, to just fly to Cancun. Still, I'd never be making that journey again.

Martin Swann lives a quiet life in a ramshackle hut on the beach near Tulum. Martin Swann doesn't even have electricity, but that's OK, coz he charges his phone up at work. He works behind the bar in a much-lauded restaurant where his chief occupation is preparing the limes for the house cocktails. He now speaks fluent Mexican Spanish and his nickname at work is Chino, because the boss refuses to believe he is anything other than Chinese. Oh, the irony. His life is simple again, straightforward, and the family he left behind is but a distant memory. Losing them was tougher than he thought it would be; it was like going through a period of mourning when he first got here. But they say time's a great healer. And it has been.

Until that night. The place was heaving. December, the area gets overrun by fashion wankers, and it was clear that the table in the corner was full of cokeheads. That instinct has never left me. Plus, it was only the models who were ordering any food.

And then I saw her. Heading to the bogs with some other skinny rake. She didn't see me. I look so different, with the beard and the ponytail and the year-round tan. And I dress for ease, looking like something blown in from a Goan rave. But it was definitely her. And in that second, my world and head exploded.

I'd worked so hard to push all thoughts of the family to the outer reaches of my brain.

And here she was. So elegant. So tall. A woman. Fuck.

And she was going to the toilet to do coke. Any fool could tell that a mile off. I told the boss. She got them kicked out. It was pandemonium. I ran out the back and hid till it had blown over.

I was all over the place after that. I practically stalked her. And then I heard her on the beach. Talking to Natalie on the phone. I just knew she was. And then she told that bossy black bird she was with that her mum was coming out to see her.

My family. Here. In Tulum. This didn't make sense. It's about as far away from England as you can get. How? How did this happen?

I stopped eating.

I stopped going to work.

My daughter was now a fucking MODEL. How did that happen?

And why was she here? And why was Natalie coming here?

I felt like my head was about to explode.

I hid away in my hut.

Were they onto me? Had they had a tip-off?

I'd spent years avoiding looking at the internet or Googling to see what had gone on in my absence. Was I front-page news? Had I just slipped away unnoticed? It was too much. Was Owen coming as well? I was making myself ill, unable to stop obsessing about it all. Lying on the mattress in that dark hut fretting, picking at the sore that was my life. Knowing I had to get away.

And that's when I had the idea.

It had been theatre last time.

This time I'd do it properly. There was a beautiful symmetry to it, the more I thought about it. I was meant to have died five years ago. Now I actually would.

Danny had become Jimmy had become Danny had become Martin had become Chino had become . . .

A cry in the dark.

A whisper on the breeze.

Then gone.

Natalie

I had a phone call from Raymond Lee the other day, sexy police guy, saying there'd been a development in the case. Someone had contacted the police in Brighton to say they thought they'd found Danny's necklace. A friend had found it on the beach years ago but hadn't seen the publicity about Danny's disappearance, so hadn't seen the detail about the necklace. It was only when showing it to this friend, and her seeing the engraving, that alarm bells of familiarity started to ring. Raymond was going to have it sent back to me.

If only that beachcomber had handed it in all those years ago. I'd have known he was dead back then.

I now hate my new house. Been there but a few months, and it feels grimy with stalactites and stalagmites of despair.

I know. Pretentious or what? I hate what I'm becoming.

I've never needed a holiday more.

Mexico's a bugger to get to. Because I booked so late I couldn't get a direct flight, and I have to change at Philadelphia of all places. Our air stewardesses all have tinsel in their hair. One of them is called Pepper. I'm not sure why that tickles me, but it does.

Cally told me she'd been about to do some cocaine with someone from the modelling shoot and they were kicked out of a bar and it's caused all kinds of drama. I think she thought I'd kick, scream and shout but I didn't. I just felt this huge compulsion to get over there and give her a hug. I'll kick, scream and shout at a later date.

Of course, she has no idea what her dad did for a living when I first met him. And she doesn't need to know, frankly.

I've told Owen he can stay at the house while I'm away. I really don't know how I feel about him. I'm hoping to get some perspective on this trip. I think I'll be washing my hands of Dylan and Lucy, though. Every time I think of them, I'm hit by a wave of nausea.

It's about forty-five minutes from Cancun airport to Tulum, where the hotel is. It's baking. All along the coastal road, I stare at the sea from the back of my cab. Eventually the dual carriageway becomes more of a dirt track, and on either side are hippy shops and boutiques, achingly cool restaurants, art galleries.

We stop to let a man cross the dirt track with a goat. A goat, in this heat, the poor thing.

There's another cab on the other side of the road, heading towards the airport. I wonder where the person in there is going. Have they found some perspective in Mexico? Or is their brain as fried as mine? I can't see much in that cab as the windows, like this one, are all blacked out. Must be about the heat. Our two drivers know each other, and give each other a little *brap* of their horns.

Brap! I like that. It's like a klaxon sounding for the good times to happen.

And I feel something I've not felt for so long. I feel a rush of elation.

I'm excited. For the first time since Danny left, I am looking forward to the future. Now that I know he must be dead, it feels like a weight has been lifted from my shoulders. The cab driver stalls. He tries the key in the ignition. Eventually we drive on.

Danny

I take a taxi to the airport. We stop en route to let that weird fella with the goat past. I've spent my last dollars on the flight and this cab. I've nothing else in the world except a few bits of change for water. When I get to Acapulco, I will walk up to the cliffs there. Finish what I started. They say when you're about to die, your life flashes before your eyes. I've got a four-hour flight ahead of me. I can take my time thinking about it.

I feel excited. It's weird. But then, I guess I've never been dead before.

Always good to try new things, eh?

Natalie

I could charm the birds from the trees. They always used to say it was Danny who had the gift of the gab, but I can pull it out of the bag when I need to. It became quite clear that the restaurant Cally had been kicked out of was the only place to eat round here, so I popped in one daytime and had a word with the owner, who was completely charming and apologetic (God knows why) and a bit at sixes and sevens because she was training a new guy to do the limes. Seriously, people need to be trained to do that?

Anyway. Now the people from the shoot have gone home, we've been allowed in there to eat. It's some of the best food I've ever tasted.

Cally's like a different person. It's like she's finally starting to grow up. She tells me about this boy she saw a few times but now his family have gone back to England because their room got broken into, or something.

We have a bit of girly chat after we've ordered our meal. I'm going to try the lavender prawns and we're sharing a bottle of rosé. Well, it's nearly Christmas.

A loud American on the next table is spouting forth about suicide rates in Mexico and how it's a preferred place for Americans to come to kill themselves.

Jolly.

I tell Cally what's happened with Owen, and I'm brought up short about how young she is because she gets a complete fit of the giggles about it and is almost crying with laughter by the time I've finished.

'It's not funny, Cally.'

'I know. Sorry.'

And she's off again. Slightly hysterical now.

Then I tell her about the necklace. The laughter turns to tears. But fortunately they don't last very long.

'So you think he's dead?' she asks in a soft voice, quite unlike her.

'Yes, darling, I do. I think he did something silly. Had an affair, I don't know. Felt very guilty about it. And jumped off that cliff.'

She stares at me. I think she might start crying again. And then she sort of makes this sighing noise, like something is frustrating her.

'What?' I ask.

'Well . . .'

'Go on. Say it.'

'Well, he was a bit of a selfish cunt really, wasn't he?'

And now it's my turn to laugh. Really laugh. Belly laugh, like she did, till I'm almost in tears. The loud American looks at me.

'It's not funny, Mum!'

'I know. Sorry.'

But I'm off again. Slightly hysterical now.

I try a sip of wine. Will that silence me? But I just have to give in to it.

I can't stop laughing. Cally looks thrilled. And she starts laughing too.

All She Wants

There are some things in life you can always rely on.
Living in the shadow of your 'perfect' brother Joey,
getting the flu over Christmas, and your Mother
showing you up in the supermarket.

Then there are some things you really don't count
on happening: a good dose of fame, getting completely
trashed at an awards ceremony, and catching your
fella doing something unmentionable on your
wedding day.

This is my story, it's dead tragic.
You have been warned . . .

Jodie X x

'Utterly original, sharply written and very funny'
JOJO MOYES

The Confusion of Karen Carpenter

Hello.
There are two things you should know about me:

1) My name is Karen Carpenter.

2) Just before Christmas my boyfriend left me.

I'm not THE Karen Carpenter. I just have the most embarrassing name in Christendom. Particularly as I'm no skinny minny and don't play the drums.

I can't even sing. I'm tone deaf. I work in a school in the East End. (Where I came third in a 'Teacher we'd most like to sleep with' competition amongst the Year 11 boys).

My Mum's driving me mad. She's come to stay and is obsessed with Scandi crime shows and Zumba.

Oh yeah. The boyfriend. After eleven 'happy' years he left me. No explanation, just a letter Sellotaped to the kettle when I got in from work. I think I'm handling it really well. I don't think I'm confused at all.
What was my name again?

'I enjoyed it HUGELY . . . a total page-turner,
very entertaining, then very moving'
MARIAN KEYES

The Girl Who Just Appeared

LONDON – THE PRESENT

Holly Smith has never fitted in. Adopted when just a
few months old, she's always felt she was someone with no
history. All she has is the address of where she was born –
32B Gambier Terrace, Liverpool. When Holly discovers that
the flat is available to rent, she travels north and moves in.
And in the very same flat, under the floorboards,
she finds a biscuit tin full of yellowing papers.
Could these papers be the key to her past?

LIVERPOOL – 1981

Fifteen-year-old Darren is negotiating life with his
errant mother and the younger brother he is raising.
When the Toxteth Riots explode around him, Darren
finds himself with a moral dilemma that will have
consequences for the rest of his life.

Moving between the past and the present, Darren
and Holly's lives become intertwined. Will finding
Darren give Holly the answers she craves? Or will
she always feel like the girl who just appeared?

'Absolutely delightful. Jonathan Harvey
writes with all his heart and all his soul.'
LISA JEWELL

It's time to relax with your next good book

THEWINDOWSEAT.CO.UK

If you've enjoyed this book, but don't know what
to read next, then we can help. The Window Seat is
a site that's all about making it easier to discover your
next good book. We feature recommendations,
behind-the-scenes tales from the world of publishing,
creative writing tips, competitions, and, if we're honest,
quite a lot of lists based on our favourite reads.

You'll find stories and features
by authors including Lucinda Riley, Karen Swan,
Diane Chamberlain, Jane Green, Lucy Diamond
and many more. We showcase brand-new talent
as well as classic favourites, so you'll never be
stuck for what to read again.

We'd love to know what you think of the site, our books,
and what you'd like us to feature, so do let us know.

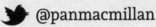 @panmacmillan

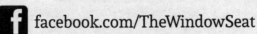 facebook.com/TheWindowSeat

WWW.THEWINDOWSEAT.CO.UK

extracts reading groups
competitions books new
discounts extracts
competitions
books
new
events books
extracts
new titles reading groups
interviews
discounts
new books events
events new
discounts extracts discounts
www.panmacmillan.com
extracts events reading groups
competitions books extracts new

reading groups
events
reading groups
extracts
discounts
extracts
events
reading groups
books
events
interviews
new books
books
extracts